ORPHAN MONSTER SPY

SHORTLISTED FOR THE COSTA BOOK AWARDS 2018
A WORLD BOOK NIGHT 2019 TITLE
SHORTLISTED FOR THE BRANFORD BOASE AWARD 2019

"Timely as well as tense." *The Sunday Times*

"Deeply disturbing and chillingly good."
Elizabeth Wein, author of *Code Name Verity*

"A thought-provoking and incredibly page-turning debut."
The Irish Times

"A story that twists, turns and threatens to stab you
in the back." Non Pratt, author of *Trouble*

"*Orphan Monster Spy*'s Sarah sits alongside Lyra and *True
Grit*'s Mattie Ross as one of the best spiky, clever, daring,
unyielding protagonists I've read."
Martin Stewart, author of *Riverkeep*

"*Orphan Monster Spy* weaves one heroine's courage through
a spectrum of darkness, and the effects resonate long after the
final page." Ryan Graudin, author of *Wolf By Wolf*

"I devoured this book. It is insanely good! Action-packed,
thrill-a-minute, so make sure you pick this one up."
No Safer Place

FOR THE VERY MANY WHO HAVE SUFFERED SO MUCH AT THE HANDS OF THE VERY FEW

First published in the UK in 2020 by Usborne Publishing Ltd., Usborne House, 83-85 Saffron Hill, London EC1N 8RT, England. www.usborne.com

Text © Send More Cops Ltd., 2020

The right of Matt Killeen to be identified as the author of this work has been asserted by him in accordance with the Copyright, Designs and Patents Act, 1988.

Cover geometric pattern © Shutterstock /PollyW
Cover seamless wavy pattern © Shutterstock/L. Kramer

The name Usborne and the devices ♀ ⊕ ᴜsʙᴏʀɴᴇ are Trade Marks of Usborne Publishing Ltd.

ISBN 9781474942393   FMAMJJASOND/20   04766/1

Printed and bound in Great Britain by CPI Group (UK) Ltd, Croydon, CR0 4YY.

MATT KILLEEN

DEVIL DARLING SPY

USBORNE

CHAPTER ONE

23RD AUGUST 1940

THE SIREN SEEMED MUFFLED. It was absorbed by the seemingly endless hills of mud, or it fled into the big grey sky and was gone. Either way it didn't seem particularly auspicious. It couldn't even startle the few disinterested seagulls that continued to squat on the grey metal tube, as if it really was just a drainpipe left lying on the side of a hill. They failed to notice the cables and wires that straggled into the mire along its length, or the branches and offshoots of pipework welded into the main cylinder at regular intervals.

However, the grey tube and muddy slope did have a more interested audience elsewhere. The cables trailed away to form an intricate path of black rubber lines, down into the valley and back up the facing slope. At their end, five hundred metres away, was a concrete blockhouse sunk into the hilltop. Through a small slit running horizontally across its length, a dozen eyes watched and waited.

The darkness inside managed to be both stuffy and damp.

The boards covering the floor were ill-fitting and filthy, marked with muddy footprints, the walls bare and unadorned. A rusty radio hid in a corner, emitting a quiet metallic hiss.

"*Zehn*," a voice crackled through the speaker.

The men straightened up and crowded towards the light. Their uniforms varied in colour and design but shared a predominance of gold and silver braid, medals and epaulettes, and a thick sense of entitlement.

"*Neun... Acht... Sieben...*"

Even the least theatrical jackets had a great number of hoops, lines and decorations. One man stood apart, in a dark suit, expensive coat and hat.

"*Sechs... Fünf...*"

The man stared over someone's garishly braided shoulder-board at the opposite hill, his bright blue eyes piercing and unreadable.

"*Vier... Drei... Zwei...*"

There was a shuffle of anticipation.

"*Eins... Null!*"

A swiftly rising whine built into separate hissing screams. Then sparks escaped from each of the pipe's tributaries in an almost simultaneous cascade, creating one roaring sound from a chorus of individual howls. Fire exploded from the pipe's summit with an unmistakable *thunk*, moments before the opening belched a cloud of thick black smoke.

The squarking of the scattering seagulls filled the sudden silence. There were a few tuts and disappointed noises from the assembled officers. Certainly the event seemed deeply anticlimactic.

"Did it work?" complained a portly *Luftwaffe* officer.

"Of course it worked, *Oberst*," snapped a *Heer Generalmajor*. He looked to one side. "How far?" he barked.

A nervous soldier sitting next to the radio coughed.

"One moment." There was some excited chatter through the speaker. He adjusted his headphones. "Approximately seventy – seven-oh – kilometres, General."

The general swung around and, with a triumphant smile, opened his arms to the waiting officers.

"Seventy kilometres, gentlemen. Seventy...and this is just a quarter-sized scale model. As you can now appreciate, a full-sized example would have a range of some two hundred and forty kilometres, deliver a shell weighing some *half a ton...* and fire every twenty seconds..."

"...if it's reliable enough," whined the *Luftwaffe* officer.

"The *finished* cannon will fire *every twenty seconds* and unlike the Paris Gun, the K-Five or any other traditional artillery piece, this gun barrel will not degrade and will not be damaged by repeated fire..."

"If it *can* be fired repeatedly..."

"*On-kel!*"

The distant scream tore through the room and stopped the argument dead.

A *Schutzstaffel* officer leaned towards the viewing window and started. "What on earth?"

Across the muddy valley a small figure in a red coat could be seen running from the cannon towards the blockhouse. She skidded and slid, almost toppling over in the deep sludge, but she remained upright and began to climb the hill.

"*On-kel!*"

She was pursued by two soldiers, themselves incapable of staying on their feet, twice falling into the sludge in their haste. The child's beret fell off as she clambered up the slope, long braids of golden hair swinging as she moved.

"*Gottverdammte...*" swore the man in the dark suit loudly. "Herr *Generalmajor*, that is... She... Take me out there immediately."

He turned for the door and began shooing the officers out of the way. They tried to move, but the room was crowded, so they bumped into one another in the gloom. Those furthest away were confused and everyone began asking questions. By the time the door was opened and the man reached the top of the steps to the open air, trailing the *Generalmajor*, the girl had summited the brow of the hill.

She was maybe twelve years old, small and slight. Mud was plastered up her legs and the hem of her coat was thick with sludge. Her eyes were red with tears and her face was contorted in hysterical panic. Glistening snot ran from her nose.

"*Onkel...*" she howled, spotting the man and charging the final few metres towards him. She leaped onto him, forcing him to stagger back a few steps, almost crashing into the collection of officers who had gathered behind him. He managed to catch her weight in his arms and hugged her close.

"Ursula! I told you to wait in the car."

"You were gone so long I didn't think you were coming back," she wailed, hyperventilating and hiccupping in her rush to spill the words out. "So I went looking for you and there was a big bang and then these soldiers started yelling at me and—"

"Apologize to the general at once!" the man in the suit growled.

"Herr Haller..." The general coughed.

"*Now*, Ursula..."

"What was your daughter—" the general tried again.

"My niece, Herr *Generalmajor*..." Then he snapped at the girl: "Ursula!"

"Sorry, Herr *Generalmajor*," the girl wailed and, with a shriek, began to sob again.

"We must leave... Gentlemen." The man nodded to the crowd of uniforms behind the general and began to stride away over the hilltop.

"Herr Haller..."

"A most exciting test, Herr *Generalmajor*. I look forward to the contract," the man called over his shoulder and the crying of the little girl.

The general found himself staring at the retreating figure, as did the guards and officers. After a moment the spell broke and everyone shambled back to the bunker, murmuring as if nothing had happened at all.

The man closed the car door and started the engine. The Mercedes grunted in the cold air and came to life. The little girl in the passenger seat stopped crying and tossed stray hairs away from her face. After a long, wet snort, she snapped her fingers at the man. He handed her a folded handkerchief that she shook loose before blowing her nose noisily.

"I'm getting too old for this *Quatsch*," she spat.

The man smiled. "Did you get it?"

"Of course," she murmured, pulling what looked like a large grey firework from her coat.

"Then you aren't too old."

She made a face before holding the device up to the daylight that limped through the windshield. "I don't understand the fuss. This is just an oversized firecracker."

"Rocket-propelled shells. Bad news for London," he said, and then glanced down at something else that Sarah was holding. "What's that?"

It was a piece of porcelain, like part of a large cereal bowl.

"They were everywhere," Sarah said, holding it up to the light. "Hundreds of pieces. Is it important?"

"Maybe... You measured the barrel?"

"Hm-hm." She teased phlegm from her hair. "And I'd have rewired it, too, if that *Schwachkopf* hadn't stumbled into me."

"Language."

"Yes, right." She laughed.

"Seriously. You better not talk like that at the next party, Sarah Goldstein of Elsengrund. What will the cream of Berlin high society think?"

"Don't worry, I won't be there. I'll be bringing Ursula Haller, the sweet little National Socialist darling instead."

CHAPTER TWO

SARAH HAD INSISTED THEY LEAVE the apartment behind.

It didn't matter how much she had scrubbed, disinfected or bleached the floor, she could still see Foch's blood there. It was like a glossy, dark and stagnant lake that reflected the room. In this mirror world, the moment of his murder in her arms repeated endlessly. The SA officer had unmasked them and had been about to shoot the Captain; but self-defence or not, she had been complicit in the horror.

She had eventually rubbed off the varnish and begun to tear into the surface of the wood, but she could still see the blood. It was on her shoes, under her fingernails, in the creases of her skin. She couldn't tell where the remains of the SA *Sturmbannführer* ended and her own raw and bloody fingertips began. As for the bathroom where the Captain had dragged the corpse and then emerged over the course of two days with a series of old suitcases... Sarah couldn't even enter that room.

The Captain was reluctant to move at first – the apartment had several advantages for an agent, including an escape route, radio antenna and false walls. But returning one day to find Sarah had torn up the floorboards and was bleaching the undersides, he was finally convinced that a fresh start was needed. Besides, that minimalist apartment was no place to entertain.

Sarah passed through the halls and palatial rooms of their new townhouse as the staff busied themselves around her. She paused here and there, to have chairs rearranged or to make a suggestion, but in reality their work was practised, seamless.

The parties she and the Captain had held as the spring of 1940 turned to summer had been a huge success, as Germany had celebrated a seemingly endless series of military victories. Any initial concern among the German people about what this war might cost in men or resources had evaporated as the days warmed. The national atmosphere was buoyant, jubilant. For the generals and staff officers at the Captain's soirées, the mood was triumphant and overwhelmingly self-satisfied.

They had good reason for this. The Third Reich, and its allies, had swollen and consumed Europe. It now stretched from Poland to the Atlantic coast of France and north through Denmark and Norway to the top of the world. It was all actually happening.

Sarah caught sight of herself in a mirror and looked away. At almost sixteen, she still looked twelve, dressed like a Hollywood child star, with frilled ankle-socks and a knee-length dress with puffed sleeves and petticoats. The Nazi Shirley Temple. The Little Princess of the Reich. Darling of the *Wehrmacht* and Berlin high society.

It put the men at ease. It made them feel grown-up. Superior. Magnanimous. They talked to her without thinking, answering her precocious or innocent-sounding questions with a chuckle. Or they talked around and over her like she wasn't there. She didn't understand half of what she heard, but this hadn't made it less valuable – according to the Captain.

Sometimes, the men took a *special* interest. They brought her gifts. They wanted her to sit with them, on them. They wanted her to talk about meaningless things, or sing to them, but sometimes they wanted her to listen as they unburdened themselves of their darkness. They wanted to hold someone. Someone pure? Or was it something else?

The proximity made the saliva turn sour at the back of her throat. It made her want to hurt them.

But it was the job.

In truth she wondered how much longer she could play this part. Nine months of good food had given her an extra six centimetres in height. Her body was filling out. No amount of tight blonde curls and ribbons could conceal what was coming. She was watching her little-girl act receding like a railway station platform, and she needed to stop leaning out of the train window.

By the mirror were the two leather armchairs where, at their party three months ago, Sarah had goaded the portly *Luftwaffe Generalfeldmarschall* in his garish white uniform into a wager that had backfired. He had waved her over to join him and a surly looking *Generaloberst,* who did not welcome the distraction.

───────

"Come and sit on my knee, *Prinzessin...* I'm just telling Walther here how he should deal with the fleeing British."

"I don't need any advice, thank you."

"Certainly you do. You want to risk your tanks in the streets of Flanders?"

"I want the enemy out of action, yes."

"Nothing puts a defeated army out of action like bombing them into surrender."

"They've got their backs to the sea and they've no way home. They've abandoned all their heavy equipment, they're going to surrender anyway. We just need to press the point."

"Yet you want to waste German lives at the hour of our victory. Let the *Luftwaffe* deal with it."

"This is all hypothetical—"

Sarah interrupted. "Walther, it sounds like you should let him try."

"Sorry?"

"You say they can't go anywhere, what does it matter if you let him bomb them into surrender?"

"See, Walther. The little girl has courage that you lack."

"Yes, *Generalfeldmarschall*, but you need to risk something, too..."

"Yes! *Jede Wette!* Leave them to me and I'll have them

surrender in three days. Shall we say a hundred Reichsmark? *Prinzessin*, you shall be the bookmaker..."

━━━━━━━━━━━━━━

Sarah hadn't seen the *Generaloberst* – Walther – to give him his money. The crumpled fifty Reichsmark notes sat unclaimed as most of the British Army slipped across the Channel from Dunkirk in little boats, battered but undefeated by the *Luftwaffe*, while the tanks had sat and waited. Had she done that, even in some small way? According to the gossip, Göring, now the *Reichsmarschall*, was busy failing to defeat the Royal Air Force in the skies over Britain, as he had failed at Dunkirk, so maybe he needed no help making his mistakes.

But mistakes from the German military had been thin on the ground. Despite everything Sarah and the Captain had apparently achieved, the secrets they'd uncovered, the nebulous manipulations they had wrought, she couldn't shake the feeling that the work of one British spy and his...apprentice, a small Jewish orphan, didn't amount to anywhere near enough.

She felt they were standing waist-deep in a fast-moving river, trying to stop the current with their fingers. It swept over and around them like they weren't even there. And all this time, Sarah wore pretty dresses, curled her tresses and ate sumptuous food. She might have stopped Professor Schäfer and his bomb – her first mission alongside the Captain – but that hadn't prevented the *Wehrmacht* from tearing across the fabric of the earth.

However, it was what Sarah saw on the streets of Berlin that affected her the most.

The Jews had been on curfew and denied wireless sets, jobs, businesses and citizenship. Now they were at risk of being rounded up for no reason, ordered to train stations with one suitcase each, and disappearing. They lived in fear, increasingly hungry and desperate.

Sarah the Jewess, posing as Ursula, the Nazi's Aryan darling, watched all this from the wrong side of the glass. She wore the finest clothes at lavish dinners, when just a year before she had worn rags and eaten scraps from bins.

But what made her most uneasy wasn't the guilt, as much as its absence.

Those dresses – the softness, the crinkling thickness and gentle perfume – had become routine. She had to admit to liking it all at first, and it was an important part of the job. Then she had come to expect the pampering. But this wasn't what Sarah Goldstein was – whatever that really meant – this was *Ursula Haller*. Sarah increasingly struggled to reconcile the two.

Even the food – the greasy, tender, fluffy, flaky, sweet, sour, crunchy nourishment at all times of the day and night – had begun to pall, turn bland and insipid, no matter how much Sarah pushed into her mouth. She remembered the hunger and knew she should be feeling guilty about eating while others starved, about feeling nothing while others endured that aching, empty desperation.

Sarah had stolen and lied to survive before and had felt no guilt. But this was different.

She had once kept a box deep inside her in which she locked every horror and humiliation, every trauma and fear, so that her mind was clear enough to think without dread and anger. Since leaving the charnel house apartment behind, she didn't seem to need that any more. Increasingly Sarah felt…not nothing, but intense shades of grey rather than colours. She knew that this should frighten her, but the emotions appeared to just pass through her. She was like a wireless set with the volume too low, rather than switched off. She was aware of the vibrations, but could make out no detail.

Likewise, the violent visions she had been experiencing from time to time since her stay at the Schäfer estate had ceased to bother her. It was like the drone of beehives on a summer's day that you stopped noticing after a while. Was this boredom at the uniformity of her new life, the normalization of constant fear, or had she suffered so much she had broken herself? She saw the same thing in the Captain, who only came alive when he was in danger.

Now Sarah could hear raised voices coming from the stairs to the kitchens. Frau Hofmann was vexed about something again. The housekeeper used her terseness to control the motley collection of part-time staff, porters and other domestics wheeled in for the parties. But this time, her anger had a serrated edge to it that Sarah had not heard before. She descended to investigate.

"I don't know what you're thinking bringing that *Schornsteinfeger* here. This is a decent house, not a *Hottentotten* encampment," the woman barked.

Frau Hofmann stood with rough hands on hips, dominating the kitchen, while in front of her stood Herr Gehlhaar, the little man from the domestic agency. A step behind him and to the left stood the so-called chimney sweep: a young black girl.

She was very young for a servant, no older than fifteen or sixteen, Sarah's real age. She was slight in a way that Sarah recognized as underfed. She watched the floor intently, again a tactic that Sarah knew all too well from a childhood dodging vengeful Hitler Youth and inquisitive stormtroopers. She could have been looking at herself a year ago.

"*Meine Frau.*" Herr Gehlhaar sighed and ran the rim of his bowler hat through his fingers. "There are no restrictions on the employment of—"

"Yet."

The young maid glanced up. Her eyes were full of fear, the look of someone trapped and on the verge of panic. Sarah remembered the Captain wore that same expression of a cornered animal on the docks a year ago, and she had been unable to stop herself from helping him then. There was something else there, too. Anger.

"Frau Hofmann, she can stay," Sarah called out.

The woman spun around, glaring, but seeing Sarah, checked herself before replying. "*Fräulein*...this is nothing to concern yourself with, let me take care—"

"Oh, then I could fetch my uncle," Sarah interrupted, eyebrows raised.

"I think, considering tonight's guest list," the woman pressed on, "having a young *Neger* about the place—"

"Well, she can stay down here. There's plenty to do. And I'm sure she knows her place," Sarah added, feeling an unpleasant tug inside as she said the words.

"But, *Fräulein*, this is a *Rheinlandbastard*. What if one of the soldiers from the last war sees her..."

"Girl?" The maid was already staring at Sarah. "You'll stay out of the way...promise?"

She nodded vigorously. Sarah had imagined gratitude, but all she saw was the same fear, or fury, as before.

CHAPTER THREE

THE AVAILABILITY OF CHAMPAGNE in the summer of 1940 was a symbol of Germany's victory and the subjugation of the hated French. Herr Haller's parties, where the traditionally rich and powerful – *the Upper Ten Thousand* – rubbed shoulders with industrialists selling things and the military who bought them, made a statement of it. The Captain ensured that a guest could have bathed in the yellow bubbles and still drunk their fill afresh afterwards, so most were inebriated shortly after arriving. Drunk tongues were, after all, loose ones. Sarah watched a neglected bottle on the carpet, pulsing its contents into the pile. The smell made her feel both nauseous and vulnerable.

By 9 p.m. the party had become an animal. It bucked, roared, went quiet, stretched, shook and rested, before staggering to its feet once more.

The Captain leaned against the drawing-room mantelpiece, simultaneously towering over the room and yet hidden from it, like a long forgotten park statue. His habitual mask of disinterested amusement sat crookedly on top of another expression as he noticed her, one that Sarah had come to understand in the last few months as a look of faint disapproval. Sarah obediently drifted over for her admonishment. He acknowledged her, and then they stood side by side.

"Frau Hofmann tells me we have a *Neger* in the kitchen," he murmured.

"No doubt *defiling* the Strudel and mongrelizing the Schnitzel, like a bad little *Untermensch*."

The Captain snorted before leaning towards her. "It's compromising. Even dangerous."

"Like acquiring a Jewish orphan, you mean? Come on, she's a *servant*. And we're not running an *underground railroad*," she added in English. "Anyway, there's no law against it."

"Yet."

"Well, Captain Jeremy Floyd, maybe we need to decide what kind of Nazis we're going to be. There doesn't seem to be much alternative any more."

"That's pessimistic."

"I mean, it's all over already, isn't it? Just that one little island. Against *everywhere*."

He shook his head. "Britain is more than a little island. It's an empire that covers the globe. Do you know how many soldiers the British could muster in India? Don't underestimate them because they're *brown*; that's Hitler's mistake. And the Royal Navy is better than anything that the Reich can dream of. The *Wehrmacht* thinks it can invade by floating over the Channel in *barges* and the British are just going to watch."

"Which is why you're selling them barges?"

"Of course. They're going to get *slaughtered*. And how do you think I'm paying for this house? No, it's not over, Sarah of Elsengrund."

He fell silent as a group of officers, reeking of beer, stumbled over to shake his hand. Sarah smiled beatifically and curtseyed. A swollen hand patted her head and even before she could picture herself sinking her teeth into the thick fingers, it was gone.

The Captain waited a moment and continued. "If Britain can get what it needs past the U-boats, that is. However, *we* have a more pressing problem. What's wrong with this party?"

"It's really dull."

"No," he said flatly.

"It is, trust me."

"Look around, tell me what's wrong. From our perspective."

"Oh, I like this game." Sarah chuckled.

She scanned the room.

It was heaving with uniforms, of different ranks and colours. Flushed, sweaty faces, laughing too loud, drinking too quickly. There were plenty of civilians, too, businessmen and chancers, the well-connected and the want-to-bes, side-by-side. Crowds of wives and mistresses, exchanging glances of jealousy and pity.

The drinking songs had not yet started, but the piano was already lost in the hubbub. The room stank of cologne and alcohol.

Uniforms.

"What do we have...not so many *Luftwaffe*. Busy over

Britain?" Sarah asked. The Captain nodded. "All right, *Kriegsmarine* out in force... Oh, who is that coming in? Lots of gold braid on his shoulders?"

"Admiral Canaris. We'll get to him in a moment."

The admiral did not command a lot of attention on entering. He had the look of a small, kindly old man, which made Sarah instantly suspicious. His skin was a little yellow and unhealthy, with age pulling at his jowls. His eyebrows were untidy in a way that suggested someone meandering his way to retirement, but his pristine dress uniform did not. It was the darkest navy blue, so dark it was nearly black—

Sarah looked around the room again. "No black. There's no *Schutzstaffel*, no SS. Presumably no *Gestapo*?"

"Exactly," the Captain said, clapping. "Although you don't see them in black any more – they want to wear grey like real soldiers. We have here a very narrow subset of the Nazi machine. One of the reasons our parties have proven popular with the *Wehrmacht* is the absence of the monsters. They make people nervous. This is somewhere they can feel free to have a good grumble about everything. But this means that we have, inadvertently, chosen a side."

"Monsters who don't like monsters?"

"Different circles of hell," the Captain muttered.

Sarah huffed and narrowed her eyes. "Have you actually *read* Dante's *Inferno*? There's a whole ring for the Jews because they lend money. The same circle as the murderers, the war-makers, thieves and tyrants. It's *Quatsch*."

"I'm not sure that's what Dante meant, or where God puts the Jews."

"God doesn't put the Jews anywhere, Captain Floyd. We have no hell." Sarah relaxed a little. "Just shame, in the here and now. Do you know where Dante puts the traitors against the state?"

"In the ice."

"In the ice," she agreed. "Up to our necks, eating each other. For ever."

"They're the traitors," the Captain said, waving at the soldiers that surrounded them. "Not you."

"So you keep telling me."

"Talking of traitors..." the Captain said, straightening up. "Here comes the messenger of one in particular."

Admiral Canaris's young naval adjutant was weaving through the crowd towards them. He was evidently sober and his politeness was an impediment to his movement, surrounded as he was by swaying, braying drunks.

They found a set of armchairs by pulling rank on some junior *Kriegsmarine* officers.

"Admiral, may I present my niece, Ursula."

Sarah curtseyed and conjured up her widest winning smile. The admiral looked at the Captain in momentary confusion, then nodded to Sarah. The Captain waved her onto the floor next to the admiral's chair.

"A fine party, Haller," the admiral declared. "Thank you for the invitation. Holstein, find me something that isn't champagne."

The adjutant seemed about to ask a follow-up question,

then realized his absence would be sufficient.

"We're honoured by your presence obviously," the Captain said.

"That's nice for you," the admiral said, before stretching, a pretext to look around before speaking. "I received your gift earlier today. I must applaud the quality of your industrial espionage." He leaned in slightly. "Haller, I know from our time in Spain that you can be counted on to get things done, outside of official channels of course."

"Of course," the Captain confirmed.

"You sent me a fragment of a ceramic bomb. These are used to drop disease agents on your enemy. They are the work of our anti-Bolshevik friends, the Japanese. In particular, one Shirō Ishii, an army surgeon in Manchuria. I'm guessing you got this somewhere closer to home?"

The Captain nodded. Sarah stared at the Captain, trying to understand the unfolding events. He gave the fragment she found to an admiral—

Shush. Listen and learn.

"The Reich has any number of research projects, some of which are independently funded," the admiral continued more softly. "There is a preoccupation with *Wunderwaffen* – rockets, giant cannon, *Superbomben* – which our leaders encourage, none of it very well organized. It seems one of our chemists blew up his own house recently." The admiral chuckled and shook his head like a tolerant uncle.

Sarah had to squint against the white light of her memory. *The house vanishing in an instant, taking with it Schäfer's body and his work.*

She shifted her weight and settled back onto the floor. The admiral continued.

"One of my...*colleagues* in the SS, one Kurt Hasse, has been empire-building in this fertile, clandestine area. He and Ishii met in 1929 and I'm...*interested* to discover that Surgeon Colonel Ishii is in Berlin right now, at the same time as his bombs, and they're meeting at the Japanese Embassy tomorrow night. I would very much like to *play the mouse* at that appointment, but all my usual friends there have been asked to make themselves scarce after 10 p.m. Haller, you know people who aren't above a little burglary, don't you? Maybe have a listen to something in the ambassador's office?"

"I'm surprised you don't know someone yourself..."

"This isn't something that I can involve myself in directly – the armed forces keeping tabs on the SS? That would not go down well. In this case, *you* are the person I know."

"What might they be discussing, that you need to know so much?" the Captain asked.

"Hasse has been communicating with a group of German missionaries in Africa. They have been there for some years researching tropical diseases—"

Sarah was having to make herself concentrate as Canaris spoke. Like much that she overheard, it seemed dull and parochial, or too distant to be of interest. She knew this made her a bad spy.

"If they've stumbled on something especially nasty in the jungle," he continued, "there are those who would like to use it. Being outside the Reich, their activities fall under my purview. I find myself *responsible* for them but cannot draw attention to them because, of course, our sagacious Führer does not believe in gas or germ warfare—"

"Why not?" piped up Sarah, her curiosity overcoming her caution.

Canaris paused, staring at her. He seemed to hover somewhere between ignoring and indulging her, before answering.

"Our war hero was gassed by the British in 1918. I think he found the experience less than pleasant."

"No war is pleasant though, surely?"

Canaris laughed and slapped his thigh. "I think, in a rare moment of pragmatism the Führer has grasped that the British have a large gas stockpile and were we to use something similar, it would just *stab a wasps' nest*. We supply our armies using horses, and horses cannot wear gas masks. However, he may be persuaded to use something untraceable or at least apparently natural in origin. In fact he might already have been so persuaded. And that is an unpleasant thought. *Jesus...*" Canaris noticed something behind them and sat back in surprise. "Your clientele just expanded."

Sarah turned and started. Like finding three crows at the window watching you with unblinking black eyes, she saw three SS officers in meticulous dress uniforms by the door. Sarah had once been told what the collective term was for crows in English. *A murder.*

"May I introduce *SS-Obersturmbannführer* Kurt Hasse," the admiral murmured with a sigh.

"A coincidence?" the Captain asked.

"No such thing," growled the admiral.

"The monsters are here," Sarah said, under her breath.

CHAPTER FOUR

THEY STOOD BEHIND THE GLASS DOORS to the stairs and watched the crows move through the party. The soldiers drifted aside as they approached and closed ranks behind them. Sarah had once seen a cat pad across a town square of pigeons who acted the same way.

"So the SS came. That's lovely," Sarah said brightly.

"Not especially. That one, next to our new friend," the Captain said, pointing to the older, better-fed of the three crows. "*Sicherheitsdienst*, SD, SS intelligence. We are now being watched."

For a moment, a sliver of a second, and for the first time in months, Sarah felt fear. It was like someone had opened a door onto a winter's evening, then abruptly shut it. It woke her from her stupor. She could feel things coming alive inside her mind, like warming valves in a wireless set.

"Who said, 'There's only one thing worse than being talked about, and that's not being talked about'?" she mused.

"One day, Sarah of Elsengrund, you'll quote a famous British homosexual in the wrong company."

"Until then, life will continue to excite... So, who does Admiral Canaris work for?"

"He is chief of the *Abwehr*. Military intelligence."

Sarah's mouth dropped open. "Military intelligence?" she growled. "We work for *German military intelligence*?"

"No, we work *with* German military intelligence."

"Whose side are we on?" she cried. "Whose side are *you* on?"

"Remember what you told me from the *Arthashastra*? 'The enemy of my enemy is my friend'? Well, Admiral Canaris is an enemy of Hitler."

Sarah pointed back into the drawing room, where a disordered marching song was breaking out. She watched champagne running down a well-fed face.

"Oh yes, the German military looks *horrified* at what's happening."

The Captain placed a finger against his lips and moved closer. She had been getting careless in the last few months, so secure had their operation seemed.

"Not everybody is happy, but nobody feels comfortable to speak out...and some don't *get involved in politics*."

"*They don't get involved...*" she mocked. "Politics is *everything*." She stopped so she could vocalize the next thought coherently. "I heard some of the soldiers talking about Poland, about the *Einsatzgruppen*? They rounded up school teachers, priests, Gypsies and Jews...and shot them. Thousands and thousands. The army *helped*."

"And that was enough for Canaris," the Captain told her. "An eye-opener for the professional soldiers. They don't like Slavs or Jews, but shooting civilians *en masse...* This is not what they signed up for."

"Still doing it though, aren't they?" Sarah snarled. She waited a moment for some guests to pass them. "Look me in the eye and tell me that this admiral is on our side."

"He's not. He's on *his* side. He's a right-winger, and I don't know if he's more upset by the murders or because the army got involved. But either way, if he's worried about Hasse, Ishii and these missionaries, then we should be, too. This is not the first time I've heard them mentioned."

"Who does he think *you* are?"

"A businessman, a fixer, more interested in money than politics but with no love for Hitler for practical reasons. I do the odd job for him."

"What do we get out of this arrangement?"

"Good question. We're being fed information. We're undermining the National Socialists and we get help when we need it."

"How? How do we get help? How do I tell people that I'm *actually an* Abwehr *agent*?"

"Well, you don't do that for a start."

"How do I ask for help?" she insisted.

"There's a code word. *Die Drei Hasen.* The three hares."

"*Der Hasen und der Löffel drei...*" Sarah sang, thinking of the stained glass they'd seen at Rothenstadt, the school for the Nazi elite that she had infiltrated to get to Schäfer. "Is that for me? Am I the three hares? My, you've got sentimental."

"Not really, it's quite descriptive. We have limited resources and we make it count double."

"But what—"

"For god's sake, can't you just accept—" he snapped, then stopped. Sarah noticed the line of sweat on his top lip.

"I'm—" he began.

"It's fine," she interrupted. She waved her hands at him. "Go do what you need to do."

He turned and headed for the stairs. *Again? How many times has he lost his temper recently, over nothing?* she thought.

The clock rang out as he climbed. Only 11 p.m.

And it's happening earlier and earlier.

Sarah pushed open a heavy door that made a sighing groan as if unwilling to move. It chivvied her into the dark space as it closed. Enough moonlight seeped through the papered windows to illuminate the contents. Furniture, paintings and rugs slept under dustsheets, as pots of paint and ladders waited.

Like everything else, this arrangement was a sham. There was no grand furniture under the sheets, just piled junk and cheap chairs. No decorating was going to take place. Beyond this suggestion of renovation lay empty rooms of peeling wallpaper and crumbling decay. The house, its luxury and expensive sumptuousness was a theatre set.

Sarah felt an absence at odds with her usual need to be left alone. She found she needed to talk. Not about anything in particular. Just talk. When the Captain could not, and he had been increasingly unavailable, Sarah struggled with the isolation of her secret life.

She had once had other voices in her mind, that argued and

berated. They had been still for a long while, and she missed them. She also struggled with that silence, because the mission that took her to Rothenstadt had, for all its violence and terror, given her other people to think about, to care for.

There was the Mouse, the tiny, weak, bullied little girl who had clung defiantly to Sarah, even as the monsters had circled around her. Then there was Elsa, a monster only because her father was one, who had betrayed Sarah but saved her at the end.

Sarah had sent Elsa away out of necessity, to get the hysterical, damaged girl to safety, but the Mouse... Sarah wanted to see the Mouse, to reach out, knowing that the girl would eventually stop talking about puppies and listen. Sarah desperately needed to unburden herself upon someone.

Sarah was lonely.

She entered a third room that was pitch-black, but she walked into the gloom, confident of her steps. She reached out for the back wall and ran her fingers across the torn wallpaper, until she found a crack. She pushed the wall and, finding it immovable, she felt for a small hole at waist height.

She crouched and, sliding two hairgrips into the opening, cocked an ear to listen.

Click.

Click.

Click.

CLICK.

A section of the wall swung towards her, the room filling with a blinding yellow light.

Inside, surrounded by whirring, clicking, moving machines, a man pointed a revolver at Sarah where she was crouched.

"That door was locked for a reason," he growled.

"Come on, it was barely locked," Sarah scoffed as she entered.

The man lowered the gun and dropped it onto a table. He pulled a pair of oversized headphones over his curly hair as he muttered to himself and scratched his beard.

Sarah walked among the racks of machines, watching their matching metal discs spinning and lights twinkling. They buzzed and rustled. The air smelled like the inside of a wireless set, like electricity and thunderstorms.

"Anything good tonight?" she asked.

She leaned in and gently turned a knob on the nearest *Magnetophon*, watching the dancing needle grow more frenzied.

The man pushed past her and returned the control to its original position.

"No. There are too many people here," he complained. "I can't make anything out. I've said this before, I don't know why no one listens to me."

"Nothing at all?"

"Stukas are too slow to fight over England, but we knew that. Fighter Command knows that. By the time we tell anyone, they'll have been withdrawn."

"So this is a waste of time?" she enquired, half statement, half question.

"No, this is a brilliant plan, really badly executed."

Sarah flicked a switch and the room filled with noise. Drunken singing, tinkling glasses, a distorted piano, two distant voices—

"*—insistent on withholding strategic bombing, or rather he has to be the one to order it.*"

"*No, it has to be the airfields—*"

He turned the speaker off and glared at her.

"That sounds useful—" she ventured.

"Well, it's not," he snapped.

He was a small man, but there was a fury behind his eyes that made his presence unnerving. Sarah pushed on.

"What is your problem with me?" she demanded.

"Other than you coming in here to needle me?"

"I'm not needling you," Sarah stated calmly. "I just want to know—"

"You're dangerous and I don't trust you," he blurted out. "You're at best a child, who can't be expected not to make mistakes, and at worst, you're some kind of plant. Where did you come from? How did you get your claws into him?"

"*I'm* dangerous?" Sarah was incredulous. "What about you, walking around Berlin with that accent? You might as well be in a British uniform, *Sergeant Norris.*"

"I'm not a Jewess swanning around dressed as a doll in a room full of Nazis."

"At least I don't sleep in my clothes and forget to bathe," she sneered.

"You're going to get us all killed. They'll torture us all first, then they'll kill us."

Sarah looked at him, trying to see past the anger, the unkempt beard and the sweat spots. "But you're a wireless operator. If any of us are going to be arrested it's you. A short life expectancy is in the job description. I can't be that much more threatening." Sarah paused, her mind cycling through the options. "No, you aren't scared of what I'll do, it's something else."

Norris opened his mouth to speak but stopped. Sarah saw the uncertainty behind the rage.

With a snap and a flutter, the nearest reel sucked up the last of its tape and accelerated to a blur. He switched the machine off and began to remove the spool.

"Haller. He's...different. You've changed him. It's like he can't take any risks any more." He thrust the large metal reel into Sarah's arms. It smelled of nails. "Always double-checking, weighing the options—"

"What? He's more dangerous because he's more careful?"

"He's thinking too much, not acting on instinct. Like he doesn't trust himself. Those little windows of opportunity that he used to seize upon, they're gone before he can make a decision." Norris pulled the new tape through the rollers. Under, over, under, over... "One day that's going to be an escape route that he dawdles next to. Second thoughts *kill*."

"He's not *committing to the move*," murmured Sarah.

"And these parties – they're just an excuse to have the house. He wanted a *house*. He's *sleeping* at night—"

"You mean he's *happy*...?" Sarah laughed.

"No, I mean he's become emotional. The danger used to be a piece of mathematics, a puzzle to solve. He liked it. Now it's a threat. He's more preoccupied with you than the job. As for that bullet he took," Norris continued, "he's a shell of the man he was. If you can't see what's happening to him, you're more stupid than I thought."

Sarah *had* seen. She just didn't want to think about it—

There was a noise behind them. They spun round to see the new maid standing by the open door.

CHAPTER FIVE

For a moment no one moved. Then everybody moved at once.

Norris lunged for the maid as she took a step backwards. Sarah tried to stop him but couldn't prevent him dragging her back into the room.

"Close the door," he growled.

Sarah pulled the door closed and turned to find the maid held around the middle, arms pinned to her sides. Somehow Norris now held a knife, a long, thin spike like a knitting needle. He pushed it under her chin.

"NO!" Sarah screamed.

"She's seen too much."

"She has a name!" shouted Sarah.

Norris paused. "Well, what is it?"

Gottverdammt.

"Girl, what's your name?"

"Clementine. My name is Clementine." Her voice reminded

Sarah of the Mouse. The fragility was the same. "I'm sorry, I didn't see anything, I won't say anything—"

"You're right there, *Clementine*," Norris interrupted.

"You can't—" Sarah cried.

"If you hadn't unlocked the door, I wouldn't have to..."

Sarah leaned into the storm of culpability she was experiencing. *Not another innocent death. Not one more...*

"Don't do it to punish me... Look at her. LOOK. AT. HER." Norris glanced down as Clementine looked up, wide brown eyes full of panic. "She's just a little girl."

He sneered, but looking again into Clementine's face below his, he hesitated.

"Have you ever killed anyone before, Norris?" Sarah asked more quietly.

One of the reels pulled the last of the tape from its machine and spun wildly, the tail of the tape making a *phut* noise with each revolution.

Phut.

Phut.

Phut.

"I've killed chickens."

Phut.

Phut.

Phut.

"Did the chickens have names?"

"Yes," he hissed.

"Did the chickens look at you like that?"

Phut.

Phut.

Phut.

"No."

Another machine ran out of tape.

Phut. Phut.

Phut. Phut.

Phut. Phut.

"But if she tells *anyone* about this, anyone at all..." Norris groaned. "I'll make it quick." He closed his eyes.

"NO!" shrieked Sarah. She thought quickly, carelessly, looking for a way out. She clasped onto the first idea— "She can join us, work for us..."

"You're kidding."

"No... Clementine, listen." Sarah took a deep breath. "We work for the *Abwehr*, for military intelligence. We listen in to the army, make sure there are no traitors to the Führer. Do you understand?"

Phut. Phut.

Phut. Phut.

Phut. Phut.

Clementine nodded carefully, glancing down at the shining blade.

"Do you want to help?" Sarah continued, edging closer to Norris. "Do a special job for the Reich? Work for Herr Haller?"

Clementine nodded as emphatically as she could.

"But it's secret," Sarah stated clearly. "No one can know. Ever."

Another nod. Sarah reached up and gingerly pushed the steel spike down and away from Clementine's throat, feeling its wafer-thin edge on her fingertips.

"So that's it, we just let her go?" Norris muttered.

"No, we don't just let her go," Sarah said in exasperation. "We keep her here until the end of the party. *My uncle* speaks to Herr Gehlhaar and she moves in. If she's useless, you can kill her then."

"Haller decides. Not you," he conceded.

"Fine. But you know he'll agree with me."

"She could be a spy."

"Then she's in good company."

Sarah objected to locking Clementine up, but there didn't seem much option until the guests had gone and the Captain had resurfaced. The room was little more than a broom closet, but it had a light and it was warm. It would have to do.

Before she locked the door, she stepped inside.

"This is just for a few hours," Sarah whispered. Clementine appeared downcast and motionless. "Are you all right?"

The girl reached out and shoved Sarah against the wall. "Who are you, *Evangeline St. Clare*? You think you're *my little Eva*? Get your daddy to buy me up and live happily ever after? You read too many stories, Nazi girl." Clementine released her and stepped back with a derisive noise.

Sarah stood, shocked and open-mouthed. She was also confused by the reference to *little Eva*, until she remembered *Onkel Toms Hütte*, and the little white girl who befriended *the slave* Tom.

"Didn't I just save your life?" Sarah protested finally.

"Oh, and I should be *so* grateful that now I can be your

Hausneger," Clementine mocked, putting her hand across her heart. "Well, thank you, I'll be a subservient, well-behaved little punching bag from now on."

Clementine curtseyed in melodramatic fashion.

"You weren't so mouthy with a knife at your throat," Sarah said.

"You want the quiet little girl? Get a knife."

Sarah began again, still thrown off-balance. "If we're going to make this work, I'm going to need you to—"

"I get threatened *all the time.* I am not scared of you," Clementine spat.

"You looked scared earlier," retorted Sarah, getting irritated again.

"I can pretend. It makes people like you and Herr Hairy feel more important. Less likely to cut me open with a knitting needle. So get yourself a knife, Nazi girl."

Sarah was lost for words.

She stepped out of the room, wondering what she had done bringing *this* Clementine, rather than the one she thought she had met, into the house.

She locked the door, tempted to turn off the light as she did so.

CHAPTER SIX

24TH AUGUST 1940

AS EVERY NIGHT SINCE THE OUTBREAK of the war, there were no street lights and no illuminated windows in Berlin, but even in the waning moonlight Sarah could clearly see a dozen ways into the incomplete Japanese Embassy. It would soon slot neatly into Speer's new fake-classical Berlin, but for the moment the unnecessary columns and sharp edges were softened with scaffolding and rough fences.

The car was becoming cold, so Sarah rubbed her legs to keep them warm.

"You should have let Norris kill her," the Captain declared. "It would have been the sensible thing to do."

He was bright and alert. Maybe a little intense.

"So that's who we are now? Murderers of little girls? You didn't kill me back in Friedrichshafen. I was like her. What did you call me? A witness, *a loose end.*"

"I needed a little girl. I don't need two. Where is she now?"

"In the servants' quarters. Norris is keeping an eye out.

Herr Gehlhaar was happy for us to take her off his hands. Frau Hofmann was not. Clementine is happy to be getting twice what she was being paid—"

"*Twice*?"

"She wanted three times as much...she's, um, forthright," she finished weakly, as the Captain shook his head. "We could always use a maid," Sarah tried. "Having to bring in agency staff is a security risk—"

"Oh yes, it's a great time to have a black maid. Soon we won't even need to pay her, just remember to lock her door at night." He sighed.

"What's a Rhineland bastard anyway?"

"Ha, I do like you having limits." The Captain chuckled. "The Rhineland was an occupied zone after the last war. The French troops stationed there made themselves at home, including the colonial troops, the *Tirailleurs Sénégalais*—"

"I see," Sarah interjected.

"Despite what you might hear, they didn't force the women—"

"Yes, I get the point," she interrupted, squirming away from the thought.

"Most women married their French boyfriends, some had accidents, and the children of those relationships are *die Rheinlandbastard*. National disgrace, evil foreign blood defiling German youth, et cetera. She must be the very last of them. The French left in 1925."

"We've needed an extra pair of hands," Sarah said. "On the inside of what we do, I mean."

"Do we? And she's not on the inside. She thinks we're the *Abwehr*."

"You told me that's the same thing right now."

"So my choice is go along with this or kill her, now that you've told everyone she works for us—"

"I can't live in *another* house where another person...*dies*," Sarah burst out, with more feeling than she intended. "And I don't mean do it somewhere else. I need...to not have caused this."

The Captain studied the glowing dials of his watch before speaking. "She opens her mouth, breathes at the wrong time, she's dead," he said quietly and with complete seriousness.

"She puts us in danger, I'll kill her myself," Sarah snapped, instantly regretting the words. She thought of Stern, the SS guard who she hadn't stopped as he walked back into the inferno of Schäfer's lab, of Foch who she had hugged as the Captain opened up his throat, and a cold wave of nausea lapped around her belly.

She looked at his watch and again at the moonlit construction site attached to the Embassy.

"Why am I doing this?" Sarah complained. "Why aren't you going in as a builder?"

"At 1 a.m.?" the Captain replied, fidgeting.

"Why is a little girl awake at 1 a.m.?" she continued, but her heart wasn't in the argument. She wanted to do this – no, she needed to do this. The sense of sitting and waiting idly as the Third Reich swelled and absorbed the world gnawed at her being. The challenge at hand felt like picking up a sword and charging into that fight.

There was also a feeling that Sarah at first struggled to identify and then immediately felt guilty about. She was excited.

The steps up to the doors from the road were gentle, almost an affectation. There were plenty of trees and the square columns of the entrance would obscure much of the gardens. There was no guard visible. The two lampposts were off for the blackout, but even with the moonlight there were plenty of shadows to inhabit.

If there had been a pie cooling on that colonnade, I would already be eating it, she thought. The starving girl who had run across the Viennese rooftops in search of food awoke for the first time in months.

The seconds passed.

"Let's get on with it," she moaned, tapping the door's handle impatiently.

"He isn't late, yet," the Captain chided, but Sarah could feel his discomfort, and not just because they were parked up in the heart of the deserted diplomatic district.

She wondered about what Norris had said, that the Captain couldn't commit, that his caution would get them all killed. Was the Captain as excited as she was to be doing things instead of just being?

"How's your Japanese?" he asked.

"*Sonzaishinai*," Sarah replied.

The Captain snorted.

"It means nonexistent," Sarah said with a chuckle, before continuing more quietly. "I can sing you a folk song. My mother had friends…"

"Just remember, the guards will assume you're with him. You have no reason to be here if you aren't. But that works both ways."

A car screeched around the corner in front of the Tiergarten and then accelerated towards them, its masked headlights just glowing slits.

"That's a Nazi driver right there," Sarah mumbled, turning back to check her faint reflection in the window. Braids, uniform coat of the *Bund Deutscher Mädel. Dumb little monster.*

The approaching car growled past them before pulling up at the kerb in front of the embassy with great drama.

"Wish me luck," Sarah grunted, turning the door handle.

"Take no chances," answered the Captain.

Sarah stopped and looked back at him. There was no fear in his face, but there was an absence of confidence that made Sarah feel vulnerable.

She slipped out of the Mercedes.

The asphalt here was fresh and perfect, and Sarah's feet passed silently across it. She was grateful for its smoothness underfoot, as she wore noiseless ballet slippers, dyed black to pass as school shoes. She kept low to the ground and moved quickly towards the other car.

Its uniformed driver opened the rear passenger door on the kerbside as Sarah approached. The SS officer Hasse climbed out.

Don't look around. Don't look around. Don't look around.

He straightened up and stretched out his shoulders—

Don't look around—

—and walked towards the embassy doors. Sarah reached the car and crouched behind it. Peering through the windows, she watched the driver, trying to guess his next move. Hasse was starting up the staircase—

Commit to something, gottverdammt. Stay or go.

The driver moved around the front of the car to the driver's door. Sarah bolted the other way and up the steps behind Hasse, keeping to the shadowed side of the path.

There was a flash as light spilled down the shallow stairs. Two great oak panelled doors now stood ajar at the entrance, flanked by guards in military uniform. Silhouetted by the lights inside, an official in a tailcoat waited. Sarah slowed as Hasse reached the door. She couldn't make out the exchange but saw the official bow to Hasse's salute and a moment's confusion ended in nodding. They entered the building and the doors began to close.

Sarah accelerated to a skip and emerged from the shadows. *Just a bit behind my adult. Catching up.*

The guards were dressed in dark brown uniforms with red markings. As she approached, she tried to read their faces – were they bored, alert, tired? – but their expressions were fixed, martial and staring. They wore cloaks, even in the warm summer air. *They're trained to stand immobile. They are ceremonial,* thought Sarah. *Perfect. Not paid to think.*

She skipped towards them, beaming and nodding.

Catching up. Sorry. Arigato.

She stepped onto the colonnade and one of the guards moved across her path—

Sarah cursed herself. *So sure of yourself.* Her body tensed and quivered as it prepared to run—

The guard caught the closing door and pulled it wide open. His stony visage slipped as a half-smile lit up one side of his face and he winked.

"*Arigato gozaimasu*," Sarah burbled quietly, her heart thumping in her chest and ears.

Hasse and the official were already halfway down the brightly lit hallway, but she had to slow her breathing or she would be overheard. Sarah slowed to a crawl. There were doors to either side, and she tried to overlay the architectural plans on top of what she was seeing. The carpet was thick and her feet made no sound, but that meant that no one else was making any noise either...

She glanced at the closing front door. There was no one behind her. The embassy was deserted, sleeping, *vulnerable*.

She veered to one side and crouched next to a sideboard as the others disappeared through a door at the far end of the corridor. She saw herself once more in the polished black lacquer. She was less a dumb little monster and more a scared little girl. *Oh, verpiss dich, Schwächling*, Sarah tutted at her reflection, reaching for the nearest door.

Although Sarah knew the way, in theory at least, the offices and waiting rooms were unlit and windowless. Several times she collided with furniture and had to pause, bruised and aching in the dark, waiting to see if anyone had heard her. Once she scattered a pile of papers across the floor and, not being able to see to tidy them up, became conscious that she was leaving a trail for anyone following her. She picked two locked doors on her journey and wondered whether to lock them behind her, but she did not have time – the meeting was probably already underway.

Besides, tonight the building was out of bounds to the staff. Hasse did not want his visit to the embassy to be noticed or remarked upon, and apparently Imperial Japan was equally happy for the meeting to be unobserved.

She hurried up a dim back staircase and emerged at the end of a long, empty and brightly lit corridor. The ambassador's office was halfway down, and Hasse must already be inside. She moved swiftly along the carpet, counting doors against the building plan in her head. Men's bathroom, first secretary, military attaché (*spy*), file room, ambassador's secretary. The sign on the door was, for Sarah, unreadable.

大
使
個
人
補
佐
官

Sarah stopped, wondering if the plans were up to date, whether the offices could have been swapped around.

Commit to the move.

She dropped down and gently laid a shoulder against the door. She gripped the handle and pulled slowly, before turning. The latch bolt slid silently back, and Sarah let her weight open it. No lock. But as wood crossed carpet it made an audible swish that announced her arrival. She froze.

A typewriter and some more complex printing machine were lit by one green desk lamp; the rest of the windowless room of dull filing cabinets and minimal decor was illuminated by the corridor behind her. There were two internal doors. One, leading to the waiting room, was bordered by thin, white light. Faint noises could be heard through it. The other, to a bathroom that led onto the office itself, was dark.

So near now—

As Sarah entered, she noticed she was breathing heavily... or rather she found herself aware of her breathing, sensing the air rushing through her windpipe and exploding into the atmosphere in a way that couldn't possibly go unheard. She closed her eyes and inhaled deeply through her nose, holding the lungful for a moment before letting it out through her mouth in one long, slow release.

Not for the first time, Sarah waited for another voice to chide, cajole and pester her, but nobody spoke.

She opened the door to the bathroom, noticing at once the acoustics change. The room was unfinished and filled with boxes of tiles, copper pipes and anonymous white ceramic items in wooden crates. There was an aroma of sawn timber and sewage. The murmur of voices, now clear enough to be understood, came echoing from a rectangular outline of white light at the far end of the room. She stepped inside and found that the floor was littered with sharp fragments that immediately attacked her feet. She took one last look at the jagged landscape in the light of the office, scrunched up her toes to minimize any damage and closed the door behind her.

Sarah moved slowly towards the entrance to the ambassador's office, reaching out for the boxes she knew to be there. Someone was speaking in perfect German, but with an American accent, so Sarah guessed it was the Japanese ambassador.

"...the beginning of a more extensive and profound relationship between our empires—"

Something sliced through her slipper into the sole of her foot. Sarah wanted to scream and hop and hit things. Instead she stuffed a wrist between her teeth so she didn't reveal herself. She waited, panting silently for the waves of shock and pain to ebb away.

"...cooperation that goes beyond the military, that our shared goals..."

She tried to put weight on the foot. It hurt, but she could bear it. She doubted that she could run if she needed to and, more worryingly, she could feel something serrated moving around in her wet sock.

Her destination wasn't a door at all, but a sheet of wood nailed into place while work was carried out. It was ill-fitting and as Sarah squatted down next to it, she could see a sliver of the room. By leaning forward and back she could see the whole meeting.

The large room was brightly lit by a chandelier and was a mixture of Germany's marble minimalism, some luxuriant furnishings and a smattering of Japanese *objets d'art*. Hasse stood in its centre, cap under his arm, his grey day-to-day uniform seeming out of place among the tangible expense of the room. His face was a mask of affable tolerance.

Behind an extensive desk, and dwarfed by it, sat the Japanese ambassador. He was a small man who grinned as he talked. His eyebrows seemed too big for his face and too high up his forehead. Coupled with his moustache and glasses, the resemblance to a Jewish comedian Sarah had seen in a film when she was little was startling. She half expected him to begin waddling around the room.

The almost comic stature of the ambassador was in sharp contrast to the officer of the Imperial Japanese Army who sat impatiently to his right. Dressed in simple khaki battledress but sporting thick braids of gold on his red collar patches and long, spotless boots rather than the puttee wrappings of the guards, he reminded Sarah of Trotsky, the communist driven out of Russia by his Bolshevik friends. At not much under two metres tall, he towered over both the ambassador and his desk. Merely by tapping a foot in irritation, he seemed to dominate the space, a personality on the verge of explosive expansion. This had to be Shirō Ishii.

Behind both of them sat a Japanese woman dressed in a Western style, head bowed and taking notes. So still was her body that Sarah almost overlooked her entirely, until she turned a page of her pad.

The ambassador stopped to take a breath in his speech and seemed ready to go on, but Ishii interrupted in terse Japanese.

"In German, for our guest, please," the ambassador scolded after a pause of surprise and disappointment.

Ishii sighed and then repeated himself in halting German.

"I think we get the idea, Your Excellency. Now I think the *Obersturmbannführer* and I need to have a confidential conversation." He nodded towards the exit.

The ambassador looked at his assistant and then smiled.

"Oh, Fujiwara-kun is entirely in my confidence," he scoffed gently. "A lady of a great house. You may speak in front of her."

"No, Your Excellency. I need to talk to the *Obersturmbannführer*. Alone."

The ambassador's expression froze and then fell into a

scowl, as the insult hit home. He began to growl in Japanese, repeatedly tapping his finger on the desk.

"Not in German for our guest?" Ishii sneered in German and then replied in Japanese. The argument continued.

Secrets. Authority. Military. Hierarchy. Mine. Courtesan—

The ambassador stood and slammed a fist on his desk, rage reddening his face. But he fell silent.

Courtesan. The suggestion that had ended the argument.

The seconds ticked by.

The smaller man turned to Hasse, his face under control. "*Obersturmbannführer*, it was a pleasure meeting you and I hope you have a fruitful *military* meeting," the ambassador managed.

Hasse nodded as the ambassador bowed minutely and then strode from the room without acknowledging Ishii. He was followed by his secretary, who had glided to the door in his wake, but found herself on the wrong side as it closed. She waited for an awkward few seconds, head down, until the ambassador returned to open it for her.

When the door finally shut, both Hasse and Ishii broke into raucous laughter. The German sagged and placed his hands on his thighs as if struggling to breathe. The Japanese officer leaned back and hissed through his teeth.

Finally, he stood and waved the SS man into a nearby armchair, before perching on the edge of the desk.

"Politicians," Ishii scoffed. "Diplomats. How much more we could achieve without them."

"My friend," Hasse said, holding a finger in the air while he sat. "I am a political animal, as are you. Is not war just politics by other means?"

Hasse was now mostly obscured by the back of the chair, and Sarah had to press up against the wooden partition in order to hear him clearly.

"Yes, yes, true, true," Ishii conceded. "I just have no time for indecisiveness. That our countries are not yet formally allied and we must meet under cover of darkness is a nonsense. Come," Ishii exclaimed, clapping his hands together. "Let us not follow their example. You have something for me? How did my ceramic bombs work?"

"They have been useful, and we are in your debt. There are still problems with our cannon, but—"

"I know they work!" Ishii interrupted. "We just completed some field tests over Ningbo. That Chinese city is now enjoying an epidemic of the bubonic plague."

Enjoying.

"Excellent..." Hasse soothed. "But, if I understand, metal shells or explosives kill the bacteria or insect vectors. What if you had a virus that could survive the blast?"

"Viruses...too difficult to work with," Ishii dismissed the idea. "And you can't improve on smallpox."

"For which there is a vaccine! What if I could get you something *better*?"

Sarah felt, rather than heard, something behind her, as if pushed by a breeze, and she caught a crisp, chemical scent of jasmine and rose. She looked around, but her eyes hadn't adjusted to the darkness before a hand wrapped itself around her mouth.

CHAPTER SEVEN

SARAH TRIED TO PULL AWAY, but her right foot, now sodden, slid across the tiles, and she fell into the body behind her. Another arm coiled around her, and she was dragged backwards. She squirmed and tried to open her teeth to bite the hand, then realized she would only alert the men behind the partition. Their voices continued uninterrupted beyond it.

Stay still, she screamed to herself, as her feet bumped painfully over the threshold of the door to the assistant's office and onto carpet. She remembered that smell, though—

The door closed with the smallest *swish*, and the arms released Sarah onto the floor. The desk lamp came on.

Standing above her was the ambassador's secretary, Fujiwara. Her expression was concentrated, revealing nothing, but the smallest series of blinks revealed the effort required to not give anything away. Sarah looked at the exit that led to the corridor. Even from the floor she might get there first... but looking at the dark red streak her foot had left on the light carpet, she knew she couldn't outrun the woman as far as the staircase. Even a woman in high-heeled shoes. Wearing Chanel No. 5.

Fujiwara saw the look to the exit. Silently and slowly she shook her head, before raising a manicured index finger to her lips.

Her other hand held a gun, a weapon so small that Sarah hadn't identified it as such until then, it being just a glint of silver and dull white pearl. The woman looked at Sarah, then placed it on the desk and reached over to a box next to the typewriter.

She flicked a switch and the voice of Hasse oozed into the room, as if heard on a wireless set.

"—*this mission on the edge of the Congo has been receiving money from some friends of ours in the United States, friends whom I have been helping fund.*"

Fujiwara leaned against her desk and readjusted hair that had come loose in the struggle, without looking away from Sarah.

"*These friends obsess over Wunderwaffen, and always want to know what horrors can be dug up from the dark continent,*" Hasse continued excitedly. "*But I believe that these missionaries really have stumbled upon something marvellous...*"

The woman seemed to have come to a decision. She crouched, pointing at Sarah's right foot, before making a *give it to me* gesture with her fingers. Hasse's voice droned on behind her.

"*...it is highly infectious,*" Hasse burbled happily. "*Guaranteed lethal, and if this virus is truly airborne—*"

The ballet shoe slid off her foot to reveal a sock saturated with blood. Just that movement made Sarah wince and clench her teeth. She glanced at the gun on the edge of the desk. She could kick Fujiwara in the face with her other foot, get to the—

The woman shook her head and gently squeezed the sole of Sarah's foot through the sock. The pain was jagged, sharp, piercing, like a flashbulb light, like vinegar in a papercut. It left Sarah panting.

"*Kangaenasai...*" the secretary whispered, tapping the side of her head.

"*Do we want a virus that's one hundred per cent fatal?*" Ishii's booming voice crackled, distorted by the desk speaker. "*If the enemy doesn't have to care for the sick—*"

Sarah's sock was teased from her foot, and Fujiwara tutted at the sight of the wound, before standing and rummaging through the desk drawers.

"*My friend, you are thinking too small,*" said Hasse, quieter, more distant. "*Imagine the expanse of China...entirely free of the Chinese. That long, difficult war you've been fighting, using up all your strength...over in a few weeks. No garrison required, just ten million square kilometres of a new Japan, with all its resources and no sub-humans littering the land...*"

Sarah had been distracted up until that moment, by the pain in her foot, by the actions of the secretary and by the peculiarity of the situation. But that sentence, the matter-of-fact, mundane coldness of it, stopped the racing train of her thoughts like a fallen tree.

The woman had also stopped and was staring at the speaker.

Ishii exhaled. The sound through the intercom was like the snort of a horse.

"*We'd lose a workforce...*" Ishii mused. "*We'd have to import more Korean forced labour.*"

Fujiwara's mouth had fallen open as she heard this, outrage and distaste overtaking her. Then she glanced at Sarah to see her staring back. The woman's mouth closed, sealing away the visible emotion. She pulled a first-aid kit from the desk.

"*It's what we call here Lebensraum,*" Hasse pontificated. "*A bit of room for your people to live. You'd be doing them a great service.*"

The secretary crouched again, and after a moment's preparation began to swab alcohol onto the sole of Sarah's foot. She was in her late twenties, Sarah guessed, but her eyes seemed older, more tired. There was something very familiar there, but Sarah wondered if she just recognized suffering.

"*You'll obtain samples for me?*" Ishii grunted.

"*And you will do the field trials? Although it sounds like they're doing that already,*" Hasse continued with a laugh. Like sandpaper on steel.

The secretary gripped something embedded in Sarah's foot with a pair of tweezers.

"Shush," she whispered to Sarah, and pulled.

Sarah hissed once more as she saw the flashbulb light again and felt the tearing stab. She squeezed her eyes shut against it.

When she opened them again, Fujiwara was holding up a serrated sliver of white tile, two centimetres long.

She mouthed *Wao*, and dropped it into the kit. She looked very young at that moment. Very alive. Sarah marvelled at how much this woman was concealing.

"*You see, until we invade the Soviet Union, I don't have*"

anywhere to do them," Hasse explained. "*Poland is too small and too full of Germans. Italian East Africa is too near to the British. Your unit in Manchukuo is perfect. You have human test subjects, the 'logs', do you not?*"

As the woman bandaged her foot, Sarah could see her mouthing the odd word or phrase coming from the speaker, as if committing it to memory.

"*You're making a lot of assumptions,*" Ishii growled. "*And you're still allied to the Soviet Union—*"

"*You and I are adults, Ishii. We both know how worthless that alliance is to Germany, even if Stalin apparently does not. And you have nothing to lose here. Do you want to go on poisoning rivers and giving children contaminated sweets, or do you want to create something truly destructive? A weapon to conquer China? Even the United States?*"

"*I should strike you for your impertinence,*" Ishii said quietly.

"*But you won't because you know I'm right. I have some nerve gases you might be interested in, too—*"

"*Yes, I've read those papers, thank you. Not exactly secret. Why don't you use them on Stalin?*"

"*If I controlled them, I would.*" Hasse laughed. "*You met Stalin once, didn't you?*"

"*No, but I did see his work. He's as intent on wiping out his people as you are, if the starved corpses in the streets were anything to go by.*" Ishii paused. "*They did claim to be making smallpox, tularaemia, typhus, glanders...but they also said they had a grain surplus.*"

"*Either way, they won't be alive to use any of it.*"

◆　　◆　　◆

The men talked of their families, then of their favourite *Laufhäuser* in Paris before they left noisily.

Fujiwara leaned against her desk, smoking and watching Sarah struggling to put her damp sock back on. She listened to the men's voices fading away to nothing, and when she was sure they were gone, she stubbed out her cigarette and straightened up.

"So," she said out loud at last, in quiet, fluent but heavily accented sing-song German that reminded Sarah of something. "Who would send a little girl to spy on the Japanese ambassador to the German Reich?" She pushed her gun idly in a circle on the desk with a manicured finger, repeating the word *Reich* until the *R* hardened, and continued. "That's not very ethical, is it?"

Sarah picked up her shoe, which was a flat and sodden dripping mess. She tried to tease the wet satin upper from the sole.

"Ethical like a secretary listening into her bosses' private conversations?" Sarah replied, uncertain of how to proceed.

"Well, *Rikugun-Gun'i-Taisa* Ishii Shirō is not my employer, and the *Obersturmbannführer* is *gaijin*, a foreign agent," Fujiwara stated in mock solemnity. "His Excellency will be delighted that I can report extensively on the meeting that he was ejected from. From. *From.*" She walked around her desk and opened several drawers. "Tell me, little Nazi girl, who will be delighted that you can do the same?"

She tossed two flat-soled shoes at Sarah, who let them bounce to the floor before thinking better of it and retrieving them. They were only two sizes too large and Sarah could depart, if she was departing, without leaving a bloody trail through the embassy.

Lies will eat you up, she thought.

"I work for the *Abwehr*," Sarah stated, pulling a shoe over her injured foot.

"The *Abwehr*!" Fujiwara cried out melodramatically, looking to the heavens and placing both hands to her face, an expression that, again, Sarah found oddly familiar. "We're being spied on by the German Army! That would be simply awful..." She dropped her hands, cocked her head to one side and made a sad face. "If it were true. But it's not."

"It is true, *it is*," Sarah found herself saying.

"You are telling me that, er...*German military intelligence* is now employing little girls? *Jewish* little girls?"

Sarah felt paralysed and cold. She fought the rising panic and the urge to repeatedly inhale.

She forced a smile that could turn into a snarl and, shaking her head, she managed a dismissive snort. She rose to a standing position, ready to leave, to bluff it out, to seize the gun.

"I'm not a...*Jew*, that's ridiculous...and an insult. Whatever gave you that idea?"

"Yes, you are. It's passed down by the mother, yes?" The woman leaned into her. "And you're Alexandra Edelmann's daughter."

Sarah took a step backwards, the shake of her head no longer voluntary.

"You are Sarah Edelmann...no, Sarah, Sarah, *Sarah Goldstein*, your real name. That's you."

Sarah lunged for the gun and closed her hands around it,

but her foot gave way and she collapsed to the floor. She fumbled the tiny, heavy piece of metal, trying to hold the stock and aim the barrel but failing. Fujiwara smiled and kneeled down next to Sarah, neatly swatting the weapon from her hands. Sarah was hyperventilating as she crawled backwards.

The woman's face softened and she began to sing in a gentle, lilting timbre, a melody both foreign and utterly, wholly part of Sarah's being.

"Kono-ko yō-naku, mori-woba ijiru—"

"Lady Sakura?" Sarah gasped.

The woman blinked and held a hand in front of her mouth to hide a wide grin, but it could not hide her dimples.

"It has been a long, long time since somebody called me that."

The music got louder. The laughter more raucous.

Sarah covered her ears with her hands, but it was no longer enough. The dull stabbing through them made her want to collapse in on herself, to fold her head into a clenched fist. It was the second night of the earache, a constant blanket of fever, warm pus and pain.

Someone sat on the piano keys, and when this drew a laugh and a burst of applause, they did it again. And again.

Sarah rolled her lower body off the edge of her mother's bed and let her weight carry her feet the last few centimetres to the floor. She stood, shivering, her nightgown damp with sweat. She was small, not much taller than the vertiginous bed, and the ceiling seemed like the distant vaults of a great hall.

Tottering unsteadily and fighting the dizziness, she made her way down the hall towards the noise and lights.

She passed two men with glazed eyes slumped against the wall and skirted a wide pool of clear liquid and broken glass. Emerging into a packed piano room that was thick with tobacco smoke and intensely bright, she searched for her mother.

A woman, half-dressed and with streaked make-up, sat bouncing on the piano keyboard, laughing hysterically. An enraptured audience of middle-aged men clapped along. Gramophone records were crushed underfoot, empty bottles were strewn, spinning on the sticky floor, and those who were not unconscious on the furniture were shouting to each other over the noise.

Sarah saw her mother talking to a tall man from the theatre. Struggling to pass a gyrating dancer who was sloshing a yellow liquid out of a green bottle, Sarah called out.

"*Mutti*—" Sarah began.

Her mother turned, eyes red, saturated in irritation. "Sarahchen, go back to bed at once. It's very late, very late...very early in fact. Too early to get up."

"*Mutti*, it's really loud. I can't sleep and...my ear really hurts and—"

"I'm *working*, just go to bed," her mother hissed. "Or join the party, I don't care."

A single tear rolled down Sarah's cheek. It cooled as

it travelled, to become cold and uncomfortable as it gathered on her chin for the final drop.

"I'll see to her, Alexandra-san," said a sing-song voice. *Alexandla*. "Alexandra. *Alexandra*."

Sarah turned to see a mountain of brightly coloured fabric gliding across the floor towards her. There were robes upon robes of silks and patterned cloths, rising to a wide sash of bundled material and ties, before erupting over the top with two wide sleeves. The vision had a porcelain white face, the features and expression seemingly painted on, while her hair, jet-black buns as smooth and perfect as polished ebony, was adorned by combs, flowers and streams of falling petals.

Then the vision suddenly grinned, cracking the blankness of the mask. Above the edges of her smile, small dimples formed, and warmth flowed from them. The face under everything, her true face, was little more than a teenager's.

"Sarah-san, take my hand," she said. "I am Lady Sakura."

"Hello, Lady...but my mother..."

"Your mother is working, she has asked me to care for you. She tells me you are sick. Come..."

Sarah thought that this wasn't how it had happened, but she felt weak and unable to argue. She reached out for the woman's hand, which was long, slender and as soft as anything she had touched.

The woman bent down and swept Sarah into her arms. There was the scent of clothes badly stored, a touch of mothball, the tension of bathed skin and poorly laundered material, and the crisp jasmine and rose tang of what Sarah could identify as Chanel No. 5.

They flew from the crowded room, the partygoers melting away in front of them.

It felt quieter and cooler in her mother's room than it had before. Even the bed felt less monolithic and softer, being laid on it by two caring arms.

"You're Japanese?" Sarah wondered aloud as she wriggled under the covers.

"I am. A visitor to your country," Lady Sakura murmured, feeling Sarah's brow and making a clucking noise. She reached for a tumbler of water but did not like what she found there.

"Are you a *geisha*?" Sarah asked, remembering the word.

The woman placed a hand in front of her mouth to conceal a smile, but her eyes creased under the white make-up and the grin danced across her dimples. "No, I am not. I am a professional fake." She chuckled. "*Hitsuji no atama, inu no niku.*"

"What does that mean?"

"*Sheep head, dog meat.* I am not as advertised. I am just a dancer and singer, and a...courtesan."

"What is a *courtesan*?"

The woman paused and shook her head. "Not a geisha. Geisha are artists, respected, refined. Once, long ago, I was *Maiko*, an apprentice geisha. Now..." She paused. "Now, I am just a showgirl," she finished with a joviality that Sarah did not believe.

"Is there anything wrong with being a showgirl?" Sarah ventured. "All our friends are show people..."

"I wanted to be a geisha, then to travel the world like Madame Sadayakko, *the Sarah Bernhardt of Japan, bewitching theatres of Westerners.* To return home, cherished. But the world does not need two Sada Yaccos. Just more cheap, exotic dancers in inexpensive kimonos...so people can mock their eyes." Lady Sakura added the last sentence almost to herself, then leaned forward and whispered in a conspiratorial stage whisper, "This *obi*, my sash, is a curtain from a boarding house in Hamburg."

She began to laugh, not trying to cover her mouth, or maintain her tranquil aspect. It was a deep belly-chuckle that set her shoulders quaking. It made Sarah smile for its joy, but that made her wince. Lady Sakura settled onto the bed next to her.

"*Mimi no itami?* Pain in your ears?" The woman sighed and made a deep noise of profound sympathy. "Come, I will help you sleep. This is a lullaby from where I grew up, so close your eyes."

She gathered Sarah into her right arm and began to sing in a flute-like voice of penetrating gentleness.

"*Kono-ko yō-naku mori-woba ijiru...*"

Sarah fought the song's soporific effect.

"That's beautiful," she managed when it was over. "And sad, really sad. What does it mean?"

"The lullaby is sung by a servant girl, looking after

another family's baby, who is crying." Without the melody and her voice, the words are dark and painful. "She is tired and without sleep, and she pleads with the baby to rest. She wants to leave, to return to her own family, but she cannot, she has nothing. She is ashamed."

"Why can't she go home?" Sarah complained, burdened by the misery of the story.

Lady Sakura looked away.

"She is of the *Burakumin* people," she began. "She is an *eta*, as they used to say, the lowest of the low, worth just one seventh of a *real* person. The *Burakumin* have long done the dirty work – burying the dead, slaughtering animals, making leather. That was all they were permitted to do, but they were shunned because they did it. People no different, treated as outcasts, for their whole lives... The girl in this lullaby is lucky to have that job. *Lucky.* She should be *grateful.*"

Her face was in shadow and painted to a blank slate, but her voice betrayed anger and suffering.

"Are you one of the buraku...is that why you aren't a geisha?"

"It's a long story." The woman sighed and shook off the question the way that Sarah noticed so many adults did. "But in part, yes. It's all supposed to be different now, but it isn't. There are registers, lists, you can't keep your caste secret. It haunts your life."

There was a crash, screaming and laughter from outside the bedroom. When Sarah looked back to Lady Sakura, it was as if the clouds had parted and there had never been any rain. In its place, a smiling young Japanese woman in stage make-up.

"What is your name? Your real name, I mean?" Sarah asked, yawning.

"Atsuko. Takeda Atsuko."

"Mine's Sarah Goldstein... We're Jewish really, but *Mutti* doesn't like people to know. Could you tell?"

Atsuko nodded with a smile. They shook hands formally, but did not let go.

Sarah squeezed Lady Sakura's hand and rested her head against the thick, rough embroidery of her obi. She drifted, ready for sleep, but fought the urge. She was waiting for her mother to come to say goodnight.

But she never came.

———

Sarah clung on to Atsuko for a long minute, the mission, the danger, all forgotten.

"How are you here?" Sarah asked finally, blinking back the tears. As ever, angry at their ungovernable wantonness. "Of all the people, in all the world—"

"Wait a minute, that was my question." Atsuko laughed, letting go of her. "Your mother has you working for the Nazis?"

"My mother died," Sarah said flatly.

"I'm sorry. She was a...good woman," Atsuko managed.

"You don't have to say that."

"No? Well, she tried, but she drank like a...brush maker? Is that what Germans say?"

"Yes, that's the phrase." Sarah felt she was being disloyal, felt she should not be saying anything negative, even to someone who knew the truth.

The truth.

Sarah looked at the face of the woman in front of her, suddenly so familiar, a tiny but very real part of the *good* inside Sarah. Yet, she was not the babysitter of ten years before, much as Sarah wanted...*needed* to share something with her. The gymnast in Sarah stood on the edge of a balance beam, ready to tumble, but frightened to.

Commit to the move.

"I work for a...spy, I suppose. He's British." Sarah pushed on, as Atsuko opened her mouth. "He and the *Abwehr* have a common enemy."

"Ah, Kurt Hasse and his nasty tricks department!" Atsuko smiled.

"They – *we* – wanted to know what he knew, what Ishii was doing here."

"Now you know," the woman said, spreading her arms.

"And what are you doing here?" Sarah insisted.

"I'm working—"

"*Fujiwara-kun of a noble house*?" Sarah interrupted derisively.

Atsuko laughed. Dimples and dancing eyes.

"Indeed. Did you find out what a courtesan was?" Sarah nodded, and Atsuko continued. "So the noble-born secretary *Fujiwara-kun* is just an excuse for a high-ranking official to have me here. Few people are fooled. Ishii certainly was not."

"But why would you make that happen?" Sarah shook her head incredulously. "Why would you want to be here?"

"Can't a man find me attractive?"

"I'm guessing any man would find you attractive if you wanted it..."

Atsuko laughed, the belly-chuckle of that bedroom long ago.

"Things have not improved for the *Burakumin*. And now the empire is in the hands of those who see the Japanese as superior beings, led by a living God. People like Ishii. People willing to give diseases to innocent civilians, because they think those lives are worth nothing. They've done it in Manchuria, they'll do it in the rest of China, Russia, Singapore, Philippines...they won't stop. The Americans don't want to get their hands dirty, and the British are dangerously overstretched. But the empire has to be stopped, or there will be no equality for anyone. No one will be free."

"You're a communist?" Sarah asked.

"No, I work for the *Suiheisha*, the Levelers Association of Japan, fighting for our rights. But I *do* pass information to the Soviet Union. The Nazis aren't the only people who have a marriage of convenience there. It's only a matter of time before Germany invades Russia. Then we'll all be on the same side."

Sarah wanted that.

"We're both spies now." Sarah laughed. "You'd have got long odds for that."

"We've both had to play a role our whole lives. We are both dog meat, pretending to be a sheep's head," Atsuko said quietly. Then she held something up. "Here, a gift. If you're going to stop Hasse, take it with my blessings."

Sarah took the pistol, a tiny derringer, little more than a collection of silvery-blue metal pieces barely wider than her palm, maybe three hundred grams in weight. She looked into the woman's eyes and saw, for the first time, fear there amid the determination. Atsuko opened her arms and gathered Sarah in to her.

"In Japanese, we say, *the weak are meat.*" The woman squeezed her and continued. "Be strong, Sarah Goldstein. Be *strong.*"

"And then she just walked you out?"

"Well, limped. Past the same guard. Singing. *Arigato gozaimashita.*"

The Captain finished the stitch knot and, lifting her foot, bit the thread to break it.

"There are scissors in the kit for that purpose," Sarah said through gritted teeth.

"Force of habit, sorry," he murmured, laying her leg back onto the bed.

"No scissors in the British Army?"

"With the *Hejazi*, not so much," he murmured as he began rebandaging the foot. He sighed. "Very dangerous telling her about me. The Soviets are technically our enemy."

"She's a friend. She's *family,*" Sarah insisted with a vehemence and certainty that surprised her. Maybe she was just tired. Maybe she just didn't want to argue about it.

"She's someone you knew ten years ago, when you were five? Six? And what if she's captured? By the Germans? By the Japanese *Kenpeitai*?"

"It's done. If you can work for Nazis, I can have friends who are Soviet agents," Sarah finished and then began to giggle, so ridiculous was the sentence. "This is quite a vocation we've got for ourselves, isn't it?"

The Captain knotted the bandage and smiled. He was *really* smiling. Work always made him feel better. Maybe that was all he needed.

"So, what will the admiral think of this?" Sarah yawned.

"I think he's going to send me to the Congo to look for these missionaries," the Captain replied, with an almost jolly sigh. He carefully repacked the medical kit.

Send him. Weakened. Unstable. Unable to commit. Unable to go a day without—

"I don't think that's a good idea," she managed.

"He won't want any of his people going. That risks open war with the SS. I'm deniable."

"No, I mean..." Sarah struggled for the words. She was frightened to dampen his renewed enthusiasm. "Are you fit enough for that kind of work, alone?"

"I'm fine," he bristled quietly, closing the tin with a snap. "I was shot ten months ago."

Sarah struggled for the next thing to say, but the Captain shook his head suddenly. "Hang on, I missed something. What did she call your mother?"

"Alexandra Edelmann. That was her stage name."

"*Your mother was Alexandra Edelmann? The* Alexandra Edelmann?"

"You've heard of her?" Sarah was surprised. Nothing

remained of her mother's career; she didn't even know how many films she had made or what roles she'd played onstage.

"Yes. Cinemas are good places for meeting contacts – dark, mostly empty in the daytime. I've watched *a lot* of films."

CHAPTER EIGHT

25TH AUGUST 1940

THE NEXT AFTERNOON, THEIR MERCEDES pulled away from *Abwehr* headquarters along the *Tirpitzufer* and followed the canal towards the *Zoologischer Garten*.

Sarah waited as long as she could and then spoke.

"You're bringing me," she said with all the calm strength she could muster.

"Hang on, this is *Africa*. This isn't a boarding school or a cocktail party—"

"And you've been to Africa?"

"Yes," he said with certainty. "Egypt...Libya," he added with less conviction.

"Not the Congo, then? Oh, is the Congo in Egypt? You know, I'm sure I read—"

"You've made your point, thank you," the Captain said tersely. "I just think" – he held up a hand to stop her interrupting – "a blonde girl will draw too much attention on a continent of black people."

"You're blond," Sarah said defiantly.

"You're a girl."

"Am I? That explains *a lot.* Only the other day, I was looking and thinking, *Where is my Piephahn?* and—"

"It's dangerous," the Captain said, talking over her. "A dangerous place. And a dangerous mission."

The meeting had been short. Sarah had made her report while the admiral gazed out of the windows, hand on his chest. Then he sat forward, tapped his battered desk and began talking.

"Very well. These...missionaries...scientists...are in Vichy territory about to fall to the Gaullist Free French, and therefore into British hands.

"One, as an agent of the *Abwehr*, you're going there to stop the research ending up with the British. I don't want to give their scientists at Porton Down anything they might be tempted to use. Get the people back here and under the control of the *Wehrmacht*.

"Two, as Helmut Haller, High Society's Fixer, you're there to stop them being interned as a favour for an old friend.

"Three, and most of all, prevent the research from reaching Ishii, by whatever means necessary. As quietly as possible. I will not start a war with the SS...not yet. Start in Chad, travel south through French Equatorial Africa and follow the bodies."

Follow the bodies, the admiral had said.

"So you should go alone? So I can discover, weeks – months?

– later that you're dead? I'm a Jewish girl with fake papers, I'm in danger here as well."

"Knowing you as I do, you'd be fine."

Sarah was thrown momentarily by the implied compliment but rallied. "Thank you, *but* if that's what I wanted, I'd have taken your money and left you in that barn near Rothenstadt to die and saved us all a lot of trouble. You need to bring someone...and I don't mean taking that idiot Norris. Take someone useful."

The car slowed as it approached a checkpoint where a *Blockwart* was checking whether car headlamps were ready for the blackout.

"Is this because you want to do *spy things*?" he asked.

"You mean, *for fun*?" she sneered. "When I said those words last year, it was because I wanted *purpose*, not excitement. *Spy things*, Captain Floyd, are what I do. It's what I am. I don't have any other usefulness, unless surviving is its own reward. I'm not anyone's child, anyone's sister, anyone's playmate or pupil. If you left me, yes, I would cease to exist, but no..." She was almost shouting now. "That is not why I want to go. It's because you need someone with you and *I'm all you have*."

The car seemed extra silent when she stopped. The *Blockwart* waved it through the checkpoint.

"And my foot hurts," she added.

Sarah was exhausted. She couldn't sleep after infiltrating the embassy. Once in bed, she had been practically shaking through fear or excitement, she couldn't tell which.

"We should take Clementine as well, if only to keep an eye on her," Sarah continued into the silence.

"Why not? Shall we bring Frau Hofmann, too?" the Captain muttered.

"Taking a black spy to Africa sounds prudent," Sarah countered.

"If Norris hasn't killed her already..."

He had said *Shall we*. "We". Sarah had won but was too tired to revel in it. *Maybe this will be good for him*, Sarah thought. Or maybe they should be staying somewhere safe until he was healthy...

There had been something else to their orders:

"Oh, and find out who Hasse has been talking to in the United States. There's a little nest of vipers there somewhere... I need to know who they want to bite and why."

"You think they're friends?"

"They're Nazis. We're all Nazis..." said the admiral. "For the present."

"This better be important," Sarah grumbled.

"Do you know what happens if the British discover that Germany has used a *disease* as a weapon?" the Captain said. "We'd have mustard gas dropped on Berlin. Then chlorine dropped on London...and so on, until there's nothing left. It would be the end of everything."

Through the window Sarah watched the people in the sun-drenched *Tiergarten* – the children and the mothers, the young women flirting with the soldiers, and the elderly walking the aches from their old bones. Unbidden, her imagination set everyone writhing, choking, and spitting up bloody foam.

Sarah closed her eyes and on the paper of her mind, began to write.

Dearest Mouse,

It does seem strange still calling you Mouse, when your name isn't really <u>Mauser</u>. But I think that maybe some things just fit. Ruth HeißStöck...no, that doesn't work. Mouse it is. But then I'm not really writing this at all.

We hold these parties. Soldiers and politicians come and get drunk, and when my uncle isn't selling them radios or barges or French wine, you can hear them talk.

They talk a lot when they're drunk.

They've been talking a lot about Poland.

They've been talking about rounding people up and shooting them. Not Polish soldiers. Just <u>people</u>. Women and children, too. So they're not all partisans, you see. They're just killing people for the sake of killing people.

Sometimes it's because they're Jewish. They pushed two hundred Jews into a synagogue and set it on fire. Children burned to death.

The Führer sent the army in "to kill without mercy and reprieve all men, women and children of the Polish race". He said that, in so many words. He means the Poles aren't real people.

I watch the people listening to this. Some are upset, angry and sick under their silence. Some are pleased, happy, <u>enjoying it</u>.

You can see the line between the two. It's like a new surgical incision — it's small and neat and almost invisible, but you know it's going to be pulled open and torn bloody. You know that even if it's stitched back together, it will be ridged and jagged like a mountain range, that the dirt will still be there. It'll grow septic and weep pus and it'll infect everything and everyone.

Alles Liebe,
Ursula

CHAPTER NINE

30TH AUGUST 1940

THE JOURNEY BEGAN IN SOME SPLENDOUR. The polished walnut and chrome of Berlin's Tempelhof Airport with its gloved and deferential waiting staff felt like moving through Sarah's lost childhood, when money and food were plentiful. However, that childhood of theatre people had seemed to Sarah to be open and welcoming to all, back when Jewish people could walk the streets unmolested and work and marry whom they wanted. Black performers had been treated as a curiosity by some, but there had been no malice among her mother's friends. Clementine's presence here, even as a servant, drew reproving glances and snide comments. Sarah noticed them and it needled her.

"The way people are looking at you..." Sarah sighed.

"Am I embarrassing you? Well, sorry, *Fräulein*," Clementine spat.

"No, I mean it's not right."

"You're offering me *sympathy*?" Clementine said, looking up.

"What kind of a Nazi *are* you?"

"I just—" Sarah began and stopped.

"Look, this isn't *Huckleberry Finn*. I'm not here to teach you an important life lesson about us. I'm here because servants have no choice, so look for your self-improvement somewhere else."

"You've read a lot of American books," Sarah pointed out, her irritation getting the better of her.

"Clearly so have you. What did you expect, me to be climbing trees in my spare time? Picking fleas or pushing bones through my nose?"

Ursula Haller should be acting like the perfect little monster, but instead Sarah wanted to be *nice*, while maintaining her cover. Something about Clementine's attitude made that an almost impossible line to tread. Sarah found herself saying what she thought, without any filter at all.

"This is...stupid," Sarah managed, uncertain of what she meant.

"You know what's stupid? Me helping military intelligence. I should have let that man with the weird accent kill me."

This is why I don't like people, Sarah thought. *They're difficult and complicated.*

And Clementine was turning out to be very complex. She was no poorly educated domestic. As well as proving to be a terrible maid in almost every way, her fierce intelligence didn't fit her story. While the ferocious attitude made more sense, it seemed so reckless to Sarah, who had spent years keeping silent out of a sense of self-preservation.

It was on the plane, a brand-new Junkers Ju 52/3m whose

ridged silver metalwork glittered in the morning sun, that the voyage began to go wrong.

Sarah was fine, even excited by the prospect of flying for the first time, right up until the moment she fastened the seat belt. The interior reminded her of a bus and the large, rectangular, curtained windows made it feel light and airy. But the act of strapping herself down, even across the waist, made her feel trapped.

The door closed. The handle turned and locked.

Sarah tensed.

The engine on the right wing started up with a stuttering, coughing bark and, after a moment's splutter, exploded to a caustic roar. Sarah was startled and her breathing quickened. The other two engines joined the cacophony, and it felt like competing orchestras of percussionists, coming together and then slipping out of sync with a clatter.

Something about the noise, all around and filling every space, made Sarah want to flee, and the fact that she was restrained from doing so was a solvent to her intellect. She became a small mammal with one imperative.

Lauf. Run.

When the Luft Hansa airliner finally started along the runway and the engines opened up, the howling rose through two octaves and swelled to an ear-splitting intensity.

The airport began to slide past, and the ground became a blur, before falling away with a lurch.

Sarah waited for her mother's voice to cajole or sooth her, but she was still silent.

Sarah had to deal with this alone.

She watched the buildings become toys, then dots on a shattered chessboard, before the ground began to fade to white. Looking at the surrounding clouds she suddenly imagined falling through them, like she had taken a misstep on the red roofs of Vienna. But this time there would be no impact, just more and more white air, sucking her stomach through her mouth as she dropped.

She closed her eyes and dug her fingernails into the rubber armrest. She tried to be the inner voice herself.

Rip yourself together, Sarah.

She couldn't hear herself over the inner screams of panic.

Clementine leaned around Sarah's seat.

"What's the matter?" she yelled through the roar. "You're talking to yourself."

Sarah looked around, shaking, sweat stinging her wide eyes.

"God, you're pathetic." Clementine sighed.

She reached out and took Sarah's hand. The skin of her palms was rough. Rough in a way no child's hand should be. But it was warm and strong, so Sarah gripped it tightly.

The Ju 52 carried them to Rome in an eight-hour rattling cocoon of noise and panic.

The Hotel Victoria was stuffy, the corridors dark and crammed with paintings in lieu of windows, scenes of Rome committed to canvas so no one need ever go outside.

Sarah was physically exhausted by so many hours trapped on the edge of terror but found that her brain – soaked in that same fear – was now hissing like a frying pan. She dearly wanted to sleep, to cut her engines, but she couldn't.

The hotel had its priorities. The bar was fully stocked, but it did not have a library so much as a bookcase. The lounge was deserted, but the chair next to the shelves was occupied.

"I'm not here on your time," Clementine stated, looking up from her book and frowning.

"I know, I'm not going to stop you."

"Not that you could," Clementine muttered with raised eyebrows.

Sarah did not know what to say, so she said nothing. She looked determinedly at the spines of the books, not really reading the titles. Something about Clementine, or her attitude, meant that Sarah felt obliged to try and...what was she trying to do? To convince Clementine of her good intentions? To convince her she *wasn't* a Nazi? To *win*? What would she be winning?

Was this how the Mouse felt all the time?

Having decided she wasn't going to order her around or treat Clementine like *the Black Shame*, even if the little monster Ursula would, Sarah was highly irritated that Clementine was being so...*rotzig*. The starving Sarah, the hunted Sarah, the abused Sarah...she had made herself small. Clementine was the opposite of this. Maybe this is what they meant when they called the *Neger* feral and primitive—

They. Sarah shuddered at the way that thought appeared, unbidden.

"The servant quarters are hot and the company is terrible," Clementine mumbled.

This was the first volunteered piece of conversation, and Sarah didn't know what to do with it.

"The rooms aren't much better," Sarah laughed.

"Is that what you think? You spoiled bitch."

Anger flared in Sarah and consumed all sensibility in its fire.

"Think I haven't lived in poverty? I've slept with cockroaches and eaten potato peelings and made bread out of sawdust, so get off your high horse."

"When were you poor?" Clementine scoffed. "I've *seen* your house."

Gottverdammt. Think it out.

"My mother was very sick," Sarah said as sombrely as she could muster. "Things got very bad for a while, until my uncle came for me" – *don't lie if you can avoid it* – "and he's not really that rich. It's all about looking wealthy."

"Rich enough." Clementine laughed, but her tone had softened a tiny bit, like throwing a sheet over a rock.

"I would like us to stop fighting," Sarah said quietly. "We've got work to do and real enemies—"

Clementine snorted without looking up. "I told you, you want a *Hausneger*, get a big knife."

"How have you survived this long as a servant?"

"When they get the whip out, I stop. That's always done the trick." Clementine sighed theatrically. "Fine, we can *stop fighting*. But if you think I'm going to give you absolution, Nazi girl, think again."

"What are you reading?" Sarah tried again.

"Maigret. Read it before."

"Did your father teach you French?"

Clementine's head snapped upward.

"I taught *myself* French," she growled. "Taught myself everything. You think I could learn anything at school while the children chanted *bimbo, bimbo* at me for hours on end..."

Clementine seemed to struggle with something behind her eyes and then continued more calmly.

"When I was two, my father took my mother – his *wife*, his *German wife* – back to Senegal to set up home. Their ship, some *beschissener* cargo freighter, sank with all hands just outside Dakar. My grandmother in the Rhineland was *overjoyed* to have to raise her family's greatest embarrassment permanently and made sure that I understood, on a daily basis, just how difficult that was for her... I learned French to irritate her," Clementine added, shrugging. "All I got was this camera." She waved to a black-and-brass Leica on a side table. "He was going to get his things later. Things like his daughter."

The lounge clock ticked.

"You read this?" Clementine said suddenly, waggling her book. "Simenon has this whole thing about masks and alternate personalities. Who are you, really?"

"Well, I'm a spy of sorts, so..."

"What exactly is your job?"

"I'm just cover," Sarah said, shrugging. "They see a little girl, it makes them dismiss me, dismiss my uncle."

"You aren't going to get away with that for much longer, you know?"

The train rolled out of the station. The little girl waved at Sarah as she pulled away.

"And you? Who are you really?" Sarah demanded. "With

87

that education, that camera and that attitude? Not actually a maid, are you?"

Clementine looked to be on the verge of saying something vicious and cutting but then appeared to relent.

"I am...*employed* as a maid occasionally. These big parties, you can avoid doing any work easily enough. But I'm nosy and sometimes I find out things that people want to buy. Rich people have dirty little secrets. They *hate* me for being a *Rheinlandbastard* and a *chimney sweep*, and they treat me like dirt. But they're all rotten to the core, and I punish them for it. And make money," she added.

"It's enough that there are secrets to be had..." Sarah mumbled to herself. "So you didn't *accidentally* follow me to the recording room?" she asked out loud.

"Sorry. Now you're buying my silence, and I'm not living with my grandmother any more. You stopped seeing the scared little maid because you became my primary customers. I hit... what do they call it in America? *Pay dirt*. Pity you're Nazis."

"You could have been killed, you know? Norris would have killed you—"

"If you hadn't been there to save me. Little Eva, are you proud?"

"Another *spy*..." Sarah mused, ignoring the provocation. "Are you any good?"

"Well," Clementine said, dropping the book onto a nearby table. "The fifth floor is supposed to be closed. But there's someone in 502. A communist. The owners of this hotel are anti-fascist sympathizers. Is that something the German Army wants to know?"

"Maybe. We'll...put it in the report. Thank you. See, that wasn't hard, was it?"

"Or maybe I should tell the SS officer in 306?"

"There's an SS officer—" Sarah stopped herself, there was too much concern in her voice. "Well, there's an inter-service rivalry there." She laughed awkwardly. "I suspect the *Abwehr* would rather know first."

"Why do you trust me?" Clementine asked abruptly.

"I don't trust you. At all. I just don't *distrust* you enough to let someone push a needle into your brain to be on the safe side."

"Probably makes you a terrible spy. I'd have killed me."

Sarah walked along the road, conscious that there should have been glass underfoot.

"MUTTI!" she howled into the mist, but there was no reverberation, no sign that the sound had carried. She stood at the broken fence by the warehouses.

Her mother was gone. The car, the crash, the dogs that had pursued her...all gone. Instead, in the centre of the road was a hospital bed. Strapped to it was Elsa. Her hair was wild, eyes red, skin pale.

"Where's Mutti?" asked Sarah.

"Where's Mutti?" repeated Elsa, her voice cruel. "Like everyone else, she's gone. Do you see what you do? Where you go, lives end, people suffer. I should have let my father—"

"But you didn't," Sarah talked over her, gagging. She tried to free her, but the leather straps were tied, wrapped around

themselves, the knots too small for her fingers.

"You think you're helping, but you're not," Elsa snarled through clenched jaws. "See, you're not the innocent little girl."

"No—"

"You're the grinning maid at the port hotel..."

"No!"

"And you're counting the dead. As. You. Go."

Elsa was free. She wrapped her hands around Sarah's throat and dragged her down into the sheets.

"Now...or later?" Elsa screamed.

Sarah sat up in bed, teeth gritted, trying to pull Elsa's hands from her neck.

Gottverdammt.

She lay back in the darkness, panting, and imagined a letter.

Dear Mouse,

Oh, Mouse, would it help to know that Schäfer's dead? That Elsa shot her father before he could do...anything... to me? Or does that make you angry that no one came to save you? He can't do what he did to anyone else, ever again. Does that help?

Elsa was taken to a hospital and she hasn't come out again. Do you think that's deserved? Is it punishment for all the lambs she led to the slaughter? Nobody thinks she killed her father, so if she can recover herself, she can have her life back...or _a_ life back...a new life, anyway.

I know you tried to warn me, the best that you could. I know that talking about...it...is hard. Even now I can't put it into words. All those moments when you were quiet or staring into space, I had no idea what horrors you must have been reliving. I'm sorry.

Maybe Elsa got her due, _hat ihr Fett wegbekommen_, after all.

A little bird twittered that Rothenstadt has closed and that Bauer has been taken to a camp outside Munich. Did you do that? I'm not criticizing you, that was always your job. Is your father proud now?

Alles Liebe,
Ursula

CHAPTER TEN

31ST AUGUST 1940

SARAH COULD HAVE EASILY IMAGINED that Rome was a hot summer's Berlin. The smells, the parks and most of the buildings could have been transplanted from Italy back to the Reich.

Tripoli was something else entirely, the most alien place that Sarah had ever been to. It felt like somewhere she should not be.

The heat was dry and endless, and the air tasted of the dust that collected in every fold, crease and pocket. Amidst that sand, there was the scent of burned toast and the smell of cinnamon.

Tripoli appeared marshalled, landscaped, coiffured. The streets were wide, straight avenues of newly planted trees and heavily watered gardens, decorative walls and staircases, but these boulevards were an Italian facade, spliced onto the complex city behind it. Here the white-clad subjects of Italian Libya milled and crowded in the available space, a living, breathing host to the Italian parasite.

Likewise the Grand Hotel was a fantasy of a building from the *Thousand and One Nights* seemingly created to pander to the white colonial masters and their sense of theatre. It was inside this building that Sarah felt the sense of trespass most keenly; not just that *she* shouldn't be there – the Jew, the spy, the actress – but that *none of them* should be there.

The further south they had travelled, the more the porters, maids and waiting staff seemed to carry servility like a weight, and their treatment at the hands of their white patrons worsened, as if they weren't people at all. Here in Tripoli, Sarah wondered what separated them from slaves. They weren't "slaves", there was no *slavery*. But those were really just words.

As breakfast arrived on pristine crockery, Sarah wondered if this kitchen was run by a proud and argumentative Frau Hofmann, angry and damaged Clementines, or enslaved people? Arriving with a black maid, she felt complicit in the orders, the obsequiousness and the fear. Sarah had watched the Nubian staff in Rome through a back alley door, sharing a cigarette and a joke, like their fez-wearing exoticism was an act for the tourists. She could draw no such comfort here.

"Something wrong with your eggs?" the Captain murmured.

"They're bought with the blood of the oppressed."

The Captain spat his coffee back into his cup and coughed into a handkerchief. "So where's Clementine? Stealing secrets somewhere?" he asked.

"Off taking photos. She wanted to see the market, the *Suk El Turc*... Why did you bring her?" she asked suddenly.

"Do you mean why did I let you *make me* bring her?"

"All I wanted was for her to be able to work, because I felt sorry for her. Then I didn't want her to be killed, which is why I was too scared to leave Norris with her, and too scared to have her loose in Berlin with what she knew, and...and..." Sarah stopped before continuing, shocked. "Why *did* I do all this?"

"This is how she operates though, isn't it? Look, there's no harm done. She won't sell us out to the Gestapo now, we pay better, and she's too involved. And you were right, we do need an extra pair of hands. She's a born spy...there *is* a communist in 502."

"I got caught up in her *liking me*..." Sarah said incredulously.

The Captain snorted, then softened.

"You are...human, Sarah of Elsengrund. It's rare in my – *our* – line of work that this is a positive, but your talent comes from that place, I think..." He trailed off, on the cusp of a compliment. "Look, we've been *spoiled* of late. Got sloppy, got away with it. This trip is going to be good for us, you'll see."

Sarah stared past his shoulder. "If Kurt Hasse was somewhere at the same time as us, that might be a problem, right?"

"It would make things interesting, yes."

"Because he's standing. Right. Over. There."

The Captain picked up a knife and while examining it for dirt, used it to see the room behind him.

"He's coming over," Sarah whispered.

"Yes, he is. Stop whispering."

"Herr Haller, may I introduce myself?" The SS officer stuck out a meaty hand. "I am Kurt Hasse. We've nearly met a few times, but I've never had the pleasure. Mind if I join you?"

"Hello, erm…*Sturmbannführer*?"

"Oh, never mind that, Haller, *dummes Gewäsch*," he said, grinning before continuing in English. *"A lot of stuff and nonsense!"* He switched back to German, supremely pleased with himself. "Can I call you Helmut? I'm a big fan of your work."

He sat himself at the table, with a wave of strong men's cologne. He was wearing an immaculate civilian's safari suit and clutching a pith helmet. It made him look like a tourist dressing for the tropics. Sarah suspected this, along with the extra weight he carried, was a deflection, a way to make people dismiss and underestimate him, in the way that his SS dress uniform had been worn to give the opposite impression.

"Oh, and there I was thinking I was a capitalist parasite…"

Hasse laughed heartily. *"Ends*, Helmut. The ends are important, not the means. We need wireless sets, you make wireless sets. We need barges for a suicidal and doomed invasion, you find barges."

"You don't think *Unternehmen Seelöwe* is going to work?" the Captain murmured.

"Shush, Helmut, that's supposed to be a secret name." He laughed. "No, Operation Sea Lion is not going to work. That fat *Stück Scheiße* Goering is merrily failing to establish air superiority and if they think that they can bomb the English into submission, they don't know them very well. You know they're bombing London now? I spent many happy years on that blessed isle – do you play cricket, Helmut?"

"What is *cricket*?" the Captain replied after a moment.

"Never mind – no, they're not the types to surrender. Everyone thinks we can do to England what we did to the

Communists. You were in Spain, weren't you?" The Captain went to answer, but Hasse continued. "They're a strong people, Helmut. No, we're going to need an alternative strategy to take them out of the war before the Americans decide they're going to be *the Seventh Cavalry* charging over the hill. They need to find a burned-out homestead when they finally get there."

"I thought you liked the British?" the Captain interjected.

"Just a metaphor, dear Helmut. So, what brings you to Tripolitania?"

There was a millisecond's pause. *Lies will tie you up*, thought Sarah.

"I've been asked to escort some German missionaries home."

"Interesting use of your talents."

"Well, I have some experience of moving across lines from my days in Spain. Someone, mentioning no names, of course, is concerned about a family member in the party. They seem to think that the territories of our new French allies are due to pass into the control of more radical elements—"

"And they're right," Hasse interrupted. "The *Afrique-Équatoriale Française* is siding with de Gaulle as we speak."

The Captain nodded sagely. "And it is very useful to be owed favours by senior figures in the party. *Ends*, Kurt. You know."

"Of course." Hasse frowned. "Yet, you're bringing your niece? And your *Neger*?" He looked around for her.

"Time was the cream of German youth would have travelled the world, perhaps visited the outskirts of our empire. I want Ursula to have experience of that. This is not really a demanding endeavour. And" – he laughed – "someone has to clean."

Sarah's eyes narrowed before she could stop them.

"Indeed. And perhaps if you wanted someone to blend into a dark continent, you'd want someone dark." Hesse began to cackle.

The Captain shrugged and smiled. Sarah wanted to lift the silver spoon from the table and scoop out this man's eyeball.

"And why are you here?" Sarah enquired, with mock attention.

Hasse flinched. It was so slight, Sarah wasn't sure it happened, but the riotous laughter that followed was just that bit too forced, too enthusiastic.

"*Gosh*," he began in English before switching back. "German manners aren't what they were! Replaced by a rapacious curiosity, I see. *Fräulein*, I am on my way to Abyssinia, to see how the glorious *Regia Aeronautica* used our gas to defeat the natives, carrying spears. See what we can learn from the experience."

"The Führer doesn't like poison gas," Sarah interrupted.

Hasse stared at Sarah. "Our leader has the luxury of scruples. Those of us in his service do not," he said seriously. "*Ends*, you see," he added quietly.

Oh, shut up, dumme Schlampe. He would have underestimated you, now he's wary of you. Well done. Good job.

"Forgive my niece, she's a zealous National Socialist. She has yet to learn about the shades of grey, or *ends*."

Oh, verpiss dich, thought Sarah, regret and resentment in equal balance.

"Well, my flight takes off at midday," Hasse declared. "I must finish packing. Should have brought a *Neger* to do that

97

for me, hey?" He stood, guffawing, and bowed. "Enjoy your trip, Helmut, *Fräulein*."

They watched him leave the dining room.

"He seems nice," said Sarah.

"Oh, yes. Delightful."

"What's *cricket*?"

"A very dull sport that I haven't played in almost twenty-five years..."

"'Your niece', he said. He said it first. We didn't tell him," Sarah said slowly.

"I think he knows a lot about us that we didn't tell him." The Captain placed a small bottle in front of Sarah. "Here."

"What is that?"

"Chloroquine, from a friend at Bayer. We have enough problems without getting malaria."

"Shall I share this with Clementine?"

The Captain froze. "Yes. I'll...find some more."

CHAPTER ELEVEN

3RD SEPTEMBER 1940

THE LIGHT WAS BLINDING. From horizon to horizon there was nothing but searing white sand, and it hurt the eyes.

Sarah vomited again into the paper bag, nothing but bile. It was nearly full, and the smell made her retch again.

The pilot nudged his navigator and they laughed. They called the constant falling and climbing *aidtirab*. The Captain, now dressed as a missionary, translated into German – *Turbulenz*.

The brightness, the endless ups and downs, the incessant thudding, howling drone of the engine, the stench of oil and sweat, added to the unceasing broiling, suffocating heat was too much for Sarah. The cramped *Storch* was so small and fragile-looking that even before she had been pushed on board by the Captain, her body had gone into panic mode and stayed there. It was as if every gram of energy and fluids had drained from her body. Her head was sandpaper, and she felt like a dried-out fruit skin.

Clementine rubbed Sarah's back gently.

"I'm not your Eva," muttered Sarah.

"Shut up," Clementine said, sighing.

"Don't close your eyes, you'll just make it worse. Look at the horizon," the Captain called out.

"Too...bright..." muttered Sarah. The Captain leaned over and pushed a pair of white-rimmed sunglasses onto her head. They had a visor of some kind over the nose. It was uncomfortably warm, but the pain in her head eased slightly.

The co-pilot seemed preoccupied with something outside. Sarah almost wished there was something wrong with the wing. Death seemed preferable to continuing a moment longer.

He nudged the pilot and after a moment's conversation, they both stared out of the starboard windows.

Eventually, the pilot turned and called out.

"نحن متباعون"

"What are they saying?"

"I'm not sure," the Captain replied.

"You speak Arabic," Sarah groaned.

"I speak classical Arabic. This is Libyan...something else." The Captain screwed up his face before replying. "*Seguiti? Nous sommes suivis?*"

"*Oui,*" the pilots shouted together.

Followed.

The Captain made a flat, circular motion with his finger, and the pilot shrugged. The plane banked slightly to the right, and the landscape tipped up and began to slide slowly to the left. Sarah fought the ripples of nausea and pressed her face to the glass to look behind her.

Against the blinding white and blue, the aircraft's black tailplane looked like a piece cut out of the world. The featureless sand seemed to be crawling uphill from the heart of this void.

A tiny black shape appeared from behind the airframe. It looked like a bird, but its wings did not move and it hung in the sky in a way that gliding or hovering raptors did not. Sarah watched it slowly slip along the horizon until it was level with the wing.

"*Là*," called the pilot.

The birdlike dot shifted orientation and began to drift back towards the tail.

The Captain and the pilot began to bicker in a quick succession of hybrid Arabic, French and Italian phrases. The pilot tapped a nearby fuel can and the co-pilot shook his head in support.

Catch-up, pursue, frighten...limits, consumption, burning, risk.

The Captain tossed them a bundle of banknotes. The pilots began to argue between themselves.

"What's the problem?" Sarah asked.

"The one on the right doesn't want Reichmarks," the Captain replied.

"No, I mean, what don't they want to do?"

"They don't want to chase our friend out there," the Captain answered. He had pulled something heavy from a bag and was beginning to unwrap the cloth that surrounded it. The pilot turned and shouted something back. The Captain nodded. "Put your seat belt on."

"Why?" complained Sarah, who couldn't think of anything

worse than to be bound to this bucking, shaking animal and lose the illusion of escape.

"Because you're going to get hurt otherwise."

He was assembling something made of three black metal and brown Bakelite pieces. Something from behind his shelves of forbidden books. Sarah began scrabbling for the straps behind her.

The pilot called out.

"جاهز؟"

For the first time Sarah saw something other than carefree, grinning, oily insouciance on his unshaven face. She tightened her belt.

"*El-an-a*," the Captain commanded in Arabic.

The plane lurched, rolled and dived for the ground, engines screaming. The airframe rattled and shook as the desert landscape filled the windows. Sarah's sunglasses shot from her face, but she managed to grab them before they disappeared onto the floor. The plane hung, weightless, above the sand for just a moment, but it felt endless.

Then it rolled onto its back and pulled up sharply. Desert. Sky. The colour drained from everything.

They were now low over the dunes and rocks. Watching them flash by, Sarah was suddenly aware of their speed and her own fragility. The Captain clicked a magazine into the submachine gun and opened a window.

The cabin filled with a howling wind. Sarah's hair pulled free of her clips and braids and attacked her face, so she pushed her glasses tight onto her nose. Clementine had her eyes tightly shut and hands clasped, seemingly in prayer.

A shadow passed over the plane.

"Now!" called the Captain.

The engines rose in volume, and the plane started to climb. Sarah was pushed back in her seat and found she couldn't move her arms. Panic started to seep through the seams of her control. The sun filled the cabin and then vanished as they turned.

"*Là*," the Captain shouted, pointing at something Sarah couldn't see. "*Plus proche.*" The pilot shook his head and pointed up. "*D'accord. Vite, vite.*"

Sarah placed her hands around her fear and squeezed, using its energy to regain control. *Take the fear and use it.* The pressure eased on her arms as the plane levelled out. She unbuckled her seat belt and leaned towards the open window. She could now make out the aircraft ahead. A black cross shape, with the wings, body and tail making one sleek whole. It looked like a threat…but it also looked uncertain. It waggled its wings in indecision before slowly descending before them.

The pilot began to shout, an excited babble of French and Italian.

"He says it's Italian…look at the white cross," Sarah translated. "*Regia Aeronautica.* Italian. Messerschmitt Bf 108. They're friendly."

"Yes, but to whom?" the Captain said. He turned to Sarah. "Remind them that they're mercenaries. They don't have any friends."

With difficulty, Sarah climbed to the front. "*Pas d'amis. Vous êtes des mercenaires.*" Sarah jabbed a finger towards them. "*Pirata…*"

The co-pilot yelled to his friend.

"الاقراصنة!"

And they broke into laughter and pushed the throttles forward.

The target grew in the cockpit windows with the Sahara Desert laid out behind it, like a yellow canvas. Sarah took it in and swallowed it whole, owning the terror. She found she was panting.

Closer. Bigger. Until it filled the windows and Sarah thought they'd plough into it.

The Captain opened fire.

Thrack. Thrack thrack thrack thrack thrack thrack.

Shell casings were tossed across the cabin. One bounced off Sarah's arm. It was hot.

The Bf 108 shuddered and seemed to spring a leak. Something black and spotty tumbled into the air as it shrieked and banked sharply away.

Thrack thrack thrack thrack thrack.

"Down! *Giù!*" the Captain called as he grabbed Sarah's arm and tried to pull her back to her seat. She shook his hand loose and pushed his arm away, burning her hand on his gun as she did so.

"No," she growled. She clasped the metalwork above her firmly and rode the descent, feeling the lightness in her feet and the pressure in her face. She wanted to see, to be part of it, rather than it be something that just happened to her. The other plane was now clearly visible against the sky, dragging a tail of dirt and smoke in its wake. It was looking for them, a wounded hunter.

The Captain was reloading and calling to the pilots in Arabic. Whatever he was saying was not going down well, but his voice was commanding and brooked no argument. They shrugged and turned the plane back towards the enemy.

The 108 turned tighter and moved into profile. The *Storch* straightened out. Both planes were close to the sand dunes now and heading right for each other.

Sarah looked at the man at the controls. He was rigid in concentration. The 108 seemed to swell in the cockpit windows with terrifying speed.

The copilot was chanting something.

"دعب سيل"

It sounded like lay-sabad-o.

"دعب سيل"

The 108 was huge, black and demonic, trailing its tail of filth behind it. Surely someone would move out of the way?

"دعب سيل"

Sarah could now see the figures in the opposing cockpit and its pilot, taking in his round, surprised mouth.

The Storch climbed slightly, showing every sign of breaking off. Sarah exhaled in relief.

"آلان!"

El-an-a.

They dipped back in front of the other plane.

Thrack, thrack, thrack.

Then their plane tipped into a vertical climb and turned on its tail.

As the 108 screamed under it, the *Storch* stalled immediately and dropped belly first towards the sand. The wings caught the air, the plane bounced twice on the sand, throwing Sarah through the cabin, and with a roar of strangled noise it staggered into the air. A drunk on his way home from the bar.

Sarah lay among the cargo between the seats, staring at the ribs of the ceiling, uncertain if she could move. Clementine's face appeared.

"Put your *gottverdammten* seat belt on, Eva," she sneered. "Get up, you're missing everything." She pulled on Sarah's arms and manhandled her onto a seat.

"Where's the other plane?"

Clementine pointed out of the window as the *Storch* banked, revealing the 108 at the end of a long dirty streak in the sand, its nose resting in a dune. No one had yet emerged.

"This is quite a little aircraft, isn't it?" Clementine smiled. "Safe as houses, huh? No need to be so scared."

Sarah was still scared. The terror was deep in her toes. She just had command of it.

The co-pilot turned and put his chin on the seat back. He waved a finger to the Captain, who was stripping his gun, and spoke to Sarah in broken Italian.

"He says that was an impossible shot you made with that," Sarah recounted. "You scare him."

"Good."

"He also says that we need to land soon. We've used too much fuel...*having fun*, he says...to get to Al Wigh."

"Also good."

Sarah looked at the Captain, noting the sweat on his upper lip and the very slight tremor in his right hand.

"Are you all right?" Sarah asked.

"I'm fine," he snapped. "Just leave me alone," he added more quietly and looked away.

Sarah closed her eyes and sitting back, began to write.

Dearest Mouse,

You know how you tried to tell me about Elsa's father, but something stopped you actually saying the words?

I had trouble talking to my mother about the things she did. These were not secrets, these were things we both knew about. We just didn't talk about them. About what they did to us. What they did to me.

I swore that I wouldn't ever do that again. I swore I wouldn't keep denying something that I knew to be true and pretending it would go away.

Yet, here I am.

Is it because we were little more than children that we let that happen? Is this just the way that the world works? Are we broken?

IF WE TALKED, IF WE COULD NOT BE SILENCED, THEN PEOPLE LIKE ELSA'S FATHER COULDN'T DO WHAT THEY DO. ROTHENSTADT COULDN'T HAVE RUN. ~~THE NAZIS~~ EVIL COULDN'T EXIST, BECAUSE WE'D ALL BE POINTING AT IT, SCREAMING, WARNING EVERYONE ELSE.

Every girl, every woman calling out danger and then dealing with it.

But our lives are full of secrets, aren't they?

I have a secret, something that can't be screamed out.

And that's how it starts, doesn't it?

<u>Alles Liebe</u>,

Ursula

CHAPTER TWELVE

3RD–14TH SEPTEMBER 1940

THERE WERE TEN STOPS. MAYBE MORE. Sarah lost count.

This night, in a tiny oasis near the border of French West Africa, the swirling sunset of purples, oranges and yellows brought more than a steady breeze. It was accompanied by a long, sustained humming. It sounded like a choir of bass voices or the vibration of a distant airplane.

Sarah stood up and walked to the edge of camp, wrapped in a blanket. She scanned the skies for the 108, but although the booming rose, swelled and faded, it wasn't uniform like a plane. And it droned on and on.

"What is that noise?" she wondered aloud.

"الرمل يغني," the pilot called out from the fire. "*La sabbia, sta cantando,*" he added.

"The sand...is *singing*?" Sarah laughed incredulously.

The Captain appeared at her side. "If the conditions are right, the drifting sand makes this sound." He was wistful and alert despite the hour. "I didn't know it did this outside of Arabia though. Special, isn't it?"

If it was a choir, it would have been vast and inhuman, an orchestra playing string instruments the size of the earth. The words, if there were any, would have been dark and primal, the tale of the world since the dawn of time. It was beautiful and frightening in equal measure.

"I won't be able to sleep," Sarah managed.

The pilot heard this, understood and laughed. He began to sing in Italian, an aria about a sleepless princess and her wakeful kingdom.

Some of the Imazighen around the fire began to clap along, giggling. These desert travellers had welcomed them into their camp. They had little to fear from the Captain's party, as they were all heavily armed. They were, the pilot explained, a long way from their usual routes and eager for news. But there was no shared language to converse in. They were reluctant to unwind the long blue *tagelmust* headgear that obscured their mouths in front of guests, which made reading their expressions difficult, so they settled for sharing their food.

Sarah couldn't stomach the *liwa*, the millet porridge they offered, and the *akh*, the goat's milk, made her retch, to the amusement of their hosts, but she wolfed down the flatbread, *taguella*, that they made in the sand under the fire, even managing a trace of the meat paste that went with it. Her nausea had not driven away her need for food, and she was grateful to find something dry and warm to satiate and reduce the cramping sensation.

As the pilot's voice struggled into the next section of the song, the Imazighen began chanting in accompaniment, and the clapping grew more complex, shifting with the sound of the sand.

"I just need a piano," Sarah said with a sigh. "Our friend Hasse was in that plane?"

"Almost certainly."

"Is he dead?"

"Doubt it. We've given ourselves a head start, that's all. It'd be easier to stay ahead of him if we knew exactly where the scientists are, but hopefully he'll have the same problem…"

"Do you…" Sarah began and stopped. She tried again. "Do *we* have everything we need?"

"Yes. Why?"

"I don't want us to run out of anything."

"Alles in Butter." The Captain smiled and held his arms out widely. He turned and walked to his tent.

The song at the fire grew ragged, with much cackling and clapping.

Clementine appeared at Sarah's side, cradling her camera in one hand and a tin canteen in the other. "I brought your water," she said, proffering the bottle.

"I'm not thirsty."

"When did you last have to pee?"

Sarah thought about this.

"If you're having to think about it," Clementine continued, "you're dehydrated. Drink."

Sarah took the bottle. The water was warm, unpleasant, and her throat resented it. Once swallowed, Sarah had to admit her body relented.

"Your uncle has a 'medical' problem—" Clementine began.

"I know," Sarah interrupted.

"I'm just saying—"

"Well, don't," Sarah snapped.

"I love being on the same side as you," Clementine mused sarcastically. "You're right, it makes all this more pleasant."

The pilot was trying to persuade the campfire to accompany him on something else. The language barrier led the Libyan to switch between Italian, French and Arabic with much arm waving. His co-pilot laughed at his efforts.

Sarah needed to say something to make things better. To gain absolution.

"Do you feel closer to your parents here?" she asked.

"You really are an ignorant *Hure*, aren't you? Dakar is about three thousand kilometres away. We're probably nearer to Germany."

"You know, for just *a second* you could try not to be such a *bitch*."

Clementine curtseyed. Something heaved inside Sarah, like she was about to be sick again. It bubbled up and, as she stooped and opened her mouth, a chuckle fell from her lips.

Clementine grinned and they watched the singing sands slowly turn blue.

She took a step towards Sarah and spoke quietly. "I get why I'm here now, why you brought me. He's falling apart and you need someone to help you, so you aren't alone when he messes up."

Sarah stared at the darkening horizon, becoming angry and relieved simultaneously, seeing the truth in Clementine's words.

"But I'm curious why spies for German Intelligence are shooting down Italian aircraft," the girl went on.

"I told you. There are traitors."

"Yes, yes, there are. And I think I'm with them."

The campfire had fallen silent behind them, and only the singing sand and the shuffling of livestock could be heard.

Sarah knew that Norris, for all his hesitation and weakness, would have killed Clementine, right here and now. Would the Captain? She felt the weight of the derringer in her pocket. *It would be easy and over quickly, they wouldn't even have to hide the body—*

"It's complicated," she managed. "Trust me, we're on the right side."

"That might be true. But one shouldn't trust traitors."

"What do you care? You're a blackmailer. You're being paid...to do nothing much, to be honest. I mean, what do you want, Clementine? To report us to the Gestapo? Be left in the middle of the Sahara Desert?" Sarah paused. "A punch in the mouth?"

Clementine began to giggle. "I want the truth," she said once she had finished laughing. "In your rather pathetic way, you are far too nice to a *Rheinlandbastard* like me. You might wear a BDM uniform, but it doesn't wear you."

"You want me to be nasty to you?"

"I want you to go piss yourself."

Lies will tie you up. Sarah found a different lie, but a ready-made one she could regurgitate, with a seam of truth she could access.

"All this racial *Quatsch*. It's a sideshow. It's all things that the Führer said to galvanize the population. He doesn't care, we don't care, *I* don't care if you're a *gottverdammter Schornsteinfeger* or a Jew or an Englishman, *if Germany wins*. It's not just the SS that do pragmatism."

"You *really* believe that?"

Sarah shrugged, before she continued. "I just need you to keep your *gottverdammtes Maul* shut and pretend you're a maid. Maybe do some of that snooping for your country."

"That's better. You almost sound like a National Socialist now. Almost." She folded her arms against the breeze. "Get some sleep."

As Clementine walked back to the fire, leaving Sarah more confused than ever, she turned and called back, "And if you ever want me to show you how to fire that tiny thing in your pocket, just let me know."

As the plane flew ever southwards, the desert looked, at first, like a face growing stubble. Soon these dark patches joined to form ripples, like the edge of the beach as it meets the surf, and among these swirling patterns trees sprouted. Kilometre after kilometre the vegetation came, first black and then green, to consume the darkening sand.

The illusion was that Fort-Lamy, the capital of Chad on the banks of the green Chari River, marked the boundary of the untamed desert, but it was just a trick of watered gardens and irrigation. However, it was the first expression of European colonization for some two thousand kilometres.

Neat rows of white buildings fanned out like spokes on

a wheel, growing ragged and brown towards the edges. It was an enticing image of civilization, how the wild and that famous darkness were being brought under control and placed in good European order.

Sarah thought of the "ordered" demolition of the synagogue in Munich, to make a *parking lot*. What had this white town removed?

The *Storch* bounced onto the airfield, and she stopped thinking about anything for a while.

Waiting by a truck so old it seemed inconceivable that it still functioned, stood a large black priest. He smiled a wide toothy grin and opened his arms as if in thanks.

"*Bonjour, mes amis*, and welcome to Chad." He turned to Clementine and said, "Girl, make sure all the luggage gets onto the truck."

Clementine looked ready to disobey but then complied with a shrug.

When she was out of earshot, the priest's face changed, like someone had thrown a switch. It was now distrustful, guarded, cunning.

"Jeremy. Are you collecting little girls? What the hell?"

"Good to see you again, Claude. May I introduce my niece, Ursula...an intelligence operative in my team."

Claude stared at Sarah, seeing the dishevelled, pale and washed-out girl she felt she was. "If you say so. And what about the *bamboula*?"

"The maid-cum-operative. I don't know yet. She's been

told we work for the *Abwehr*, but I suspect she no longer believes us."

"Oh, well, not at all complicated. *Jésus*," Claude swore.

Several Gendarmes were walking over the field, eyeing the *Storch*'s markings suspiciously. Claude nodded to them.

"A sign of the times, Jeremy. A few weeks ago, Félix Éboué, the governor, walked into city hall and declared for de Gaulle. You are now in *La France Libre*," he said.

"How did that go down?"

"Not massively popular, but no one wants to end up in jail, so they're bending with the wind. Besides, everyone needs to trade with the British over there." Claude pointed to the west. "And you can't do that as Germany's ally. Money talks. Anyway, your plane has Italian markings, so I have to make this go away, excuse me."

The priest walked towards the policemen, calling out in a big, friendly voice.

Sarah was about to head for the truck, then remembered Clementine and turned back.

"Leave her," warned the Captain. "She's supposed to be the maid. You be the little girl. Little girls don't help maids carry luggage."

"But I'm not a little monster any more. Aren't we missionaries now?"

"You think that doesn't make you a monster here, too?" the Captain said, frowning. "Being European? Believing in God?"

The pilot caught Sarah's eye and then waved her over with two fingers. Sarah was curious, so she approached him. The Captain shrugged and headed for the truck.

"Thank you for..." she began in Italian, and then tried to recall the Arabic. "*Tayaran?...*" She realized to her embarrassment that she didn't know his name.

The pilot grinned, about to correct her, then stopped. His Italian was patched and sewn together but understandable.

"You know my song? At the oasis? You know what happens next?"

"No, no I don't, *sadiqaa*," Sarah replied.

"The hero is trying to win the hand of a cold Chinese princess. She wants to guess his name so she can execute him. To protect his secret, his young maid, who loves him, kills herself. You...watch out for yourself little *Tanit*."

CHAPTER THIRTEEN

"So, my old friend, what brings you to the *Afrique-Équatoriale Française* at this most interesting of times?"

The rumbling truck trundled across the rutted track, sounding its horn to hurry Chad's pedestrians along. The crowds of people, most wearing baggy white shirts and embroidered skullcaps, shuffled out of the way. Sarah tried to see their faces as they passed, but they went by too quickly and the motion made her feel sick again.

"Do you know anything about new diseases between here and Libreville?" the Captain asked.

"Ah, you want *Le Diable Blanc*, the White Devil."

"I'm sorry?"

"It's a story, almost a folktale, but it's something supposedly happening *now*. A demon, dressed in white, visits wrath on the unholy. Where he stalks, pestilence follows. Always in the jungle, never near the towns. If you actually see him, *you're already dead*. For the Christians, he's Satan. To the natives, he's whatever *connerie* angry tree-god they worship. But dressed in *white* though? That's some symbolism there." Claude grinned.

"So how do I find this White Devil?" the Captain asked.

"I've heard of some Germans, missionaries from the Congo, who might know the truth. They've been following the latest plague south, trying to save each village as they come to it... Or offending the ancestors and causing it, depending whether you're an ungrateful *natif* or not. But they're mostly heading south because they need to stay out of Allied territory. Oubangui-Chari, Moyen-Congo, even Cameroun, are all for de Gaulle. Only Gabon left now, the coup failed there. Collaborating Vichy *salopes*," he spat.

"So there is a plague?" Sarah interrupted.

The priest sounded his horn again to disperse a crowd in the road. He made a dismissive noise. "There's always a plague. Men mucking about in the jungle where we're not supposed to be. It wakes up the monsters."

"You do believe in monsters, then?" she asked.

"*Dégagez!*" the priest screamed out of the window. The pedestrians shuffled into the mud at the side of the road. He looked around at Sarah before continuing more gently. "Real monsters, yes. This continent is a world *de merde*. Hiding in the trees and caves. Malaria, sleeping sickness, snail fever and worse. It's not some vengeful god..." His voice tailed off. "Except, maybe, the real God *is* punishing them." He shrugged. "I mean, why would good men come here?"

"Where are you from?" Sarah asked.

"*Paris*, little girl," he growled. "You think I'm one of these *sauvages*?" He eyed Clementine before continuing. "You think I'd have ended up *working for the Abwehr* if I were from here? I'm bringing civilization and the one God to this piece of France. And what are you, *bamboula*?" he said in French to Clementine.

"I'm German, and *allez se faire foutre*," she swore passionately.

Claude looked at her like she'd spat at him. Then he grinned, the widest grin of the day.

"I like her. I like them with some spirit."

Their first port of call was a French mission house, south of Mandjafa. The building next to the tatty church had all the bricks, stone and white-painted wood panelling of Chad's administrative buildings, but in the way that flour and water were not bread, the various items piled on top of one another did not evoke the same gravitas.

Here on the banks of the Chari, the nights failed to bring the desert chill, and the heat was growing moist around the edges. The patio to the rear of the mission house, away from the road, was the coolest place, but the insects of an entire continent gathered to feast on Sarah and the Captain as they watched the darkening sky over the scrub-like savanna. Clementine had declared herself too sensible to be dinner for the mosquitoes and had retired, but Sarah thought she was missing out. The stars here were already twinkling and fizzing to life in a way Sarah had never seen at home. Millions and millions of them, so thick they painted a brushstroke across the sky.

It was the first new experience that had not made her want to vomit, sweat, pass out or cover her eyes.

The Captain was now in a white linen suit and clerical collar with a straw hat covering his eyes. She wondered if he was still awake.

"He swears a lot for a man of God." Sarah smirked. "Does he believe in anything at all?"

"Claude believes in right and wrong. I met him in Arabia. He saw what we did there, how our countries lied and broke our promises. He turned to God for answers. It seems God has not answered."

"Good excuse to be an *Arschloch*, I suppose," Sarah thought aloud. "But he's not a Nazi? With an attitude like that?"

"He's here to help the population, who are not of a mind to be helped. They are not interested in his brand of civilization as it tends to carry a *chicotte*—"

"A what?"

"A whip, made of animal hide. This lack of cooperation enrages him. This attitude isn't that of a Nazi, it's a colonial, an imperialist...*a white man*."

"Sounds the same," Sarah said. "But he's *black*...?"

"Indeed. Only he's not African, he's *French*. He doesn't identify with the population here. They're savages, while he's metropolitan, a Parisian. He is *superior*. There's a pecking order. The governor here is black and Guianese. The church-educated middle classes? They think they're superior, that the rest of the black population would do better working harder and doing what they're told faster. Claude always struggled with being a second-class citizen in the land of *Liberté, égalité, fraternité*. He found that *égalité* was dependent on having white skin, so after the war he went somewhere he didn't have to worry about those principles at all."

"How did you deal with what your country did?"

"Like Claude, I went somewhere and pretended to be something else. I, too, don't belong in my country."

"You're not black or Jewish – where *don't* you belong?" Sarah sneered.

The Captain shrugged. *Shutters down.*

Gottverdammt. What a terrible spy you make. Mouth always moving, ears never listening.

Sarah pulled something with wings out of her iced tea. "Tell me I don't have to fly any more." She sighed.

"You don't...but I don't think you're going to like the alternative."

The word *road* had certain connotations for Sarah, raised in a Berlin suburb and a resident of two big cities. Paving came and went on the way to Moundou, but the promised highway never appeared. The truck wove through pedestrians, carts and herded animals, with Claude leaning on the horn and turning the air blue through the open windows.

But the bumpier the ride, the faster they went and the wind blew cool onto Sarah's face. The Captain's sunglasses and nose visor kept the dust out of her eyes, and a wound scarf kept her hair in place. Even this noisy and vibrating, shaking and twisting journey through the very centre of Chad's population was better than flying.

Chad was a patchwork of woody bush and grey-brown grassland, like life couldn't quite reclaim the desert. The baobab trees had the thickest trunks of any she had seen before, yet their foliage was threadbare and comically small in comparison, like a bald man covering his pate with strings of long hair.

Sarah's instinct was to recoil from the mud, the dirt, the apparent squalor and poverty of the brick-and-thatched villages, but it took her just a moment of thought to recognize the piled garbage, cockroaches, hunger and grime of Berlin and Vienna as different parts of the same thing. This place, these people, were not the deficiency. It was just the sharp end of what society did to people everywhere.

She watched the people of the *Afrique-Équatoriale Française*, the subjects of the AEF, as they passed. They worked, they smiled, they talked and the children played. For all the differences, except perhaps the decorative facial scarring, they could be anywhere in the world.

Something occurred to Sarah.

"There's no war here?" she asked Claude.

"In a way. For these people, whether they're part of Vichy France or Free France, it doesn't matter. They won't feel the benefits, only the deprivations. Until we round them up to fight for us one way or the other."

"So there is a downside to being a French colony then?" Sarah smirked.

"No, they're lucky. They could be Belgian. Then they'd all be chained to a rubber tree until they rotted."

Sarah looked at Clementine, who rolled her eyes, nodded in

Claude's direction and made a curious waving motion with her fist. Sarah shook her head, not understanding.

"Congo Free State, he means," Clementine interjected.

Sarah shook her head again. She didn't like ignorance. It didn't suit her. Clementine rummaged in her bag and pulled out a torn and creased book, *Red Rubber*.

"Read this, then I'll tell you why he's a *branleur*," she swore into Sarah's ear.

The Captain heard the word and snorted.

Sarah opened the book but quickly found that trying to read made her nauseous. The words shook into indecipherability as they ate the kilometres east.

They followed the path of the Chari River before turning south at Mondo, and away from its water the land became arid once more. But this time farms and plantations held on and slowly, steadily, the landscape grew green and verdant, until they reached Moundou, where at last the grass replaced the sand.

Sarah's on-the-road adventures with the Captain in Germany had been difficult. The tension of the drive to Rothenstadt school and the beginning of her mission there; the fury-saturated journey back to Berlin after Christmas at the Schäfer Estate, with the sweating, agonized Captain recovering from his bullet wound, a journey that ended in the death of the SA officer—

Sarah recoiled from the memory.

But she understood now that there had been some small joy shared in his car. A pleasant buzz had accompanied the pair as they drove, engaging in covert devilment, jousting and competing for points. She had felt...safe? Definitely capable of closing her eyes and resting, free of the dogs or ghosts.

This truck allowed none of that. Unable to be herself or speak her mind, she had a surprising and growing desire to climb into the Captain's lap, to bury her head in his neck, to be held and reassured. This need was nothing to do with the prickly tactility, comfort and absolution that she provided at the parties. Meeting Lady Sakura after all these years, receiving again the unconditional comfort and protection that she had once supplied, resting in those willowy arms...it seemed to have weakened Sarah somehow. It identified a need and dragged it into the world. The woman's touch was like medicine that Sarah needed over and over, leaving her weak and fragile in-between.

She remembered the Mouse crawling into her bed, neither holding her nor flinching away. The warmth and closeness in that fragment was an illusion, she knew. The situation had been fraught, surrounded by peril, and the girl's presence had in reality felt like an invasion...yet the sensation of comfort remained.

Sarah wanted to be held again, held by someone she could *trust*.

She looked at the Captain, weaker and more fragile in these days since the bullet that had nearly ended him. There was *faith*, conviction in his intentions and no small measure of affection. But Sarah had to be one step ahead of what he was thinking for her own self-preservation.

Sarah did not *trust* him.

She watched the foul-mouthed and prejudiced priest. She glanced at the snoring Clementine, her claws momentarily withdrawn. A liar and a spy, by her own admission and not to be trusted.

Sarah was alone.

She closed her eyes and waited for the clean, smooth paper of her mind to stop moving before she began to write.

Dear Mouse,

I wonder where the Ice Queen is now? Now she's graduated and no longer the ruler of a school, how do you think she's coping with being back in a world that sees her as a walking womb? Did she get to walk through the streets of Paris after all, when the army rolled in, just as she wanted? Or is she sitting at home, baking or something? I don't think there's a more fitting punishment for the things she did at the school than losing that control over her life.

Then again, if she hadn't started <u>der Werwolf</u>, the secret society, and if Elsa hadn't been part of it, would Elsa have had the strength to stand up to her father at last?

When I joined <u>der Werwolf</u>, I vowed that I'd drag all of them to hell before I was done. Is that what's happened? Are Elsa and the Ice Queen in hell? Did I do that? The Jews...some Jews, believe that hell is in the here and now.

What about you? Are you in hell? Did I put you there, too?

I ask you a lot of questions. Do you have the answers?

<u>Alles Liebe</u>,

Ursula

CHAPTER FOURTEEN

17TH–22ND SEPTEMBER 1940

SARAH DIDN'T OPEN THE BOOK as they passed out of Chad into Ubangi-Shari, or even as they entered the Congo Basin above Carnot. She found herself too dizzy on the move and too fatigued to read once they stopped. The movement became everything. Alien as it was, Sarah grew disinterested in the landscape, even as it slowly changed. There was just so much of it, so many trees, so many people, so many kilometres. Everything contracted to a slow green blur.

Jungle. Mud. Wood. Whitewashed stone. Mud. Jungle.

She saw no animals, except insects. The atmosphere grew ever more oppressive, more muggy, until it was like wearing a hot, soaking blanket over her face and even the wind through the truck windows became wet.

Jungle. Mud. Wood. Whitewashed stone. Mud. Jungle.

Their clothes became moist and uncomfortable, with every motion chafing and irritating.

Was this how people came to hate this place? Like the priest?

Jungle. Mud. Wood. Whitewashed stone. Mud. Jungle.

Then something caught Sarah's eye, causing her to climb out of her little well of negativity.

The truck trundled past a line of men, several hundred strong, shuffling along by the side of the road, backs bent. At the head of this column and dotted alongside, were a few armed men.

Sarah saw them – better clothed, better fed – for what they were. Guards.

"Are these prisoners?" Sarah asked Claude.

"No, just workers. Miners, I think," he answered, distracted.

"Why are there guards?" Sarah continued.

"They don't want any deserters."

"Deserters? How can leaving a job be *deserting*?"

"They're slaves, Nazi girl." Clementine sighed.

"They're not *slaves*, it's a *prestation*," Claude growled. "They probably can't pay their taxes."

"Why were they being taxed if they didn't have money?" Sarah pressed the point.

"Slaves," Clementine insisted.

"Shut your mouth, girl," snapped Claude, becoming irritated.

"No, hang on," Sarah shouted back over the engine noise. "They don't have money, so they're being *made* to work? Are they being paid?"

Claude was silent.

"*Slaves*," Clementine restated.

"It might be an administrative punishment... And there's a war on," Claude said more quietly.

"There's been a war for about two weeks...how long has this arrangement existed?"

"About five hundred years..." Clementine sneered.

"Girl," Claude said, turning to Sarah, "they're African. They're natives. They're lazy and uncooperative. If they wanted to work, they wouldn't have to be pressed into it."

"But—"

"They are one step up from animals," Claude interrupted. "They need to be told what to do, looked after."

Clementine laughed.

Claude reached over and slapped her face with the back of his hand. She jerked away, eyes wide.

"They need *discipline*, as you do," he snarled coldly.

Sarah's first instinct was to grab Claude, to drive her fingernails into his eyes...but he was still driving at speed, the line of miners still flashed past the window.

A hand appeared on her chest. Gentle but firm.

"Enough, Claude." The Captain was awake now and sitting up. "You don't touch my help, or my niece. Ever."

"You've changed, *mon ami*," sneered Claude.

"So have you," stated the Captain dispassionately.

Sarah looked at Clementine. One tiny dribble ran from her nose. In the light the blood seemed almost black against her skin. Sarah reached over with a handkerchief to clean her face, but Clementine swatted her arm away, with the eyes of both a terrified child and a warrior set to burn the world.

She had been too late to stop Sarah, though, who looked at the white cloth in her hands, stained bright red.

Sarah watched the tail of the column through the window,

and the bare backs, scarred by the whip. She felt a tingle in the rough skin of her own back, the permanent souvenir from her time at Rothenstadt, a tiny window into their all-consuming misery.

The next stop couldn't come soon enough. It was another shabby mission house on Claude's list, each apparently built with the same aspirations, and the same shortcomings.

Clementine was bent over a trough behind the house, cleaning her nose.

"Are you all right?" Sarah asked.

"Go away," Clementine grunted.

"Nope. You work for me," Sarah insisted.

"Am I on the clock?"

"All the time now. Let's face it, I can't let you loose in this place, can I?"

"Are you *looking after me* then?"

"Like any good imperialist, it seems..." Sarah said, and watched her fingers twiddle in front of her, for somewhere to look. "I had no idea what happens here, not really."

"Oh my God, we *are* in *Huckleberry Finn*. I *am* here to teach you a lesson..." Clementine put two fingers in her mouth and made a vomiting noise.

"Don't flatter yourself. I'd have got there on my own, and I wouldn't have got a smack in the face doing it."

"Only because you're white," muttered Clementine.

"Hey," Sarah moaned.

"It isn't my job to make you feel better."

They stood, side by side, leaning against the trough. There was so much moisture in the air, Sarah wondered why they bothered with troughs at all.

Something occurred to her.

"Why are you out here?" Sarah asked.

"He won't let me inside."

"We'll see about that."

Sarah seized her hand and pulled her towards the door.

Inside Claude and the Captain were sitting with two men. Their host, an elderly white missionary, sat back from the table, arms folded, but the other, a young African sitting sweating in his Sunday-best clothes, was in deep conversation with the newcomers. His French was incomplete, but his meaning was easy to follow.

Claude looked at Sarah and Clementine but didn't want to interrupt the visitor. Sarah settled cross-legged on the floor next to him and, pulling Clementine with her, began a quiet game of *Backe, backe Kuchen*, allowing them to eavesdrop more easily.

"After the White Devil had gone, one villager grew sick. It started with one man, then his family and then those who tended them. They grew fatigued, then feverish, then, confined to bed, they started to bleed from their noses, mouths, ears and eyes. Their friends and family withdrew in fear.

"Then the German missionaries arrived. At first the villagers were happy the Germans had come to help with doctors and European medicines, but soon everyone left in the village was sick and one by one they started to die. They were not permitted to tend to their dead and when the sickness spread, they feared..."

The storyteller glanced nervously at the minister.

"They feared that the ancestors were growing more angry and—"

The minister tutted and glared at the young man. The Captain motioned him to continue.

"And that was why the plague was threatening the area. The Elders demanded that the missionaries leave, but they would not. To save the area, they said, they finally...erased the village—"

The storyteller didn't have a French word. He spoke at length with many hand gestures. The elderly minister squirmed uncomfortably before speaking.

"*Un lance-flammes*," he murmured.

"What's a *lance-flammes*?" Clementine asked Sarah quietly.

"A *Flammenwerfer*." Sarah had seen the gun and its jets of fire on the newsreels. She thought about the streaks of glowing silver from the screen and had a sudden, unbidden sensation of the fire in Schäfer's lab, of the skin of her arms reddening and blistering and falling off—

"They used the flamethrower on the villages and the surrounding bush. But it was too late. They discovered the sickness had spread to the next district, and the Germans went to help."

"How many villages? How many people?"

"Two or three...hundred."

The Captain sat back and hid his face behind a teacup.

The elderly minister thanked the man for his testimony.

"The same story was told to the other German."

Claude and the Captain exchanged looks and began talking at once.

Sarah concentrated on the rhyme and the pattern of handclaps.

> *"Eier und Schmalz,*
> *Zucker und Salz,*
> *Milch und Mehl,*
> *Safran macht den Kuchen gehl."*

She had played with few children and was clumsy, but Clementine was having the same trouble coordinating her hands.

> *"Schieb in den Ofen rein..."*

"The German who came a few days ago."

Their hands collided, and they made themselves laugh before beginning again.

"How much longer do we have to travel with that lunatic?" Sarah complained as she paced beside the Captain's bed.

"Well, unless you have a truck and an intimate knowledge of the missions between here and Gabon, then all the way to Libreville where we can get a boat."

The Captain was, somehow, dressed in a silk robe, while Sarah squeaked in her wet clothes. It annoyed Sarah in ways she couldn't quite fathom. He was looking very relaxed, to the point of passing out. She wished he was more awake, more interested.

"He's some friend of yours. Hitting women—"

"He hit a black servant." He raised a hand to stop her protest. "This is where you are now. Getting wound up about it is a waste of effort."

"These people, the French people, are supposed to be our allies, right? British allies, I mean," Sarah clarified.

"Yes, please tell the whole mission that. In fact, a little louder would be great."

"*Our allies* keep people as *slaves*. Call it what you will. Work for free that you can't leave is *slavery*."

"At home convicts do hard labour—" Again he raised a hand to quieten her. "It's the same difference. Those men have fallen foul of the laws. Yes, it's not fair, and when this war is over maybe we do something about it, but right now—" He waved away her frustration. "*Right now*, we're fighting a war. You think the *two or three hundred* dead villagers we heard about tonight would have cared who we were friends with if we could have stopped their deaths?"

"Do you think they were made sick on purpose?" Sarah couldn't quite believe it. That level of malice seemed inconceivable. Then she thought about Poland. She thought briefly of Schäfer and his bomb – Sarah squirmed away from that memory but pushed through it. His bomb, powerful enough to flatten a city. A weapon ready to be used. She thought of Ishii, of Ningbo *enjoying* their bubonic plague, of children being given contaminated sweets.

"Even if it was natural, someone is out here studying it," the Captain replied. "Maybe these German missionaries, maybe not. But don't you wonder why missionaries have a flamethrower?"

"Hasse is here, too?"

"Seems so, and he got in front of us."

"Are we going to look at these villages?"

"I'm afraid so."

CHAPTER FIFTEEN

Sarah had left her mother safe on the roof, despite her protestations. Sarah had someone else she needed to check on.

The moon was a day or two past being full, but Sarah didn't need that light to navigate. Everything was bathed in a flickering red glow from the streets beneath. The smoke was tickling her throat and causing a pain in her chest as she danced from rooftop to rooftop, up the eaves, along the ridges, down the valleys and gables and hips. Bare feet on red tiles, hands propelling her from chimney stacks and flashings, until she was in the heart of the Jewish Quarter. Somewhere below, among the screams and smashing, was her friend the butcher.

She straddled the drainpipe and slipped, slid and clambered down the five storeys.

Don't look down, don't look down, don't—

She bounced off the ground, hurting her back in her haste, and shuffled, crab-like, into an unopened doorway.

The windows of the shops, all of them, were shattered. The belongings of a dozen apartments lay broken or burning in the street. Groups of whooping Hitler Youth and SA stormtroopers ran back and forth, boots crunching through the debris, but there were others, young and old civilians, happily destroying, stealing and chanting.

The butcher's shop was gone, an empty wreck, and on the street outside, on his hands and knees, was the *shochet*. He was cast in shadow but instantly recognizable. Even laid low, he almost dwarfed the stormtroopers and other troublemakers around him, but they seemed to have tied him with several ropes. As they moved, Sarah could see he had been brutally beaten. One cheek and eye had bloated, changing the shape of his face, while his nose was twisted and hanging loose. Something dark dribbled through his swollen lips.

Even now he swung a fist at his tormentors' legs, defying them in the only way he could. But the action unbalanced him, and the crowd, jeering, pulled at his ropes, trying to topple him. Around his neck was tied a crude, outsized Star of David, roughly hewn from a shop sign and painted yellow, a swear word scrawled across it.

A boy from the Hitler Youth walked up to him, trailing something on the ground, like a rope. He turned when he reached him, and Sarah recognized Bernt. A teenager. A boy not much older than Sarah, but a bully, her serial tormentor...and someone with a grudge against the *shochet* and a score to settle. In his hand was a whip, a whip like nothing Sarah had ever seen, with a long tail trailing from the handle.

"*Eins!*" Bernt shouted.

The boy raised his hand but the whip moved too fast to see.

Crack.

"*Zwei!*" yelled some of the others, laughing.

Crack.

"*Drei!*"

This time the cracking noise was wet. And several of the others flinched as something splashed in their faces.

"Stop," called the butcher.

"Stop? What do you mean, stop? You don't give orders here any more, Israel. I'll have to start again!" cackled Bernt.

The whip flew and snapped across the butcher's back, drawing a scream.

"*Eins!*"

Sarah climbed to her feet and, feeling the shriek of incandescent, howling, spitting wrath rise from her groin to her chest that bleached out all other feelings or thoughts, picked up a thick piece of timber and stepped into the light. It didn't matter if she only got one swing at Bernt, she would make it count, after that she didn't care.

Then strong arms wrapped themselves around her and lifted her up and back into the shadows, her legs cartwheeling in helpless fury.

"Be still," hissed the body behind her.

Sarah screamed and tried to wield the wood on her jailer, but a second pair of hands caught the lumber and twisted it free from her grasp. Those hands then clamped themselves over her mouth.

"*Zwei!*"

Crack.

Sarah, to her horror, began to cry, a pounding, heaving sob, that sucked the power from her struggles and rendered her feeble in those arms. Her captor felt her surrender, and the soft fingers covering her mouth slid away.

"*Drei!*"

Crack.

"I have...to...help him," she gasped.

"You can't," a man's voice behind her said.

"Why don't you...do something?" she implored.

"We are, *Liebchen*. We are."

"*Vier!*"

Crack.

Scream.

Sarah turned her head. He was a man of maybe fifty, beard greying, skin wrinkling, eyes awash with a blue watery sadness. Next to him, a small woman of similar age, a single tear visible on her cheek.

"Go home. Hide," the woman insisted. "Do what you

need to do. There'll be food to steal from our window sill again tomorrow night. And every night."

"It's not *enough*," Sarah howled in anguish, looking into the flame and the twinkling glass, the blood and the vomit, the hatred and destruction. "You aren't doing enough."

"*Fünf!*"

Crack.

Scream.

"I don't think we have any more to give."

Sarah closed her eyes.

She opened them as the nightmare dissolved to find them filled with real tears. The pain in her belly was just the same, two years later. Sarah swore and pulled the sweat-soaked sheets off her, before turning up the lamp and digging into her pack for Clementine's copy of *Red Rubber*.

Sarah slammed the door open, and the Captain started, shoving something under his pillow.

"Have you *read* this?" she shouted, waving Clementine's book in the air.

He squinted with tiny pupils at the cover. Then he shrugged. "Yes, many years ago."

"How do you sleep? How does anyone sleep? The Belgians. The *verfickten* Belgians are supposed to be on *our* side—"

The Captain made shushing eyebrows and Sarah attempted to sit on her rage. She failed.

"It's *not* that long ago," she continued. "And Clementine

says nothing has changed and that much the same thing was happening here. Children, *children* getting their arms chopped off because their parents didn't work hard enough. CHILDREN—"

The Captain lost his state of calm and made an almost violent downward motion with his hands. His face contorted into something frenzied. Sarah paused and took a breath.

"Sit and shush," he hissed.

Sarah felt like she might throw the book at him. Then she let her arms drop to her sides. Her eyes continued to burn. She sat on the edge of the bed and folded her arms over the book, her nails pressed into its surface.

"*Red Rubber* – rubber bought with African *blood*. Floggings with dried rhino hide were routine. *Routine*," she growled. "Work as tax...that's slavery. In the twentieth century. Villages burned to the ground and men flogged, women...they...for objecting. They couldn't farm, they *starved*, worked until they died...*severed hands acted as currency*. Is this true? Really true and it's what happened?" She whined the last part, wanting him, someone, to tell her it was a horrible myth.

"Yes. It's all true," the Captain said quietly. He lay back on the bed.

"This wasn't a few villages; half the population of Congo Free State died... Clementine says *ten million people*. And the French? The British? Much the same?"

"Probably, I don't know...and for the love of god, *shush*," he moaned.

"Then who am I fighting for? You've already rounded up people and put them in camps. Already worked whole villages to death. Why are the *Wehrmacht* so upset? All they're doing in Poland is what everyone has done here."

"It's different," he mumbled. "We wouldn't do that now."

"Now? What are we now?" Sarah demanded.

"Look, they're just Africans—" The Captain stopped.

He was actually panting.

Sarah stared into his face.

She wanted to grab it and push her fingernails into it.

"And I'm just a Jew," Sarah said quietly.

"No, you're more than that—"

"*More* than? You mean that's not enough? I, they, don't qualify as human unless they're *more than that*?"

The Captain's face hardened and he pushed himself into a sitting position.

"You know what," he whispered angrily, "there have always been people, humans, who are worth less. Not because they actually are, but because someone has put themselves on top, and someone has to be at the bottom. It's the Jews, or the Negroes, or the poor...always the poor, and it's wrong, but this is how humanity functions."

"So what are you fighting for?" She gave an exaggerated shrug. "Why bother?"

"You know as well as I do that the Nazis represent something more, something new. Like having the Congo's *Force Publique* on the streets of Europe."

"So, that's special, *different*. We can all go to war for Europeans, for Jews or *white people*?"

"You think they'll stop with the Jews? You think the Nazis ruling Africa is going to be better than Congo Free State was?

Do you think a government who thinks Slavs are subhuman is going to let them live happily and peaceably? No, Sarah of Elsengrund, you want to change the world, start with the most overt, obvious, enemy and worry about them first."

"We're hypocrites."

"Maybe. I don't know about you, but I'm not a politician or a statesman. I'm a soldier...a spy, an assassin. A murderer. I'm doing my job, my bit...and I'll continue to do what I can, as long *as you keep your gottverdammte voice down.*"

CHAPTER SIXTEEN

25TH SEPTEMBER–12TH OCTOBER 1940

SOME PEOPLE ON THE ROAD tried to stop them. In broken French and with frightened eyes they shouted, pushed and waved.

Turn back. Death. Disease. Cursed.

There wasn't much to see. The flamethrower had done its work. Some of the villages had brick and concrete buildings that were now charred ruins, without doors, windows or roofs. But any other sign of habitation – huts, tents, shelters, paths, the belongings of many dozens of people – was gone. There was just a wide blackened circle that left no tree, shrub or bush.

Something else bothered Sarah, but she couldn't put her finger on it.

The Captain and Claude were picking their way gingerly through to the centre of the clearing. Sarah and Clementine had intended to stay next to the truck but found themselves drawn onto the burned ground.

"Well, this is cheery." Clementine sighed and wound her camera on.

Sarah tried to imagine a place where people lived. Where they met and smiled and danced, where children had played, where workers had returned to their families every day. Her imagination failed her. The people were abstract numbers. She looked up and tilted her head to one side.

"No noise...no birds, no animals," Sarah wondered. She hadn't noticed that their noise had been a constant on their journey, until now.

"White girl, jungle expert..." Clementine mumbled behind her, the shutter on her camera snapping open and closed.

The ground, up close, was not black but grey; a layer of ash had settled over it, and it snapped and cracked underfoot. Sarah pushed something with her shoe.

"These sticks have survived...stone sticks?"

"Not sticks. Not stones," Clementine whispered.

Something went crunch under Sarah's tread, and with it went her confidence, detachment and inner quiet. She slowly raised her leg out of the way to see what she had broken, increasingly sure she knew what it had been.

In the ash, half flattened by her footprint, was the grey, flaking, incomplete but unmistakable shape of a human skull. Half a face. Watching her.

Sarah let out a tiny, involuntary cry and stepped backwards. Another *crunch*, another rib, another leg bone, another—

She looked at Clementine, who was cradling an almost complete skull.

Sarah turned and ran.

Everywhere she looked, there were bones. Flensed, cracked, broken, blackened, scattered pieces of people.

She backed away to the truck and pressed against it, but even here in the long grass there were charred fragments. The villagers were all around her, with stories to tell.

Were they all dead when they were consumed by the fire? Had they welcomed it? Why was it they had to die? Did they have their own questions? *Where are my children? What happened to my father? Why? How could this happen? Why? Why? Why, Sarah—*

Sarah found herself in Schäfer's laboratory, lying on a tiled floor, too hot to touch, surrounded by flames, her skin peeling and popping, the air itself too scalding to inhale, rapidly turning opaque…

"*Ursula!*"

The sound came from the door, the *Ausgang*, where the air was cooler. But the voice was Schäfer's… *Every girl wants to know that she's beautiful. Desirable…* And in the way stood Stern, who burned like a torch—

"*Hey, white girl!*"

Clementine was holding her face, a cheek in each cool hand. Her brown eyes were wide and, Sarah realized, for maybe the first time, sincere.

"*I'm just a little girl,*" Sarah remembered out loud.

"Yes, you are. It's all right. It's over."

Sarah began to scratch her arms, but the skin didn't flake off. It wasn't blistered and raw. She was sitting in the moist grass, leaning on the warm tyre of the truck. She blinked the water from her eyes.

"I was somewhere else. In a fire."

"Well, you weren't here," Clementine said, letting go and backing off. "I think you might have a fever."

Next to Clementine on the ground was the skull she had been holding moments earlier.

"That was someone. A person," Sarah managed, her voice breaking.

"Just a *black* person," Clementine scolded, her barriers, her defences restored. Sarah had thought that she had control over how she felt. About the war, about the disappearing Jews in her neighbourhood, about the stories of Polish atrocities. They were all just terrible facts that merited a rational, negative reaction, bar the simmering sense of injustice and spikes in her temper, quickly contained. She had thought the wheel of emotion was stationary. Sarah now grasped that it was spinning so fast she had only mistaken it for a lack of movement. She was careering, unbridled, down a hill with the untrammelled weight and dread of her experiences waiting below. No barriers. No box for her horrors.

She felt the dread like cold shivers.

"*Fräulein* has a fever," she heard Clementine declare.

"Have you been talking your chloroquine?" the Captain.

Sarah nodded vaguely.

"Not everything is malaria, *mein Herr*," Clementine snapped.

"Do you want me to whip this one?" Claude called.

"You can try…" she growled.

"No one is whipping anyone. Girl, *shush*," ordered the Captain.

Sarah closed her eyes and surrendered to the fire.

◆　　◆　　◆

She shivered, burning, through the night, imagining the cleansing, murderous fire and the distant laboratory consumed in flames. She was dimly aware of some initial panic. The others were uncertain if she should be quarantined just in case, and an argument began, heart versus head, caution versus compassion. There were a million harmless things it could be, the Captain declared. He refused to countenance leaving her behind or sealing her up somehow and became belligerent, that much Sarah remembered. But when her fever broke the next morning, Sarah found Clementine curled up in a chair next to her bed and the Captain was snoring in another room.

The relieved party travelled south, Claude tight-lipped on what he had suggested but still wary of Sarah's recovery. They found the sites of another six outbreaks and ten razed villages. They spoke to locals from the nearest settlements, and the story remained the same. But behind the facts, the spectre of *Le Diable Blanc* grew more powerful and fantastical. He was a demon beast that travelled the Ubangi River, brought to life by King Leopold's crimes. He was an emissary of a troubled spirit world sent to punish the wicked. He was even the ghost of a murdered white man, driven to reap souls of the natives who killed him.

The itinerant missionaries arrived soon after the outbreak. Sometimes the locals were initially grateful, then concerned, and finally distrustful as the medicine and clinics failed to save or heal. Not being able to prepare and bury their own dead caused resentment and even resistance. Sometimes the missionaries were suspected as the source of the disease and chased out of the area.

Always, the flamethrower dealt the final blow, usually against the explicit wishes of the surrounding community. Nobody who caught the mystery disease lived to tell the tale.

It was always a remote settlement, never close to a town or plantation where authorities could be found, never a major source of labour for surrounding farms or mines. By the time anyone knew about an outbreak, the missionaries were already in place behind a *cordon sanitaire*, and fear discouraged the curious.

The other German – sometimes a French official, sometimes a British medic, but clearly the same person, with the same questions – was following the trail, but he had not been everywhere. Whatever sources Hasse was using to track the disease, it was not as effective as the chain of churches that Claude was tapping into.

Sarah couldn't help totting up the death toll, no matter how rough or precise their estimation.

1,532. Give or take a few hundred.

Give or take a few hundred.

When she closed her eyes, she saw charred eye sockets staring back at her.

CHAPTER SEVENTEEN

13TH OCTOBER 1940

"WHERE ARE WE GOING?" Sarah asked again.

"It's a mystery tour..." Clementine declared, a grin lurking and a skip in her step. "All the best journeys are."

They were walking into town, unaccompanied by the local priest or Claude and his *chicotte* or the Captain, who was snoozing in his bed, and Sarah was beginning to feel self-conscious. Out of place.

"There is no point having a *Neger* who can move unnoticed through the locals if they don't share their discoveries with you," Clementine added.

"I don't *have* you," Sarah moaned. "You're employed, by my uncle actually. And can you stop using that word about yourself?"

"My alternative was the hairy one running me through with his knitting needle." Clementine grinned. "You say employment, I'd use kidnap and hostage. And as for the word—"

"You just say those things to get *me* to say things, so *you* get to look clever."

"You're learning...and I did it again, Huckleberry!" Clementine said, then switched to English and an exaggerated American accent. *"Chickens knows when it's gwyne to rain, en so do de birds, chile."* Then she smiled broadly, her mouth pushing into her cheeks. There was something odd about that smile recently, Sarah thought. Something *unaffected*...

Clementine continued: "Your uncle thought that maybe we needed to cheer ourselves up, just a bit. A night without, you know, looking for disease and death. No skulls..."

It was bright. Berlin had been wrapped in a curtain of precautionary gloom every evening since the previous September, so it was shocking to see crowds passing under an open night sky lit by dozens of buzzing electric bulbs, a sound that was a counterpart to the fizzing of the nearby forest.

The same whitewashed wooden buildings with verandas and palisades dominated, mostly by virtue of their height. But between them shacks and constructions of iron, wood and thatching had sprouted like something living had grown across them. Here were the bars and shops where the town lived, reverberating to a soundtrack of laughter and the looping, plucking thrums of string instruments.

People *were* looking at them. Some people were staring at them, but most nodded and looked away.

Sarah was not scared, but she was uncomfortable with its unfamiliarity. Normally, she avoided her own ignorance. She resented it.

"Am I, are we...safe?"

"You mean, are you going to be kidnapped into white slavery?"

Sarah sighed, unwilling to play that game. "I notice you didn't bring your camera," she murmured.

"I wouldn't walk through Berlin holding a camera this time of night, *Fräulein*," said Clementine, tutting. "Do you know what would happen to an African who hurt a white girl? What would happen to their family, their town?"

"You've assimilated very quickly," Sarah muttered, begrudging the turn that the conversation had taken.

"I've *talked* to people. Have you? Or have you really only listened to that *stück Scheiße* Claude?"

Sarah stopped in front of a stall of wood carvings. After a moment she pushed her knuckles into her forehead and turned to Clementine.

"You don't have to be a sanctimonious *Arschloch*, all day, every day, you know? You can be right and you can be nice."

"I'm going to let that one go," Clementine offered. "Because you know what I'm going to say."

"See, that wasn't hard," Sarah replied, looking up and smiling. Clementine scowled, but her heart wasn't in it and it became a long slow smile.

"My, my, it's *Ngontang*. I don't know if I should be honoured or scared," said the stallkeeper in French, hands on hips.

"I'm sorry, *Monsieur*?" Sarah replied.

The man thought better of his introduction and shook his head and hands as if to reset the conversation.

"Does your *Madame* have money with her?" he said to Clementine.

"My *Madame*—" Clementine began, scowling.

"*Boah ey!* You are really bad at acting a part, Clementine." Sarah laughed incredulously. "*Madame* has Reichsmark," she added to the storekeeper.

He made a face, shrugged and then opened his arms over his wares.

Each carving was a symbolic naked figure, twenty to sixty centimetres in height, sanded, oiled and polished to a shining black or dark brown. There were diverse styles and techniques, with different shorthand for coiffured hair and features, different priorities in proportion. Some sat, some stood, toned or muscular with expressions of disapproval or antipathy, while others were slender and elegant with faces of intelligence, concern or grief. Their cone-like navels were exaggerated, as were the genitals or breasts, in a way that Sarah had never seen in a work of art. But for all their visual differences and styles, the figures depicted were all *waiting*. Ready. On guard.

Some of the work was basic and clumsy, but some pieces were works of astounding craftsmanship, compelling creations of patience or warning.

"These are *Bieri*, reliquary guardians. You attach them to the bark chest containing the relics of your ancestors. They face down the evil spirits and protect your family."

"Are these all yours?" Sarah asked in wonder.

"Did I carve them? No. I buy these from the surrounding villages and sell them on to the Fang who live in the towns, people too busy to carve their own. They might go to church on Sundays, but few risk leaving their family's bones unguarded."

"The Fang?"

"My people," he answered and then made a circular gesture. "All these people...except him." He waggled a finger at the shopkeeper next door. "He's *un étranger maudit.*"

His neighbour grinned and made a rude gesture.

"But for you," he continued, "a memento of your voyage. Perhaps your father is a collector?"

"I couldn't take anything sacred," said Sarah.

"Nonsense, they mean nothing as they are. Set them to guard your ancestral relics, *then* they're powerful." He laughed. "*Tout est nul*, of course. Superstition."

"Tradition is important," Sarah replied. She was thinking of the butcher, of his skills, his customs and of how strong his faith had made him. *How vulnerable that made him in the end.*

Clementine leaned in. "Now he's got you defending them," she whispered in German. "He's smart. But what should a little Nazi be thinking of these primitive objects? You're also playing a part, remember?"

"I get it, they're like cartoons, caricatures," Sarah mused. "These are the aspects that are most important, if you want to scare evil spirits away. Strength, resolution, determination. Or maybe that's what you want your family to stand for. I'll bet they could make them look like real people, they just don't *want* to. Like Picasso."

"So, they aren't just savages, they're *worse*. They're *degenerates. Nature as seen by sick minds*, that's what Herr Goebbels would say. You are a terrible, terrible Nazi, you know that?"

Sarah looked at Clementine. Again, behind the faux-solemnity

155

there was a hint of a smile, a shared joke that she was not just the butt of.

"I'm sorry," Sarah said, turning to the shopkeeper. "What was it you said, *un-gong-tang*, or something?"

"That was rude of me, *Mademoiselle*, I apologize." The shopkeeper looked at his feet.

"Tell me."

He motioned back into his shop, to a wooden mask that hung in the shadows, coloured white with clay and pigment. It was adorned with moon-design carving and a long, narrow nose. It had none of the compassion or strength or determination of the *Bieri*. It was almost weasel-like.

"It's just a dance costume, a recent tradition," he said awkwardly. "The nose is hard to reproduce, so it's a challenge to—"

"Tell me about what it means," Sarah insisted.

The man paused anxiously but continued.

"That is *Ngontang – the White.* The mask of...the young... European girl. The spirit that interferes with nature's balance... who brings violence, change, disease and suffering. A trickster, a liar, with a foot in the worlds of both the living and the dead. Sometimes there are two faces, because..."

"I understand, thank you."

"*Mademoiselle—*"

"Thank you for your time," Sarah said with a nod and thin smile, before turning away from the storefront.

"That's *the White Devil* right there, isn't it?" said Sarah to Clementine. "How many more peoples have their own *Ngontang*? It's not superstition – it's caution, it's...fair warning.

It's like a copy of *Red Rubber* containing all the horrors. And that's what they see when they look at a white person...a white girl. Not a demon, I mean, but—"

"A trickster, liar, bringer of suffering and disease?" Clementine shrugged. "And as you've put yourself at the centre of that statement, that is why, yes, you are safe here."

Sarah looked around at the town going about its business, at its inhabitants stealing glances at her. Were they looking out of curiosity? Or out of fear – the way that the Jews had looked at the stormtroopers?

"Is that what you wanted to show me?" Sarah asked Clementine, feeling the prickling of despair and sadness under her eyes.

"No, no! I have a...nice surprise. Promise."

Clementine took Sarah's hand and led her through emptying streets. They bought some strips of meat smeared in a sauce of oily nuts and roasted over an open fire. Something about it made Sarah think of her beloved pot of peanut butter, now containing just a streaky residue that could still be induced onto a slice of bread with a bit of effort. The meat was less easy to identify.

"Is this chicken?" Sarah asked in French.

The chef answered in Fang-okah, and repeated the word several times, with Sarah trying to say it.

"Sure, chicken. Sure," he said finally with a shrug.

They thanked him and walked away, the food wrapped in leaves. Clementine sniffed the package.

"I think it's monkey," she said. Sarah snorted and this made Clementine giggle, until they were both laughing uncontrollably.

"No, seriously, it's called *bushmeat...*" she attempted to continue, tears in her eyes.

"Why not? The French eat horses." Sarah chuckled. Then stopped. "Is this horse?"

They came to what looked like a barn made of corrugated iron. From its dark interior came the sound of a cheap piano and the noise of many voices talking quietly.

Clementine paid a man at the door and he ushered them inside.

The space was lit by one light bulb strung in the rafters, but Sarah could see the people inside were sitting on the matted floor, facing a brick wall that had been painted white.

"It's a cinema. You've brought me to a cinema." She smiled at Clementine and nudged her arm.

Sarah beamed inside. The darkness, the anonymity and the sparkle of silver shimmering light...she had sought sanctuary in the cinema many times over the years. There she had been safe from the *Hitlerjugend* for a while, in a place where people dropped sweets and half-eaten fruit. This was an alien version of that experience, but it promised to bring the dark and the shimmer and a place to hide, from herself at least. She could only guess how Clementine might have come upon so perfect a gift.

An empty space appeared for them to sit near the front, whether from ill-gotten respect or fear, but shortly afterwards the light died to general applause, hiding Sarah's discomfort from view.

Behind them a machine spluttered and clattered into a rattling, thrumming rhythm, and the wall crackled and coruscated into a white rectangle.

The piano started up in a good imitation of a Hollywood theme and an old-style title card appeared.

UNIVERSUM-FILM
AKTIENGESELLSCHAFT PRÉSENTE

Le temps de l'innocence

It was a German production – not that it made any difference as it was a *Stummfilm*, not a talkie. Sarah felt a moment's disappointment, but she consoled herself with the prospect of hearing the pianist providing the whole soundtrack. To create the moods, the tension, the themes and more while improvising always seemed to Sarah to be next to magic.

She looked around to find the musician, but all she could see were the dancing shafts of white light twinkling and cycling through the tobacco smoke.

Clementine leaned over. "Did you see that?" she said, digging Sarah in the ribs with an elbow. "Jewish names, must be really old."

"What?" Sarah murmured as she looked back to the screen, not having heard properly.

She read the subtitle. *New York. 1870.*

Two prominent families of good name were about to announce the engagement of their children. The quality of the picture was poor and the sets were lost in the background blur, but the period clothes were sumptuous and complex.

"*Now* I know who you are really," Clementine gasped.

"Who am I, Clementine?" Sarah replied distractedly.

A cousin, now a Polish countess, has left her husband and returned to New York. Scandalous. The families are concerned for their name. The hero will let nothing stop his union with his betrothed...

The story was really familiar. Drawn by something in the music, she stopped following the intertitles to listen.

"The two families have their own refrains, that synchronize when played together," whispered Sarah glancing behind her. "If the pianist wrote that himself, he's a genius."

"Your uncle told me to take you to see this film, this *particular* film, when he heard that it was on nearby." Clementine continued, "I didn't know why then, but I think I do now."

"It's a nice thing. I love movies, I couldn't get to the theatre much because—" Sarah stopped, suddenly cold in the heat. She was aware of the danger of her words, of the conversation that was actually happening, as if for the first time. "Because... my mother lost all our money when she got sick."

A party to announce the engagement. Cousin Ellen will be there. The Countess.

"Because you weren't allowed to go," Clementine said. Not a question. Sarah could not see her expression in the dark.

Our hero turns and sees the Countess, his childhood friend, a child no longer—

Across the brickwork screen, lit by flickering bulb, emerging from ageing, scratched celluloid, standing two metres high and glistening silver, stood Sarah's mother.

Clementine was still speaking, but Sarah didn't hear her.

Sarah had never seen her mother on film. She had never seen her this beautiful, this valuable, this full of *life*. It left her breathless and unable to swallow.

Watching the film unfold, the damage that Sarah always denied was there, the deep wound of pain and suffering, was not removed or reduced. But watching *the Countess*, the character – who was not just glamorous and desirable, but strong, determined, caring and passionate – to see her embodied by her mother... Sarah understood in that moment that this was the closest she had ever come to *loving* her, unconditionally and without the fear and disappointment.

In this moment the criticism, the aggression, the blame, the vindictiveness, the self-pity, the self-destruction and delusion, even the stench of a human going bad that had never left Sarah's nostrils, paled against the warmth and brilliance of her performance. Like the stars are bleached away by the sun, Sarah could pretend those things weren't there. Because for the very first time Sarah discovered that *Alexandra Edelmann* was every bit the actress that *ihre Mutti* had thought, had insisted, that she was.

What must it have been like to have had *all this* taken away from her? No wonder she had disintegrated as the Nazis took her fame, her money and her livelihood.

She shouldn't have come apart. She should have been stronger for them both. But it made more sense why she could not.

The tears streamed down Sarah's cheeks, as she rose and fell on the waves of love and loss in which she was floating.

The Countess left for New York, leaving her love behind, refusing to destroy his life and family, knowing that he would always carry her in his heart. She was strong for both of them.

The film finished. There was a smattering of applause as the lights came on. People slowly clambered to their feet and left. Sarah could not move.

"She was your mother?" Clementine asked quietly.

"Yes," Sarah replied, staring at the wall.

"She was Jewish. So you are Jewish."

Sarah didn't answer.

Clementine sat back with her arms extended behind her and whistled a descending note.

Sarah was struggling with an emotion, an old, dusty, unused thing that she couldn't identify. Something that was both buoyant, and a weight.

Pride. Sarah was *proud*.

CHAPTER EIGHTEEN

15TH OCTOBER 1940

THAT MORNING, THE PREGNANT DARKENED clouds that had been collecting in the sky for weeks tore open and emptied themselves over the forests and fields – sluicing the mud of a continent into the roads and tracks and threatening to end the expedition where their wheels spun. The forest itself sagged under its weight and shook its head in exhaustion.

Their world closed in. The tree canopy, already impenetrable, turned dark, and the track ahead was obscured by a gauze of water. The mood in the truck grew tense, the bickering verging on nasty, and the sweat was sour on the tongue.

Then during a brief respite in the deluge, they found what they were looking for.

The barrier was makeshift, fashioned with saplings and tree branches, but it was tall and countenanced no intrusion, at least not by automobile.

One large yellow sign was tied to its centre and in bright red paint it read: DANGER: MALADIE INFECTIEUSE.

A middle-aged woman sat crying by the side of the road, surrounded by pots and pans. Her distress was palpable and vocal to the point of it being a lament.

Claude stopped the truck well away from her, as if the misery, like the disease, might be catching. The Captain examined the barrier and found that it rocked if pushed. Clementine's shutter clicked, open and closed, open and closed.

"This could be moved," he suggested. "Should we just drive on…or do we do this on foot?"

"We're just walking into this?" Claude replied, revealing the merest sliver of vulnerability. "They could be infecting people on purpose… Even if they're really helping, it's dangerous…we don't know—"

"We're here to find that out," the Captain interrupted.

Sarah moved away from them towards the wailing woman on the roadside, who looked up at Sarah in renewed hope. "*Mademoiselle*, I made them soup. Let me take it to them, please," she implored in French. Her eyes were like puddles and the lines that ran to them were deep with panic, a human long since overwhelmed by circumstance, dissolving in tears.

"Who is stopping you?" Sarah asked.

"The *Madame*…she says no."

"You have friends there?" Sarah pointed beyond the barrier.

"My sister and her family. Please," she implored. "I'm a healer, I can help."

"The *Madame* didn't want help?"

"Not my kind of help, she said."

"Come on, let's go and see her," Sarah said.

Sarah bent down and helped the woman up. She smiled, just an uncertain glimmer of a thing, and then she began gathering her pans. She busily described their contents.

"Ursula." The Captain beckoned from the middle of the road.

Sarah excused herself and returned to his side.

"Sarah of Elsengrund," he whispered with a special intensity. "Do not...touch...another person here, do you understand?"

"She's not sick," Sarah scoffed.

"You don't know that."

"She's outside the, what...*cordon sanitaire.*"

"Is it manned, is it holding? Is this spread by animals? Who are these people really? Until we know something...Don't. Touch. Anyone."

His voice had acquired a steel, a certainty that she had not heard for some time.

"I'm going to help this woman up the hill," Sarah said firmly. "Do you want to yell at me now, or do you want to save that for later?"

"Let Clementine do it—" the Captain called, causing Clementine to make a rude noise and fold her arms.

"Yell at me later, all right?"

As they climbed the slope, with the others trailing in their wake, the woman chattered. The village had become sick just over a week ago. The missionaries came a few days later and stopped anyone coming near. There was anger, but also fear among the scattered locals. There were few relatives who dared approach the village.

"What would you want to do?" Sarah asked.

"The elders would say, leave everyone in their huts. If they come out, good; if they don't, you burn them where they lie. *Two precautions are better than one.*"

"But would *you* do?" Sarah said, smiling.

"They're old men, easy to stop caring when you're that old," the woman said scornfully. "These people need looking after, by their own."

"You don't like the missionaries?"

"They're like the elders, it makes for easy decisions when it's not your family."

"But they've brought medicines, haven't they?"

"I work in a town twenty kilometres from here. There's a hospital and some good people in it. But the white—" She stopped talking, paused, then restarted. "The French, the British, they have no cure for death. But death quakes in the face of love, it laughs when love is withheld. We need to be involved here, our traditions exist for good reason. You can't swap that for an injection. Even after death, call it a *Christian burial* or the final rite of passage, you don't have to believe that the unburied dead will upset the balance of the world. People just need to say goodbye to move on. It's important."

"Have you heard of the White Devil?" Sarah asked.

The woman stopped. "That's a lot of superstitious *connerie* – sorry, pardon my language, *Mademoiselle*. People get sick, sometimes it's catching. It's not a demon, or a God. It's the way of things...but you know, when you stop people following their traditions and don't explain anything, it makes them suspicious and irrational."

They crested the top of the rise where the track turned a corner. There, in a fierce patch of sunlight that had stolen through the clouds, stood a figure in a green coat and apron, long rubber gloves and boots, mask and goggles over a cloth hood.

Sarah took an involuntary step back. She heard the camera aperture click open and closed behind her.

The figure pulled off its gloves and dropped them to the side before reaching up to its head and pulling the hood, mask and goggles away.

It revealed a small white woman in her early thirties, with a look of intense concern on her face. So unlike the steel and gilt of the Ice Queen's malice, or the shadow-soaked blonde cunning of Elsa, this woman wasn't *beautiful* in that way, nor was she handsome like Marika Rökk or any other film star. But in those green eyes there was not just a fierce intelligence, but a warmth that echoed the round, dimpled attractiveness. There was also immaculately applied make-up.

As the strap of the goggles came free, her hair escaped from a tie and shook loose down one side of her face. Despite the sweat and tangles and strap marks, her hair was a vibrant gold with flashes of auburn brown that actually glittered in the light, like tiny pieces of gilt were threaded through it.

A look of deep sadness and profound pity overcame her expression. She walked up to Sarah's companion.

"Oh, Millie, *Liebling*. I told you...well, you're here now. Why don't you set those down there and I'll make sure they get to...Marlène, isn't it? She's good, you know, she's hanging on. I'm really hopeful..." The words poured out in French and German. Millie tried to talk over her, but the European reached up to touch the other woman's face. Her hands were red and chapped. "No, *Süße*, I know, I know. What kind of doctor would I be if I let you get sick? You've children, *three* children, right? We have to protect them." Millie was still talking, but somehow everything she said was lost in the woman's speech. Soon she was facing back down the hill and departing.

The woman watched her go, hands on hips. She spoke to Sarah and the others without even acknowledging them.

"*Lieber Gott*, that poor woman. Every day. Every day she comes here. She is such a brave one."

"You could let her see her sister," Sarah ventured.

"Her sister died three days ago." It wasn't a rebuke, it was a quiet cry of controlled anguish. "What am I supposed to say? Maybe I can save a niece or nephew, offer her something at the end."

"Can you save them?" Sarah asked.

The woman turned and looked Sarah in the face. One lone tear had escaped her eye, taking a rivulet of mascara down one cheek.

"I haven't so far..." she murmured, before apparently coming around. "*Gottverdammt*, there goes what's left of the make-up. Do you have any eyeliner?" Sarah shook her head. "Maybe your girl?" Clementine raised her eyebrows. "Sorry, silly question. Talking of questions..." She turned to the Captain and Claude. "*Bonjour mes amis, nous sommes des citoyens Suisses, agissant sous les auspices du La Société Missionnaire de l'Église—"*

The Captain raised a hand and interrupted.

"We're not the Free French authorities. Which is a good job, too, as I don't think your Swiss passports, if they even exist, will pass muster, as you're German. We're looking for Professor Bofinger."

She relaxed and then became a very different kind of suspicious. She cocked her head to one side.

"Who's asking?" She turned to Sarah. "Who's asking, *Liebchen*?"

"The *Abwehr*," Sarah replied.

"Ursula!" the Captain moaned. Clementine sniggered and Claude rolled his eyes.

The woman chuckled in a way that made her cheeks invade her eyes.

"*Heil*, to the agents of the *Vaterla-la-dingsbums...*" She turned and bowed to Sarah. "And greetings to young Ursula. My name is Dr Lisbeth Fischer. Who is the fake priest?"

"Which one?"

"Oh, she's funny. The fake one." She pointed at the Captain and then at Claude. "He's real. I can spot a true believer a mile away."

"That one" – Sarah gesticulated at the Captain – "is my uncle."

Lisbeth turned to him, a burst of concern overtaking her. "What are you doing bringing children here? Did you know *why* you'd been sent here?"

"I'm here to talk to Professor Bofinger, and I'll use any

assets I have to, in any way I see fit."

The Captain had the edge to his voice that Sarah had come to know only recently. It was the voice that grew impatient. The one that made mistakes, that forgot to charm and ingratiate.

"Dr Fischer, do you know the Herr Professor?" Sarah asked, moving into the silence.

"Rudolf Bofinger is my *stepfather*." Lisbeth turned back to the Captain. "He's not going to want you here. As for you, true believer, get some gloves and a mask and start tending to the sick."

"It would take the devil to make me do that," Claude replied in perfect German.

"Well, true believer, the devil is here, all right."

"You don't go into the village without mask, gloves and goggles. Don't remove your mask, gloves or goggles in the village, at any time, for any reason. If you do, you're staying there," Lisbeth stated in a voice used to giving orders. "When you're done, gloves in the bleach, all the way in, that'll clean your hands. *Then* take off your mask and goggles. Hands in the bleach again, and let them dry in the air. Get that wrong and you stay in the village. You cause me any trouble, you stay in the village. I've only lost one nurse so far. You endanger that record and you *stay in the village*. Am I being clear enough?"

"*Glasklar*," Sarah replied. She caught Clementine's eye, who made a vomiting gesture.

The table of buckets, gloves on hooks and other protective

gear ran alongside the new path that led to the village from the mission encampment, itself the size of a small village. Sarah counted twenty tents at least in the camp, as well as two large marquees. In addition to the white mission staff, a small army of servants moved from shelter to shelter. Horses were corralled next to carts and behind that sat two large trucks. For something so evidently temporary it seemed oddly like Fort-Lamy, a statement of intent, of privilege and power.

As they approached it, Sarah noticed that the clearing they had set up camp in was not natural but built from scorched earth and ashes.

Lisbeth called to a porter and talked to him in Flemish Dutch.

"Take their girl and fetch their luggage. On the way, burn the gloves on the path and...empty the soup out into the bushes. Carefully, so it won't be seen. Leave the pots by the barricade."

The Belgian waved to Clementine to follow him, who did after an insolent delay.

"Not eating the soup?" Sarah asked.

"I'm...too scared, to be honest. I'm not sure we've got all of this bottled up here."

"You touched her face," Sarah mentioned quietly.

Lisbeth shrugged. "She needed to be touched..." Something occurred to Lisbeth. "You speak *Dutch*," she said with a smile.

Sarah's command of languages, one of her mother's few gifts to her, came so easily that she sometimes forgot what she was listening to. She was going to have to be more careful around the doctor.

"Now I see why he keeps you around," Lisbeth continued. "What does he want, Ursula?"

The Captain hovered, but Lisbeth ignored him, turning her back to him as he moved. Sarah struggled momentarily to unpick the truth from the lie, the cover from real mission, uncertain what that was.

"You're in enemy territory, you need to be escorted to safety," she managed.

"Well, enemy territory is where we're needed right now," Lisbeth replied.

"You've research that's needed at home."

"Oh, *screw* that. It's meaningless there if people are still dying here."

"I think they're interested in what you've uncovered."

Lisbeth stopped and swung around to face Sarah. "*They're* interested... *Gottverdammt*, Father..." She spun on her heel and stomped towards one of the big marquees, before storming in.

There were raised voices, which quickly settled.

"What did you say to her?" the Captain demanded.

"Just that we're here to escort them back and—" Sarah stopped as the Captain pulled a face. "What? But that's the cover story."

"But we don't know their intentions!" he snapped. "We don't know who or what the Reich—"

"And we're not going to find out with you arguing with everyone," Sarah interrupted.

"*Herrgot*—" the Captain snarled, then stopped, breathing heavily.

Sarah fizzed in irritation. She saw him beginning to struggle, to lose trust in her, to fail as a spy. Evening was approaching, and he was in trouble. His skin was already pale and the whites of his eyes growing sallow. This was a play she had seen over and over, but she had stopped questioning the script. She knew the final act but never waited to see it, believing that if she ignored it, it would go away. Norris knew, Clementine knew, and not letting them talk about it hadn't stopped it happening.

She took a deep breath. "I'm not sure you should talk to anyone at the moment," she managed quietly. "Go...do whatever you need to do."

She winced at the phrase she had used before, over and over.

He looked like he was going to argue. Then one of the mission staff emerged from the tent. He was wearing a lab coat and a mask that concealed his features.

"Welcome to the Bofinger Medical Mission. You are all invited to dinner at 8 p.m. You will be shown to tents where you can dress appropriately. Please be punctual."

He turned and walked back into the marquee. Several servants had taken their cue and began beckoning to the visitors.

Sarah rubbed at her face, feeling the weight of the air tighten around something in the centre of her forehead. It was like the dirty sky was pushing down and threatening to crush them all.

CHAPTER NINETEEN

THE DINING TENT WAS the pulsing heart of the mission encampment's pretension. It was as lavish as Sarah had seen, even in early childhood or at the Schäfer's poisoned banquet hall. The huge table was solid beneath the tablecloth, the chairs were no camping stools but high-backed mahogany antiques, and the place settings were gleaming crockery and silverware. There was even a chandelier suspended above it, fully laden with freshly lit candles.

Sarah could barely conceive how the contents of this room were transported, how many porters and servants, carts or trucks might be required to drag it from one piece of the jungle to the next, keeping pace with the work of the White Devil. They also needed to keep away from the Free French authorities, who could decide that even missionaries from an enemy nation like Germany might be safer under lock and key.

However, the grandiose sense of scale was choked by the atmosphere. The darkness and the candlelight just added to the sweltering heat, saturated air and intense pressure. The claustrophobic space made Sarah feel short of breath, that she might asphyxiate or drown where she sat. The thick stench of sweat from the assembled diners was just a minor discomfort in comparison.

"You're late," growled a man at the head of the table, gripping the arms of an oversized chair like it was a throne. It wasn't possible to guess his age. He seemed both youthful and impossibly old all at once. There was a fire in his eyes that spoke of a childlike vitality, but they sat in a jowl-laden face, skin tanned and wizened by ten thousand suns or more. He had the thick, curled moustache so beloved of older men, now a silver-white, but that hair sought escape from such control. With the thinning mop of strands perched on his head, it risked being comic. Something in his expression of intense disapproval and reprimand suggested otherwise.

Behind him hung a flag that it took Sarah a moment to identify. It was the war flag of the Kaiser's German Empire defeated in the last war. It made a change from the usual swastika, she thought.

"They are almost exactly fifteen minutes late, as decorum demands, *Vater*," Lisbeth chided, rising and turning to the guests. She was now wearing a cream evening dress, something Sarah recognized from her early childhood as being almost twenty years out of fashion. The lace was yellowing and the material had been darned and repaired, yet she made it look like she was on the cover of the latest *Filmwelt*. Sarah also noticed she had fixed the mascara trail and restored a perfectly powdered complexion. On a leather strap around her neck was a long, thin necklace carved out of one piece of white stone.

"Almost is not good enough," he complained. "If you want meat from my table, you need to be timely. We're not savages here." He stared at Claude for a moment and then made a dismissive gesture.

Lisbeth rolled her eyes theatrically and waved the Captain, Claude and Sarah to their seats.

"Where's Clementine?" Sarah whispered to the Captain.

"Yes, let's bring our servants to dinner, that's not at all weird," the Captain said witheringly. To Sarah's relief, his eyes were clear, his skin healthy.

"Ursula, sit next to me—"

"Boy, girl, boy, girl—" the host grunted.

"Shush, *Vater*," Lisbeth interrupted.

There were another half-dozen guests, all but one men of various ages. Most seemed less than delighted to be there and one, the youngest, looked positively terrified. The servants began to serve water and a dull series of dishes of chicken and potatoes, but the food was *hot* and there was enough. Not many of Sarah's meals on the long drive south had been.

"Thank you for your hospitality, Herr Professor—" the Captain began.

"So my *step*daughter tells me that Berlin wants my research," the professor interrupted. "To which I say, about time—" He stopped and looked away. "By *heaven's will*, Klodt. Stop fidgeting with that cup," he shouted at the scared-looking youth with too much oil in his hair. The boy was holding his water like it might reach out and strike him. "It's water. Our water. Clean— Oh, never mind, drink the wine and dehydrate, see if I care."

Bofinger took a second to gather his thoughts before continuing.

"Yes, forty years wiping the *Popos* of these savages." He made a circular gesture with a hand. "And finally I seem to have something important to the Fatherland."

"I'm not sure at this point what you may have found—" the Captain managed before Bofinger interrupted him.

"Well I am. A more virulent pathogen has never been discovered. Cut a swathe through our party before we could control it."

"But, Lisbeth—" The words were out of Sarah's mouth before she could stop them and now everyone was looking at her. "I mean, Dr Fischer said you'd only lost one nurse."

"And we did, a good man."

"We also lost twenty-two native workers, Ursula," Lisbeth said quietly, fiddling with her necklace. "Before we knew what we were dealing with."

"And a fair few since," the professor went on as if no one else was talking. "Bofinger's Disease has a nice ring to it, don't you think? I'd name it after the first patient, but he was some meaningless *Platzverschwendung*—"

"Father!" Lisbeth cried.

"*Some poor subject of the Belgian Empire*," he corrected himself sarcastically and went on. "And I don't even remember what toilet of a river we were near at the time, something running off the Ubangi River or somewhere. Can't call a disease *Ubangi*, no one would take it seriously. I'd seen it before anyway, or something like it, off and on for the last ten years. But this...it's better, stronger, more infectious, takes longer to appear in a host, kills slower...this is something worth having—"

"Father, *enough*," Lisbeth snapped. "I'm sorry, my father is an old warrior, and he occasionally forgets to be anything else."

"Yet we're at war again, stepdaughter. A time for warriors. Do you think Berlin's sudden interest in our work is altruistic?"

Sarah wondered if he were drunk. That would have made her feel better about this conversation, that it could be dismissed as an alcohol-fuelled rant, like her mother's admonishments and threats. That there would be a time of tears and apologies and regret. Yet the man seemed steely-eyed.

"Time was it didn't matter what the cost," he continued. "Didn't have to pretend that we cared, or that we were doing things for *their* own good. Back when Germans went into *Südwestafrika*. We wanted the land, we took it. We wanted the cattle dead, my father killed all the cattle—"

"*Father!*"

"If there was research to do, someone needed a human skull, my father would just walk into the concentration camp and take one—"

"Father, *please*," Lisbeth insisted. "Stop talking about *that*."

There were now tears in her eyes. Sarah wondered at this woman, living with someone who seemed to revel in his inhumanity. *Like attending Rothenstadt for ever.*

Something occurred to Sarah, who looked around the tent.

There were six servants present. Six *people* for whom this was also a reality, who were the *subject* of this story.

Bofinger looked at his daughter with a mixture of pity and disgust. He sighed, as if disappointed. "So, Haller, isn't it?" The professor changed the subject. "What do you bring me from the Fatherland? Men? Money?"

"I'm here to assess your work and bring you to safety. Then to Germany, where I'm sure—"

"Then you're useless to me. I don't know why I'm feeding you and your *Neger*." He glanced at Claude, who visibly bristled. "I'm not coming home now to have this taken off me by some upstart. No! I'm coming home a hero, with a weapon to win the war, or not at all."

Lisbeth was shaking her head angrily, gripping her necklace with white knuckles.

"You are now surrounded on all sides by enemies of the Reich," the Captain said. "Free Belgians to the east, the British to the north-west, the Free French everywhere—"

"Do you know how many times this benighted piece of land on the edge of a stinking continent has changed hands in the last forty years? The only difference is where the money goes. Doesn't matter to the natives, to your priest over there, or even the lowly servants of the German Empire like us. We're just treating the local sick, like good little missionaries." He looked at Claude. "Not that anybody here is naïve enough to still believe in God," he muttered, and then tapped the table. "I'll come back when I'm good and ready."

"Well, will you at least allow me to stay and report back on your progress?" the Captain asked, with just the right level of disappointment and need in his voice. "I can spread the word."

Sarah had forgotten how good he could be when he was able to concentrate.

"Very well." The professor sighed magnanimously. "I'll let Lisbeth show you round the local petri-dish."

Lisbeth made a face and closed her eyes.

"Have you heard of the White Devil?" Sarah asked.

Bofinger stared at her – that same look of incredulity tinged with both amusement and anger. Then he laughed.

"Of course I have. *Gottverdammte* superstitious savages. Still, stories travel faster than news; it's a good way of getting to the next outbreak in time."

"So you don't think someone is deliberately infecting villages?" Sarah asked.

There was a brief silence in which looks were exchanged and the dinner guests squirmed.

"Shush, child," ordered the professor. The amusement was gone, leaving just the incredulity and anger.

Lisbeth put a red hand on Sarah's. Reassuring. Calming. Warning. The skin was rough and oily where she had recently applied a cream, but it was wonderfully warm.

Dearest Mouse,

Men and boys. Everywhere there is a problem, everywhere there is something bad happening, everywhere there is damage and pain and suffering. Men and boys.

There are bad women, I know, and you and I have met many of them. Maybe I've become one of them. But for every dictator like the Ice Queen, for every attack dog like Rahn, for every twisted teacher like Langfeld and her stick, there seem to be <u>dozens</u> of bad, dangerous men.

And these men have all the power. They have the opportunity to be worse, or the chance to be bad on a bigger scale. Maybe that's the problem? If we had power, might the world not be better?

The <u>history of the world</u> is the story of men and it seems like history is the story of death, greed and destruction. Great towers built on the backs – and the corpses – of the poor and the weak. It sets the tone, the world that women like the Ice Queen and Elsa have to live in, to survive in.

In fact, <u>history</u> is the history of <u>Western</u> men. <u>White</u> men.

Do you think...maybe...that there's nothing superior about Aryan men? Really, I mean? Other than enough nastiness to do the horrible things necessary to always be the winner?

Do you think that maybe being the fittest and surviving shouldn't be an aim in itself?

Those are dangerous thoughts these days. They shouldn't be, Mouse. They shouldn't be.

Alles Liebe.

Ursula

CHAPTER TWENTY

LISBETH WALKED THE GUESTS back to their tents. Outside of the path and its pale oil lamplights harassed by clouds of small insects, the darkness was total. The jungle chittered, hissed and vibrated, keeping its secrets until dawn.

"What camp is your father talking about?" Sarah asked.

Lisbeth shook her head. "My father is wrong to talk of such things, I'm sorry," she said sadly. "Especially around you, Ursula. It's not right."

"It's fine. I'm quite hardened."

"So it seems. But little girls shouldn't be."

"Well, you seem pretty strong," Sarah ventured.

Lisbeth laughed, cheekbones and eyebrows. "Strong, hard… these are not necessarily the same." She smiled. "But you're right, I was hardened, and that wasn't really a good thing."

"Was it living here?"

"Lord, no, I love this place, every muddy, dusty, stingy, buzzy bit of it. This is my home. Africa made me strong."

"Then what—"

"My mother died," she said quietly, holding her necklace in one fist. "Back in the Fatherland an illness took her away, as the defeated troops came home, the streets burned, and you needed a bucket to carry the money to buy a cup of tea. That made me hard...but not hard like my father, my *step*father I mean. He doesn't...care. That's actually useful in a man, especially one dealing with this disaster. I get upset, he gets busy."

"Nothing wrong with getting upset."

Sarah didn't believe this, or couldn't allow herself to believe it, but it seemed like the right thing to say.

"Good, now you sound like a little girl again," Lisbeth said, smiling.

"Can your father be persuaded to come back with us?" the Captain interjected.

"I'm not sure I want you to take him."

"You would come, too, of course," the Captain added.

"Oh, *would I?*" Lisbeth's voice grew cold.

"I'm sorry." The Captain held his hands up. "What does he want?"

"If you appeal to his vanity enough, and you have something concrete to offer him, then maybe. He doesn't feel valued by Germany any more. When the empire was taken away at the end of the last war, and we were driven out of our homes, nobody cared what we'd lost. We got back here under our own steam. He has some plans, but they don't involve Germany much."

"Doesn't he understand what the Führer has built in his

184

absence? People like your father *are* valued now," the Captain gushed. "In the Third Reich your father's work would bring him prestige and fortune."

"You've seen his flag. I don't think anything after 1918 means anything to him."

"It's an empire of hard people, people who don't care. It's the place for him." The words were out of Sarah's mouth before she had time to think about their consequence.

Lisbeth made the face again, but when she opened her eyes the anxiety was gone.

"What do *you* want, Dr Fischer?" the Captain asked.

"To do *my* work, achieve *my goals*," she said defiantly. She stopped as they reached their tents. "Well, goodnight, Herr Haller, *mon Père*."

The men, dismissed, murmured their farewells and disappeared.

Lisbeth stood with Sarah. It was only for the briefest of moments, but being in each other's company felt...*right*. Sarah couldn't think of any other way to express the feeling.

"Thank you for dinner," Sarah said.

"Well, thank you for being there. It gets very dull, the same eight faces every night. Klodt thinking he's going to get sick drinking the water and Father shouting at him."

"What are your father's *other plans*?" Sarah asked.

"He has friends in the United States. They share his ideals, and I believe they do actually support the new Reich, but they make a lot of promises."

Elsa had once said, of her father's American friends, *America is full of Nazis. More dangerous, more secretive.*

Sarah shuddered. She thought it was on the inside, but she began shivering.

"You're getting cold. You should go in," Lisbeth suggested.

"I'm sorry about your mother...my *Mutti* is..."

Sarah dug into the grief of her mother's death to support the lie. She found that soil dry and dusty, like the feelings hadn't been watered in so long they'd died off. She grabbed hold of her new and raw pride and felt the jolt of its power.

"In an institution. She's gone." Sarah hugged that truth and rode the wave of loss. "She doesn't know who I am any more," she finished.

Lisbeth's face filled with the same sympathy, the same concern that she had shown Millie, but this time there was a quiver around her mouth, accentuated by the thick lipstick. She reached out jerkily and, when Sarah didn't flinch, she placed her hands on the girl's shoulders and slowly gathered her in.

Until Sarah was reunited with Atsuko she hadn't been held, other than for the purpose of deception or violence, for much more than a year. Before that her mother's touch had been such a conditional thing, so often tinged with violence, accompanied by the scent of alcohol, and later vomit or urine or both. The available comfort had also needed to flow uphill to the adult who should have been supplying it all.

This was different.

The arms were uncertain, but that caution came from care. They wrapped themselves around her gently and then squeezed slowly, to a point nearing discomfort, before relaxing. The smell of perfume, strong but clean, was like a sunlit garden, masking the underlying trace of bleach and disinfectant.

And the embrace was warm. Not like the surrounding muggy, oppressive heat or the aggressive dryness of the desert, but a warmth born in the heart.

In that moment, Sarah of Elsengrund was no longer solely responsible for her survival, for her happiness, for her life. She felt a fissure open deep within her and through it raw untrammelled emotion oozed out, a slight trickle that might retreat at any moment, like canned milk from too small a hole.

She had thought that she felt nothing, that the empty box of horrors meant that there were no emotions to deal with. Then she thought she was sliding towards them, on wheels spun by anger. Now the sudden awareness of all the pent-up sensation that she stood on, the perception of that tide of feeling washing around under that skin, made her see that she was *in* the box. She lived in that small space, and the emotion and the horrors were in the walls and floor all around.

"Get strong, don't get hard," Lisbeth whispered.

Sarah pulled away, as gently as she could, feeling the loss almost immediately.

"Thank you," Sarah said with a sincerity that she hadn't needed for a long, long time.

Sarah felt her way into her tent. She could hear Clementine's breathing.

"Nice fancy dinner? Do you know what they gave me? Half a potato," her voice growled from the darkness.

Sarah was all at once deeply, profoundly tired and was struggling to find the entrance to the mosquito net.

"That's...sorry," she murmured.

"Want to know what I've learned, or do you just want a *Nickerchen* in there?"

Sarah gained entry and slumped onto the cot. Then she rolled back towards Clementine. "Do tell," she managed.

"The money from the missionary society doesn't begin to cover what they're spending here, not that there's much religion going on. Someone else is giving them money...the pay is good. It's why no one has left, despite the danger. And some of the Africans are a long way from home now, unlikely to ever make their way back to Angola or South West Africa—"

"Did anyone say what the professor was doing in *Südwestafrika*?"

"Long time ago. There's an old man, Samuel, who was there...the Africans think Fischer is an angel and Bofinger is a monster. They think *the professor is* the White Devil."

"I think they might be right," Sarah said, rubbing at her cheek where Lisbeth's make-up had stuck to her face.

"Your uncle, what's he trying to achieve here? I mean, he's not here for the *Abwehr*, not really...not with a Jewish girl in tow."

"No one said I was Jewish," Sarah said, rolling away from Clementine. She stuck to the line, not knowing what else to do.

"Fine, but..."

"Doesn't matter who we're working for," Sarah insisted. "He needs them to leave and as quickly as possible so we can stop all this."

"Before the SS officer from the hotel catches up?" Clementine asked after a moment. Sarah was silent. "Your uncle is a terrible

te and hammered into the ground like a nail into soft
ter, looked like parasites or infections on the surface of the
ng village.

But the village was living no more. No one moved in its
eets, the gardens were overtaken with weeds and the fruit
 the trees was unpicked and turning. It would have been
sy to assume that the community had fled, except for one
ing.

Above it all, there was one long, continuous vocalization, as
he remaining inhabitants moaned, gasped, cried and sobbed,
ointly and alone.

It came from the huts, it came from the people lying under
the canvas shelters, it seemed to inhabit every piece of the
clearing.

Clementine was busy taking photos and counting her
remaining shots. Sarah wanted to make her stop but wondered
if they'd be all that was left of the village in a week's time.

Through the mask, through the chemical sting, the smell
was an assault. There was all the sewage and vomit stench of
a bad hospital, but added to this was rotting vegetation and
something else, something sweet and repellent. Something
that made Sarah want to stop and turn back.

Sarah had expected beds, chairs, curtains, the equipment
of a hospital, but the shelter was just twenty or more patients
lying on blankets in ordered rows. Lisbeth kneeled down next
to one, murmuring to him and gently taking a pulse. The man
looked at her, but through her, as if she was not there.

He was bleeding from his nose, mouth, ears and eyes…eyes
that were no longer white but a putrid red.

diplomat. He's crashed into every conversation so far and
offended someone. You might as well ask Claude to do it."

"He's overcompensating," Sarah murmured.

"What does that even mean?"

"He's…afraid and he knows that's bad, so he's trying to be
more impulsive."

"Oh, I thought it was because he needed more morphine,"
Clementine said quietly.

Sarah rolled back to face the darkness where Clementine
sat.

"He was shot last year. He was in a lot of pain. It became
a habit, I suppose."

"It's going to get us killed, *I suppose*."

"Did you learn anything else?" Sarah said carefully,
changing the subject.

"You know what they're calling this disease? *L'hémorragie…
the Bleeding*."

*The tent was bathed in blue-grey light and every detail of its
inside – the two cots, the mosquito nets, Clementine snoring
away and their baggage – was clearly visible. On the end of
Sarah's bed, sat the Mouse, half in and half out of the netting as
if it wasn't there.*

*The little girl, because Sarah always thought of her as such,
was nodding excitedly to nothing, as she often did when she was
about to say something. She was slight and all eyes, on the verge
of laughter or horrified tears, as Sarah remembered her.*

"Hello, Haller," she said.

Sarah tried to sit up but found she couldn't move. "I've been writing to you, did you get my letters?" she managed.

"Only in your head, silly." The Mouse giggled.

"You look happy, Mouse," Sarah said.

"Because you are, I think. I'm here because you're feeling guilty. But you aren't really guilty, or you don't think you're guilty...I don't understand."

The Mouse delivered this with a shrug and a little head wiggle.

"Everything that happened to you, I'm sorry—" Sarah began.

The room darkened like a cloud had passed over the moon.

It looked like the Mouse was gone and then she reappeared, leaning forward and looking at Clementine.

"Older girls...fathers, mothers...sisters. Finding people to take their place...you should be careful, Haller. You think this is all wonderful and by the time you realize it isn't, it'll be too late."

"You said that once before...no, Mouse, Mauser, Ruth, come back, talk to me—"

The Mouse was fading.

"Keep writing, it'll help you figure things out," she interrupted. "Do you like kittens or puppies best?"

"I don't—"

She was gone. The room grew darker and darker until Sarah could see nothing.

CHAPTER TWENTY-O[NE]

16TH OCTOBER 1940

EVEN CONSIDERING THE WEATHER CONDITIONS, [...] unbearably hot in the apron, gloves, mask, boots and g[...] Sweat ran freely down the inside of Sarah's clothes, [...] collecting, squelching and sloshing around the soles [of her] feet. The mask stank of bleach and disinfectant wher[e the] insides had been soaked in caustic liquid. It made her [nose] and mouth burn. The eye-pieces kept steaming up, and Sa[rah] had to constantly remind herself not to wipe at them with [her] oversized gloves. They flapped as she hobbled along in boo[ts] four sizes too large.

Then they reached the village and she forgot all about that.

Clearly, this had once been a thriving hamlet with dozens of large huts, each made of intricately woven raffia with a high, rolling thatched roof that dropped to the ground on either side. Behind each house was a fenced-in vegetable garden or a small orchard.

The mission's temporary structures and shelters, uniformly

The blood seeped around his face and gathered in a dark sticky puddle underneath him, stretching from his head to his hands and onto his feet. Flies buzzed about him and feasted in the pooled fluids.

Lisbeth flapped at the insects to move on, before turning to the visitors and beckoning them close. She made a *not now* gesture to Clementine as she raised her camera to her eye. The woman's voice was muffled through the mask, and she had to shout to be understood.

"They get a headache, they get tired, then they get a fever, they vomit, then they start to bleed, inside and out. Anyone unprotected who touches them catches it. Wildfire," she added.

"How is it transmitted?" the Captain called out.

"Blood, fluids, definitely, but I think we have to accept now that it's airborne."

"Airborne?"

"Like the flu. Didn't used to be. That's what everyone wants though, *isn't it*? A good *weapon*?" she sneered. "Can you *stop*?" she called to Clementine, who was leaning into another patient to take a shot.

"What can you do?" Sarah asked.

"Fluids, maintain blood pressure, morphine for the pain..." She brushed a finger softly along the man's cheek, an affectionate gesture. He did not react, and the skin moved unnaturally like it wasn't attached to the head beneath. "But they all die in the end."

She shook her head and climbed to her feet, wiping her hands on a soaked cloth.

"Did anyone not catch it?" Claude grunted.

"They're infectious for two to three days before showing symptoms. We quarantined the healthy, then took out the sick, quarantining fewer and fewer each time. We have two left," Lisbeth called, pointing up the hill to a distant tent at the treeline.

Sarah was looking at a large pile of woven material behind the furthest hut. There were lots of blues, reds and yellows in the mound, it was the brightest part of the village. It seemed to shimmer. Then she saw the foot...then all the feet and arms.

All the feet and arms.

The sparkling was a cloud of insects, whose buzzing was lost in the noise of the living.

Lisbeth stood in her way, hands up, as if to block the view.

"We've been taking the bodies away and burning them, but we can't spare the gasoline any more. It makes no odds at this point, sorry," she apologized.

"They want the dead..." Sarah said, pointing to the horror. "Millie wants to do the rites of passage—"

"They are just bags of infection now, it's not safe," Lisbeth interjected.

"But—"

Sarah was interrupted by a small shriek from a nearby shelter.

"What's that tent?" Sarah pointed to the tent. Inside there was feverish activity around a high table.

"The morgue, post-mortem...that's really dangerous. I can't let you in there," Lisbeth stated, shaking her head.

"What was that noise?" the Captain asked.

"The nurses are very frightened. If they get upset from time to time, I let that go," Lisbeth said firmly.

Claude looked at the village, hands on hips.

"These people don't work for the French, then?" he asked.

"The Bateke are very independent. They stay out of the way of the French."

"That's very convenient," Clementine mumbled into Sarah's ear.

The quarantine tent was large and the fact that just two men sat on the ground in one corner was chilling.

Seeing the visitors, one of them, little more than a teenager, jumped to his feet and walked towards them. He began to talk, incessantly, strenuously and with no little fear. The language was swift and insistent, with a syncopated rhythm and punctuated with small explosions of syllables. It reminded Sarah of jazz music.

"I don't speak Kiteke, but he wants to leave. That much is clear," the approaching nurse called.

Claude yelled at the man. An order. He pointed to the blankets and held his finger there, part command, part warning. The teenager stopped talking like he had been struck and retreated, a mixture of anxiety and rebellion in his eyes.

"You keep them here against their will?" Sarah asked.

"Otherwise they'll leave, they'll infect another village and this goes on for ever," the nurse complained.

"How many have you saved this way?" Sarah demanded.

The nurse's eyes narrowed behind the goggles and he turned away.

Clementine snorted. "No one," she growled.

"This strain is so infectious, we've lost everyone, every time." Lisbeth's shoulders were sagging as she talked. "But Kubsch is right. We are at least stopping it from spreading."

Sarah watched the nurse preparing to take some blood from the other patient. This man was approaching middle age, dressed in a simple, patterned wraparound fabric that showed muscles beginning to lose their definition. His expression was too complex to read, complicated by a scar on his right cheek, but the sorrow sat upon him like a lead weight. He had not surrendered, but his will to fight lay under that handicap. Sarah wondered if he was resigned to his isolation, or saving his strength.

He barely flinched as the hypodermic needle slid into his forearm. It was an ageing steel syringe, well worn. Sarah was struck by the complexity of some of the equipment that the mission needed, over and over again. She thought of touching the syringe, touching the sick, touching others, the impossibility of not spreading whatever this was.

"How can you keep everything clean out here?"

"Chlorine bleach is powerful stuff; it gets a scrub between uses," Lisbeth asserted.

"End of every day," chimed in the nurse, squeezing the drawn blood into a bottle.

"But each syringe gets cleaned after each use," Lisbeth added, her eyes narrowing behind the goggles.

"Yeah, mostly—" the nurse burbled.

"What do you mean, *mostly*?"

"Well, *mostly*. We're going through a lot of needles, we haven't time…and your father—"

"You mean, here or *there*?" Lisbeth pointed back down to the village.

"Well, I mean, ideally they're separate—"

"*Ideally?*" Lisbeth screamed.

The teenage patient watched this exchange, not following the words, but the tone. He became increasingly agitated until the doctor's explosion. At that moment he bolted for the tent flap, hanging open where the visitors had come in.

"Stop him," howled Lisbeth, but he was out of the tent before anyone reacted.

By the time the party was outside, the patient, who was young and fit, was halfway down the hill and heading for the path to freedom.

"Kubsch!" called Lisbeth, and the nurse stepped forward.

He pulled a machine pistol from under his apron, raised it and aimed. Clementine raised her camera.

"No!" screamed Sarah and rushed forward.

The Captain wrapped his arms around her and dragged her out of the way.

"No!" she screamed again.

The youth had reached the path.

Kubsch pulled the trigger, and the gun made a snapping noise.

The top of the teenager's head vanished and he crashed to the ground, a mess of arms and legs, finally sliding to a stop.

The buzzing vocalization had stopped. The jungle all

around answered with a burst of howling, hooting and distress calls.

The medical staff stood, staring at the corpse, before turning as one to look at Lisbeth.

She doubled over, fists balled, before she began screaming.

"*Scheiße, Scheiße, Scheiße...*" she hissed, before turning on Kubsch and slapping him chaotically. He staggered back, covering his head with his arms. "Look what we did! Look at him! Just because you couldn't be bothered to wash the needles every time. How many others are dead because of that?"

Eventually, one of her punches made contact with his chin. There was a crack and he fell.

Lisbeth stood over him, rubbing her hand. For a moment Sarah thought she was going to kick him, but instead she turned and marched towards them. She seized Clementine's camera and shoved her over onto the ground.

She swung on her heel and strode down the hill to the village, pulling the film out of the Leica in a series of violent actions and dropping the camera on the ground next to the corpse. The waiting medical team, who had been watching this unfold, suddenly found things to do.

CHAPTER TWENTY-TWO

THE BLEACH DIDN'T HURT, at first, and everyone was just happy to take off the protective gear. But in the few minutes it took to get back to camp, Sarah's skin had begun to flake. The joints in her fingers grew red, cracked and sore. It was oddly excruciating, like nails bitten down too far.

"It's an occupational hazard," Lisbeth said sadly. "Come with me."

Sarah looked back to Clementine, who could barely control her rage. Sarah made an apologetic face but followed the woman.

The inside of Lisbeth's tent was much the same as the one Sarah had slept in, except this shelter was home to a huge dressing table and mirror, bigger than anything her mother had owned at the peak of her success and wealth. The table was laden with pots, bowls and tubes, sponges and brushes – the tools of high fashion and the theatre.

As Sarah entered, Lisbeth was already seated in front of it, having lit some candles and beckoning her in with a wide and conspiratorial smile. She glanced at her reflection and swore softly as she noticed that her goggles had made marks in her make-up. Sarah sat on the cot next to her and took the jar of cream that she was offered. She scooped a few fingers full of the oily white substance and began to wring her hands with it.

The cream stung dully as Sarah worked it in. Lisbeth chuckled at her expression.

"You have to force yourself past that, it'll get better, I promise," she said, leaning into the mirror and smoothing out the goggle marks. She was silent for a few moments as she worked, then stopped and looked at Sarah's ashen face, still in shock at what she had seen.

"I'm sorry you had to see that." Lisbeth sighed. "This place is too dangerous, you all have to leave—"

"My uncle would say, not without you and your father," Sarah managed. She was shaking now, the rush of fear and shock beginning to seep away. "We've a job to do."

"So have I," Lisbeth said with finality. "I've people to take care of, a problem that has to be solved."

Sarah sat, unable to create an opposing argument, uncertain even what they really needed to do for the best. She knew that being close to Lisbeth was advantageous, to learn what she could, but everything she had seen was occupying too much of her mind, forcing her thoughts into blind corners. Part of her demanded that she find the flamethrower and destroy everything and everyone, right now, so this would stop and never happen again. But Sarah knew that she lacked the ruthlessness to make that happen, to torch the innocent and the guilty as one.

Be the little girl, she thought. *That's your job. Do it.*

"Is all that make-up?" Sarah asked.

"The very best that money can buy... Actually no, that's a lie. It's the second or third rate at best, but you can't do this work and expect the Hollywood treatment. I've heard about some new stuff created by Max Factor, called Pan-Cake. Promises to get rid of the 'flexible greasepaint' for ever. Once I get my hands on that, all this goes in the bin."

"All this is American?"

"Some of it. Presents from my father's *friends*." She turned. Her skin was once again flawless. In the candlelight it was eerie. "Want me to make up your face?" The conspiratorial smile returned.

Sarah's strategy was working – they were growing closer. But she felt a little thrill that made her suspicious and uneasy.

"Yes – I think." Sarah laughed. Her mother had never offered to show her how. In fact she remembered once having applied her mother's lipstick as little more than a toddler and being beaten for it.

She allowed Lisbeth to tie her hair back with a headscarf and then waited while the woman fussed over her pots and tubs.

"Who are they exactly? Your father's friends, I mean," Sarah ventured.

"I don't know really. They're *true believers* of a sort. They believe the United States should be joining the war on the side of the new Reich and seem pretty intent on it."

"Why are they interested?" Sarah asked.

"Who knows? I think they don't like the Jews very much... but who does?"

Sarah closed her eyes, not certain she could keep the reaction from her face.

Little monster. Dumb little monster.

"I think they like what Herr Hitler has achieved," Lisbeth suggested. "They think that America should follow his example." She began to dab something onto Sarah's face. Forehead. Nose. Cheekbones. "I don't care as long as I get to do what I need to do. What do you think of the Führer's work?"

"I don't..." Sarah began, her head abrubtly full of street beatings and broken glass.

Little monster.

Lies will tie you up and eat you.

"You know," Sarah said after a pause, "I go to the meetings and sing the songs and throw the books on the fire, but..."

"I know what you mean."

"You do?"

"Politics...just causes trouble, doesn't it?"

Sarah smiled and started to nod, then stopped herself.

Politics was ordering the Jews of Berlin into the street at midnight, one suitcase each. Politics was rounding up villagers in Poland and shooting children. Politics was turning girls into women like the Ice Queen. No one had the luxury of dismissing politics as troublesome and ignoring it.

"Do you think reusing the syringes has really killed people?" She was still irritated as she spoke but regretted what amounted to an accusation the moment it left her mouth.

The woman exhaled and began smoothing the cream into Sarah's face.

"Yes, it probably did. It may mean that it isn't airborne after all. Lost research, lost people." Lisbeth paused and sighed. "You were very smart to spot that. It's the kind of thing that doesn't occur to an experienced medic, but you thought of it straight away, didn't you?"

Sarah quivered her shoulders non-committally, as she couldn't really move her face. Lisbeth had begun another layer of something else, but it vexed her.

"*Gottverdammt*, Leichner," she hissed, waving the stick of Leichner greasepaint at Sarah. "Piece of *Scheiße*. You know that Leichner left Max Factor waiting in reception all day when he came to see them in 1922, so Max stopped selling their crap and made his own. Who's laughing now? Max Factor was a *verflixter Pole*, you know? Look what the United States did with him, what we could have had a piece of. And look what the Reich is currently making."

Lisbeth dropped the stick of greasepaint onto the dresser with a clatter.

"Just make-up, though, isn't it?" Sarah winked.

"Bullets, guns and bombs get made in the same factories by the same people. When the German Army goes over the top with Leichner sticks and find the Americans armed with Pan-Cake make-up, that'll put an end to the Führer's Reich."

"Maybe we need the United States on our side after all," Sarah muttered.

"Damn right, we do... Hey, stop flinching."

Lisbeth was pushing something into Sarah's eye.

"What is that?"

"Eyeliner, stupid girl." Lisbeth laughed.

Sarah froze and allowed the point to close in on her face.

"Lisbeth..." Sarah began, conscious of the sharp stick next to her eyes. "*Is* someone causing these outbreaks? Deliberately, I mean?"

Lisbeth bit her lip as she swept the pencil effortlessly under Sarah's eye.

"It looks very suspicious, doesn't it?" Lisbeth said. "But that would take someone who was very driven, who could murder hundreds of natives to get what they wanted and not worry about it. Could a normal person imagine killing...*massacring* all those people? Could you bring yourself to do that?"

"Maybe dead natives is what they want. We dropped bombs in Spain and didn't worry about who they hit. And have you read *Red Rubber*?"

Lisbeth stopped and considered this, before continuing. "Eyes closed, please...yes, but that was money. People do horrific things for money. Or revenge. And what is a little girl doing reading *Red Rubber*?" Lisbeth added.

Sarah felt very vulnerable but the question needed to be asked.

Commit to the move.

"Do you think your American friends might pay for... someone to do that?"

"What are you saying, Ursula?" Lisbeth hovered the pencil right next to Sarah's eye.

Commit.

"You don't think...it could be—"

"It's not my father, I promise you *that*." Lisbeth sighed, almost relieved. "He's very driven, yes, and nasty, but even he couldn't do this. And he's always here. He never leaves." She spoke with total certainty. She swapped to a small brush and began to paint Sarah's eyelids. "No. I think there's a reason it's always in the bush, away from the towns and moving south like this. I think it's an animal disease, like the flu or rabies. Maybe it's birds or bats or some creatures on the move."

Sarah wanted to believe her, to think only good things of her. The feeling was so strong that it surprised her, overwhelmed her. Threatened to drown her.

Her mind shook itself like a wet dog. She looked at what remained and made herself go there.

"Did you have to have the man shot? Couldn't you have caught up with him?"

Lisbeth sighed. It was deep, filled with sorrow. "And have him pull someone's mask off? Scratch someone's face? Worse, let him go and reach the next village before we're ready? Do you know what triage is? It's when the doctor selects patients to treat from multiple casualties. It means giving up on people you can't save in order to save someone you can. It's horrible, miserable and it kills me every time."

"But you're keeping these people here against their will," Sarah said, unable to stop herself. "And not letting them tend—"

"These people are our children and it's our duty to care for them," Lisbeth asserted. "We have to worry about the science, not the superstition. Grown-ups have to make hard decisions."

"Do *you* have children?" Sarah began again.

"Do I *have* to have children?" Lisbeth had stiffened. "It's expected, isn't it? Marriage, children, *Hausfrau. Kinder, Küche, Kirche...*"

Her voice had acquired a hard edge, beyond which the atmosphere grew dark.

"I'm sorry," Sarah murmured.

Lisbeth brightened. "Oh, don't be sorry. It's not your fault, is it? No, no children, no husband. I'm married to my work," she stated theatrically. "I'm sorry about your girl's camera. I just got cross. I hope it didn't break it. You really shouldn't have given her a 1932 Leica II though, far too good for mucking about with... Now, lips. Do this—" Lisbeth widened her mouth into a large *O*, revealing bright white teeth.

Sarah did her best to copy her. She hadn't thought about Clementine at all while she was having her face done, and now felt uneasy about it.

"*Eye-oo-oo-air-ache-uh-ih-uhs-huht...*" Sarah began.

"Wait, *Dummkopf.*" Lisbeth chuckled. "Now you can talk," she said sitting back.

The lipstick felt gooey and thick as Sarah contracted her mouth. It tasted faintly soapy. And grown-up.

"I said, why *do* you wear all that make-up in this heat?"

"Pout, please," Lisbeth insisted and leaned back in.

She busied herself around Sarah's lips and hummed tunelessly to herself. The woman looked at Sarah's face and then set about it with a fluffy brush. The powder tickled Sarah's throat and the feeling of weight on her face increased.

She had begun to wonder if Lisbeth would answer the question, when the woman placed her brush on the dressing table, reached around Sarah's shoulders and drew her in to look in the mirror.

Sarah inhaled sharply, taking in some floating powder and coughing.

The little girl was gone, irrevocably extinguished by this window into adulthood and the appearance of a woman in her place.

Not a woman, not a real one, she understood that. The mask of one, but a mask so compelling she wondered if she could bear to take it off.

"Feel it? Feel the power?" Lisbeth rested her chin on Sarah's shoulder.

Her mother had been beautiful, once. Sarah knew that for sure having seeing her onscreen. With the exception of those final sober days, now flecked with her blood, her make-up had seemed a function of her descent and demise. The cracks, the faults, the failure to use it properly, all drew attention to the artifice, revealed its fakery. This face that Sarah wore was immaculate, like it was sealed over her own.

She was, her face was, the mask was…stunning.

Somewhere inside of her a little child – a smart, capable, cynical beast who had looked into the mouth of a real monster and seen her utter destruction and enslavement there – stamped her foot and howled at the superficiality, the rootlessness of this feeling. Sarah ignored her.

"I see it, but the work involved…the discomfort." She laughed hollowly as a bead of sweat broke on her brow.

"It's civilization, Ursula. We wear clothes, even in this heat, because we're not savages. These things give us authority."

"But is anyone looking?"

"*We're* looking. We are. This is for *us*."

Sarah looked at the mask. At her face. This was *her face*. She cleaned lipstick off her teeth with her tongue and smiled.

Dearest Mouse,

What does it mean to be a woman?

Is it wearing make-up and going to parties? Is it bearing children? Is it becoming the Ice Queen? Does it mean drinking alcohol, all day and all night?

I don't know and have no one to ask, except you... or the paper I'm writing on, which is really the inside of my own head when I close my eyes. Maybe that might change.

Schäfer wanted to do <u>something</u> that was to do with being a woman, but I was not a woman. You were not a woman.

The things that happened to you, that were done to you...

<u>I don't know what happened to you.</u>

I can't even think about <u>it.</u>

When I think about what happened to me, what nearly happened, I just get really angry and confused, and my brain speeds up until I can't think and I want to hurt people, or myself. I want to hurt the world.

Because that was not for us, like a Schnitzel is not for a baby. It was wrong. It was a crime.

One day it might be for us, but I wonder if that is still possible?

<u>Alles Liebe,</u>

Ursula

CHAPTER TWENTY-THREE

SARAH WALKED BACK to the Captain's tent with a skip in her step. She marvelled at this expression of confidence and joy, so tied to the little girl yet fuelled by the mask of the adult. She didn't care. She was smiling. So much it made her cheeks hurt.

She walked into his tent and all that seeped away.

"It's gone," he said, an edge of panic in his voice.

He was sweating profusely, soaking his shirt to the point of transparency. His eyes were wide and round. She had never seen him this agitated. When he had lain dying, infected and feverish on the floor of a barn, when he was near to his own death, he had been calm and pragmatic. That had vanished.

"What's gone?" she asked.

"You *know* what!" he snapped.

"The gun?" she whispered.

"Don't be dense, child."

The carefully constructed self-delusion that Sarah had been relying on evaporated in that moment.

In the months following his recovery from the gunshot wound, the Captain had suffered. He concealed it, but Sarah could see that the injury was limiting. It disturbed her to know that they could no longer rely on his physicality. She was strong for her size and nimble, but she was no match for the Captain and his skills. Worse still was the idea of trusting the surly Norris, who she wasn't sure would step up, even if he could.

Then one day, he'd seemed better, stronger, brighter and back to his pre-shooting self. The change was so sudden it had piqued her curiosity, but something made her pause and feign disinterest to herself.

After six months, a short temper coupled with sweat and an intense frown, became the nightly routine. His irritability – the pain – whatever it was during this time, made him do questionable things. *Stupid things*, Sarah thought. Later that evening, or the next morning, he was his usual self.

Sarah had chosen to overlook this coincidence and then tried to forget that choice.

Neither was an option now.

"Where was *it*?" Sarah asked him.

"It's not there now—"

"I am *trying* to help you...where might it have fallen out, been placed, I don't know..."

The Captain stared at her, as if seeing her for the first time. "What the hell happened to your face?"

"I've been ingratiating myself with the mission target, *Arschloch*. What have you been doing except losing...*things*?"

Claude stuck his head into the tent.

"It's very noisy in here," he growled.

"Your friend is being a *branleur*," Sarah snapped.

"What happened to your face?" Claude asked, confused.

"Don't you start. My uncle needs help finding something and apparently doesn't need my assistance," Sarah said, pushing past the priest and out.

The air was really no cooler outside. The skies were growing pregnant with moisture and the clouds were pleading for a storm. But it was a relief to be out of the Captain's tent. Maybe the problem would quickly resolve itself...but maybe it wouldn't. The idea of continuing the mission without his... guidance? Connections?

She wasn't even sure she knew how to achieve the mission goal. She thought back to Canaris's office and the three parts to the job they were given, each apparently contradicting the others. She had assumed the Captain knew what had to be done and what their own personal goals would be. Did she need to stop the disease, or stop the White Devil, or just stop Hasse? Did she need to stop Bofinger meeting with the Americans? How important was that afterthought? What did she need to destroy?

Claude was an agent for the Allies, but being on his side made her skin crawl.

Did she need the flamethrower?

She felt very alone.

"I told you that your uncle had a problem." Clementine's voice came out of the darkness.

"I know. I knew," Sarah replied quietly. "And there are no medals for being right."

"That's a shame. I thought this espionage stuff was all military. They like giving medals."

Clementine caught sight of Sarah's face in the light of a nearby lamp. She pouted and made a short rising whistle.

"The good doctor is giving lessons," Clementine said slowly.

"It's stupid," Sarah muttered.

"No, not really. You look like a woman. A big, grown-up white—"

"What have you learned?" Sarah interrupted.

"Well, it seems to have escaped *your* notice that the people here are monsters. Kidnapping, murder, vivisection... This is the Congo Basin, famous for atrocity, but you've only been here a few weeks and yet you're apparently happy to play dress-up with them. That was quick."

Sarah couldn't trust herself to speak, angry at both Clementine and herself, with warnings thumping in her ears.

"Trust you, you said," Clementine continued. "We're on the right side, you said. But which side is that?"

"The *Abwehr*—"

"Yes, I've heard that *Quatsch* already. You're Jewish."

Lies will tie you up and eat you... Find some truth.

"There are those who don't approve of the way the war is going, how it's being fought," Sarah managed. "They don't care what I am. Or they don't know."

Sarah was standing on treasonous ground now. She couldn't read Clementine's face, which was shadowed. The lamp behind lent her a halo, where the orange light caught her tight curls.

"Things are happening that are..." Sarah continued. "Like *this*." She waved her hand about her.

"So you're not here to take this weapon back to Germany," Clementine whispered carefully.

Commit.

"No."

"So you *are* the traitors."

Sarah measured the distance between her and Clementine. Her pistol was in the tent, so Sarah wondered if she could get her hands around Clementine's neck before she could react. She thought – *she knew* – that she could murder her, here in the middle of the camp, and that there would be no investigation, no police, no consequences. Her body could just be rolled onto the pile of arms and feet. Just another *African*.

What had Clementine just said? *That was quick.*

She was waist-deep in the monstrosity that was that thought. Her life didn't even depend on Clementine's silence. She could walk around the camp screaming the truth, and they might be able to talk their way out. There would be no arrest, no Gestapo basement. But with the Captain out of action, Sarah's fear was beginning to take over, and it drove this putrid line of thinking.

Act now before it's too late.

"He's having trouble making the weapon," Clementine stated. "He's stockpiling diseased blood samples, but they don't last long enough. Two weeks, maximum."

The relief was like a cold shower.

"Show me," Sarah said.

◆　　◆　　◆

The professor's lab was deserted, but the lamps were still lit above the workbench. One was sputtering as the oil ran dry.

To the left was a large glass box, like a fish tank, with two circular doors in the side. Rows of test tubes and other arcane equipment sat next to it, along with scattered papers and jumbled rubber tubes. There were two cabinets that looked like kitchen iceboxes, one cold and one warm to the touch. Both had stencilled warnings to leave well enough alone. Sarah pulled on a pair of gloves and undid the latch on the heated cabinet. Inside nestled dozens of eggs. An incubator. Clementine shrugged. The cold box was full of labelled glass bottles, containing a dark red liquid.

"This is it?"

"I don't know. Looks like it."

Sarah wanted to seize them – smash them – and at the same time recoiled from their touch. How could they be destroyed? Underneath the workspace, open buckets of bleach filled the air with their distinctive odour. Could she pour the bottles into the disinfectant without being infected?

But over that caustic smell they could now make out the unmistakable scent of animal. They turned to the blanket-covered crates lining the right wall of the tent. Small movements could be heard within.

Heart beating, Sarah gripped the first blanket and slowly pulled it away.

The crate seemed to be a dirt-filled birdcage with a ceiling that appeared to have quivering leather pouches suspended from it.

"Bats," Clementine murmured, replacing the cover.

The second blanket covered a stack of mouse cages, their contents scurrying and rustling in wet straw.

As Sarah drew the third cover, two bloodshot human eyes stared back at her.

She started and took a step back.

Crammed into a cage far too small for it was an ape, a chimpanzee. It looked at Sarah with an expression of the deepest, most profound sadness, like it would lean forward and tell them the miseries it had seen. The aspect was so much that of a person that it was Sarah who leaned in and looked back into those eyes, overcome with sympathy and sadness.

The ape threw itself at the cage door so violently that the cage nearly toppled onto the girls. As they jumped away, it bared its teeth and screamed, pounding its fists against the wire and hooting. The eyes now spoke of only horror and pain and rage.

Someone pushed past and threw the blanket over the cage. The hooting and the crashing died away, as if the ape felt the pointlessness of the exercise, but all around them the jungle answered.

The figure turned. In his hand was a small revolver, and Sarah took an involuntary step back. He was one of the black mission staff, but he had an air of authority and seniority reinforced by his silvered hair and beard. *But not invited to dinner*, thought Sarah.

"What are you doing here?" he asked quietly.

"Samuel. Tell her what you told me," Clementine ordered.

"It's a long story," he replied with a shrug.

"She needs to hear it," Clementine insisted.

Samuel folded his arms as if refusing, but then quietly, carefully, began to talk. Sarah had to move closer to hear him over the rustling of the animals about them.

Samuel was a Herero from the south-west of the continent. There was an unforgiving stretch of coastline that the Herero called "the land that God made in anger", and this inhospitable barrier of rock and marsh had protected the pasture inland from the attentions of the Europeans for centuries. Finally, it attracted the German Empire, who was obsessed with acquiring colonies and feared missing out on the party.

The Herero and the nearby Nama people ignored the scattered German settlers, disinterested in so-called protection treaties or trinkets. They were farmers, tending huge herds of cattle on land owned by everyone. The settlers found them educated and sophisticated, with a taste for European clothes. Not what the Germans expected at all. They were also wealthy and could buy what they needed from any number of traders.

Then the diseases came. *Rinderpest*, the cattle plague, annihilated the Herero herds. Their whole wealth and economy vanished overnight. People began to starve. This was followed by an outbreak of typhoid and malaria. Thousands of malnourished Herero and Nama perished.

Rinderpest killed everything it could, so finally it extinguished itself. Some herds returned to full strength, but many of Samuel's people had lost everything and were now dependent on the settlers. They were put to work enriching the colony and, sensing their desperation, the settlers bought cattle at knockdown rates and sold goods at sky-high prices. Some of the Herero leaders had even started to sell land –

which was not theirs to trade, but once the deal was done it was too late. The principle had been established.

It took a minor war between the Herero and the Nama, in which a panicky leader swapped a huge strip of land in return for help defeating their enemy, to really change the balance of power, but the die was cast.

"So, you're saying these diseases weren't accidental?" Sarah interrupted, with more incredulity than she really felt.

"Well, at first we thought it was just convenient for them. There was a drought, too, and no one believed that this was the work of a German. Think about it, how could anyone do that? Risk killing so many people. It defies the imagination, doesn't it? It sounds ridiculous...but let me tell you how I came to work for Herr Professor Bofinger."

What followed, Samuel explained, would often be justified by saying that the natives needed to be civilized or protected from themselves, but there was nothing noble about the crimes the Germans committed. They grew more confident, more greedy. Treaties were ignored. Lands were taken. Cattle were stolen. The settlers all but enslaved the local population in the form of forced labour that was rarely paid.

There were murders, beatings and rapes, and nothing was ever done about it.

Even peaceful resistance was met with horrific ferocity. When the Germans attacked the settlement of Hoornkrans, the soldiers didn't follow the retreating Nama fighters, but set about slaughtering their elderly, women and children, before enslaving eighty women.

Planned reservations for the Herero and Nama that would

have meant surrendering the rest of the lands were the final straw. They knew the settlers would never be content while the Africans owned anything or had any say over their affairs, so the rebellion began. Even then, the opening shot was engineered by the settlers.

The Herero and Nama, now reconciled, knew their land and the Germans did not, so the invaders suffered several humiliating defeats. The Herero and their allies fought with honour, sparing and protecting German civilians. The Germans did not.

The victorious Herero were encouraged to negotiate for peace and gathered on the edge of the Omaheke Desert to wait for a German delegation. Instead they were encircled by a reinforced army, now armed with machine guns and cannons from home. There was nothing the warriors could do against that kind of firepower.

The Herero survivors retreated the only way they could, into the desert, and the pursuing enemy prevented them from breaking off from the main column. There was no water and no food. As each man, woman and child stopped from exhaustion or thirst, they were executed by the German Army.

This was a *specific order* from General von Trotha.

Samuel stopped and closed his eyes. He recited something long committed to memory. Something he knew he must never forget.

"Any Herero found inside the German frontier, with or without a gun or cattle, will be executed. I shall spare neither women nor children. I shall give the order to drive them away and fire on them."

He opened his eyes and exhaled, knowing he had remembered correctly. He paused, as if summoning the strength to continue. It was the only clue as to what recounting the story was costing him.

The Germans sealed off the desert, he continued, making it impossible to return.

Any Herero appearing was shot or driven back to die of thirst.

Fifty thousand people had camped on the Waterberg before the battle. Only a handful survived.

The Nama suffered a similar fate. The army swept the bush for survivors and took them prisoner. Many were tricked into returning with promises of good treatment. There was a fake settlement where supplies were plentiful and its inhabitants were sent out to draw others in. But the final camps were not homes. They were what the British in their second war with the Boers had called *concentration camps*.

And they were prisons. Labour camps. Places of death.

The inmates were barely fed, worked too hard, and were whipped for even gathering scraps from the roadside. But there was a worse fate than starving.

Samuel stopped and unfolded his arms.

"This was a place I called home," he began again softly.

He had met Bofinger in Shark Island Concentration Camp, a windswept, freezing piece of land surrounded by water, where Bofinger's father was the camp doctor. Samuel was intelligent and educated, enough for the boy to see Samuel as something other than cattle. He slowly, carefully, made himself indispensable to the doctor and his son in their work.

Their work was not to care for the prisoners but to use them in their research. Inmates were injected with poisons in an effort to cure scurvy, infected with malaria and typhoid to study the diseases and how they might be used as weapons.

There was a roaring trade in shipping human skulls back to the Fatherland. There were plenty of corpses, and if there weren't on that particular day, then Bofinger Senior just took a live inmate—

"Stop," Sarah interrupted, now nauseous.

"Four thousand people died on Shark Island. More than sixty-five thousand people were exterminated by the German Empire in my country in just three years," Samuel continued in a calm, level voice, the voice of a man who had long since resigned himself to the role of spectator. "The young Bofinger grew up dissecting bodies for fun. Some weren't even dead—"

"Just stop," Sarah pleaded.

"Infecting villages isn't a big leap." Samuel sighed. "Africans are not really human to him. That Germany would let him, would encourage him, would want to turn this into a weapon? I think we know the answer to that, too."

Sarah had a hand over her mouth, because she didn't want to vomit or because she couldn't trust herself to speak – she didn't know which.

"Your girl suggests that you are here to stop him?" Samuel asked.

"Why have you stayed...? Why haven't *you* stopped him?" Sarah managed.

A woman appeared at the tent flap, one of the white nurses. She was a slim woman in her late forties, brown hair pulled back into a ponytail, with a no-nonsense demeanour. Yet she carefully closed the flap and came to stand behind Samuel. Laying a hand gently on his shoulder, she muttered in his ear. He took her hand and muttered back before they both looked at Sarah again.

"I stayed for Emmi," he said, and the woman smiled at Sarah, squeezing his shoulder. "Realistically, there is no other place we could be together. And before he found this disease we did care for the sick, even if it was just to keep the workforce healthy. I hoped we would again, one day. But we have not stopped him because the consequences for the African staff involved in harming a white mission, whether among the French, Belgians or Germans, would be dreadful. People have families to protect. We have been trying to sabotage his work, but there are always more samples... Will you help us?"

Sarah wanted to agree, to help, to burn the tent that instant. Then she thought of the Captain and his chances of survival in this state, of the road home, pursued by Hasse and Bofinger, of returning to a *Gestapo* cellar in Prinz-Albrecht-Straße...

She felt overheated and breathless.

"I don't know how yet." Sarah turned for the exit, her mind full of broken glass.

CHAPTER TWENTY-FOUR

CLAUDE WAS WAITING BY HER TENT when she appeared, rubbing her temples and panting.

"Your uncle is…sick," he said, shifting uncomfortably.

"My uncle has lost his *Stoff*, Claude," Sarah chided impatiently. "He's a *Morphiumsüchtiger*. Let's stop pretending." Just speaking the words was freeing, a liberation. "They have morphine here, don't they?"

"It's all gone. Used up last week."

Things were beginning to fray at the edges.

"Can we find some more?" she asked.

The sound of an approaching truck engine reached them as Claude thought about it. "Maybe, but he's lost his Pervitin as well."

"Pervitin?"

"A stimulant. Everyone in Germany is taking it, apparently. It wakes him up after he's taken the morphine. That's how he functions. We won't get that here."

"I take it he's going to suffer now?" Sarah wondered aloud. "Like drying out?"

"Yes, maybe two weeks."

Two weeks. Could they wait two weeks to act? How many more people might die? What if Hasse arrived?

Sarah rolled her eyes, letting the action push back against the rising tide of panic and helplessness. There were shouts elsewhere in the camp. She spoke quickly to conceal her nerves. "Okay, first job for you is to find some morphine. We'll tell people he has malaria."

"I don't take orders from you," Claude spat.

"Oh, enough of the self-importance," Sarah snapped, allowing her irritation to drive the ship. "You're his friend, an allied agent, right? Just do it."

The nearby shouting continued. *Wake up. Attention.*

Claude opened his mouth to speak, then stopped and turned away. Sarah wondered momentarily whether he felt bullied by his own *Ngontang*, but she struggled to feel sorry for such an appalling human. Before she could regret that thought, he grumbled over his shoulder.

"I'm looking forward to not having you in my life."

Out of the gloom, Samuel appeared, a haze of agitation hanging over his calm shell.

"Excuse me, *Monsieur, Fräulein*...the Free French are here."

Sarah pushed into the Captain's tent. He was sitting on the edge of his cot, his eyes wild and darting.

"What's going on?" he said.

"Don't you hate being right all the time? The Free French troops have appeared and want to know who we are and what we're doing."

He was already pulling at his bag and removing the parts of the gun.

"No, no shooting, no more *death*—"

"I'm not going to shoot anyone," he interrupted. He placed the metal pieces on the bed and reached back into his bag, producing an envelope. "Read, quick."

Inside were two French passports. *Émile and Élodie Poulain. Marseille*—

"You can't do a Marseille accent," Sarah growled. "What were you thinking?" She struggled to fix the cadence in her head, the patter of consonants like a military band and the *ooo*ing of the vowels...

"Don't do the accent, we're too travelled."

"What are we doing here?" She passed him back his identity card.

"Saving the savages from themselves. We're not *Gaullists*, but we're not Vichy either, got it? We've been away the whole time."

"Daughter?"

"Yes."

"Promotion! What are you going to do with that?" She gestured to the gun. She could seize it, walk the camp, and— She shook her head to lose the fantasy.

"Hide it," he said. "But this one" – he produced an old revolver – "is French."

He went to stand but doubled over, and Sarah had to catch him. They staggered back until he regained his feet.

"I'm fine, I'm fine," he muttered.

"You're clearly not," she snapped. "Get in bed, you have malaria. Go."

He sat back on the cot, too tired to argue, too agitated to marshal his thoughts. There was shouting and hurried feet all about the tent. She looked at the flap, at the sliver of the night outside.

She grabbed at the situation, which was shaking and twisting like a wet dog. She held on as options and possibilities fell away, trying to contain her fear and her rage, which pulled in different directions.

She leaned in to the Captain.

"Tell me, *why* don't we just hand all this over to the French now? Put the disease in the hands of the Allies..."

He lay back and covered his eyes with one hand, beckoning her with the other.

"One, these troops are allies now, they were enemies a month ago, friends before that. Next week? Who knows... Two." He stopped to cough. "Two, who are they, how smart are they, will they even know what to do? Three, that would be it for us, cover blown. We couldn't go home. Four..." He panted slightly and paused. "We need to know who the Americans are. If they can bankroll all this, then they're a real danger. And if they're the same friends of Schäfer..."

Sarah experienced a sudden urge to hit something.

"I don't care who they are. No, we have to stop *this* now," Sarah growled.

"How will you do that?" he snapped back, shaking now. "We don't know everything—"

"We know enough."

"Do you? Really? Have they sent samples to Germany or the United States already? Have they been in touch with Hasse? Is there actually a weapon here yet? Who is making it—"

"We *know* who's making it—"

"Maybe, but the rest? We need to play for time. Please, just see what's going on. Just that."

Sarah looked at the entrance again. She felt pressure in the front of her head, from the weather or the decisions, she couldn't tell.

"For now," she stated and left.

There was a stand-off where the road met the camp. Lisbeth, at the head of a small delegation of mission staff, was talking to a surly-looking French officer, who was clearly not convinced by anything he was hearing. His squad stood behind him and around the French military troop truck, a new Renault.

Sarah tried to surmise their intent. Black troops with soft fezzes. The red-hatted soldiers were bored, even resentful at being out at night. Three white officers in the French, stiff, flat-topped *kepi* hats. One was disinterested and leaning on the truck. The one who was doing all the talking was incredulous, officious and condescending. However, the officer behind him was silent and watching. Sarah couldn't read his lapel badges but she was sure she'd identified the senior man.

Sarah could sense, rather than see or hear, intense activity in the camp behind them, probably because she had spent a night there listening to its usual rhythms and sounds. She hoped the soldiers couldn't tell. *Or did she really want that?*

Sarah looked round for Clementine but could only see Claude. She moved over to where he stood and spoke quietly.

"We're French now. My *father* is sick in bed."

"I know...look." He nodded towards Lisbeth as she remonstrated with the officers. "They're not listening to her because she's a woman. They want to speak to a man."

"Where is Bofinger?"

"Who knows?" He shrugged and made a dismissive noise.

With that Claude approached them and began to speak over everyone in an unnecessarily loud voice.

She watched him work and had to be impressed. He immediately made everything about himself, then turned that self-centred bonhomie on the officers. She remembered back to the airfield at Fort-Lamy and the ease with which an Italian plane had landed and the Germans aboard had sped away, unquestioned. She had on occasion wondered what kind of intelligence asset the unpleasant Claude was. Clearly his talent, his skill, was in talking. The papers that Lisbeth had been trying to show the soldiers were taken off her and Sarah noted that Claude did not actually let the officer see them, yet was not withholding them either. It was a smooth sleight of hand.

Sarah edged over to Lisbeth, who was fiddling distractedly with her necklace, and gave her a quizzical look.

"Your uncle was right, and not just about our Swiss papers." Lisbeth sighed.

"My *father*, born and bred in Marseille, has malaria, *Madame*," Sarah said deliberately.

"Well, at least one of us was prepared." She smiled wanly.

"We just need time to pack up our things here. We can move fast, but they need to go away."

"Do you have a cigarette and a lighter?"

"Erm...yes, but..."

"Give them to me now, quick."

Sarah picked her way past the confrontation as Claude gave a booming laugh and punched the officer's shoulder. Seconds later he had an arm around him. *So effective.* Such an *Arschloch.*

She walked straight up to the senior officer, smiling the most sparkly of all her smiles, thinking of the salons and thick carpets of Berlin society. His troops shifted but saw only a harmless girl. She stopped in front of him and curtseyed.

"*Bonsoir, Capitaine, bienvenue. Voulez-vous une cigarette pendant que vous attendez?*" she piped in her most endearing French, holding up Lisbeth's pack of cigarettes.

"*Lieutenant...*" he began but couldn't help smiling. He took the pack and stopped. "This is a German brand—"

"The Swiss...on everyone's and no one's side." She tutted and then laughed, trying to let it tinkle the way her mother's salon laugh could, but in this humid, close darkness, it just rang hollow. He was intelligent and thoughtful, she had to get under that, to something more emotional.

He snorted and tapped one out, gingerly putting it to his lips. Sarah thumbed the lighter, but it didn't catch. The lieutenant smiled and took it from her.

"Nice and slow, see?" The flame caught and danced briefly as he lit the paper tube.

Sarah held her breath. This was no time to cough.

"Can I ask, what's going on? No one ever tells me *anything...*"

She pulled a theatrical face and she made the lieutenant smile again.

"You're French? You're not Swiss?" he asked, inhaling deeply. He frowned and looked at the gift between his fingers.

"Yes, we met up with the Bofinger party a month or so back."

Lies. Watch where they come to rest on the floor and do not sidestep or retreat without looking.

"What do you do here?"

"Me? Not a great deal! My father is a missionary," Sarah explained. "The poor victims of this terrible sickness... They're all doctors and things here. No one was taking care of their spiritual needs."

You sound too old now.

"What are they doing? The *Swiss*?"

"Trying to treat the sick...they don't let me near, so I don't know whether they're succeeding. They're all pretty sad most of the time..."

"Never known missionaries to be much interested in anything but getting sick natives back to work," the lieutenant muttered, and stared at the glowing cigarette in his hand. "You think they're Swiss?" he pressed.

"Why...wouldn't they be Swiss?" Sarah replied, trying to sound confused.

"Just because they said so?"

Sarah made a face of curious wonder. "Why would they say they were Swiss if they weren't?"

"If they were German, for example."

Sarah burst out laughing. "You wouldn't want to be German,

we're at war with Germany!" She stopped and changed expressions like she'd said something wrong. "Or are we? Oh, are you for the Armistice, are you *pour les Fishies*?"

The lieutenant laughed out loud, causing his subordinate to look around. Sarah caught Claude's eye for just a moment, the merest hairline crack in his mask revealing his anxiety and concern.

"*Vichy*, for Vichy, you mean. You know in English you said... That's funny." He looked at the cigarette again and dropped it into the mud. "No, we are for de Gaulle, until the next meeting and then we might be for something else. But right now, I think your friends might be German. Some of them, maybe."

"Oh, you think there's a German hiding here... Oh! Can I guess who it is? Can I?" Sarah clapped her hands together.

The lieutenant sat on his haunches next to her and looked up into her eyes. Sarah was immediately uncomfortable. It was always easier playing the little girl from below, looking up.

"So who is it?" he asked seriously.

"Oh, oh, it could be... No...maybe...no... How would I tell?"

The man chuckled. "I don't think you can," he conceded. "Maybe their papers are real or they're not, but I do want to know what they're doing here."

"Oh, that's easy," Sarah piped. "There's a disease and it's spreading south. It's *deadly*. The professor and the doctor are trying to stop it."

"That's not what the locals think. They think this mission is making people sick."

"Urgh," Sarah exclaimed, making a disgusted face. "Why would someone do that?"

"Why indeed?"

"So who is going to check the papers?"

It was a roll of the dice, to present him with a reasonable option, a way out.

He smiled and nodded towards Claude. "He's a bag of hot air, isn't he?"

Sarah laughed. "Oh, yes, well, typical jumped-up *nègre*."

Sarah shuddered inside, from her feet to her hands; she had to concentrate to stop them shaking. The words came out so easily, she didn't even know if it was a calculated ploy, or something she *actually thought*.

Dumb monster.

The lieutenant grunted. "I was going to say a Parisian, but yeah. Worst mix."

He stood and barked some orders to his officers. They were moving out, taking the Swiss papers back to the town to be checked. Someone pulled the cards from Claude's hands and headed to the back of the truck.

"Oh, do you have any morphine? We've run out and it's so important…" Sarah layered every gram of syrup she could muster onto the request.

"Where are you from? Your accent is all over the place."

Sarah stiffened. "Born in Marseille. Never been back. I'm from *here*." She made another disgusted face. Again, she was guessing what might go down well.

"There's a kit in the truck, probably been stolen already but, if it's still there, it's yours."

The troops were climbing aboard the Renault. Lisbeth was struggling to hide her relief. Claude was talking the other officers away, like a beater driving birds to a hunter. The lieutenant climbed back out of the cab and handed her a medical kit. It was old and dusty but sealed.

"Good to meet you, *Mademoiselle*...?" he enquired.

"Urs...ssss," she hissed. *Gottverdammte dumme...* She held up the kit. "Sss...look at this, so old! Thank you, though." She made a show of putting it under her arm and then offering her hand. "Poulain. Élodie Poulain."

The lieutenant took her hand and gave it a perfunctory shake. "La Roux. How old are you, Élodie?"

"I'm twelve, nearly thirteen," Sarah squeaked.

"That's some grown-up make-up you're wearing," he said with a frown.

She had forgotten.

"I was just..." she managed. No suitable answer came to her.

He leaned in and touched her hair.

"Don't grow up so fast, little one. There will be plenty of time for that," he said softly, before standing. "I will see you tomorrow morning, Élodie Poulain."

"So soon, lovely," she exclaimed, smiling.

CHAPTER TWENTY-FIVE

THEY WATCHED THE TRUCK back up and take several minutes to turn on the muddy road. As it finally disappeared into the darkness, Lisabeth turned and began yelling. Her staff moved in all directions. They were leaving.

Claude was looking at Sarah. Something approaching admiration cut through his habitual sneer.

"That was...interesting," he said, seemingly incapable of following through with the compliment.

"They won't get the papers back though."

"They were bad fakes. They've done their job."

"This is for my uncle," she said, passing him the first-aid kit. "Can you see to it?"

"*Bien sûr.*"

"What will happen to the village now they're leaving?" she wondered.

There was a distant roaring. Not a gorilla or an elephant, not thunder or a passing airplane. Something else.

The clouded night sky turned *orange*.

Lisbeth looked up and swore. She began running.

The whole jungle was painted in dancing red light. From the edge of camp and up the trail to the village, the trees looked like swaying shadow puppets, telling a story of a cataclysm. The smell of burning wood was thick on the air and made it hard to breathe.

Sarah found her legs reluctant to carry her forward. Her skin prickled where she had been burned at Christmas, and she felt on the edge of hyperventilating. The air grew hot, hotter than the cloying humidity of the Congo autumn. Hot in an aggressive, violent way.

Commit to the move, she remembered. Just keep walking.

She rounded the corner in time to see Lisbeth come to a stop on the edge of what had once been the village. The sound of roaring, the low, throaty scream of the flamethrower, drowned out anything she might have been shouting. Clementine was already standing there, silhouetted against the fire, fists balled, watching the horror.

All the huts were alight, billowing painfully bright clouds of incandescence where straw and raffia had been. The gardens and orchards burned and, worst of all, the shelters that had been filled with the sick and quarantined were gone. Nothing remained that wasn't a black or smouldering pile among the flickering floor of flames.

One figure, draped in tanks and tubes and a long leather coat, conjured an immense arch of fire that almost reached its end before smoke could even fight its way free, and the flames seemed to splash to the ground like water.

Lisbeth took three steps towards the weapon's operator but was driven back by the smoking turf, heat and smoke.

"They are not sentimental, are they?" yelled Clementine as Sarah drew level. She was trying to load film into her camera. It wasn't working.

"Tell me they moved everyone. Tell me they've all gone somewhere else," Sarah howled in desperation.

"They've definitely gone, one way or another."

The roaring stopped, and the operator turned back to them, the mask and googles making him seem more demonic.

They could now hear Lisbeth screaming in rage. She advanced on the man, her anger overwhelming the sense of danger. The operator removed his mask as she approached. It was Klodt. Too scared to drink the water, frightened-looking and little more than a child Klodt. He was confused at the reception.

She whaled at him with her fists. He dropped the gun nozzle to cover his face with his gloved hands and arms.

The beating played out, more shadow puppets before the fire. Amidst the scent of burning wood, gasoline and choking smoke, there was another smell, a stronger, richer, sweeter aroma that Sarah couldn't identify.

Then she knew what it was. She just didn't want to.

The smoke made the camp darker and more opaque, like a factory smog that hurt to breathe. Ash and glowing sparks began to fall like snow.

By the time Sarah had walked the kilometre back to the tents from what remained of the village, most of them were down and packed away. Bofinger's lab had been the first to vanish. A smaller bonfire had begun on the same patch of ground, with the mission staff throwing papers, rubbish and other items onto it.

Sarah's tent had gone, so she returned to the Captain's to find him dozing on the cot and Claude packing their gear.

"He's out of it. Where's your *Neger*, girl? Why am I acting as his valet?" Claude grumbled.

"They burned the village. The whole thing, the houses, the dead, the dying, the living…everything."

Claude snorted. "What did you think they were going to do?" He shrugged. "There was only one survivor anyway."

"Just one *murder*…"

"One African, one savage, one native, it doesn't matter."

"It *matters*!" screamed Sarah. "You're an African, shall I slaughter you?"

"I'm *French*," Claude yelled, prodding his finger violently into his chest. "I might be a second-class Parisian, but I'm a Parisian. And you just try." He flung the Captain's bag at her. "Here, sort out your own *merde*."

They continued in silence for a few moments.

"What do we do now?" Sarah said quietly.

"I've not a clue, short of getting out of here. Think those Gaullist troops haven't seen that firework display Bofinger laid on? We need to be as far from these crazies as we can, or we'll all end up in the stockade."

"No, we need to follow them and—"

237

"You need to follow them, maybe. I've had more than enough already—"

"But you've got a job to do—" she interrupted, only to be interrupted in her turn.

"You've an intelligence officer who's *une junkie*, for a mission I don't understand and the only asset that remotely works is *twelve years old.*"

"I'm *sixteen*," she snapped. "And I thought you were his friend?"

"Which is why I'm driving you to Libreville or wherever in Vichy territory and you can get a boat back to Germany, but we leave this horror show behind. Maybe then I can report any of this to London in a way that makes sense. I don't know what you've done to him – I barely recognize the man."

Clementine stuck her head through the flap.

"Not sure I can hear you arguing clearly enough outside," she reproached. "Lisbeth wants you, Ursula."

Sarah looked to Claude, who nodded.

"The truck leaves in ten minutes. You, *bamboula*," he sneered at Clementine. "We're helping him onto it. Do some work for once in your life."

The dining tent was being lowered to the ground, and most of the other shelters had already gone. Lisbeth was coordinating as the last of the covered animal cages were being loaded onto a truck.

Her eyeliner had run in long streaks down her face, then been swept aside along with much of her greasepaint by the back of her hand. The effect wasn't the least comic. It spoke of pain and tragedy. Sarah noticed her knuckles were bruised. She saw Sarah and smiled sadly, reaching out for her hand. Sarah did not take it.

"Ursula, we're headed for Libreville. There's nothing to be done in Free French territory now, unless we all want to be interned. We'll just have to sit and wait in Vichy-controlled Gabon for the disease to get that far."

"You torched the village," Sarah said coldly.

"My father ordered it." She shrugged. The act was supposed to signify disinterest, but it lacked conviction. "I wouldn't have done."

"And you still think your father couldn't be infecting people on purpose?"

Lisbeth closed her eyes and winced, touching her necklace. Then she was back, certain of herself.

"He couldn't leave that place to be found by a bunch of people who had no idea what they were dealing with, to get infected and take it back to the nearest town. If this got to Bangui or Brazzaville, can you imagine? Tens of thousands of people."

"But all the Bateke..."

"The living dead, Ursula. I told you, he makes the hard decisions, while I get to be upset."

"You're upset because you know it was wrong," Sarah cried.

"It wasn't wrong. We got everything out that we needed first. It's for the greater good."

"The man in quarantine, he wasn't sick," Sarah hissed. "He was murdered."

"He...he'd had multiple tests using the same needles as the

sick, he wouldn't have lived, any more than the sick would have."

"So, what, this is triage? On a village-wide scale...on a country-wide scale?"

"If the Free French weren't prowling the countryside, we wouldn't have to leave... Look, I don't like this either, Ursula, *I am not having a nice time.*"

Lisbeth's voice broke and another tear ran down her face.

Sarah found the tear a solvent to her anger, much like her mother's anguish and lamentation. Overcome with the need to do something, Sarah took two steps forward and wrapped her arms around Lisbeth's waist.

Sarah felt larger arms wrap about her and squeeze.

"Oh, I'm sorry, you shouldn't have to look after me," Lisbeth whispered. "It should be the other way around."

Yes. Yes it should. It hadn't been, for as long as Sarah could remember, but it definitely should.

Dearest Mouse,

Does anyone look after you? Your parents, do they care?

I didn't look after you.

Because my job was so _gottverdammt_ important.

I saved dead babies and flattened cities, but I bought them with you.

I wanted my mother to care, really actually care, to make me the most important thing in the world, instead of just saying it.

Because that's how it's supposed to be, isn't it? That's the story we're told.

But in the end I let you down, for the job, for _the show_, for what I needed to get done.

Just like my mother.

I am trying to do better. I am trying to look after my friends. For you.

Alles Liebe,

Ursula

CHAPTER TWENTY-SIX

17TH–22ND OCTOBER 1940

THEY ARRANGED TO MEET in Libreville a week later. Lisbeth did not want to go home, but she accepted that the Captain might be able to help them when they got to Gabon's capital. Sarah just hoped they would show up. She trusted the doctor, but Bofinger might have other plans. Sarah would have stayed with the mission, but knew she couldn't leave the Captain in his condition and could not care for him alone. Claude might just dump him somewhere for all she knew.

The Parisian, anxious to put distance between them, drove north, hoping to find a better road into Gabon. The jungle of the Congo Basin sat like an implacable obstruction all around. The movement of the truck over the ruts and holes and mud should have made Sarah motion sick, but now it was as if all of her nausea had been exhausted.

The sky was lightening ahead of them, but Sarah couldn't help but look back. The flames and glowing ash were now far behind.

"We should have gone with them." Sarah sighed. "We may not find them again."

"If they're not intending to show up in Libreville, then they're up to something and maybe we don't want to be around when that happens. We also don't want to get interned with them. Your uncle needs medicine. Hospital care. He needs it *now*. You're lucky I'm considering going south-west at all."

Clementine looked agitated. She sat up. "Are we heading east now?" she asked.

"Still north," Claude replied, looking at his compass.

"Then why is the dawn light *ahead* of us?" she enquired.

As they drew nearer they could see that the light was reflecting off a column of black smoke, then they could see the flames, and finally they rounded the last corner to see a blazing truck blocking the track.

Fanned out around the burning vehicle were a dozen bodies. There wasn't enough left of the truck to identify it, but most of the surrounding corpses had survived the inferno. Even in the dark and at this distance, they could tell it was a squad of French troops, maybe the same Free French squad that had visited the mission earlier that night.

Sarah had the door open and was leaping out, even before Claude had stopped.

"It could be an ambush—" he shouted.

"Yes, and we've missed it," Sarah called back as she hit the ground.

The fire was still intense enough that it hurt to approach it, but Sarah pushed through this, through her own fear. *Back into Schäfer's burning lab, looking for the axe to break down the door.*

She identified one of the white officers, the surly, obnoxious one, and kneeled down next to him. Like his subordinates around him, he had a neat hole in his face and lay in a pool of black liquid. Someone had walked through the wounded and dying and shot each one in the head.

"I'd say this was some locals panicking, but look," Claude said, gesturing to the ground under the truck. "Landmine... then they gunned down the survivors as they left the truck." He bent down and picked up a spent cartridge case. "It's all French ammo, nothing unusual there. It doesn't tell us anything. Troops loyal to Vichy, or..."

"Bofinger did this?" Sarah wondered.

"But why torch the village, why leave at all if they were going to stop them like this? They've taken their weapons...it could be bandits."

"Or it could be Hasse. Protecting the mission from the authorities," Sarah said quietly.

They looked at each other and into the thick jungle on every side, suddenly feeling very vulnerable. They started to back away.

"We should go," Clementine called from the truck.

"Yes, yes we should," Sarah replied as Claude nodded.

It took five days to cross into Gabon, taking a long route through Cameroon, recently pledged to de Gaulle. They practically begged for morphine from the few hospitals, towns and missions they passed, but that process was hideously expensive. Persuading people to part with medicine as the

Free French troops were mobilizing and war was coming to the AEF took almost every franc they had brought. Their Reichsmarks were worthless. The Captain was managing, but each dose made him sleepy for hours after, and the window of useful, calm wakefulness was hopelessly narrow.

French tanks and troop transports were gathering on the new frontier, blocking the roads and swamping the small settlements with excitable soldiers – almost exclusively Africans led by a tiny minority of white officers. Whenever they were stopped, their French passports should have been enough to continue their journey, but the question was asked over and again: *Vichy* or *de Gaulle*? They found noncommittal smiles and shrugs the most politic response when talking to troops barely able to answer that question themselves.

Claude always found a way through. *God willing there will be no bloodshed, and we'll be together with our brothers again,* was the sermon he preached as they went.

Finally, they were past the last Gaullist pickets and into Gabon.

The soldiers on the Vichy side this far north were fewer in number and less tolerant of alternative viewpoints. France was France and anyone who supported de Gaulle was a traitor, a warmonger. But in the end they were more concerned about their identically dressed and equipped counterparts over on the Congo side of the line than in cross-examining some travelling missionaries. Their passports were undeniably French, and they were in French territory.

Sarah was weary. They hadn't had a hot meal for days, and sleeping in the truck was no substitute for a bed; even a cot in a tent had been preferable. There were no rest stops to be had on this leg of the journey. The churches and missions on Claude's list were now full of billeted troops.

The jungle was thinning out as they moved into Gabon and climbed out of the Congo Basin, but if it was possible, the weather had grown more oppressive, more humid and darker, even at midday. There was a constant vibrating tension in her jaw and at the top of her belly. Every limb felt heavy.

The Captain had once talked about war, about the days and hours before a battle you knew was coming. She recognized this pause. At the end of this road would be Bofinger and the decisions they would have to make. Complex problems with consequences unfolding like a *Himmel und Hölle* paper fortune-teller. But until then there was nothing but cold meat and discomfort, haunted by the idea of Hasse in pursuit... or maybe waiting for them along the way.

Sarah was desperate for the Captain to wake, to return to normal, to take some charge.

Clementine slept. She seemed to be able to sleep anywhere, at any time.

Sarah was getting a headache. She reached for a canteen to slake her thirst but found it nearly empty. She couldn't figure out how she could still be thirsty.

Clementine offered hers. "Little Eva, you look like crap," she said. "Like someone is putting you back on a plane."

"Well, thank you. I'm sure you look equally unpleasant."

"Am I still getting paid?" she asked. It took Sarah a good

few seconds to start laughing, joined by Clementine. "That was the deal you know, I'm not in it to save the world..."

But Clementine seemed chastened by their experience somehow. Quieter, less acerbic. They leaned into each other by choice as well as necessity and took comfort from it.

They were sitting in the truck as Claude haggled noisily with a roadside trader for gasoline. They needed more and more, with less and less, and Claude had grown louder with every last franc. Sarah wondered if, when all the money was gone, he could buy fuel and food with the power of his voice alone.

She was ever so tired but incapable of sleep. Her body ached and she couldn't focus on anything. She felt bloated and her belly was cramping up.

Sarah watched Clementine fussing over her camera. Something bothered Sarah, and she couldn't put her finger on it. Clementine noticed Sarah's attention.

"That *Zicke* broke it, I think. Just can't get it to work."

"Do you have any of your photographs with you?" Sarah asked.

"None of mine," she said, then she brightened. "I have my father's album though. Would you like to see it?"

Clementine dug deep into her pack and pulled out a thin, creased and flaking photo album. Within it, in blurry monochrome, a series of vignettes revealed a white mother and black baby outside a modest house. Clementine burbled about focal lengths and f-stops. There was a dull Rhineland landscape, a group of *Tirailleurs Sénégalais* looking glum or bored in their light uniforms and floppy fezzes, and at the back a family portrait. Serious soldier, proud mother, small child. A toddler. No, older.

"When did your parents leave Germany?"

"I don't remember exactly," Clementine said, shrugging.

"The last of the French left in 1925."

"If you knew, why ask me? I'm the one that sets traps to make you look stupid, thank you."

"So you're three in that photo? Four? In 1925. How *old* are you? Really?" Sarah asked, gripping the photo album tightly.

Clementine returned her stare and said nothing, the look of fear, fury and the trapped back in her eyes.

"1925..." Sarah thought out loud, something else crystallizing through the fatigue, its corners becoming clearer. "But that camera was made in 1932," she finished. "Lisbeth said it's a Leica II—"

"It's not my father's camera, *all right*?" Clementine snarled. After a moment she flung it at Sarah. It hit her arm and spun into the footwell. "And that's *not my family*." Clementine was almost spitting the words. "Are you happy now, you screwed-up Jewish Nazi lunatic? Is that what you wanted to hear?"

Sarah sat stunned by the revelation she had stumbled into without even looking for it. She had no idea what to do next.

"I'm a real, genuine *Rheinlandbastard*," Clementine cried. "The French troops were little darlings and courteous and well behaved, *but not my father*, oh no, whoever the hell he was. He *had* my mother and then disappeared back to Africa. Is this what you wanted to hear? That the stories about blacks in the Rhineland were true? Pleased that I grew up in an orphanage after all? Does that make you feel superior at last?"

Sarah waited. The Captain hadn't even moved. Claude was staring at the cab of the truck, unable to see inside.

"I don't care about any of that."

"Everybody cares about that. And now I'm angry and feral and uncontrolled, which is *just typical of people like me*," she snarled.

"I knew you were a liar. And a thief. Why would any of this make me think of you differently?" Sarah ventured a small, at-the-edges-of-the-mouth smile. "You want sympathy for this, is that it? What would you say if I said, 'Oh, how terrible, I'm sorry'?"

"I'd tell you where you could stick it," Clementine said softly.

"Exactly. I'm a Jew, pretending that a *gottverdammter* British spy is my Nazi uncle, because my drunkard mother got herself shot. I'm *also* a liar and a thief. Why would I judge you? How could I? There's a queue of miserable life stories and you're clearly ahead of me, but you are not in this line alone. I am right behind you."

Clementine said nothing. Which was as close to an apology, truce or admission of defeat as Sarah was likely to get, but she didn't want any of those things. She tried to hand the photo album back, but Clementine shook her head.

By the time the truck rolled into Libreville, the rains had finally come. The water fell, heavily and unceasingly, in sheets that kept the streets empty. The town announced itself with a painted water tower, just visible in the fading light. This promised running water and Sarah could think of nothing else but getting clean.

This capital city was more of a small town, and Libreville felt less like an imposition than Fort-Lamy. Its colonial buildings nestled among the palm trees as if they belonged there, something Sarah had to remind herself wasn't really true. It seemed as if the gardens and flowers had been there all along, not a frontier town but a collection of Berlin lakeside properties.

The three-storey Central Hotel was different and promised all kinds of luxuries. It hadn't been built for expediency – the large double staircase to the veranda on either side of the entrance was a statement of wealth and permanency.

"This is the best hotel in Libreville. Even has indoor plumbing," Claude said, handing Sarah and the Captain room keys. "We don't have money for it, but I'm heading back inland to round up some funds. Tip well and hopefully they won't figure out that you're broke until it's time to pay the bill. Try not to attract attention. You," he said, turning to Clementine and handing her an older, rougher key. "You go to the back door."

"You didn't use the back door," she snarled.

"Because I sound like a middle-class West African. You sound like a German from the gutter when you speak French. You're supposed to be a servant, so play your part, girl."

"She can help my uncle in and then find her quarters," Sarah said gently.

"Oh, can I? Really? Why, thank you, *Miss Eva*." Clementine spat the words.

"I'll walk myself and everyone can shut up," the Captain growled. He opened the truck door and unsteadily climbed down.

Clementine watched him, then sighed and slid out of the door in his wake. Sarah watched her try to help the Captain and his efforts to fend her off.

"What will we do with him?" Sarah said to Claude.

"He goes...*cold turkey*...isn't that what the Americans say? Lock him in his room. He can sweat it out. Tell the staff he has malaria. He'll be human again in a week or so."

"*Or so?*" Sarah howled.

"What do you want from me? We've no money, there's a civil war about to kick off, I'm two thousand kilometres from home. This is the best I can do. They'll bring you food, and when I return I'll find a boat to get you back to Germany."

"What do I do about Bofinger?"

"Screw your mission, girl. It's over."

Sarah opened her mouth to argue, but she was just too tired.

Sarah closed the door to her room and leaned back against it. This was no palace of fantasy like the Grand Hotel, or fading threadbare artifice like the Hotel Victoria, but it had been swept and had a clean-looking double bed and mosquito net. It was the best hotel room Sarah had ever seen.

Too tired to find a bath, she staggered to the bed and, barely opening the net, she fell onto it. It was cool and smelled of soap powder. She lay in silence, listening to the rattle of heavy rain filter in through the window. She knew she had to use the latrine before sleeping but couldn't face moving another centimetre. Not just yet. She also had to close the window, because she was beginning to get cold. She rolled over and dragged a blanket over her. Fixed.

The final stages of the seemingly endless journey had been beyond uncomfortable. She had been constipated after weeks of diarrhoea. The cramping in her belly had got more intense, until she couldn't sit properly, and no matter how much water she drank she felt dehydrated. The headache just wouldn't go away.

Even now it wouldn't leave her alone...and she was still cold. She really had to get up, just for a second...

CHAPTER TWENTY-SEVEN

23RD–28TH OCTOBER 1940

SHE WOKE, BLINDED BY THE DULL DAWN LIGHT that shimmered on the ceiling. The noise of the rain extinguished all other sound. She was freezing and found her body was soaked in sweat. The clothes and bedding felt like they had been hanging in the rainstorm. She tried to move her head and found that any change in its orientation felt like a series of punches. The fever was back. This time there was pain in her chest and belly, where...

She had to make it to the toilet.

She sat up and a wave of nausea overcame her, her mouth filling with cold saliva. She tried to pull herself off the bed, but something was holding her back and she couldn't figure out what it was. Like ropes, flat ropes, material—

She thrashed her way out of the mosquito net with arms that felt like lead weights and fell off the bed onto the floor. She was gasping now for breath and couldn't focus on the commode in the corner of the room. *Quick*, screamed her mind.

She crossed the floor on all fours...

She was sitting on the toilet bowl, but she couldn't remember how she had got there. Her body was clearing itself out, the rushing, pouring, painful satisfaction of passing water. She was breathing heavily and holding herself up using the wicker armrest.

She looked at the floor.

There was a series of small dark drops leading to the bed, all the way from the latrine. There was a partial handprint on the wall next to her. Her right handprint.

She turned her right hand over. It was stained red. She looked at her knees and her feet for scratches, but there were none. Her thighs were covered in brown dusty smears—

She slowly opened her knees, feeling the pain in the joints, the shivers of her fever and the pounding of her head.

Her underwear was soaked in blood, and the toilet bowl was splashed in red liquid.

She heard Clementine's voice like she was in the room.

"You know what they're calling this disease? L'hémorragie... the Bleeding."

She got back to the bed, but first she managed to lock the door. If the others weren't already sick, then she wouldn't knowingly infect them. She looked at the sliver of Libreville visible through the open shutters and the rain. How many people lived here? Ten thousand? Twenty?

No, she wasn't leaving this room any time soon.

She wasn't leaving this room.

Her canteen was full, as was the jug on the nightstand. Enough for...

You're not leaving this room.

The headache, the cramps, the constipation and then diarrhoea. Now she was bleeding. She'd been sick for days and hadn't realized.

She pulled her wet outer-clothes off and wrapped herself, shivering, in the blankets, ignoring the bloodstains she had missed earlier. She closed her eyes and let go, momentarily wistful as to whether she might open them again...

She opened her eyes. She was still alive.

It hurt to move, and moving made her shiver, so she lay listening to the rain. She wasn't bleeding from her mouth or nose – she assumed that would come later. But she could feel her insides dissolving. How long did Lisbeth say her patients lasted?

She didn't.

There was a hammering on the door.

"Ursula!" It was Clementine.

Sarah sat up and immediately wished she hadn't. The motion made her vomit water through her hands and into her lap. *No blood, yet.*

"Go away," she croaked.

"I need your help with your uncle. He's screaming the house down. Threatening to leap out of the window if we don't let him out. The staff are...upset."

Sarah wanted to tell her everything, to open the door,

to accept her help. *To be held—*

But she knew that Clementine would die if she did.

"You can handle it," she managed. "Leave me alone."

Clementine swore and complained, but eventually she went away and Sarah was alone.

She was going to die.

She wanted to be *held*. Sarah knew that Lady Sakura's arms and Lisbeth's touch, the warmth of another person, was itself a drug. And now, when she needed to be at her most independent, she craved more. Now, when her own touch would be a death sentence for those welcoming arms.

But a touch would make this easier. If she wasn't alone, she wouldn't be scared.

She was going to die.

She floated. If she thought too much about it, she found herself lying in the blood-stained sheets again, so she cleared her mind. She wafted from one side of the room to the other as the ceiling fan turned. Her vision was so beset by tiny sparks and stars that the walls became an infinite white space to sail through. But each time she travelled, no matter how long she journeyed, she always returned to this same room and the stench of faeces and blood and pain.

◆　　◆　　◆

She was going to die.

There was a terror in that thought. A state of non-existing. A state that she couldn't imagine, but would not be able to feel once it had happened. It was the ignorance that scared her. Everything she had failed to learn, she had sought to belittle, to ignore. But this could not be disregarded, or neglected.

She was going to die.

She wondered if she had led a good life, knowing that in the last year alone she had caused the deaths, or worse, of half a dozen people. All her achievements were selfish actions of survival that destroyed, blundering through people's lives, breaking, wrecking, ruining.

She immediately rejected that thought. Her life had been one misery and torture after another, brightened only by spiced sausage or coffee or *peanut butter* bought by a monster. A good life or a bad life, all of this had happened *to* her. There was no judging her. She would not be judged.

She wondered if she would end up in the Seventh Circle of Dante's Hell, with the murderers, the war-makers, thieves, tyrants and *all the other Jews*…and she started to giggle.

Her lips felt both dry and wet. With great effort Sarah touched them and found the tips of her fingers were bloody. Not long now.

She was going to die.

Tears welled up in her eyes and she let them. It was a vast

and terrible thing, this sadness. As huge as a storm cloud and just as insubstantial. A vague emotion that was unmissable in its sheer scale, yet couldn't be touched.

Mutti, she called into that cloud.

She was going to die.

She was angry now. The desire to scratch and slap and punch, to hit bullies with rocks and wound the nauseating men and their cloying, greasy desires, to push that butter knife between the ribs of the man who drugged her, to paint herself with his blood, to seize Elsa's gun and pull the trigger again and again, each time whooping with the tearing, vaporizing destruction it wrought. To set upon the White Devil in his rubber overalls, to rip the mask from his ageing face and beat it bloody. To make Bofinger pay for the thousands of dead *people*, to pay back the French for the *corvées* and *prestations*, and the Belgians for the mutilation and *chicotte* floggings, and the Germans for the annihilation, and the Nazis for their hate and their spite and their whippings and acid baths and marches to the woods and the people who let that happen—

Sarah wanted to burn the world and felt the flames consume her first as she sat on her bloody throne.

The Mouse stood by the side of the bed. So small and frail and yet so alive, with those eyes so wide and round, ready to be lost in tales of puppies or kittens or gossip, so near to fear yet so removed from it.

258

She was fiddling with her uniform skirt, which was too big and had to be folded over at the top. Sarah wondered why she hadn't noticed this before.

"Mouse!" cried Sarah. It hurt to open her mouth and making a noise was like swallowing a knife.

"Hello, Haller, how are you?"

"I'm sick, Mouse," Sarah managed.

"Yes, you are. They should take you to the sanatorium, Frau Klose will give you something for it."

"There isn't anything I can take for it, Mouse. It's the Bleeding. I'm dying."

"Oh, that's a shame. Does that mean you won't be back next term?"

"I'm sorry, Mouse."

"Why are you sorry?"

"I didn't listen to you."

"I didn't say anything, Haller."

Sarah thought she could hear snuffling and scratching at the door.

"Everything you went through…" Sarah managed.

"Yes, and then you left me. But it's all right. You had a really important job to do."

There was a yelp and a growl. The door shuddered.

"Really? You know about that?" Sarah said breathlessly.

"No, Haller," she said, her voice hardening as it had the day that Sarah turned her back on her. "I don't know that at all. I'm not really here. All I know is that you left me. That you didn't care."

The dogs at the door began howling and barking. The wood began to splinter.

"I'm sorry, Mouse, really I am."

"Tell yourself what you need to, *meine Schlafsaalführerin.*"

"Oh, Mouse..."

"I didn't hate anyone until I met you, Haller. I didn't even hate Schäfer; he was just a man and all men are monsters, but you, you were a sister...and now you're going to die. You loved *der Werwolf* so much – let them have you."

The door flew open and the dogs came. Sarah could not wake, because she wasn't asleep and the dogs tore into her and ate her where she lay.

◆　◆　◆

CHAPTER TWENTY-EIGHT

29TH OCTOBER 1940

SARAH FELT SOMETHING SOFT between her fingers. Something like…hair.

Her arms were around something soft and warm, that smelled of French perfume and expensive make-up. She was being held by strong arms. She opened her eyes with difficulty, with the same sensation as pulling the skin from an orange. The door lay in pieces on the floor, and there was golden and auburn hair between her fists.

"No, no, no, no, no…" she croaked, a feeling of failure consuming her.

"Shh…it's all right," Lisbeth purred.

"I'm dying – you'll die," Sarah managed.

"You're not dying, you have malaria."

She felt a shaft of sunlight, of hope, immediately shadowed.

"But I'm bleeding…it's *l'hémorragie*."

Lisbeth relaxed her grip. "Lie down, *Liebchen*."

Sarah struggled to lie down, the pain in her head worse than it had been.

Lisbeth rearranged the sheets around her, lifting them out of the way. "Relax," she whispered, and placed her hands on her knees.

"What...?"

"Trust me."

Sarah let Lisbeth open her legs. Then she carefully placed them back together and covered Sarah with a sheet.

"You don't know what this is?" Lisbeth said gently. "Your mother hasn't told you?"

"I don't understand."

"*Mein Engel*, you're menstruating."

The word flitted through Sarah's raw and battle-scarred mind, in search of a connection. *Something to do with mammals.*

"I still don't..."

"*The Regular Bleeding? Strawberry Week?* It's very heavy but, it's normal."

Sarah was just shaking her head now. *Something other girls at Rothenstadt had talked about.*

"*The Red Pest?*" Lisbeth added.

"*Scheiße!*" Sarah's whole body was shaking now. "This is *the Red Pest*? This is what happens...all. The. Time?" She was hyperventilating now.

"Oh, *Liebchen*, come here." She gathered Sarah in and rocked her back and forth as the girl began to cry. "No, you have malaria, that's the fever, aching and the squits."

"My lips..." Sarah touched them, quivering.

"You're dehydrated, quite badly. Your lips are cracked. And you're anaemic. I'm going to put you on a drip."

"I thought I had your disease. I sealed myself in here. I...I..."

"You're very brave," Lisbeth whispered into her ear. "That was a really courageous thing. I'm...proud of you."

Sarah kept shivering, not with fear or fever now, but with something else. Relief? "How long...?"

"You've been in here six days I think. What did you drink?"

"Rainwater, it hasn't stopped, I used the canteen... Six days?" Sarah tried to pull away. "My uncle..."

"Your uncle is fine. Well, he's sick, too, a very different kind of sick."

"*Ein Morphinist...*"

"Well, there it is."

"He was shot, he nearly died. He has a lot of pain," Sarah said, wondering at her need to defend him.

"I'm sure...but he distracted me from you for too long."

"Will he be all right?" Sarah asked.

"He's nearly over it, but you're my focus now. You've a lot of tablets to take."

It took over a week to recover to something approaching normality, fed a steady diet of chloroquine and iron tablets. Her strength seeped back into her veins via a bottle hanging above her bed. Lisbeth soothed her, bathed her and read to her, as she overcame the disease and the unanticipated attack of her own body.

Sarah stopped worrying. They had money, or rather Lisbeth

had money and was happy to feed them. The Captain was being taken care of, although Clementine was far from happy.

"You're a stupid, stupid, idiotic..." Clementine's vocabulary failed her. "Sealing yourself off to die, with something that might have killed you *only* because you locked your door on me. *Dumme Schlampe.*"

Sarah looked up sharply, filled with a sudden rage. "I was trying to watch out for people like you."

"People like me? What do you mean, *people like me*?" Clementine growled.

"People, humans, the team, my *servant*, whatever."

"So I was supposed to be happy you were dying?"

"I didn't think you'd care," Sarah muttered.

"Of course I care," Clementine grumbled. Then she stopped and looked down. "I mean, who's going to take me home if you die? *Herr Morphinist*, the wonder-spy, who can't get out of bed?"

"Well, you could have broken down the door yourself... or climbed in through the window."

"Oh yes, black African servants breaking things on purpose aren't beaten or dragged off on a *prestation* at all. Unheard of, in fact."

"And the window?"

"I don't like heights. Planes are one thing, shinning up the shutters to the third floor is another." Sarah looked at her through narrowed eyes. Clementine made a face. "Hey, I'm not perfect. Never said I was."

"How is the wonder-spy?" Sarah asked.

"He's a mess."

But Sarah felt reborn. Not in a joyful or celebratory way that might greet good news or a pleasant change in fortune, but in the shocking and traumatic way that a baby is ripped from the warm into the cold outside world and slapped into breathing. The rest of her life had been unexpectedly returned to her, but she had no idea what to do with it. She was newly and suddenly aware that she hadn't known for some time.

Away from Clementine's acerbic presence, Sarah smiled at Lisbeth's face and giggled at her jokes in a way that she couldn't remember doing for a long, long time…if she ever had.

And they cried. Sarah told the story of Ursula's mother, reaching deep into her sorrow to make the story seem real, seeing her own mother's slide into aggressive helplessness and swapping out the names and eventual fate. But the emotional weight of this, once so great Sarah staggered under it, was now like the end of a tray of ice cream. It required constant, repeated scraping to gather enough to be useful.

And Lisbeth talked about the Red Pest, about pads and bandages, about the nurses in the *Weltkrieg* and what they discovered about battlefield dressings that had changed everything.

"What is that?" Sarah said suspiciously at the tangle of elastic and metal pins that Lisbeth was holding up.

"It's a, you know, belt, for holding everything in place." She began to giggle.

"You didn't have any barbed wire to spare?" Sarah smiled and sighed. "I don't think I'm going to enjoy being a woman."

"You and me and all the rest, *Liebchen*."

And Lisbeth told her story.

"At the end of the *Weltkrieg*, I was eighteen. Germany had to surrender its empire – not that anyone else felt the need to decolonize, but Germany had to be *punished*." Lisbeth practically hissed that. "We had to leave our homes – driven out of the place I grew up – and go back to Germany.

"The country had been *destroyed*. There was no food and no work, the communists and the *Freikorps* were fighting in the streets, killing one another and anyone in their way.

"And *we had nothing*. We were missionaries without a mission, and everything we'd saved was swallowed as prices rose. The banknotes were so worthless you needed a wheelbarrow load to buy a loaf of bread. That was when we got sick.

"Have you ever seen anyone with smallpox?" Lisbeth asked.

Sarah shook her head. "Just photos," she murmured.

"A face full of sores and blisters, highly infectious. It's terrifying. No one got smallpox in Germany back then. There were just 136 cases in the five years before the war, but after 1918, people were poor and malnourished and the hospitals and doctors were overwhelmed. The disease spread through the slums and my mother, who was helping in a soup kitchen, contracted haemorrhagic smallpox. I watched her insides dissolve into a bloody mess. Then I was infected, too, so I didn't actually see her die—"

Lisbeth stopped talking and stared into space.

"This is hers, *was* hers," she said at last, fiddling with her necklace. "*Everything* went in the furnace. I stole this afterwards. It's made of stone so it didn't burn."

"I'm so sorry... How do you deal with that?" Sarah asked.

"I do this," Lisbeth answered, gripping her necklace, closing her eyes and screwing up her face. When she opened her eyes, she giggled and they both laughed. Then her expression became defiant. "And I became a doctor to do the work that wasn't done, because all France and Britain and the United States were interested in was revenge. To extract every *Pfennig* they could and all for doing what everyone else was doing – making empires, making money, causing trouble...but look where it got France. I think we'll see that the French got off lightly. What do the Chinese say? 'Before you embark on a journey of revenge, dig two graves.'"

"Confucius..." Sarah looked at the floor. "Only it's more, 'Attacking a task from the wrong end can do nothing but harm.'"

"*Oha!* How do you know that kind of thing?"

"Says the *doctor*," Sarah pointed out.

"Yes, but I'm a grown-up. Didn't you ever play?"

Sarah saw the taunts of the other children, the beatings, the hunt for food, the alcoholic mother, her belongings sold—

"In my own way," Sarah said softly.

She thought about something.

"Smallpox," she began. "The blisters, don't they...?" She trailed off as Lisbeth met her gaze.

Lisbeth blinked and Sarah saw something deep, dark and painfully desolate behind those eyes. She slowly drew a finger down her cheek and turned the tip towards Sarah, a smear of greasepaint glistening at its end.

"Maybe if I were brave, I'd show the scars off as a badge of honour. Maybe if I didn't care...but I do. So, I chose to be strong, instead of hard, and" – she smoothed the paint back into her cheek – "an artist." She smiled.

Sarah opened her mouth to speak, but Lisbeth spoke first.

"Just don't say it doesn't matter, because you're a clever girl and you know that isn't really true."

There was an edge to her voice that discouraged another question. Sarah changed the subject. "So you didn't stay in Germany?"

"It wasn't my home, and anyway, who wants a woman doctor at the best of times? Especially one that looks like this." She laughed without mirth. "Just those with no choice."

When the Captain was finally able to see her, he looked washed-out and grey, like a man twice his age.

How old is he?

Sarah dismissed the thought.

"I had no idea how sick you were," he said, with something approaching, but not quite touching, contrition.

"If you had, there would have been nothing you could have done about it."

Sarah thought about that sentence again and regretted it. She had no wish to attack him, but there was no way to say any of it without the implicit criticism.

"How do we proceed?" Sarah began again.

The Captain looked over his shoulder and leaned in.

"Bofinger—"

"No. How do *we*," she interrupted, wagging a finger between them. "How do we proceed? What can I rely on you to do?" Again, it sounded like an attack. "I mean, what are you physically capable of? Do I need to care for you?"

"You don't need to do anything," he said flatly.

"No, don't be mysterious or enigmatic," she snapped. "I want to know what we can reasonably do."

"I'm still in withdrawal. I can't hold a gun straight. I cannot lift anything or run."

"You can walk?"

"Just about."

Sarah closed her eyes and screwed up her face, before becoming aware she was echoing Lisbeth's expression.

"Fine. Now we can talk about the mission."

"Bofinger is looking for a ship to Germany," the Captain began. "He hasn't found one yet, but they might get to Vichy-controlled West Africa. Spanish territory probably means internment."

"Their blood samples last just two weeks, according to Clementine. Bofinger can't have anything left to use, can he?" Sarah asked.

"He's acting as if he has. It's possible he has nothing, but thinks I can still get him home. And they can't stay. The Free French are coming, and any German citizens will, no doubt, be locked up. Certainly their work would be over."

"So if they have nothing... Admiral Canaris sent us to stop their work, right? So all we need to do is to make sure they're here when the Free French arrive?"

"I suppose. Means we fail to uncover the American connection..." he thought out loud. Sarah shook her head and shrugged. He continued. "But I want to know for sure what they still have, what they might smuggle out. You've formed a bond with Dr Fischer. It's probably down to you."

Sarah felt a tension, a conflict in that request. Like she would be being disloyal to use the…relationship, friendship… call it what you will.

Whose side are you on?

Not Bofinger's.

"She wouldn't have anything to do with that," Sarah said softly.

"I'm sure she'd be uncomfortable, but her father has no such scruples."

"I'll see what I can do," Sarah said. She looked at her hands in her lap and fidgeted, rubbing them together like she was washing. "Did it ever occur to you, how…what might happen… when…a little girl in your employment stopped being a girl?" she managed.

"You're still a brilliant diversion. When you keep your mouth shut, people still underestimate you—"

"That's not what I meant." She struggled to put it into words. "Practically speaking…when I'm no longer a girl—" The questions came from a raw, vulnerable place that Sarah could not hold open for much longer. *Step up. Be a parent. Please.*

"You'll be a different kind of spy, that's all," interrupted the Captain.

"That's *not*—" Sarah stopped and sat back. "Did you have a sister?"

"I don't understand what you're getting at," he said testily. "No, obviously not."

CHAPTER TWENTY-NINE

8TH NOVEMBER 1940

IF YOU WERE FRENCH, wherever in the world you were, the capitulation of their army left you with two choices – to get on with life as an ally of Germany under Vichy or gamble everything for a piece of self-respect. In the *Afrique-Équatoriale Française*, where no foreign troops walked the streets, the decision had been about trade and an excuse to settle old scores.

Now the Free French army was coming for Vichy-controlled Gabon and its ports, the civil war was a real, tangible thing. Paranoia consumed Libreville. Everyone accused one another of being a traitor, and fingers were being pointed across dinner tables and desks. People were reconsidering hasty words, or making a hasty exit.

The rain didn't stop. It just kept falling, trapping everyone in the hotel, just as the approaching army was trapping people in town. In this atmosphere of humid, saturated anxiety, Bofinger decided to host a dinner at the hotel and invite the great and good of Libreville. The great and good of Libreville were much too preoccupied to consider attending but were polite enough to ensure that the vaguely substantial and average attended on their behalf.

There were three ship captains present, and Sarah presumed they were the real guests of honour. One was almost comatose drunk and another, an unshaven Liberian with only the vaguest grasp of French, seemed happy just to be there. He nodded and smiled and said *yes* to everything.

It was stuffy and unpleasant, like being under a warm, wet blanket and unable to emerge for air. Sarah marvelled at the staff who, like the guests, were in the most formal of garb and *gloves*, yet couldn't fan themselves or loosen their collars.

Clementine had not been invited, despite Sarah's efforts, and this had drawn the deepest scowl of their journey so far. But Sarah was actually the tiniest bit grateful for her absence, as it meant she could concentrate on Lisbeth, a relationship about which Clementine had been showing signs of faint disapproval, or even jealousy. For days Sarah had tried to turn conversations with Lisbeth to the disease, to the existence of samples, to the American friends, to anything truly useful – and failed. She feared risking the friendship, losing the closeness.

Now Sarah was standing in Lisbeth's borrowed cream evening dress, her hair shining in what Lisbeth had called *loosely brushed pin curls and a small pompadour*. She also had newly applied make-up and was beginning to regret that choice, as the Captain entered the room.

"What are you wearing?" he asked.

"Something more suitable to a woman of my age," Sarah said icily.

"A woman of twenty years ago," he grunted. "And you're only fifteen. I'm not sure this works."

"What does a *sixteen year old* look like, Captain Floyd? Do you know?"

The Captain opened his mouth, but they were interrupted by Lisbeth approaching.

"There's my little star," she cooed. Lisbeth was wearing a new brown silk dress with a more contemporary cut, something acquired at a knockdown rate from a fleeing supporter of Vichy. It seemed to elevate her presence to another level. "What do you think of your niece now, Herr Haller?"

"I think we're *Émile et Élodie Poulain* from now on, Dr Fischer."

"Makes sense I suppose. And who would Émile be supporting in the current crisis?"

"Whoever promised me the most money," the Captain said.

Lisbeth laughed, then waggled a finger at the rest of the room. "You and every other bastard here."

"That's rather ill advised, isn't it?" The Captain motioned to the Kaiser's war flag that Bofinger had hung above the head table. "No chance of pretending you're Swiss now."

"No papers anyway." Lisbeth shrugged. "Lieutenant La Roux won't be returning them while we're in Vichy territory."

Sarah and the Captain exchanged glances.

"No, probably not a good idea." She sighed. "But that could apply to any number of things my father insists on."

"There may be people here who won't take kindly to it,"

he said gently. "People who fought the *Boche*."

"Oh, please, some of the people here are apparently happy to live under German protection now if it means they can sell their wood and rubber. Bring on those hypocrites."

"Any sign of an outbreak in Gabon?" the Captain enquired.

"Not that I've heard, but rumours persist about the Congo side. If de Gaulle isn't careful, he'll end up in charge of the world's biggest mortuary." A waiter appeared with a tray of glasses. "Oh, wine, I've missed you." Lisbeth turned to Sarah. "Do have a drink, *Liebchen*—"

"*No*," Sarah almost snapped, before adding more gently. "No, thank you." She smiled, shaking her head.

Lisbeth shrugged. "French girls drink wine... Think of your cover."

Even the smell of the wine made Sarah want to flee.

"I'm fine, thank you," she managed.

The moment was broken by an announcement.

"*Mesdames et Messieurs*, dinner is served."

The formality of the dinner was the same as at Bofinger's camp, although Sarah noticed empty seats that she guessed the professor would find excruciating. However, the fare was infinitely better. This piece of Gabon believed itself French, and the food reflected the metropole and not the colonial possession.

After two weeks of illness and recovery, Sarah was ravenous. She couldn't get enough food in her mouth, even if she found that most things tasted of lipstick.

There was an array of shellfish, mackerel and anchovies, seasoned to perfection, with the scent of a clean sea. Next to this a pot of shredded pork, *rillettes*, that was not a paté or a meat paste or purée, yet it felt as if it was all those things and more. The vegetables were crisper, and the red-and-gold sauce for the mushrooms more enticing than anything Sarah had eaten in months, lighting tiny shimmers of satisfaction from her tongue down to her stomach.

There was more soup than could be eaten, a thin vegetable concoction with butter, cream, herbs, garlic and particles of mushroom that seemed lusciously thick on the tongue. Sarah found herself unable to eat it delicately and allowed it to run down her chin, ruining her make-up.

Then *la bouillabaisse* appeared, with slices of Atlantic fish boiled in fennel, bay, garlic and sumptuous saffron, served with broth-soaked breads that dissolved in the mouth. By the time the *plat principal* arrived Sarah was full and could do no more than pick at the salad.

Sarah wondered how a nation that gave food this amount of attention and spent so long preparing it had found time to invade and occupy anyone else's.

Slavery, thought Sarah idly, ruining her appetite altogether.

Bofinger put down his cutlery noisily and addressed those nearest to him.

"So, Haller, I'm hoping you're in better health now? 'Malaria' is *terrible*, isn't it?" Bofinger gave a knowing smile that made Sarah want to hurt him. "But let's get back to business. You came to me offering a safe passage back to Germany? Well, now is the time to deliver."

The Captain shifted in his seat. "The time to go was several weeks ago, when I could indeed have arranged it. As it is, I'm trying to get you passage to Casablanca or somewhere we can organize—"

"I thought as much. If I were that important to the Reich, you'd think someone would be here with an airplane or a naval vessel, in order to take all my work..." He looked at Lisbeth. "*Our* work," he sneered, "back to the Fatherland. But they sent you and this little girl instead. Why is that?"

"The political situation here was, and still is, chaotic. Can you imagine what would happen if a Kriegsmarine vessel were to steam into the harbour of a Free French port? All based on a rumour we heard in Berlin? You need to trust me now to get you home."

"Trust you? A *suchtkranker Morphinist* and a sickly little *Hure*—"

"*Vater*, enough now," Lisbeth interrupted, slamming her fist into the table. "*Herr...Monsieur* Poulain is doing the best he can for us. There's no need to be nasty."

Sarah stared at her plate intently, gripping her water glass so hard she wondered if it would break.

Bofinger looked like he might surrender the point, but then his face hardened.

"Oh, we should be grateful that you've got some female company and a face to paint up. You could have stayed in Germany and had a child, you know...I didn't need you here, ordering me around and making me do things. Although you might not have found anyone *dich zu ficken*, the way you really look—"

Sarah was on her feet before she thought about it, and the

water from the glass was in the air before caution or regret could form.

The liquid did not miss Bofinger entirely. It splashed onto his dinner jacket as it hit his empty plate. He flinched in surpise, then he looked amused.

"You shut your mouth," she growled. Her sweat felt cold on her back, even as her face flushed red and painfully hot.

The room was silent. All eyes in the room were on the exchange.

The Captain placed a hand on Sarah's shoulder and pulled her gently but firmly back into her seat, wincing with the effort. He leaned forward, a darkness in his eyes, and whispered.

"And what exactly am I supposed to be bringing back, Bofinger? *News* of a disease, one that's behind enemy lines. What use is that to anyone? If you don't have something to show me, there's really no need to help you at all."

"Is that so?"

The Captain waited until conversations restarted around the table. The drunk ship's captain seemed to come to life.

"Tensions running high," he slurred. "Let's avoid politics, shall we?"

Both Bofinger and the Captain ignored this interjection.

"What do you have? We left that village two weeks ago. How long do your samples last?"

Bofinger leaned forward and tapped his nose. "I have the weapon—"

"*Father*, no—" Lisbeth cried.

"But who to give it to, that's the question…"

Bofinger looked up and a wide smile slithered across his face. A loud voice broke across the room.

"I'm so sorry to be late. I know you hate tardiness, Herr Professor."

Standing at the door, in the dress uniform of the *Schutzstaffel*, was a beaming Kurt Hasse.

CHAPTER THIRTY

"WHO IS THIS, FATHER?" Lisbeth demanded in a fierce whisper. "What is going on?"

The professor said nothing, but his sickly, triumphal smile became a smirk.

Even Sarah could see that the uniform had caused a ripple of distaste and resentment among the French. It was bringing home the reality of their new allegiance. As Hasse pushed past the guests to take a seat next to Bofinger, one elderly trader stood, flung his napkin on the table and walked out.

"Ah, Haller, what a wonderful surprise to see you," Hasse cried out. "And young Ursula, how delightful. Fancy meeting you here!"

"Indeed. I thought you were going to Abyssinia?" the Captain replied with forced levity.

"Well, you know," Hasse said with a sigh, settling into his chair. "It turned out I already knew everything there was to know about gassing savages. Besides, some fool shot down my plane!"

He laughed. Not in a drunken or excitable way, it was an aggressive, foghorn-like bark of humourless noise, wearing the coat of laughter. Outside thunder broke and made the shutters rattle.

"That sounds less than ideal," the Captain managed quietly. "Do you know each other?" He gestured between Hasse and the professor.

"Oh, yes, Haller. Very much," said Bofinger.

"Father, who is this?" Lisbeth asked again, with an edge of anger that Sarah had not heard before. Bofinger shushed her before continuing.

"In fact, the *Obersturmbannführer* has proved to be an excellent correspondent and, it turns out, a much better servant of the Fatherland than you are."

"Well" – the Captain smiled – "it's not a contest. We're all serving the same master, aren't we?"

"Are we now?" Hasse commented and wagged an admonishing finger. "Sometimes I don't know about you *Abwehr* types. It seems like you've got your own agenda. I think you've been dragging your feet just a little bit, like you're not sure what to do. But now is the time for decisive action."

Thunder rolled in the distance. The drunk sailor stirred. "Did anyone hear that?" he said.

The others ignored him and carried on.

"I have an aircraft on its way to Libreville right now," Hasse continued. "Ready to take the professor and his whole team back to Germany where the weapon he has developed will be tested and readied for use."

"*Whole* team?" Lisbeth cried.

"We don't have the technology to deliver such a germ weapon, even if it were ready," the Captain responded.

"Oh, I have a special friend in the Imperial Japanese Army," Hasse said. "He's been working on this since 1932. Now that we're *formal* military allies, he'll be quite happy to share all the fruits of his labour."

"I'm not sure the Führer will welcome a germ weapon," the Captain said quietly. "And where would you test it?"

Hasse waved a hand dismissively. The wine glass in front of him vibrated, and he looked at it before continuing.

"Oh, the Führer welcomes all *Wunderwaffen*, as he welcomes anyone who brings him a radical solution to a problem."

"And what problem is it that requires such a solution?"

Hasse leaned in, as if he was to reveal a confidence. "The Führer is going to insist that we turn our attention to Bolshevik Russia very soon, whether we break the British or not. That's thousands of kilometres of land and millions of *Untermenschen* to get rid of. Herbert Backe has his *Hunger Plan* – he wants to starve them all to death by taking all their food – but we don't have time for that. Even if the *whole rotten structure comes crashing down when we kick in the door*, as our leader is so fond of saying, that will tie up millions of troops for months, years even. This weapon is a *gift*."

"So not for the British, then?" the Captain enquired.

"I wouldn't want to risk their sense of fair play. You bowl the ball at the batsman and not the wicket, they're inclined to get upset...and both teams have to bat."

The thunder broke again, louder this time.

"And the Russians will just let you do it?"

"These are not sophisticated people we're talking about. Slavs with eggs filled with cattle pox. There's no need for us to concern ourselves on that score."

Sarah noticed some of the waiting staff—

The enslaved staff, she thought absently.

—some of the *servants* were looking at one another and whispering. At first she thought they were listening in, but whatever interested them was *outside*.

One of the other guests stood and looked in the same direction.

"Whoever you are, *Obersturmbannführer,* sorry," Lisbeth complained, hand on her necklace. "This is news to my team—"

"*Your* team—" Bofinger interrupted scathingly.

"Yes, *my* team, Father—"

Whatever Lisbeth said after that was lost in the ear-splitting howl and explosion. The ground shook. The shutters shuddered and one came loose from its hinges. The chandelier rattled and developed a wild swing.

Everyone in the room fell silent as dust filled the air and their shadows rocked from side to side. Through the broken shutter they watched the rain being lit up, not by lightning but by the distant flashes of artillery fire.

The dinner had broken up quickly, as the locals had rushed back to homes and businesses, but Sarah had wanted to see the gunfire for herself. When they finally entered the Captain's room, they found Clementine, sitting cross-legged on the bed, reading by the light of an oil lamp. She looked up, as if bored.

"You have a visitor," she said, nodding to the corner of the room behind the door.

Sarah closed it and revealed Lisbeth standing against the wall. She was agitated, almost shaking.

"Can you get me to England?" she whispered.

Sarah wanted to shout, *Yes, yes, come with us.* But she bit down on her tongue and waited.

The Captain took off his jacket and dropped it onto the bed. Clementine waited a long second and then took it to the wardrobe.

"Why do you think I can get you to England? Why would I do such a thing?" he said, pulling at his bow tie and looking through the blinds to the muted thumping beyond the town.

"Because you're not...who or what *are* you really?" Lisbeth pleaded.

"Why do you want to go to England?" the Captain pressed.

Lisbeth stood, caught between two moments, like an animal who sees the door of the trap close and wonders whether another way out lies deeper into the cage.

"The disease can't go back to Germany," she said quietly. "It can't be used the way that this SS officer says."

"And what do you think the British will do when they get their hands on it?"

"I don't think they'd use it...would they? Besides...besides, who says that I'd give it to them? I just need to take it somewhere I can deal with it safely. I can't do that here. Look, I don't know what you are, but *Abwehr* or British or American, you don't want the SS to get their hands on this...do you?"

Sarah always liked the simplicity of Latin. If you expected a no, the question began with the word "num". Instead, Lisbeth's question dripped with uncertainty, longing, entrapment.

"How is it going to be transported?" the Captain asked.

"That's complicated, I'd have trouble explaining the technicalities," she sighed, shaking her head.

"Hasse has a plane coming for you," the Captain stated.

"I won't get on it."

"But your father will and he'll take everything with him."

"Not if I have anything to do with it."

Lisbeth had committed to the move.

Sarah walked up to her and took her hand. It was uncharacteristically sweaty and it contained a tiny tremor.

"Can you help me?" Lisbeth asked. Sarah looked at the Captain, but he was unreadable, beyond the fatigue and pain he now carried like an extra limb. She turned to Sarah, necklace in hand.

"We need to make plans. Go and pack," Sarah said, smiling.

Lisbeth smiled back and looked relieved. She squeezed Sarah's hand and left the room.

The Captain was about to speak and then he looked around. "Where's Clementine? I didn't even see her leave. She's like a ghost."

"So how do we do this?" Sarah demanded.

"I can't whisk Lisbeth away, how would I get her out? The ships here are going to be swamped with people trying to get to Vichy-controlled West Africa. Even if I could drive, we're on a peninsular and there are only a few roads out. I don't know the area. We'd be caught. The best bet was hanging on until de Gaulle takes Libreville...but Hasse and Bofinger won't wait for that to happen."

Sarah pushed her fingertips into her temples, her initial joy fading as her head filled with problems.

"She's committing to stop the disease, to betray her father, to turn her back on Hasse." She ran the conversation over in her mind. "But, taking it 'somewhere I can deal with it'?"

"She doesn't want us to destroy it. I think she wants to keep the research."

"She wants to achieve her goals." Sarah nodded. "We can't allow that."

She felt her betrayal, to take from Lisbeth what she needed, like it was hair torn from her scalp. It was sudden, painful, but there was no going back. Lisbeth would be angry, but the woman would forgive and hold her again.

Looking at the Captain growing pale, Sarah realized that for this evening at least, he was done. Even without the morphine, he had finite strength. There was a window of usefulness and it was now closing. She shrugged off the resentment and concentrated on the practical.

"We need to know how they've been transporting the disease, if the blood samples are supposed to be dead by now," Sarah pondered. Something else bothered her, something lost in the tension of the moment. "'That's complicated'? What wouldn't we understand?"

"Something technical... Hasse said something about the Russians using eggs?" the Captain offered. "You can make things grow inside living eggs—"

"They had eggs! Or is it in the bats or the ape? Are they the vector?" Sarah shook her head, trying to focus in on the right questions, the right answers. "They'd need somewhere to put them and they aren't here. They've only one truck outside... where is the other one? Where are the horses?"

"There are lumberyards at the edge of town..." the Captain murmured.

He was growing sleepy. Again Sarah pushed her resentment away. She needed to be at her most clear-headed.

"We need to stop this," Sarah stated. "Destroy the whole thing. Now."

Somewhere in the lumberyards was a flamethrower.

Libreville was on a peninsula. There were only so many roads into the town.

CHAPTER THIRTY-ONE

THE RAIN HAD WEAKENED to a drizzle, as if on intermission, so the sounds of the battle were clearer outside. The boom of artillery and rattle of small-arms fire were still distant, but ever-present, even closing in on the town. The odd wild round, like the one that had shaken the hotel, still dropped nearby, and this had cleared the streets.

Sarah's legs did not want to move forward, to step into danger. The act of commanding them, consciously, was making her breathe heavily.

By now she had reached the fringes of Libreville, with its newer group of warehouses, mills and storerooms. Beyond these, Vichy-supporting soldiers waited, leaning on squat tanks and smoking nervously. Both troops and officers were anxious, trying not to jump at the sound of each explosion or gunshot. Sarah understood she was looking at a group of men who had not fought before.

Walking in the darkness, through the saturated mud, Sarah

was beginning to despair of finding anything. There were too many buildings, too many side roads where the trucks could be hidden. It seemed an almost impossible task for one person, even in this small settlement, but with Hasse in town, their time watching and waiting was up. The samples had to be found and destroyed. The disease had to be ended.

Stopping next to an abandoned lumberyard, its gates closed and chained against intruders, she sagged and put her hands on her knees. The hem of Lisbeth's dress was coated in mud, and it was slapping uncomfortably against Sarah's legs. She should have changed properly before heading out, instead of just pulling on a coat and boots.

A flash lit up the sky, illuminating the street. Under her feet the road was left rutted by a hundred wheels and a thousand hooves. The rain was pooling in the tyre tracks, the edges soft and runny. Several of these tracks turned off the main road, towards the gate and under it. They weren't fresh, but, as the *crump* of the shellfire finally hit, she walked up to the lumberyard. The chain was old and rusted and the padlock was coated in mud. She turned away.

It had been raining for a week or more.

Sarah turned back and wiped at the lock with the sleeve of her jacket. Underneath the dirt it was brand-new.

She channelled her delight into action and was up and over the gate in a few seconds, cursing the awkwardness of the evening dress as she did so. It had been a while since she had climbed anything, but even in her fragile state, her muscles remembered and responded like she was scampering atop a Viennese roof.

The rumble of the battle and the sound of rain on tin roofs covered any noise she could make, but Sarah couldn't help but creep into the darkened yard. Another flash revealed one of the mission's trucks backed up to a collection of buildings at the far side.

The vehicle was empty, or at least bare of the incubators or cages. It occurred to Sarah the difficulty of finding something that might be as small as a test tube. She turned back to the buildings to see that the door of one storeroom hung open a crack. A pale orange light spilled through it.

Sarah moved towards it in a crouch, planning to peer through the gap. The sky brightened for an instant, throwing two shadows across the door.

Sarah spun around—

"What the hell are you doing here?" Clementine cried in a frantic whisper.

"I'm trying to find their samples. What are *you* doing here?" Sarah replied as quietly as she could as the sound of the explosions rattled around the yard.

"The...same... Just, you shouldn't be here, it's...dangerous," she hissed.

"Of course it's dangerous—"

"Haller, go back," Clementine said with great intensity, looking into Sarah's eyes. It was the most serious she'd ever seemed. Clementine had been furious, superior, even frightened, but all those faces had been tinged with a sardonic humour.

"You've found something," Sarah said, wide-eyed.

"Yes, yes, I have, and it's not safe. Please." Clementine was shaking her head and drops of rainwater were spinning away.

"Show me," Sarah insisted.

Clementine put a finger to her lips and leaned in to whisper. "Very well. I think there's a guard inside, so be *mucksmäuschenstill.*"

Sarah saw the Mouse, the first night that they had met, bouncing on her toes, unable to maintain her silence, even though she would be punished for it.

As they approached the building, Sarah's nose grew irritated even before she registered the thick aroma of bleach. Clementine peeked in and then pushed the door gently out of the way.

In the middle of the room, pitched by iron weights and ropes that hung from the roof, stood a large white canvas tent, glowing orange from a light burning inside. A muffled chittering, scampering animal noise escaped the folded entrance flap. Between the door and the shelter was a table of bleach and protective equipment.

Underneath that table, wearing an apron and mask, lay a body.

Sarah tried to push past Clementine, but the girl held her back.

"Careful, you don't know what's happened yet—"

"They—" Sarah began.

"They could be infected, contaminated, whatever... Wait."

Clementine walked slowly around the edge of the room, checking the corners, keeping Sarah behind her.

"Gloves and masks, I think," she suggested.

"I agree," Sarah said, nodding vigorously and pulling a dry pair from the line above the table.

The figure on the floor was face down, the back of their head a wet, dark red rose of matted hair. Sarah crouched and rolled the body gingerly with her gloved hands.

It was Klodt. His eyes behind the goggles were wide open and lifeless.

"Someone hit him. I think he's dead." Sarah sighed.

"Using this."

Sarah turned to see Clementine standing over her, hefting a large rusting pipe wrench. The jaws and teeth were spattered with drops of something dark. She fought the urge to flinch away.

"Something like that, yes," Sarah managed.

"Let's see the tent," Clementine suggested, dropping the wrench to her side and moving away.

The tent flap was protected by a large rubber sheet that had to be pulled clear with a sticky, slurping sound.

It was a small version of Bofinger's laboratory with the icebox, incubator and animal cages squashed together alongside a cramped workbench of jars and test tubes, lit by a solitary oil lamp. The atmosphere was a claustrophobic mix of chemicals, ammonia and animal faeces.

Sarah opened the icebox. It was warm and empty.

She pulled the incubator open to find cold empty racks.

"We're too late. They've taken it all," she cried.

"Let's go," said Clementine.

Sarah looked at the blanket-covered animal cages. "No, not everything."

"I didn't want you to see this," Clementine murmured and tugged at one of the covers.

The mice and rats were dead and beginning to moulder and decompose – the stench of rotting things filled the air.

"Don't be silly, I've seen dead things before," Sarah said, pulling the blanket away from the bats. They seemed alive and well.

"Do you think the bats are the...what's the word?" Sarah continued. "Are they going to bring the bats home?"

Clementine was staring at the last pen, the chimpanzee cage.

Sarah waited for her to uncover it, but she didn't. She seemed to be transfixed, hypnotized.

Sarah took a step forward and began to feel uncomfortable. She dreaded finding the beast – so human, so tortured – and suffering its wrath once more. She went to take hold of the blanket, but Clementine tried to stop her. Sarah snorted and pushed her hands away, before gripping the blanket and making a soothing, cooing noise as she did so. The cover caught at the back, and Sarah had to give it a sharp tug to free the material. It came loose with a tearing hiss and dropped to the floor.

Sarah was ready to jump back but found herself frozen to the ground, unable to move.

The chimpanzee was gone. In his place, crammed into the tiny crate, was a man.

Sarah could only see the bloodstained gag, the bruised and ruddy brown skin, the ropes that bound him, so it took her a moment to recognize the middle-aged Bateke, from the scar on his right cheek.

"It's...it's..."

Clementine pulled her mask down. "His name is Ngobila. You didn't get around to asking? I don't think you even asked what the village was called."

"Mpuru," Sarah snapped.

"That means *village*." Clementine sighed.

Ngobila opened one eye and looked at Sarah. The white of his eye was dark with blood. So swollen was his face around it that it was impossible to tell if he was aware of her or not.

Sarah tried to imagine what the last few weeks could possibly have been like for him, watching every member of his village fall ill and die, before being bound and imprisoned in this cage. When did he admit to himself that he was also going to die? Would he welcome it when it came?

These were just words and Sarah couldn't feel the terror behind them. That was something deeper and darker that she was too frightened to unleash.

"He's about to die, but he gave them the live samples they need," Clementine continued. "They were planning to ship him home for as long as he survived, but they can't put him on the plane. Everyone in it would have been infected by the time they landed. So Klodt came to euthanize him."

"How did you know..." Sarah began.

Clementine was still holding the pipe wrench. Something went very tight in Sarah's chest.

"But Hasse isn't done with him yet," Clementine stated. "He needs Ngobila – to make a fresh walking sample that Hasse can send to his friends in the United States by boat."

"Clementine, what are you doing?"

Clementine shook her head vigorously. "I'm actually really,

really sorry," she managed and her voice broke slightly on the final word. *Sorry.*

"I don't understand," Sarah managed. "You work for the *Abwehr*, for me, *with me.*" But as Sarah said it, she knew she no longer believed it. "Hasse is a *Nazi*. The Nazis will be rounding up *your* people and putting them in camps—"

"They *already* put us in camps, they *already* rounded us up. You don't even know what happened to us, do you?" Clementine cried, her anger cut with frustration and disappointment. "They ordered us into hospitals and they *sterilized* us. All of us. So none of the *Rheinlandbastards* can have children... All except one."

"You made a deal," Sarah whispered.

"Yes, I made a deal. What would you have done? What will you do when your time comes?" she asked more quietly. "The little girl thing – that's not a new trick. Hasse knew that people would spend so much time hating me or overlooking *the maid* that I'd make a good spy. The twenty year old who looks like a child. It's a great cover. And I learned things...I read and studied and understood things. That was always part of the deal."

Everything seemed clear now. Every step of their journey, every setback was rewritten.

"My uncle didn't lose his drugs...*you* took them. *You* led Hasse to us." Sarah swallowed and thought of the camera. "You've even been recording our progress for him. Clementine, these people are *evil*. Haven't you seen what they're capable of?"

"Oh, Ursula." Clementine sighed again. "The Nazis aren't anything new. The Belgians were turning blood into rubber in the Congo before we were born. What the French did in Indochina, what the old German Empire did to the Nama and Herero, what the British did *everywhere*... All of it criminal, all of it horrendous. Even the Americans who think they don't have colonies forget the Philippines and Mexico and that *they were a colony* and they exterminated the natives so they could live there *with their slaves*. All of white history is a series of mass graves. Unless you really believe we're so below you that it's only a problem now that white people and Jews are being beaten up, arrested and murdered?"

"Not everyone—"

"Not everyone?" Clementine cried, the calm dissipating. "You *woozy* sentimentalists don't stop the cruelty, the slavery, the slaughter. You read *Red Rubber*? That man, that angel, that hero who risked his life and livelihood to expose the work of the Belgian rubber trade? He was responsible for the whole Black Shame *Quatsch*. All those stories about black soldiers raping their way through thousands of innocent white women in the Rhineland, everything that made my life so miserable. He was all for *caring* for the blacks, as long as they stayed in their place, like naughty children."

"Twice false doesn't make once true, Clementine."

"Come on, how old are you?" Clementine replied.

"You'll never be equal to them in *their* world."

"And in which world would I be equal, Little Eva? In Africa run by white people? In America where they hang black people from trees for fun? I'm a *Neger*. This earth isn't designed for people like me. I have money and protection now. That's the best I can do."

"And you'll murder people to get it?" Sarah said sadly, looking at Ngobila.

"I haven't murdered anyone...much. Come on, Klodt was an *Arschloch* who kept a human in a tiny cage," she added, shrugging. "Yes, I've done bad things, but you want me to be a good little *Bimbo* and be a slave? *Scheiß drauf.*"

"You could fight them with me," Sarah begged.

"You know, I thought about it when I found out who you really were. I even got excited, but you're too feeble. Your uncle, the addict. Claude, the high priest of racism. I can't count on you... And you've already lost, Ursula. The bastards have already won, from Poland to the French coast, and on every continent on earth, long, long before you were born."

"What about those millions of Slavs who Hasse wants to *get rid of*? Don't they deserve better?"

"Ha! In Poland, there were those who were happy to round up their neighbours and do horrific things to them. The Germans only had to suggest it." Again her anger faded away. "People are monsters, Ursula Haller. All people. There's no one worth caring about," she finished quietly.

"You don't sound convinced."

"Well, forgive me for being weak. I thought I might talk you around, because you're not a bad sort, Little Eva..." Clementine stepped towards her, a pained expression on her face, and reached out a hand as if to comfort Sarah.

Sarah watched the hand, wanting the conflict to be real and the remorse genuine, so she missed the moment that the pipe wrench swung up and hit her on the side of the head.

CHAPTER THIRTY-TWO

SARAH SAW DARKNESS and an eruption of yellow-and-white fireworks. Then she felt herself hit the matted floor. The pain rolled in an instant later and was all she could feel or think about for the seconds that it took Clementine to bind her hands and feet.

"If the *gottverdammten* Free French hadn't shown up, we'd have had more time. This wouldn't be happening," Clementine said as she worked. "I'm sorry. I liked you. I really did. I didn't even tell him you were Jewish. I was just going to slip the virus into your uncle's food or do this while he slept, and he'd have never noticed. I definitely didn't want it to be you."

She pulled off Sarah's mask.

"What are you going to do?" Sarah managed to say, opening her eyes.

"A *Neger* would be too noticeable, you see. No one was going to think twice about the sick white man, especially a *Morphiumsüchtiger*..." Clementine looked Sarah in the face.

Cunning and sadness and irritation and anxiety fought for control of her expression. "But you had to come sniffing around. What were you thinking? I *told* you to go..."

Clementine stood and Sarah managed to roll over to watch her. She could feel something hot running across her face, and she tried to shake it out of her eyes. Each movement made her feel like she had been hit again.

Clementine continued. "But I suppose no one is going to look twice at the moody little white girl on the steamship to America. Maybe she's poorly and sleeps a lot. She might even tell a fantastic story, but she's *just a little girl*, so..."

"What?" Sarah cried.

Clementine was opening the cage where Ngobila was imprisoned. She had a syringe in her hand. She raised her mask. "By the time you're infectious, you'll be safely in your cabin and on your way. We'll keep you sedated, you won't know—"

"Oh, Clem, please don't do this," Sarah pleaded. She couldn't assemble a more robust thought process, all she had was revulsion and fear. "Please."

"I'm sorry, I'm so sorry," Clementine mumbled, closing her eyes. "It's just another horrible thing I have to do to survive." She opened them again, more determined. "Haven't you done things you're ashamed of? Who are *Klaus* and *Stern*? You say their names over and over in your sleep. What did you do to them? ...*Scheiße!*"

She had pushed the syringe into Ngobila's arm and tried to pull the plunger, but nothing was coming out. She pulled it free and tried again.

"I could scream for help," Sarah managed.

"And there's a war on and no one will hear you... *Beschissener* nonexistent blood pressure," Clementine swore. "Veins like noodles..."

"Didn't I...save you?" Sarah tried.

Clementine stopped trying to find a vein and turned, pushing her mask down and breathing heavily.

"You're annoying me now. A white *saviour,* rolling in to bring civilization and moral rectitude. Well, put down that burden, white girl," she growled. "I put *myself* in that position. I knew you were in that radio room. I knew you'd feel sorry for me. Not the only mistake you've made, by the way, you've missed something else blindingly obvious—"

"Please," Sarah cried. She rolled left and right but couldn't coordinate her bound legs and arms while the pain in her head was so intense.

"You've got to stop that, I'm sorry but—"

"Please. Don't."

Clementine failed to fill the syringe again. She let go of it, leaving it dangling from Ngobila's arm. She looked like she might cry, just for a moment.

"You're just making this harder..." she said, reaching in and tugging at his bloody gag. "I've got to stop you talking."

The gag came free.

Ngobila spat into her face.

It was a mouthful of blood ejected as a spray. It missed her mouth but speckled her hands, neck and chest.

Clementine staggered back with an expression of surprised terror. She looked into his eyes, to see the defiance and anger there, behind the mask of loose skin. He grunted, a guttural noise of satisfaction.

She slowly wheeled around to look at Sarah, who had managed to wriggle into a seated position.

"Is it on my face, in my mouth...my eyes?" Clementine stammered, staring at her gloved hands and rubbing them on her dress.

"I don't know..." Sarah managed. "Bleach..."

Clementine lunged for the nearest desk where a lone bucket stood among the lab equipment and, shoving things out of the way in a frenzy of smashing glass, she pulled it towards her. She took one sniff, squeezed her eyes shut, then poured its contents over her face. She spat and shrieked, before tearing at the neckline of her dress. It came away from her shoulders with a rip and she scrabbled out of it, before backing away and peeling off her gloves.

She finally sagged to the floor next to Sarah, breathing heavily.

"Ngobila has an opinion on your plans," Sarah croaked.

Clementine looked like she might strike Sarah, but a moment later, she started to giggle. It became a chuckle and finally a loud honking roar, at the very edge of hysteria.

"Guess that told me, huh?" she called out to Ngobila between whoops of laughter and frenetic inhalations. He had sagged, with his eyes now closed.

Sarah fought the sensation of relief. She knew the truce was fragile, temporary, even treacherous. She had a window, a moment to reach out.

"You didn't tell Hasse I was Jewish?"

"I knew he'd…" Clementine said. "That he'd do something to you." She winced and rubbed at her red eyes. "This *stuff* stings."

"What…will you do now?" The pain in her head was making talking difficult.

"It's you or your uncle. Or me. Hasse would hunt me down."

"Doesn't have to be either of us." Sarah was pleading again. "We can protect you."

"Mmm," Clementine mused, shaking her head and gesturing to Sarah, bound on the floor. "You can't protect yourself." She leaned in and laid a hand gently on Sarah's shoulder. "You don't really get it, do you? You think you do, Jewish girl, but I've watched what these people can do, and you haven't seen anything yet. Surviving them is going to require something special. It means compromises. Anyway, if I saved you at the risk of my own life, that would be a bit tacky – too Mark Twain, don't you think?"

Then she brightened and pointed to Ngobila. "Then again, shall I go and infect this whole town? The whole capital of imperialists, collaborators, slave owners, Nazis and their soldiers and compliant human pets? I could get on that plane to Berlin!"

"*Ach du heilige Scheiße…*" Sarah swore and began to laugh. "You're *mad*. You're actually a crazy lunatic."

Clementine feigned confusion. "Isn't that what you want, to change the world? Don't you want me to kill all the Nazis?"

Sarah saw Lise Meitner outside the cafe on the Nyhavn, asking how many innocent people had to burn to win a war. *The ends do not always justify the means.*

"Not like this," Sarah said, nodding to Ngobila slumped in a cage – a man with a life, with a family, with who knew what else taken from him in the most horrific manner possible.

Clementine looked at the gag on the floor next to her ruined dress. One tear streaked down her face.

"You're a *woozy sentimentalist*, Ursula Haller. I'm sorry."

Sarah didn't really hear the sound of the gunshot, just felt the intensity of the noise as pain in her head wound.

The matting behind Clementine erupted, and she set off on all fours for the shelter of the cages. Claude advanced into the tent, his gun stretched out in front of him. He fired again, blasting a hole in the box underneath Ngobila. Clementine vanished behind it.

The Frenchman ran the last few metres to her hiding place, then swore before turning and sprinting back out of the tent. Sarah rolled over to see him struggle out of the rubber seal.

Outside there were two more shots, and Claude swore again.

Sarah listened, waiting for any other sound, a clue as to what had just happened, but all she could hear was distant artillery fire and Claude's audible irritation.

Did you get away? For reasons she couldn't fathom, Sarah hoped Clementine had.

Claude returned and pointed his Beretta at Ngobila. The Bateke looked at the Frenchman and made an assenting grunt before closing his eyes.

"*Je suis très désolé*," Claude apologized, and fired. Sarah made herself watch. It seemed cowardly not to.

Then he picked Sarah up in one swift motion and headed

for the tent flap. He pushed his way through, banging her head against a wooden post. He dropped her to her feet in front of the table of bleach and pushed her head down into the pan.

It stung her face, lighting her skin on fire, but it was the wound on her head that was the focus of her discomfort. It felt like a long, hot needle was being pushed slowly into her brain. She struggled and thrashed, but he held her down and scooped handfuls of the liquid onto her neck and shoulders.

Finally, he released her, and she rose into the air with a roar, coughing and spitting. He freed her hands and went to work on her feet.

"Wash yourself, all of yourself," he shouted.

Sarah was stunned and couldn't think clearly. She tugged fitfully at her gloves as her feet came free.

"*Pour l'amour de Dieu*," Claude roared. He picked up one of the other pans and emptied its contents over Sarah, soaking her clothes, stinging her eyes and making her lips tingle.

"It burns," Sarah spat.

"So does *l'hémorragie*. You're not dying on me, little girl." He began scrubbing at his hands and face with the third bucket. "We have to burn this place," he grunted. "All of it."

"Did she—" Sarah began.

"Slippery *anguille*, yes, she lives," he grumbled.

"Hasse—"

"Met him, a charmer. He's packing up to leave right now, we have to move." He began searching through the piles of equipment that lined the walls of the store. "*Mon Dieu...*" he whispered, stopping. He reached into a box and pulled out a large white gas mask, practically a helmet, with huge round respirators and oversized oval eyepieces. It was the head of a beast, a monster...a devil.

He handed it to Sarah, who stared into the demonic glass eyes, seeing herself there. The helmet was oily and left a cream residue on her hands. She dropped it and watched it roll away. She rubbed her hands on her damp dress. She couldn't decide if her hands felt raw from the bleach or whether the evil of the thing had burned her.

Claude lifted a white painted diving suit from the box before throwing it back. "It's real. They did this. All of this," he whispered.

"The airfield...but he also has a ship, to get to the United States..." Sarah pushed her damp hair out of her face. Strands of it broke off in her hands.

"One problem at a time," Claude said as he turned to her, the flamethrower in his hands.

The building was already melting in on itself as Claude lit up the outside. The nearby soldiers came to watch, confused and wary, but Claude wasn't in uniform and he was accompanied by a wet-looking little girl, so they weren't obvious targets. By the time the nearest officer had decided to intervene, the building was gone and Claude and Sarah were starting up the mission's truck. As they accelerated away, scattering the waiting troops, no one felt like firing on them.

"Dr Fischer wants to go to England? She knows who you are?" Claude asked, trying to catch up. "Hey, stop crying and talk to me."

Sarah's eyes stung from the bleach, but her shoulders were quaking for a very different reason.

"I don't think she's sure," Sarah managed, sniffing. "But she knows we aren't here to get Bofinger to Germany...and you have to suppose that Hasse knows that, too."

"Did she know there was that Bateke in there?"

"Ngobila, his name was Ngobila," Sarah snarled. She took a breath and her chest hurt. "She can't have," she added, startled by the amount of hope that was shoring up her conviction. "No, she thought he was killed when they torched the camp. She wouldn't have done that."

The truck bounced through the potholes and puddles, each vibration like another blow to Sarah's head.

"Will that girl go to Hasse now?"

"No, she's...failed him. I don't think she can go back."

In truth, Sarah didn't know. She hoped that Clementine was free of him. She also hoped that she herself was free of Clementine, at least for the moment.

"You should have let me just whip her when I said—"

"Claude, *tais-toi*," Sarah snapped. She rubbed at her temples. Hair, dried greasepaint and skin flaked off in her fingers.

The other truck was gone when they arrived at the hotel.

"Find Jeremy if he's still here and I want his MP 40." Sarah looked blankly at him. "*His gun*," Claude continued tersely. She nodded and jumped out.

The rooms where the Bofinger mission had been staying were empty. They had all gone, including Lisbeth. Sarah mounted the stairs to the top floor with growing apprehension. Had they taken the Captain? Had Hasse killed him? The latter seemed more likely, if the manager hadn't seen him leave. She slowed as she reached the landing and padded quietly along the polished wooden floor. His door was in shadow, but a flicker of light from the approaching battle illuminated the inside and revealed it was slightly ajar.

Sarah held her breath and pushed as gently as she could.

The door swung open. The Captain was lying on the bed, fully clothed. She crept in, uncertain what she was hiding from, until she realized that she didn't want to know what had happened. Every extra second she took was a second where she didn't have to deal with the consequences of it.

She rounded the foot of the bed. His sleeve was rolled up and the silver syringe was still in his arm. The paraphernalia was unfamiliar to Sarah, but among the equipment she could see the morphine, which was German military issue. Hasse had supplied the perfect way to remove him from the game.

She felt along his neck and underneath her fingertips she found a heartbeat. He was still alive. Her rage boiled over the top of her fear.

"*Du dummer gottverdammter Bastard!*" she screamed at him, and kneeled on the bed to slap at his face. "You couldn't refuse junk from your *enemy*?" She swore at length, grabbing his shoulders and shaking them. He murmured and moved but didn't wake.

She stepped back and collapsed to the floor. She caught sight of herself in a full-length mirror. She was momentarily shocked by what she saw, then she sniggered at the picture.

She was still wearing Lisbeth's old-fashioned cream dress, but it was now torn and stained white where the bleach had attacked the fabric. Mud plastered the hem. The remains of her make-up streaked down her face, while her bare skin was red, raw and peeling away in dry flakes. The side of her head was a dark and gritty brown starfish with arms that ran down her loosened hair in red matted braids. She was a clown, a terrifying backstreet entertainer so long in the dark she couldn't see to apply her stage paint.

A plan. Her mother, her voice, would always want *a plan.* Still she was silent.

Sarah was a lost little girl on the far side of the world from civilization.

Whose civilization? she demanded. But she ignored herself.

A lost little girl, who would do anything to get home. *Anything.*

A lost little girl who didn't *understand anything*, who would accept *any* help, to get back home.

She looked at the monstrous clown in the mirror... and grinned.

Dearest Mouse,

If you knew who I was, who I really was...

> *You would not care.*
>
> *If you knew what I had done...*
>
> *You would not care.*
>
> *<u>Would you?</u>*
>
> *<u>Alles Liebe,</u>*
>
> *Sarah*
>
> *<u>Dirty Jew and murderer</u>*

CHAPTER THIRTY-THREE

"WHAT DO YOU MEAN, I'm not coming?" Claude was as confused as he was indignant.

"I need you to drive me to the airfield but drop me off without being seen. Then come back here and look after your friend the *Morphinist*."

"We'll probably be too late, the amount of time you took."

Somewhere behind the rain clouds the sun was rising and the sky was turning a pale grey.

Sarah had showered, changed her clothes and combed the blood out of her hair. Careful braiding had concealed the wound and she had used the Captain's cologne to mask the pervasive smell of disinfectant. It wasn't perfect, but it was all the time she could spare.

"This wouldn't have worked otherwise," she stated adamantly.

"But—"

"No, enough. You need to get my 'uncle' home, and you

can't do that if you get yourself killed. Everyone at the airfield is your enemy now."

"Then I'll burn the lot," he said, tapping the flamethrower.

Sarah looked out of the window, at the growing crowds in the street, at the people with trunks and suitcases heading for the harbour. The ease with which she could even consider this should have frightened her, but she was numb. She knew that torching everyone – Hasse, Bofinger, the mission, the samples – was the only way to be safe…but she had to save Lisbeth. The woman had asked for their help. Whatever she had been involved with, she wanted out of it. Sarah wanted…Sarah needed to hold her hand again and then everything would be all right.

Lisbeth was stopping a slaughter. Lisbeth was Sarah's salvation.

"The hotel manager talked about them having machine guns. We get Lisbeth out first, she's on our side."

"That's still easier at the point of a gun," Claude growled. "Why am I letting you boss me around?"

Sarah looked at him, almost desperate to be backed up. No, for him to be in charge and to take responsibility away from her. She looked at the priest, the angry, violent racist with a chip on his shoulder, and knew she didn't trust him. It was a lonely moment, like she was the last person on earth.

She seized on that weakness and strangled it.

"Leave this to me. I know the people, I know what I'm doing."

The truck was almost swamped with refugees now, and it was having trouble getting through. Claude sounded the horn and screamed through the window for them to make way. In the harbour there were three ships, and crowds on the quayside and pier were threatening to overwhelm them.

"I don't know why they're bothering. There's a naval blockade and two French cruisers are fighting it out off the coast. It's as dangerous out there as it is here," Claude mused.

Sarah sought out the ensigns flapping at each ship's stern.

"Liberian flag, French flag and..." Sarah stopped. The most distant ship was face on, so the flag was almost invisible until it caught the wind. She waited for the next squall to move it.

The flag was German.

She turned to Claude.

"I need money. And your gun."

Sarah ran across the airfield towards the distant truck and the tiny figures next to it. She tried to get her breathing into a rhythm, to add the acceleration that she knew was there, but the malaria and the pounding headache had taken the edge off her abilities. She had left Claude at the gate, arguing with, cajoling and distracting the guards there.

Before she had left Claude, she had turned back.

"Thank you, Claude. Thank you for saving my life."

"Jeremy brought you all the way here. Even *this* Jeremy...you must have been worth bringing. So be worth it, little girl."

Sarah laughed without humour. "He brought Clementine, too."

"No," Claude said, shaking his head. "I know the story. *You* brought her. Don't make that mistake again."

She thought about these words as she moved over the thin grass, the first time she had been able to think about Clementine and what she had done.

Sarah was wounded by the betrayal, a wide, jagged and oozing sensation of grief and loss – a loss of something that hadn't even existed. No, it *had* existed, they had been friends. But she was more angry at herself than Clementine. She played events over and over again in her mind, seeing the hundred little moments where she should have been more suspicious, more critical. When instead she had allowed Clementine to antagonize and distract her, making her second-guess herself and her motives. Had she been less brittle, had she listened more, things might have been different, before the end, when it was too late. If she had been stronger, Clementine might have felt able to join them. Sarah had failed her friend.

Clementine did what she felt she had to do to survive, and the continuation of Sarah's life had already taken innocent lives. Sarah had been right – how could there be judgement in that line of miserable existences?

And Clementine *had been right* about most things, yet so, so wrong in what they made her do. Sarah could feel her fury crushing her sense of justice and righteousness. Is this how Clementine had become what she was? To stay useful, would Sarah need to become something else?

Sarah promised herself that she would be strong, not hard.

The airfield was no more than a few hangars and ageing biplanes, but the Vichy forces were digging in around the perimeter. They were showing no signs of giving up the site without a fight. The gunfire sounded murderously close now, and Sarah felt very exposed.

They won't shoot a little girl. At least not a white little girl.

She looked to the jungle at the edge of the field and wondered if they'd stop to look.

She was close to the truck, almost at shouting distance. She could just make out the individual people, the flash of Lisbeth's hair and the taller, rounder figure of Hasse. She prepared herself, feeling again the absence of her mother's guiding voice.

She needed to cry. She dug into the recent past for sadness and loss but found only anger and rage – the razed villages, the betrayal of the dying man in a cage, of Ngobila's final weeks. She had believed herself dead...but here found only relief. She thought of Clementine, hefting the bloody wrench, but that brought only fear.

Oh, Mutti, she thought. *Where are you?*

There was a sliver of loss, of loneliness and abandonment, and Sarah pounced on it. *Feel it in the cheeks.*

Sarah began to scream for Lisbeth, letting the run pull the power from her cries to make them more vulnerable and helpless. She wanted to be with Lisbeth, to hold her chapped, greasy but warm hand, to know she wasn't alone.

The tears began to flow.

Lisbeth had turned, along with several others, but it was Hasse who moved first and began to narrow the gap between them.

"Fräulein Haller? What is wrong?" he called. She couldn't yet read his face.

"Lisbeth! Help me."

Lisbeth started forward.

"What's happened?" Hasse called. She could see his face now. Behind the mask of concern, his face betrayed a deeper anxiety. Sarah made to exploit it.

"*It's horrible!*" she howled, then let breathlessness break up her speech. "It's…it's…hor…"

Lisbeth arrived and went to hug Sarah. Hasse put out an arm to stop her. He reached down and patted Sarah for weapons. Lisbeth turned on him in surprise, then pushed past him and took Sarah into her arms.

"Oh, *Liebchen*, it's all right," she cooed.

"My uncle is *dead*. I thought he was sleeping…after his medicine…" She made her chest heave between words. "But he stopped breathing…" She pulled back from the woman's arms and turned to Hasse. "And Clementine told me to find *you* and say 'It's done', and then you'd look after me. *Then* Claude the priest turned up and shot her! Said she was a traitor…"

If Clementine had found Hasse by now, she was undone.

"When did you talk to Clementine?" Hasse demanded.

He was asking, *Are you infectious yet?*

"An hour ago," Sarah said, letting confusion cross her face. *Not infectious yet.*

He couldn't hide his relief. It was a full second before he swapped that expression for sympathy.

"Terrible, terrible. Where is this Claude now?"

"I lost him in town…"

"Enough with the questions, Hasse!" Lisbeth barked, gathering Sarah back into her arms.

A rattle-crack of gunfire made them all start.

"Back to the truck, please," Hasse ordered.

The shots restarted and stopped amidst shouts to cease fire. Sarah watched a group of soldiers emerge from the treeline, waving their arms. Strident demands for identification were being made. The two opposing sides looked identical.

They trailed back to the dubious cover of the mission truck, but Sarah held on to Lisbeth's arm to slow her down.

"Wait, we need to talk," Sarah whispered, turning and hugging the woman again, stopping her.

"I looked for you. Your uncle was in a...daze, but leaving with Hasse wasn't optional," Lisbeth said. "Is your uncle really dead?"

"Might as well be, for now. Klodt is dead," whispered Sarah, and Lisbeth winced. "He..." Sarah nodded at Hasse as he walked ahead of them. "Thinks I've been infected, without my knowledge. He's going to use me to take the disease to the United States. A walking incubator. How long before he'd have to isolate me?"

Lisbeth was shaking her head, appalled.

"Less than a week."

"Did you know about Ngobila?"

"Who?"

"The Bateke, the person who was put in a *cage*," Sarah growled.

Lisbeth closed her eyes and screwed up her face. "I didn't know. I swear that when we left the village I had no idea. I sent Klodt to...put him out of his misery as soon as I possibly could."

"Out of his *misery*?" hissed Sarah, her forehead knotted.

"There was nothing I could do for him. Nothing. It was an appalling thing that they did, but by the time I knew, it was already too late."

"*It's complicated*, you said," Sarah hissed, the venom pouring out of her, unable to stop it. "Is that what you meant? He was a father, a brother, an artist, an *Arschloch*, a drunkard, or a saint, who knows what. A person with a life, a *story*."

"You've got to believe me, I didn't know until—"

"Fräulein Fischer! Get in cover please," called Hasse.

Lisbeth went to move, and Sarah pulled her tighter.

"Who has samples?" she demanded.

"My father has—"

"I stopped Claude coming here and torching you all," Sarah interrupted. "You *must* come with me now. There's a ship to Liberia in the harbour, and from there we can get to British territory in Sierra Leone or Nigeria. You can't get on this plane *and* you've got to take the samples with you."

"We're *all* getting on that plane," Lisbeth said sadly. "Look." She pointed to the truck.

For the first time Sarah noticed the addition to the staff.

Five heavily armed men. A perimeter. Armed with machine guns. Mercenaries. Professionals. They were motionless and dead behind the eyes. One watched the two women with a lizard-like stare.

The mission staff could feel it and were nervous, fidgeting. They sensed their detention. They were prisoners.

She spotted Samuel, sitting calmly on a box next to Emmi. Then he looked up and saw her. He was briefly dismayed, then he slowly shook his head at her.

"They're going to kill everyone," said Sarah softly.

"*No*," she scoffed. "They just don't want anyone disappearing."

Sarah looked at the Herero, who stared back at her, eyes haunted by the knowledge of the past. He tightened his grip on Emmi, who had tears in her eyes.

They became aware of a distant, buzzing rumble. One by one, the waiting mission staff looked up at the grey sky.

"At last!" exclaimed Hasse, clapping his hands. "Professor, Doctor, do come with me a moment. You, too, *Fräulein*." He waved to them to join him by the truck, away from the others.

Lisbeth's eyes widened.

There was more gunfire at the treeline. It began erratically, tempered with caution, but more shots joined the chorus. There was a series of dull thuds and then an explosion that made everyone flinch.

"We should run," Sarah said.

Lisbeth shook her head and began to walk to the truck.

The deep, throbbing buzz grew.

The mercenary looking at Sarah made an unambiguous motion with his gun.

There were screams audible from the treeline. Cries for help drowned out by more firing. Vichy troops were running across the airfield to reinforce the line.

Out of the clouds dropped the huge cruciform of a Ju 52, its three engines making the air vibrate as it passed overhead.

The corrugated metal sides were unmistakable and gave Sarah a wave of nausea at the idea of being inside that tin box again, but the numbers and tail had been blacked out to hide its identity. One of the mercenaries watched it fly over and popped a smoke flare. After a moment's fizzing, it produced a billowing column of white smoke that chased after the plane.

"Aunty Ju is here!" Hasse laughed and gestured to Sarah. "*Fräulein*, come."

Sarah reluctantly followed, watching the aircraft. It almost seemed to disappear into the distance, but then banked gently and began a long turn over the town. Sarah looked back to the mission staff. The doctors, nurses, porters and servants were being herded away from the truck. Good people, bad people, side by side. She lost sight of Samuel behind one of the gunmen.

Sarah broke into a jog and reached Hasse.

"Don't do this," she pleaded.

"Do what?"

Lisbeth was arguing with her father in a quiet, angry voice, but Sarah couldn't make out the words over the rising noise of battle. *Samples. Berlin. The team.*

"Don't kill them all," Sarah pleaded. "Just let them go if you don't need them."

"If I'm to look after you like your *Neger* said, you're going to have to learn to do what you're told."

Sarah wanted to spit at him, cut herself and wipe her hands on him, something, anything that she could do that he might be frightened of. She knew, suddenly and clearly, that if she couldn't or wouldn't do something at this moment, she was going to have to live with the consequences for ever.

"Lisbeth says she needs them," she managed.

"Does she? Which ones?" Hasse asked.

She saw Samuel.

"That one, the old guy," she said, pointing. "And the woman—"

"What, some old *Hottentotte*?" He snorted. "I thought you were serious."

"I am! Lisbeth! Tell him, tell him you need them…"

Lisbeth turned from her argument, with a face so lined, so anxious, it didn't even seem to be hers. She strode towards them.

"Are you really going to do this, *Obersturmbannführer*?" Lisbeth demanded. "These are all vital members of the team."

"Professor?" Hasse said, turning to the old man.

Bofinger shrugged and mumbled something.

"Oh my God!" Lisbeth exclaimed. The first cries of alarm had started among the corralled staff. A mercenary pushed someone back. The throbbing of the aircraft engines filled the air.

"I thought as much." Hasse turned away. The sounds of the battle swelled, the cracks and bangs and screams, the mosquito whine of bullets flying wild, built around them.

Sarah tugged his sleeve. She sank into her body to make herself as small as she could and looked up at the SS man.

"Please?"

Hasse smiled and sniggered. "Your little girl act is…not convincing, *Fräulein*," he said, and then leaned down, touching his eye. "I can see kohl pencil on your eyelids."

He straightened up to watch the Ju 52, which was now face on and descending towards the airfield. The buzzing of aircraft seemed to be all around them.

"Two things," he said. "No room and...no witnesses. It's pragmatism. No one is going to miss them. In the same way, I'm going to put you on a boat to America, safely out of the way. Because if you vanished altogether the *Abwehr* might ask me awkward questions."

Sarah wanted to claw at him, to hurt him. She felt the deep panic of total helplessness.

"*Right,* enough distractions—" Hasse began as the heightened roar of aircraft engines threatened to drown him out.

The aircraft that now filled the sky were small, not much bigger than the *Storch* that had traversed the Sahara, but they seemed stockier, thicker and more threatening, festooned with bulbous projections. Face on, their wings seemed bent like those of a gull and the bulging objects fell like droppings on a seaside shelter as the planes roared, then rattled and putted past them, revealing the cross of the Free French.

One moment the ground was an expanse of flat, matted, wet grass. The next it was fountains and clouds of mud climbing to the sky, dozens of interconnecting *kar-umph*s. The blast waves from so many explosions threw everyone to the ground.

CHAPTER THIRTY-FOUR

It was like a thick blanket had been laid across everything, for all sounds now seemed muffled. As Sarah looked up, a high-pitched, whistling ring accompanied the kicking waves of hot air that rolled in across the turf. The Ju 52 swept over them, the rippled metal riddled with holes and port engine ablaze. The prop vibrated as it spun and a jet of dark liquid erupted from the casing, fading to a grey, oily smoke stream that hung in the air long after the monster had gone.

The bombing run was concentrated on the foxholes and rough fortifications at the treeline. But the nearest impacts were just thirty metres away and, rolling over, Sarah saw a few still and bloody figures among the mission staff and their captors. The rest were disorientated and clumsy, but they were beginning to come to their senses and scatter. The first instinct of the surviving mercenaries was to fall back to the truck and defend it. Sarah watched Samuel and Emmi sprinting towards the sea, hand in hand.

Hasse was on his knees, watching his plane as it struggled to maintain height and swung drunkenly out over the bay.

Sarah looked for Lisbeth. The howling noise in her ears continued and worsened as she moved. She saw the auburn-and-gold hair and she crawled towards it. Lisbeth was face down and motionless. Sarah wanted to speed up, to climb to her feet and run to her, but her body wouldn't respond to the growing feeling of dread.

She reached her and, shaking her shoulders, called her name.

Lisbeth's head jerked up from the wet grass, eyes wide with smudged make-up. She felt for her necklace and then her head dropped back to the ground.

"Lisbeth! What is it?"

The body spoke. Sarah could barely hear the words and had to push her ear into Lisbeth's hair.

"I'm fine, I'm trying not to get my head blown off," the woman shouted.

Sarah sat up, threw her head back and laughed. The explosions had made the Vichy side of the battle line a hellish channel of fire, impact and boiling wind.

The little squat planes banked off over the bay and flew over the Ju 52 as it lost the last few metres of height and crashed into the sea in a flurry of broken propellers and seawater.

The mercenaries had finally noticed that their last task was incomplete and started to fire at the fleeing missionaries, but they had run in all directions and the targets were just too numerous and too far away.

Hasse was on his feet, but his shoulders sagged as he rubbed his forehead. He regarded the truck that had lost all of its glass and blown two tyres. Then he straightened and strode over to where Bofinger was picking himself up. He kicked the man as he passed and began to yell to the gunmen.

Sarah watched Hasse's plans unravel and the little planes turning back for another pass, and she laughed and laughed in the muffled silence until it hurt too much to laugh more.

The victory was a small one, for Sarah at least. The mission staff were gone, but Hasse had acquired a new vehicle of sorts and Sarah, Lisbeth and the professor were in the back of it, ringed by his remaining mercenaries.

The roads were crowded with retreating soldiers and anyone north of the town who didn't want to greet the Free French on their arrival. No one had an interest in the rusting cattle truck with its well-armed passengers, but neither would anyone give way.

Sarah and Lisbeth couldn't talk freely in front of Bofinger. He looked vacantly into space, stunned by the turn of events. Sarah eyed the small pile of luggage at their feet, knowing that somewhere inside lay the components of a weapon that made the battle they'd just witnessed seem like a small child's game. She drew her legs back from the nearest pack.

Eventually, as the truck re-entered the town, they met refugees surging in the other direction, unaware that the Free French forces were closing in from all sides. Hasse, who had entirely lost his relaxed and affable exterior, had to abandon the cattle truck.

The gunmen pushed through the crowd, surrounding and herding Sarah and the others down the hill towards the harbour. A mercenary hit someone with the butt of his gun. There were screams and blood, but the crowd was too tightly packed for anyone to react, and the body fell under the feet of the throng. Sarah knew she might be able to drop and roll out of the moving prison, getting lost in the surge, but that meant leaving Lisbeth and the samples behind...

She leaned into Lisbeth as if needing support.

"Where are the samples? I can get away," she whispered urgently into her hair.

"No, my love. It's too dangerous," Lisbeth mumbled back.

A gunman pushed at her with the barrel of his gun.

Maybe Lisbeth was right. She'd only get one chance, one go at getting away, and failure meant the end of everything. Hasse was tolerating her because he thought she was valuable to him – a walking incubator – but she could as easily be bound and carried, even end up in a cage like Ngobila.

And she couldn't leave Lisbeth. That knowledge, that weakness, was like her own gunshot wound, slowing her, making her think too much, too carefully. Just as Norris had identified in the Captain, she couldn't *commit to the move*.

Finally, the harbour came into view. Two ships remained for those trying to escape the fighting. The French merchant was already steaming for the sea, very low in the water. Its decks and rigging were swarming with people, many more than would be safe in the South Atlantic waters.

A great booming rolled in from the ocean. The smoke stacks of two great ships were visible on the horizon, and the flash of their guns could just be seen. The curious watched the action through binoculars from a two-storey house, a reminder that many would welcome the new regime.

The German ship at the far end of the pier still had clear decks, thanks to armed sailors in the rigging controlling the crowd.

Hasse's men fought through the crush along the quay and onto the pier, forcing some people into the water. Anger boiled over, but one look from the dead eyes of the heavily armed gunmen was enough to make everyone think twice before acting.

Finally, they reached the *Ittenbach.* It was a small steam cargo vessel, just two masts and one funnel. It was old, maybe thirty years had passed since its heyday, but it was meticulously painted, patched and cared for, like it was a museum piece rather than a working ship.

The gangplank had been withdrawn to stop the refugees from swarming the decks, but the boatswain was busy negotiating with those on the pier.

The ship's captain was standing on the forecastle, leaning over the white rail. Sarah was unsurprised to see that the comatose drunk from Bofinger's dinner was really no such thing. He saw them approaching and straightened up.

"Herr Hasse, you said three in all. I see four."

"I can pay, you know that," Hasse shouted up.

"Money doesn't change my weight limits. That's a rough sea out there."

"I'll pay enough for you to leave all your other passengers at the dock," Hasse insisted.

The ship's captain grunted. "Fine, but you leave your private army here." He waved them forward, and his crew began to manhandle the gangplank back into position.

There was an explosion in a nearby street and rapid gunfire, as a cloud of smoke rolled into view. Those nearby began screaming and pushed forward into the people on the quay. To avoid being thrown into the water like some, the crowd flowed onto the pier.

The surge of people couldn't be held back and mounted the deck of the Liberian trawler.

One of the gunmen was carried away with the motion.

Sarah saw a gap. A real opportunity, maybe the last, to escape from Hasse. To find the Captain, to leave. To accept the mission had failed. It was not her fault—

YOU brought Clementine. YOU were lonely and needed someone. YOU failed her. YOU allowed her to steal the Captain's morphine. YOU led Hasse to us. YOU are responsible for this. ALL of this.

Sarah was stunned by the clarity of the thought, by the sudden understanding of her culpability.

She looked at Hasse, who was fighting off a man who had been thrust into their circle. The SS officer struck the interloper in the face and he went down underfoot.

He had to die. To protect the Captain and Norris and the millions of Slavs and...and Lisbeth. Sarah had to bring about his death.

It was a cold thought. Like an icicle had formed in her heart. So she clung to the idea of protecting the woman. She squeezed Lisbeth's rough and oily hand, hoping that it would warm her.

The gangplank was down and their guards pushed them towards it. Bofinger climbed on first, then Hasse shoved Lisbeth along it, tugging Sarah in her wake. The gunmen threw their luggage over the rail onto the deck. Sarah watched it bounce and clatter and wondered if the samples were still intact. Hasse passed a roll of notes to one of the gunmen and leaped aboard. Two of the crowd had mounted the gangplank and the mercenaries knocked them into the harbour with the butts of their rifles. Then the gangplank was raised and the gunmen vanished into the melee.

"Right!" boomed the ship's captain to the crowd on the pier. "The fare is ten thousand francs per person, in cash, hold it above your head and you can board, otherwise you can go back, right now."

The gunfire of the approaching Free French clattered in the very next street. There was another surge from the crowd. The wealthy were holding their banknotes over their heads now and scuffles broke out.

Sarah turned away from the chaos.

Hasse was looking at them, revolver in hand.

"Next stop, New York," he said, and smiled.

That smile will make this easier, thought Sarah.

CHAPTER THIRTY-FIVE

THE SHIP WAS CROWDED when it cast off. The harbour had filled with fishing boats, their captains detecting the scent of money in the air. There were even the rowing boats of the highly optimistic, so the ship pulled away carefully, sounding its horn. The sailboats had the right of way, but today, all rules were suspended.

Before Hasse waved them below, Sarah saw the swastika ensign being lowered. The crew were busy erecting canvas shelters, going to work on the hull with acetylene torches and a sailor with a pot of black paint was about to shimmy down the hull at the bow. It seemed like a lot of activity before the ship was even clear of the breakwater.

The SS officer had secured two cabins. He motioned Lisbeth and Sarah into one with his gun. It was stuffy and gloomy, and smelled of socks and fish. The lantern on the wall flickered, and the engine's rumble made the walls shudder.

"Is that necessary?" Lisbeth asked, pointing to his weapon.

"Possibly not." Hasse shrugged. "However, I've become nervous, my dear. I know you're far from happy, and I wouldn't want you jumping ship before we're clear of land. This is going to be fine. I've got some friends who will be delighted to get you back to Germany once they've obtained the samples."

"How long to New York from here?" Lisbeth protested. "Weeks? A month? The samples will be dead before then, and useless to them."

"There are solutions to all of those problems. They'll be happy to make more for you to take to the Reich."

Sarah felt like something was crawling across her skin.

She was the supposed source of this solution, but she knew they wouldn't stop with her. The samples would mean there would be other cages, other Ngobilas, bleeding out pools of useful infection.

"I would like to be dropped off somewhere, anywhere," Lisbeth declared. "You don't need me."

"No, I'm sorry. You're too valuable. Your knowledge is essential, with my friends or back in the Fatherland. You're needed by the Reich, Dr Fischer." He walked to the door. "Welcome home," he added before leaving.

The door closed and a key turned in a lock.

"He's *locked* us in, on a *boat*," Lisbeth hissed. She sat on the bunk and fiddled with her necklace. "What do we do now?" she whined.

"We could wait, lull him into a false sense of security, and make him think we're compliant."

"Or?"

"We kill him right now."

Lisbeth laughed. Then she looked at Sarah and stopped.

The ship started to roll as soon as it was clear of the harbour. Sarah had read that the waves of the South Atlantic were notoriously moody and capricious, but now they were swollen and agitated by the rainy season.

As the floor fell away, and she did not, Sarah felt her body revolting against this turn of events. She wondered how long she might be useful, before she had to vomit, before she had to lie down and close her eyes. Motion sickness was clearly incompatible with being a spy.

She slid two pins from her hair and, straightening them, went to work on the lock. It was rusty and every unexpected shift of the ship knocked her off balance enough to make her have to start again. At one point she had to close her eyes and rest her head against the bulkhead to stop the sensation of spinning that overtook her.

"He has to drop..." Sarah said, between biting down on her tongue.

Click.

"...these people off..." she continued and bit down again.

Click.

"...somewhere," she went on. "He's not going to take them to the United States..."

Click. Tchick.

The door unlocked.

"Then he'll lock me in the hold and turn me into a virus factory." Sarah turned to look at Lisbeth. "If I don't get sick, he'll help me on my way, using your samples—"

"Not *my* samples—"

"The mission's samples."

"I can't believe my father brought that man into our lives."

There was a *thud*, a sudden whining roar right overhead and then a deep, explosive splash. After that there was the sound of heavy rain on the deck above. The ship shook and then leaned hard to starboard, before slowly righting. The engines, audible as a constant thudding rumble through the bulkheads, began to slow.

They both looked at the ceiling.

"I think that is our cue, don't you?" Lisbeth said.

As they mounted the ladder to the deck, they could hear a distant booming voice but couldn't quite make out what it was saying. The cold hit them as soon as their heads emerged from the hatch, the wind whipping any warmth away with the back of its hand.

The deck was crowded with passengers, and Hasse was nowhere to be seen, so they were able to slip to the rail unobtrusively.

The sea was a rolling landscape of grey-and-green darkness, with sinews of white foam. It would itself have been breathtaking, but a few hundred metres away, and cutting a parallel line through the water as if it was warm butter, was a warship. It felt huge, as it was twice the length and height of the *Ittenbach*, and the pennant number *L37* painted on its grey side was as tall as their entire hull. If that wasn't threatening enough, a second warship, a longer, slimmer and more heavily armed beast, cut a distant perimeter around them at a seemingly unfeasible speed. At the stern of both vessels flew the same flag – a red cross on a white background, and an unmistakable British flag in its corner.

The voice, speaking in German with an English accent through a megaphone, was clearer.

"...and heave to for inspection."

From the bridge above them, a loudspeaker crackled and the captain's voice answered in French.

"We don't understand you. This is the merchant vessel, *Frère Jacques II*, from Marseille, flying the ensign of the Free French Merchant Navy...*vive de Gaulle!*"

Sarah noticed the freshly painted shelters on the deck, the new holes and shapes cut into the superstructure where the metal still smoked and glowed. There was even a second funnel shape built of canvas and wood. But it hadn't been enough to change their silhouette.

"*Dormez-vous? Dormez-vous?*" the distant voice mocked in French before switching back to German. "We repeat: you are the *Ittenbach*, from Hamburg, flying a French flag, like a commerce raider. You are ordered to heave to and submit to inspection."

"You want to board us?" the voice from the bridge continued in French.

The aft gun of the warship lit up as a ball of flame erupted from it. The concussive *thud* followed just after, and again a whining roar passed over them. Most of the passengers threw themselves to the deck. The shell impacted the water seconds later, many hundreds of metres away.

"No more games, *Ittenbach*. We are only talking because you have a large number of passengers, and we will take them aboard, along with your crew… *You might want to go down with your ship. That's up to you.*"

The last two sentences were delivered in English, as if the translator had forgotten to turn off his megaphone. Sarah wondered if the *Ittenbach*'s captain understood.

The second warship had made a tight turn and was swiftly romping through the waves towards the German ship, driving up a vast bow wave that would have swamped the smaller vessel.

A white flag was swiftly hoisted on the *Ittenbach*, as if it had been ready all along. Its captain was now shouting rapid orders from the bridge. The ship began to shudder as it slowed. Some passengers stood open-mouthed and confused. Others began to run for their baggage, and an alert few began demanding life jackets.

"Well, you wanted to go to England…" Sarah turned to Lisbeth and laughed. "This couldn't be better. We need to get the samples from your father *now*—"

"*Meine Damen*, how did you…why are you on deck?"

They looked around to see Hasse standing between them and the ladder.

Sarah struggled with the urge to attack him, to belittle him, to fight him.

"So what are your plans now, *Obersturmbannführer*? What are your orders?" she added obsequiously, so the first question couldn't be construed as rhetorical or mocking.

She was tired and the roll of the deck was worse, now the ship was slowing. She didn't have a plan and knew that giving him the initiative was probably a mistake, but she needed time to think. In Hasse's eyes, she could see the same dilemma.

"Dr Fischer, please help your father with his *luggage*. I would also advise finding some life jackets...there won't be enough to go around." He took a step to one side so she could pass him.

Lisbeth paused and then walked to the ladder. Sarah went to join her, but Hasse moved back to block her path.

"You, *Fräulein*, I need you for something."

Sarah looked at Lisbeth, who had paused at the top of the hatch. Other passengers were pushing past her. She looked disorientated, uncertain, even helpless.

Sarah nodded. *Go on.*

It was to be now.

CHAPTER THIRTY-SIX

THE DOOR OF THE STOREROOM swung open and Hasse pushed Sarah through it. One of the crew was inside gathering life jackets, and he looked up from his work. The SS officer pulled out a revolver and pointed it at the man.

"Out," he ordered.

The South Asian man – the sailors would call him a lascar – was surprised, but he didn't flinch. He picked up the remaining vests and made for the door. As he passed, he handed one to Sarah and then pointedly ignored Hasse on his way out.

Sarah looked around. There was no exit and no weapons. She dropped the heavy canvas vest over her shoulders. It was too long, too large and uncomfortable, so she worked at her clothes as she tried to make it fit.

Hasse closed the door. He placed the gun on a nearby shelf and began to empty his pockets next to it.

"You did very well, very well indeed. In fact I have a new

respect for the *Abwehr*, but I'm not convinced that you're infected at all."

"Well, we're not going to America any more so that isn't a problem," Sarah replied, not looking up.

"There's certainly been a change of plan and, I have to admit, I'm making this up as I go along. But I think you do need to contract this disease."

Hasse pulled on a pair of rubber gloves and fiddled with something that Sarah couldn't see as he continued to talk.

"A British sloop picks up refugees in Africa. One of them, a lovely, innocent-looking little girl, gets sick. That doesn't sound like a germ-warfare attack, just bad luck. One of the downsides of a global empire."

"Sounds like a workable plan. Very good work at short notice," Sarah said, still fiddling with her skirt as if she wasn't really listening.

"Thank you," Hasse replied, smiling as he lifted the syringe from the shelf.

"But I'll just throw myself overboard," Sarah declared, still readjusting her life jacket.

"No you won't. Your survival instincts are too strong. You'll go down fighting."

"Maybe," Sarah muttered. "Out of interest, why didn't you just infect Clementine?"

"Much easier to have a sick European on a ship. Easier to keep them isolated. No, a sick *Neger* would have been stuck on a mess deck, infecting the crew. They might even have thrown her overboard. Besides, I grew very fond of her."

"Like a pet," Sarah sneered.

"Yes. *Untermenschen* can be cunning, clever, and it's dangerous to underestimate them. But they will always be less than human."

He took a step towards her—

"Typical Nazi *Quatsch*," Sarah hissed. "Oh, they're dangerously smart, but they're only animals. They're dirty, lazy and shiftless, but they've still taken all the money. They're Bolsheviks, but somehow they're capitalists, too. Do you hear yourselves?"

He stopped and put his empty hand to his forehead.

"*Goodness gracious*," Hasse exclaimed in English. "You're not *Abwehr* at all, are you? I'm such a fool. You're British?"

"No, I'm a *German*," she snapped, taking a step back and planting her legs apart. She began to recite. "*Rising like vengeance…I am the last true German and my last act will be to destroy all that is within my power to destroy, kill all those it is within my power to kill, and finding myself in hell, deliver you to the devil myself.*"

"Nice speech," Hasse mocked.

"And I'm *Jewish*. You're going to be defeated by a *Jew*."

His eyebrows raised, but he didn't look perturbed. "Defeated? I'm afraid not," he said, taking another step.

Sarah drew her hand from behind her back. It had taken longer than she expected to pull Claude's Beretta from her sanitary belt, but it had finally come free and she didn't need to keep talking.

She tried to straighten her arm, to hold it in two hands, but the life jacket was getting in the way.

Hasse looked at the gun and back to the shelf, where his

revolver sat, just out of reach. Sarah was three metres away, out of grabbing distance. For the first time since the Ju 52 had crashed into the sea, he seemed uneasy. Then a second passed and Sarah hadn't fired. A new confidence lit up his face.

Do it, Sarah screamed to herself. *Do it now.*

The safeties!

Click. Click.

"Have you ever fired one of those? Have you ever actually killed someone? Can you even work that?"

Now.

Do it NOW.

Sarah pulled the trigger. There was a slapping crack and an instantaneous burst of sparks. A shell casing spun up and away. The top of the gun had shot back and torn a wound in Sarah's hand.

Hasse still stood.

He *laughed* and lunged.

Sarah closed her eyes, leaned into the recoil and pulled the trigger again and again and again.

He crashed to the floor at her feet, the syringe landing needle first into the planking.

Sarah bent over, shoving the life jacket out of the way, and pushed the shaking gun into the back of his head. She prodded him once, twice, but her finger had frozen round the trigger. She wanted to make sure, to finish it, but now the heat of the action was ebbing away.

She took a step back, but his blood had already splattered onto her shoes.

She started to hyperventilate and a shivering overtook her body.

She was no longer alone in the room. Behind her the ghosts gathered. Foch with his open throat, Elsa in her restraints, Stern with blistered and charred skin, the SS guards with bleeding gums and no hair...they crowded around the corpse. Even the Mouse was there, shaking her head sadly.

Tell yourself what you need to, meine Schlafsaalführerin, she seemed to whisper.

There was a rattle of chains and a series of thuds through the hull. The boats were being lowered.

Don't just stand there.

Hiding the pistol back where she had stored it, she snapped the needle from the syringe and, trying not to think what was inside it, retrieved the test tube of dark liquid from the shelf. All that horror, all that pain, a weapon of unspeakable power and ferocity, just sitting in her hand, separated by her middle finger.

She tried to take the revolver, but it was too heavy and she had nowhere to put it, so she tossed it into the shadows.

The door opened easily, but when she tried to close it behind her, she couldn't make it work. She turned the wheel and moved the battens, but the door kept opening.

The crewman appeared next to her, still holding the life jackets. Sarah started and stood back. He seemed only around thirty years old, but he had the same resentful resignation that she had seen in Samuel's eyes.

He looked at her shoes and stockings, speckled with blood and then at her face. She opened her mouth to speak.

He pushed the heavy door closed and worked the mechanism so that it locked, battening it shut.

"*Verfluchte Nazis.*" He snorted and walked away.

She threw the syringe and test tube as high and far as she could. For a moment it seemed as if the wind and motion of the ship might carry them back on board, but they hit the water ten metres away with a splash soon lost in the foam. They were gone. *One down… How many more are there?*

She turned to the other rail, where members of the crew were waving to her. The two British warships loomed over the merchant. One waiting, one prowling, alert to the least suggestion of impropriety from the German ship.

Both lifeboats were in the water and extremely crowded. One was already pulling away, the crew managing strong oar strokes despite the swell. Sarah could see Bofinger, sitting miserably in its bow, wrapped in a blanket and an ill-fitting life jacket.

Below Lisbeth had been scanning the rail frantically and then spotted Sarah. She stood up, nearly upsetting the boat, an expression of surprise, fear and finally joy crossing her face as she saw that Sarah was alone. She began waving frantically to her.

"Down you go, *Fräulein,*" said one of the sailors, neatly lifting her over the rail and onto the scramble nets. "Be careful now."

Clambering down the net as the ship rolled and shivered and swung from side to side would have been terrifying, but Sarah was overwhelmed by what she had just done. Her brain was replaying the final seconds over and again. Simultaneously, she had a sense of both shame and satisfaction, and the two were incompatible. She dropped into the boat, helped by multiple hands.

She fought them off, forced herself past two people and was in Lisbeth's arms.

"The samples, Hasse had the samples. Is that it?" Sarah said breathlessly.

"He has samples?"

"He *had* samples..."

Lisbeth paused, watching Sarah's face, closed her eyes and screwed up her face. Then she smiled. "Good...don't let it make you hard... I didn't know he had any! How did he do that?"

"Clementine, Klodt...doesn't matter now. Are there more?"

Lisbeth nodded.

"Did you get them or does your father still have them?" Sarah pressed.

The crew pushed away from the ship with their oars, and the boat rose on the crest of the waves before falling into a trough. The passengers gave a yelping groan as they seized the sides and one another.

"Don't worry! It's all over now. Isn't this amazing? We're going to England, just like we said we would."

"We have to get rid of all of it, we can't let the British have this either."

"My father won't give them to the British," she said, shaking her head.

"Are you sure? He just wants to be acknowledged. He isn't a Nazi, he's just a..."

"A bastard, yes." Lisbeth laughed. "He's still German. Britain is still the enemy. But we can sort all this out later." She gave Sarah a squeeze. "You did it!"

Sarah wasn't really listening. She was watching Bofinger's boat as the oarsmen battled with the rolling surf. Sarah wanted...no, Sarah *needed* this to be over, to finish the job. To destroy the last of the disease. To ensure that she had not *killed* a man for no reason.

He was going to kill you—

Because I put myself there. The British would have captured him anyway.

And maybe that crewman would now be sitting in this boat with a bloodstream full of disease...

Bofinger's boat seemed to be pulling further away. In fact, it seemed to be turning and heading in a completely different direction.

"Wait a minute, where are they going?" Sarah asked.

"What do you mean?" Lisbeth replied.

"They aren't going to the same ship!" Sarah cried, standing up.

"Settle down," shouted the man sitting next to them.

"Hey!" Sarah screamed, and pointed at the other boat. "Where are they going?"

"Sit down," someone else called.

Sarah looked around. It was their boat that was peeling away.

"Where are *we* going?" she howled.

The crewman at the tiller called out. "They want us on different ships, we're heading for the destroyer. Sit."

"No!" Sarah looked at the other boat, at Bofinger, still

clearly visible and at the pack in his lap.

"Ursula? What's wrong?" Lisbeth asked. "It's fine, we'll meet up—"

They could be sent to different places, dropped at different times. He could make it to Vichy territory, or Spain, back to Germany. She'd stopped nothing.

Sarah put her hands on Lisbeth's cheeks. "I'll see you again. I'll find you," she whispered.

"What?" Lisbeth managed.

Sarah stood, pushed past her and, before anyone could react, dived into the water.

CHAPTER THIRTY-SEVEN

SARAH THOUGHT SHE WAS READY for the shock. But she wasn't. It was cold. Colder than the Müggelsee as the sun was rising. Colder than the rain-filled ditches near Rothenstadt.

The life jacket stayed afloat and she sank inside it, swallowing a mouthful of salt water. Sarah had never swum in the sea before and her whole body revulsed at the moment, demanding that this caustic, thirst-inducing horror be expelled.

She tried to surface, but the life jacket was keeping her under and the more she thrashed the more lost in it she became. Then, just as the pressure in her chest was starting to make her panic, she pushed her head out of the green blur and took a raw lungful of cold air.

She spotted the other boat between the rollers and, ignoring the shouts and screams, she started to swim for it.

The life jacket stopped her arms from moving properly and the motion of the sea made every metre forward seem like ten lost sideways. The nausea, her body's rage at the stomachful of brine and the gathering sense that she had, on impulse, thrown away her life, all conspired to rob her of her strength and will.

The boat seemed further away than ever, then she lost sight of it. She lost sight of everything but the green and grey and foaming white that surrounded her, buffeted her and then broke over her face to sting her eyes. Again. And again. And—

The peeling white wooden fence hove into her view and arms, so many arms, slapped her and pinched her and gripped her, only to slide away again. Something tugged at her life jacket, insistently, before two thickset, bare arms reached under hers and hauled her up and out and over into the freezing wind.

Something dry was wrapped around her and stopped the ceaseless chill, but her shivering continued. She ignored the words and noises about her. Eventually, she could open her smarting eyes without them filling with tears. She feared that she would find herself back in the same boat, but looking about she couldn't see Lisbeth. She uncovered her head, immediately feeling the wind like knives on her wet hair, and leaned back and forth, looking for Bofinger.

"Hey, rest, child," grunted the tillerman, his German thick with an Italian accent. "We'll find your daddy."

"Not my daddy...a mass murderer," she said in Italian.

He chuckled and patted her shoulder. "They shouldn't have split everyone up like that."

She stood with difficulty and spotted the professor in the bow. She stumbled through the passengers to swearing, anger and protests. There was no aisle, just benches to scramble over and people to push out of the way. At one point someone grabbed her, and she swung her arms at them until they let her go.

Finally, she squeezed past the last passengers and sank into the footwell in front of Bofinger. She was breathless and quivering, incapable of talking. She sat wrapped in the blanket, staring up at him for what seemed like an age.

He seemed not to see her at first, although he couldn't have missed her arrival. But he sat, staring at his pack. He hadn't shaved in some time and his moustache had lost its curl and consistency. It had grown ragged and wild. His eyes were dark and baggy. He looked paler, older, like a shadow of the former brusque, raging narcissist.

They sat in silence, as the boat approached the smaller warship.

He raised his head. "Why are you here?" he croaked.

From under her blanket, she replied. "You know why."

"I really don't."

"I want the samples," Sarah went on. "All of them. The weapon, the experiments, it all stops now."

He looked back to his pack. "Go away, little girl," he grunted.

Sarah tugged at something under the blanket for a long minute and then pushed the Beretta through the gap in the blanket.

"Give me the samples, or I'll shoot you and throw the whole pack overboard."

Bofinger looked up again and started to laugh, a slow, coughing cackle, like a rusty gear turning and slipping.

"She fooled you as well…" he managed between wheezes. "And I thought you of all people might see through her."

"What are you talking about?"

"But then she worked hard on you, really hard."

Sarah pushed the blanket off her head, shaking her head in small quivers. "Worked hard…*on-n-n m-m-me*," she managed as her breathing grew shallow and frenetic.

"Lots of caring and compassion and *motherly* attention, just what you needed," he sneered. "Everything that fools the stupid natives and hoodwinked her team down the years."

"*Give me the samples,*" she snapped.

"I don't *have* the samples, stupid girl. My stepdaughter has the live virus."

"No." Sarah was shaking now. "She said…she said…"

"What did she say? *Exactly* what did she say?"

Sarah thought back. Had she actually stated that her father had the virus? What was it she had said?

Not my *samples—*

My father won't give them to the British.

Don't worry! It's all over now.

"She doesn't *lie*, you see," Bofinger continued. "She implies things and you think she's said something. But she hasn't. It's a rare gift."

Sarah felt she was sitting on a block of ice, and her very presence was making it melt under her. "The Bateke in the cage, that was you—"

"That was one of her staff, and when she found out she was *delighted*. It saved the whole project."

"She said…" Sarah said, tailing off.

I swear that when we left the village I had no idea. I sent Klodt to...put him out of his misery as soon as I possibly could.

It was an appalling thing that they did, but by the time I knew it was already too late.

Everything began to dissolve around Sarah.

"They said she was an angel..." she whined.

"She long since persuaded them that the things she did were necessary, even a blessing... Fools. This was her team, her minions, her followers. Provoking me, making me bitter and angry...*see, he's mad, that one*, she'd say. *He's the evil one.*"

"She asked us to get her to England..." Sarah tried again, holding on to a belief turning liquid in her hands.

"And so she would. She spotted you two, not quite what you seemed, took a guess, and bullseye!" He clicked his fingers. "She was so miserable when France fell, that they'd collapsed before she could enact her revenge, for what they did to Germany, for causing the poverty and the smallpox outbreak, for what they did to her and her mother. But Britain and the United States...she can still punish them. They're all ready for her to infect."

People do horrific things for money. Or revenge.

I think we'll see that the French got off lightly.

"She fought Hasse every step of the way," Sarah insisted, shaking her head. She was already sliding away to the edge of the precipice, the ground sucking away like water through a plughole.

"Did she? She didn't want to end up back in Germany, but she certainly took advantage of his arrival. *Oh, little girl, take me to England and freedom!*" he mocked.

"Where would she have kept samples?" Sarah said, trying to make it sound defiant.

"She's been holding it in her hands the whole time. Didn't you notice how she fiddles with it, protects it, keeps it at body temperature? That necklace is hollow."

Sarah looked round at the other lifeboat. She couldn't make out any of the individual passengers now.

"And *the White Devil*?" Sarah said quietly. She looked at her fingers that had touched Lisbeth's cheeks, at the creamy, oily residue of her make-up that was still present, even after being in the water.

He handed it to Sarah, who stared into the demonic glass eyes, seeing herself there. The helmet was oily and left a cream residue on her hands.

It's not my father, I promise you that.

Sarah fell into a pit that stretched away into the fetid darkness.

She didn't need his answer. Lisbeth was the White Devil.

Without the cathedral of belief that she had built around Lisbeth, in praise of those apparently loving arms, Sarah could see everything the way it was. Lisbeth had tried to stop Bofinger's stories only because his prejudice, his disgust, betrayed them both. She had no use for the politics when her hatred was so pure. *Politics…just causes trouble, doesn't it?* she had said. She was upset about them reusing the needles, about the shooting of the villager, because it got in the way of the science, the research, of her mission. Her revenge. Her two graves.

But that would take someone who was very driven, who could murder hundreds of natives to get what they wanted and not worry about it.

Lisbeth was that person. *The grown-up making the hard decisions* and *the children* dying because they had to.

And Sarah had helped her.

The other ship disappeared behind their destination as they drew up to its side, but it was already too far away for her to do anything about Lisbeth. The grey hull threw everything into shadow, and the air grew colder.

"Welcome to HMS *Godalming*," called a voice as the scramble nets were lowered. Sarah sat in the bow and watched the others clamber aboard. She was too exhausted, too disgusted and too defeated to move. She was the last passenger to leave and only then with the help of the crew.

"There's my little channel swimmer! Did you find your mummy?" one sailor chirped as he pulled Sarah over the rail.

"I need to speak to your captain," Sarah answered in English.

He was a little surprised that she understood him but continued genially. "Yep, all in good time, *Frow-line*. First we'll sort you some dry clothes and—"

"*Now*, I need to see him right now," she interrupted.

The sailor grinned and turned to his crewmate. "Here, got a live one. This little Kraut sounds like a duchess and she's got an attitude to match."

"I've information vital to the war effort."

The sailors began to laugh and turned away to help the lifeboat's crew aboard.

Along the deck Bofinger stood watching her, with something approaching pity. It was all Sarah could do not to take out the Beretta and shoot him. All she had left was loathing and rage, but she didn't have the energy to use either.

CHAPTER THIRTY-EIGHT

THE BRITISH SANK THE *ITTENBACH*. It was too small to be useful. Sarah watched, refusing to go below until it was done. The guns of both ships pounded away, putting holes in the hull with a puff of black smoke and sparks, until they hit the fuel tanks. There was a very small *whomp* and a ball of orange fire before a pall of smoke hid the tear in the keel. Almost imperceptibly the vessel listed and very, very slowly began to disappear under the waves.

Sarah's ship, HMS *Godalming*, was already underway before a far-off crash of bubbles signalled the *Ittenbach*'s final dive, and Sarah's handiwork – her crime – was hidden for ever.

The warship, a "*Shoreham*-class sloop" according to a chatty sailor greeting the new passengers, put distance between them and the coast. The landscape of the South Atlantic drifted past in all its writhing, graceful restlessness. The motion was, for Sarah, just about bearable, if she stayed on deck where the wind refreshed and chilled her warm brow.

The destroyer, which an officer had called HMS *Virulent*, romped to and fro, like an excitable dog circling its slower human.

Aboard that destroyer was a monster. A beast who would now travel to a country of almost fifty million people in order to make fifty million corpses, if she could. Sarah wanted that to be why she was so angry, why her impotent rage tore away at her insides with dirty claws. But that would have been a comforting lie. Sarah wanted Lisbeth stopped, *destroyed*, because Lisbeth had tricked her into caring, into loving. Her gullibility and culpability just made the loathing stronger.

Worse still was the very real possibility that Lisbeth thought that Sarah was part of what she did. That Sarah would eventually approve of her mass-murders, in return for her comforting arms.

She had to be ended, one way or another.

Sarah tried again with a young sub-lieutenant, who promised to bring the information to the captain's attention, but Sarah could see another comforting lie when it was told. He was more concerned by how wet she was, and she was quickly bundled below by a petty officer who had been ordered not to take no for an answer.

She considered telling them her mother was on the destroyer, but the message would likely be the same. *Wait until we dock.* Everyone was far too busy until then.

Finally, in oversized trousers, a sweater and sea boots that fell off if she tried to walk in them, Sarah sat against a sweating bulkhead on the seaman's mess-deck, which was crowded with the *Ittenbach*'s passengers. Having allowed them to give her bitter cocoa and something they called a *corned-beef sandwich*, whose bland, lardy stodginess was oddly satisfying, she couldn't push the fatigue away any more. She rested her head on her cork life jacket and, even though her brain continued to cycle through its reverie of failure and self-loathing, her body shut down.

So deeply was she sleeping that she didn't hear the explosion, the tearing of metal and the rush of water. It was the alarm bell that brought her to, a shrieking, painful ringing, so intense it could not be ignored. As she opened her eyes the floor tipped and she started to slide on the moist planking.

She sat up and dug her heels down, just enough to fight the gradient and struggle into her life jacket. She blinked to clear the sleep from her eyes. The room was dark, lit only by a faint green light, making it hard to see through the swinging hammocks and moving shadows. Disorientated and too confused to be truly frightened yet, she noticed that part of the alarm seemed to consist of an unsettling screaming sound.

The floor steepened with a lurch and the noise of groaning steel. The room's shapes heaved to one side and some kept falling. Sarah slipped further down the slope, but her borrowed boots were good and gave her enough friction, even as she was hit by a series of heavy loose objects, to bring herself to a stop. Something rushed past, shrieking as it went. Sarah watched the refugee hit the water that roiled under her feet and disappear into the green froth. The only lights that still burned in the room were now deep under its surface.

The screaming was not part of the alarm. It came from everywhere. From everyone.

Sarah was awake now.

She rolled onto all fours, so her back was to the rising flood, and she crawled up the steepening deck, one hand, one foot at a time, using the pipework, struts and rivets of the bulkhead.

It's just a tree. It's just a tree. Climb it.

She concentrated on the upward movement, trying not to think of the next phase of her escape. There were more cries behind her as the sound of water became the noise of a rushing river.

Don't look.

She glanced behind her to see the water level bubbling up to her heels. Arms and howling faces thrashed about in it as crates and canvas swirled around them.

She reached the top and, clinging to the pipework on the bulkhead in front of her, she shuffled to her feet. The closed door to the mess deck was two and a half metres away to her right. The wall in between was so smooth and the deck now so steep that the only way to reach it was to jump.

Sarah closed her eyes. A few months ago this would have posed no problem for her, but she felt the weakness of her limbs, the illness having sapped her strength. Worst of all was the sense of failure, of utter uselessness and inadequacy that clung to her like weights hung on a horse.

She looked down into the water. Someone was floating face down in the foam, and a woman clung to them like a raft.

Do this, or die here. Commit to the move.

There was no run-up. She couldn't even manage a proper

swing from her perch. All the power came from her legs and required her boots to keep their purchase on the moist and tilted deck.

Sarah flew.

Her arm wrapped around the handwheel of the watertight hatch. Her body weight dragged her down the slope until her elbow caught and held. The pain in that joint was almost unbearable, especially when Sarah swung her other arm to hold on to it. She gritted her teeth and hung on. *Just a tree. Just a tree. You've done this before.*

One sea boot slid away into the rising water.

She was holding the door, feet dangling against the tipping deck.

Breathe.

She pulled her booted leg up and under her to make a right-angle with the deck planks, putting all her weight into the textured sole. It held. She turned the handwheel in a series of jerking motions, too afraid to let go of it for more than a second as she fed it through her hands.

With a *thunk* the door opened, causing Sarah to lose her footing entirely. Clinging on to the handwheel, she swung away from the floor with the hatch to dangle over the water below.

Hand by hand, she dragged herself back to the edge of the door and threw an arm around it, her bare toes finding a batten to use as a foothold. She pushed on it and it held.

Then as she straddled the door, it began to swing back, and she rode the steel hatch to the door frame. The frame smacked into her head and shoulder like someone had swung a bat at her, but she used the moment to grab the edge. She finally scrambled into the corridor beyond, where red lights lit a ladder running upwards.

She looked back at the mess deck where the water was rising fast. There were several people alive in the water and clambering on the spinning debris, but the tilt in the deck meant they had no chance of reaching the hatch. If she had a rope—

A hand grabbed her shoulder and dragged her away. The sailor leaned into the room and pulled the door closed, spinning the wheel to seal it.

"There are people in there," Sarah gasped in English.

"And more up here who need time to get to the boats," he said firmly, mounting the ladder.

Sarah could still hear the screaming from inside.

CHAPTER THIRTY-NINE

"WHAT HAPPENED?" SARAH DEMANDED, as they climbed.

"Torpedo, right in the guts. We're practically broken in two. Move it now," he said with more urgency.

They finally emerged into the open air.

A bright white star was dropping from the night sky, bathing everything with an eerie pale green glow.

It was as if a giant child had bent his toy in half. Below Sarah, at the bottom of the sloping deck, the sea bubbled and frothed, claiming the centre of the ship and everything inside it. The stern emerged on the other side of the water, cracked and bleeding black oil, spouting steam and smoke from every hatch and vent. Everything stank of gasoline and burning wood.

Above Sarah on the rising peak of the bow swarmed the crew of *Godalming*, desperately working on the lifeboats. With every degree of list, the job grew more difficult and their anxiety became more apparent. The civilians were getting in the way in their panic, and a sub-lieutenant was yelling orders at them in a language they didn't understand.

Virulent steamed away in the distance and in her wake, vast plumes of water shot into the sky. The noise of the explosions rumbled in a few seconds later.

Ba-boom. Ba-boom.

Sarah gripped the rail and began the climb up to the boats when she noticed a figure hunched next to a ventilation cowl. It looked at her as she stopped.

"Ironic, isn't it, girl? You being on a British ship and then being sunk by a German U-boat," Bofinger cackled.

"That's not *irony*," Sarah sneered. "At best, it's *tragic coincidence*."

"Really? A spy being undone by anything as underhand as a submarine, after being deceived by those she sought to deceive?"

The ship groaned and the deck tilted again. The hatches of the stern spat sparks into the night, and the vents emitted a red dancing glow. The section heaved and the whole ship shuddered.

One of the lifeboats, just prised from its chocks, swung wildly from the davits and tore free from its manila-rope falls. It hit the deck on its way down, ripping the rail to shreds and crushing several sailors like snails underfoot. The wooden boat, dead men, tackle, cables and rail clattered down the side of the hull and hit the water.

The star shell hit the water and the glow faded.

Bofinger sighed. "But I don't blame you for not stopping her…I lived with her for thirty years and I couldn't stop her."

"She didn't stand a chance, having you as a father."

"I didn't make her the devil – the British and French did that. You know she won't stop if she gets to Britain, don't you? She'll travel to every city, every slum, and they're all going to die."

Sarah did not lack for imagination. She watched it happen in her mind's eye. She knew the poor would catch the disease and spread it quickly and that no one would care until it was too late. Just as the mission had cut a murderous swathe through Central Africa and hardly anyone had noticed.

But Bofinger would have happily helped Hasse exterminate the Slavs, a distinction that Sarah couldn't accept, or fathom.

The stern of *Godalming* caught fire. It spread to the leaking oil like spilled milk across a tiled floor. It danced across the waves. There were more shouts, cries and now screams from above them.

"You need to go down with this ship," Sarah whispered. "I'm not going to kill you, but you don't get to live."

The coldness of the thought process chilled Sarah to her core. Like she had walked into the snow barefoot. Not that she wanted him dead, but that she didn't care either way. She had no compassion left to spend.

"How about I take my chances in the water? Looks like that's what everyone is going to be doing anyway."

There was a life jacket at his feet. He hadn't tried to put it on.

Sarah bent down and picked it up. He didn't complain as she heaved it over the rail into the darkness. She watched it vanish.

"Goodbye, Ursula, Élodie, whatever your name really is," he grunted behind her.

Sarah turned at the rail.

"My name is Sarah Goldstein, Germany's misfortune...and yours."

Sarah saw the light and felt the wave of heat before she heard anything. The blast picked her up like a rag doll as the concussion and shockwave smacked into her.

She was unconscious before she hit the water.

She dreamed she saw a black ship turn on its end and slide into the dark sea, surrounded by little red lights that bobbed in the surf. The animal noises that accompanied it were distant and alien.

The red lights blinked and disappeared and sprang back to life, like the fireflies Sarah had once seen in the countryside.

She dreamed that the sea was filled with little boats and shouting men, but whenever she moved to look at them, they slipped away and vanished, leaves on a winter tree.

She dreamed she was warm, in a cocoon of cotton and silk, that she was being licked by a friendly dog with a salty tongue.

The ceiling of the room brightened but it was a dull, uniform grey. Sarah was bored with grey, it was *everywhere*. She rolled over so she didn't have to look at it—

Her face pulled out of the water, eyes stinging, spitting and coughing. Her teeth began to chatter and she couldn't stop them. She looked right and left, and all she could see was rolling waves and blank sky.

She tried to turn and swim, but the movement made the next wave break over her. She surfaced and coughed. The next wave hit. *Cough. Spit. Wave. Cough. Spit. Wave—*

She stopped struggling, closed her eyes and tried to relax. After a few seconds her body, buoyed by the life jacket, began to float up and over the rollers.

How long had it been? The torpedo had hit in the dead of night. Now it was bright daylight, so…hours. *Four hours? At least* four hours.

She looked round, trying to see the horizon. There was some debris. Wood, rope, clothes. The smell of oil remained along with the salted, rotting scent of ocean. No ships.

No ships.

Her tongue moved like sandpaper inside her mouth, her throat raw from swallowed seawater. Her lips smarted as the salt water burrowed into the cracks—

Stop thinking about these things. There is nothing *you can do about it.*

I need to vomit.

No you don't.

She rose and fell. Rose—

She felt the tickle of saliva in the back of her mouth.

Up and down. Up—

She threw up, getting most of it over the neck of the life jacket, but not all. The sandwich was so digested that it was sour mush and bile, but she knew she couldn't afford to lose any of it.

Stop thinking about the here and now.

How? I'm going to die—

Close your eyes for a moment. What can you hear?

The low roar of waves, pulsing, the inhaling and exhaling of something so big it couldn't be seen or understood. Her chin on the oiled canvas of the life preserver, the scratching of her ears. But there was, far away, familiar noise.

Ba-boom. Ba-boom.

She was not alone.

Sarah clung to this like it was a life raft.

I don't deserve to be rescued.

Shush now.

She was cold. So cold that she felt...warm. Like a fire dancing over her skin. Her fingers could barely move and had formed claws, incapable of holding on to the woollen sleeves she'd pulled down over them. She began to move her arms to break their stiffness. She sensed this was important. She tried to move her legs, but they barely responded.

Sarah relived the moment when Hasse lunged towards her with the syringe, feeling the gun kick in her hand. Self-defence. Then she saw herself lean down to fire the gun into his head. Had she wanted to make sure? Or had that been something hotter, more angry? Less necessary. More needful.

Who, or what, had she become? A little monster. A little monster in a different service.

CHAPTER FORTY

10TH NOVEMBER 1940

SARAH FELT THAT IF SHE WAS TO LIVE, she had to *want to*. But she also knew that *wanting* wasn't going to be enough.

Sarah waited to die.

But she didn't, and soon she grew bored.

She tried to figure out how many people she had killed.

Stern. If she hadn't set fire to the lab and lied about it, he wouldn't have gone into the fire to find Schäfer.

The guards of the Schäfer estate. They were dying of a mystery disease, the after-effects of Schäfer's super-bomb that she had detonated. The car she sent to the house...they must have died immediately in the explosion. Ten?

Foch. She had held him while the Captain slit his throat from ear to ear. Definitely.

The Bateke boy who had fled after she discovered the reused syringes.

Lieutenant La Roux and his men, whom she had talked into leaving, straight into Hasse's ambush.

Hasse. Bleeding onto her shoes.

How many of those had deserved it?

Self-defence. Necessity. This was how Bofinger and Hasse rationalized their decisions.

And what of the people whom Lisbeth would slaughter because of Sarah's blindness and stupidity?

Well, thought Sarah. *I am being punished now. Like any good Jew, in hell, in the here and now.* Was that better or worse than Dante's inferno? She was cold, colder than she had ever been, so maybe she was a traitor after all, in the lowest level of hell, frozen in the ice up to her neck.

She hadn't killed Clementine. She was still out there somewhere. Clementine was a survivor. She *wanted* to live.

But she had forgotten a death. Her first murder.

Her mother.

If her mother hadn't had a constant reminder of her lost love, would she have drowned herself in alcohol? Would she have sobered up and driven to Friedrichshafen if Sarah hadn't demanded she do something? Would she have ploughed through that roadblock if Sarah hadn't been there to protect?

She could add her mother to that list.

"Ick heff mol een Hamborger Veermaster sehn..."

Sarah hummed to herself, an old shanty that she'd heard some builders singing once across the road from her house. The language was Low German and English and this had fascinated the young Sarah, who'd leaned on the window sill, chin in hands, listening and learning.

"To my hoo...day!" she whispered rocking her head from side to side. "Her masts were as crooked as the skipper's legs...

to my hoo-day, hoo-day, ho, ho, ho, ho..."

Singing the next line in front of her mother had got Sarah a slap that had made her ears ring. She giggled and, hurting her throat, shouted it to the ocean.

"The galley was full of lice, *SCHIET* SAT ON THE SHELVES...the biscuits walked away, all by themselves...to my hoo-day, hoo-day, ho, ho, ho, ho..."

She giggled to herself.

She couldn't think of the next line.

The Schnapps was only there at Christmas Eve. That was it, the next bit.

Sarah stopped. She never wanted to think about that *gottverdammte* Christian holiday again...Schäfer, silk dresses and champagne. Gifts that were traps, a night-time visit that had left blood over the walls. She heaved, but she couldn't even find the bile to spit out.

She bobbed up and down in silence, listening to the water, the restlessness that never ended.

She threw her head back and screamed. "I...once...saw...a...Hamburg Veermaster...to my HOO-DAY."

The water listened.

Sarah dozed, not quite sleeping, so she failed to notice the growing gloom, until she realized she couldn't see the horizon. The sky was still clouded and, in a room the size of a planet, Sarah started to feel confined.

She had survived a whole day. The thirst went from desire to a draining sensation in her shoulders and cheeks. Now it sat in her head, a constant throbbing in her skull. However, the pain's very insistence made it perversely easy to forget... to drift away.

Sarah jerked awake. She was actually a little disappointed to find herself still alive. The sky had been leached of all colour. She closed her eyes again, but sleep wouldn't come.

She floated in darkness. No stars, no moon. No green glow, no white foam. Just the hissing growl of the water, the sensation of rocking, the taste of salt and a black cowl that didn't end.

She watched the first circling light in confusion, its glowing trail hanging in the air and fading slowly. She was not asleep and felt the cold water lapping at her all around. Then the iridescent line grew buds, leaves and finally flowers above a meadow that stretched off to the edge of the light blue sky.

A hare hopped into view. It stopped and cleaned its head with its forepaws, before being joined by two others. They fed on the grass.

There was someone walking towards her. Someone whose footsteps sprouted red flowers as the grass sprang back from her touch.

Sarah knew who it was before she could make them out. She had seen that walk, the stride of someone utterly at ease with themselves. This was the woman of Sarah's early years, before the bitterness and sadness had got their claws into her.

The woman came into focus.

"Hello, *Mutti*," Sarah managed, her voice little more than a croak.

"Oh, *Sarahchen*, my princess." Her mother sighed, a wide, warm and *genuine* smile crossing her face.

Sarah reached out to her but found her arms were underwater. The meadow flickered so Sarah remained still.

"I'm in trouble, *Mutti*."

"I shouldn't have left you, I'm sorry."

"I don't know what to do."

"That's all right, we'll do it together."

"I've done bad things."

"*That's my girl.*"

Sarah's mother was wearing the blood-flecked fur hat, which hadn't been there a moment earlier. Clouds rolled in over the blue sky.

A slow trickle of blood ran down the side of her face, a face older, more lined, a little crueller, less patient.

"Waiting is an art form, my darling." Her mother struck a theatrical pose. "You wait for your cue, but you don't just stand there and do nothing. You have to become that character, be that person who is listening. You wait with the impatience of someone with things to do, places to go, with words to say."

The hares began to run, around and around her, building up speed, and the clouds grew dark.

Ba-boom. Ba-boom.

"These are the lines delivered by your leading man. What is he saying? Why is he saying them?"

"Who—" Sarah said, shaking her head.

"*Himmel!* Who else is onstage?" her mother snapped.

The clouds lit up with lightning, briefly turning her mother into a silhouette.

"*A ship*, well done." Her mother continued, "The ship is talking to you. What is he telling you?"

Ba-boom. Ba-boom.

The noise was closer, louder, more urgent than it had been before.

"He's...looking for something?" Sarah asked.

"Yes!"

The hares took flight and spun in ever tightening circles around her mother, her face dripping with fresh red blood. The sky behind her lit up with forked lightning that remained and brightened until it hurt Sarah's eyes.

The hares froze mid-jump, three two-eared animals with just three ears in all. Her mother dissolved as the night sky turned to white, and the bow of the destroyer carved through the meadow, turning the grass over and into the silver ocean.

The warship, illuminated by the star shell it had fired, turned to port a hundred metres away. The wave it created in that small course correction was vast, revealing the weight and power of the monster roaring by. Sarah floated, unable to move for a few seconds, and then she began to wave her hands in the air. She tried to scream, but her throat couldn't make any noise.

It slid effortlessly by, apparently blind to the little girl floating in the artificial daylight.

The pennant number *D71* told Sarah that this ship was HMS *Virulent*. Lisbeth was just one hundred metres away.

CHAPTER FORTY-ONE

THEY EITHER DIDN'T SEE HER, or assumed she was wreckage from *Godalming*, because *Virulent* didn't stop or slow or aim a searchlight in her direction. Instead Sarah watched several barrel-like cylinders roll off the stern of the ship into the water.

Are those to help me?

The sea exploded behind the ship, a double *ba-boom* creating two huge circular mounds of white spray and at their hearts erupted two enormous fountains of dirty water. Sarah watched the sea between them bubble towards her like a wave on the shore.

It was like someone had dropped Sarah from a roof. The impact hit her submerged body, everywhere and equally, causing her heart to thump inside her chest. She sagged back into the life jacket, winded.

Killing fish?

Killing U-boats.

Virulent ploughed on, searchlights dancing around the

disturbed water. They would come back around and then they would find her. Better still, someone was already telling their captain about the girl in the water.

She could *see* the sailors aboard. The two men in the stern were working on the line of barrels there. How could they *not* have seen her?

"*Hei!*" she managed, but it came out like a cough.

The destroyer didn't turn. It just steamed on, its searchlights swinging out and away.

The star shell was almost spent, and the warship was leaving.

Sarah became panicky. Angry. She waved more frantically and found a tiny, hoarse and gravelly part of her voice.

"Come back here, you *Scheißkerle!*" she rasped at the retreating stern.

Sarah had been waiting for death, but to have been so close to rescue, to safety, even to continuing her mission and having it all torn away again was cruelty. It had made her want to live, and now she had to die all over again.

Virulent held its course.

"*Verpisst euch!*" she ranted huskily, tears running down her face. She kept swearing as if they might turn in disgust and see her. "*Leckt mich am Arsch...*"

She touched her cheek and put it to her lips. Like everything else, it was salty.

"I can't spare the water..." she moaned more quietly, but she wept anyway.

◆　　◆　　◆

The ship didn't leave entirely. It moved back and forth on the horizon, occasionally lit by its flares, bombing the ocean as it went. Sarah watched it like a dog might watch bacon being fried, and she just couldn't look away. Both *nah und fern*. She wanted to laugh, but all she managed was to bare her teeth and hiss.

The dawn brought nothing but light.

Sarah was tired now, past the exhaustion that stopped you sleeping into the realm of quiet softness that swallowed everything.

She wanted to close her eyes so she didn't have to see the blurry smudge prowling the edge of the earth any more.

Hei, wake up.

Leave me alone.

No, I didn't come back so you could just fade away like an old photograph.

Let me sleep.

No, because this time you won't wake up.

Good.

Dumme Schlampe. How dare you throw away your life?

I'm dying, Mutti.

No, Sarahchen, you're living.

You call this living?

Sarah thought about this. Her mother was right in one way. Floating alone in an ocean was as much living as being a doll. A darling. A diversion. An eavesdropper. A thief.

Certainly this was her at her least destructive. No one had

died or wound up in an institution because Sarah Goldstein was adrift in the South Atlantic.

Better that she wasn't around to hurt anyone, to make more catastrophic errors of judgement. Had she saved people? She struggled to *name* anyone.

Unless this *was* hell. Did she have more atoning to do?

Mutti? Are you God?

Her mother's laughter was long and uncontrolled.

It made Sarah smile for its unexpectedness. It had been a long time.

About twenty metres away, a piece of debris bobbed in the surf. It looked like a wooden pole sticking up into the air. At least Sarah assumed it was wood as it was floating.

It wasn't bobbing. It was still as the water rose and fell around it.

It vanished into the ocean.

Maybe it was a snake, Sarah wondered. A water snake. There were water snakes, definitely.

Do they eat people? she thought casually.

The snake rose again, nearer this time. It was black with a bulbous head. And it was turning. Sarah watched it with grim fascination. It didn't have scales, it was smooth and when its face appeared, there were no eyes, just a mouth.

It wasn't a mouth. It was a glass window.

The waves pushed Sarah around and she lost sight of it. She thrashed her arms and legs to regain her orientation, but she was weak now and it took a minute to make any headway. By the time she was facing the right way – the snake, the mouth, the window, whatever it was – was gone.

She would have chuckled to herself, but the best she could do was grunt. She was imagining things in daylight now.

The water grew rougher, swirling and bubbling, buffeting her more than usual. One wave hit her square in the face. If she wasn't able to float over the rollers, and she was too frail to swim through them, there was a real chance of her drowning, life jacket or no life jacket.

That's one way of settling things, she thought grimly.

The water fizzed around her, turning over like water in a saucepan. Sarah felt as if she was rising, being picked up by a giant hand. Something touched her foot, and this sent sparks of sensation up her numbed legs. The sea broke like the waves had reached the shore.

Then the ocean tipped itself over Sarah's head, a thundering, thudding, pummelling that threatened to sweep her away, but her feet now rested on a hard, rippled surface that pushed her up and out of the waterfall. She collapsed on something solid. She touched and gripped its edges with her clawed and wrinkled hands.

The sea parted and from them emerged a giant dark grey fish. A sleek shark of metal gratings, cables and bolted plates. It carried Sarah up and out and above the green surf with hissing growls and clunking groans.

She lay, suddenly unbearably heavy with her head propped up by her life jacket, and began to shiver uncontrollably, even as the men appeared from a hole in the beast's long snout and swarmed around her.

CHAPTER FORTY-TWO

11TH–13TH NOVEMBER 1940

SHE DRANK THE WATER and vomited. She drank more and vomited. Eventually, her quivering, blanket-wrapped body allowed some liquid into her stomach and she immediately began to feel less like a corpse and more like a sick person. Her hands and feet burned as they warmed, and she was running a fever, but this felt more like getting better than dying.

The radio operator, who was also the medic only because he had the key to the medicine cabinet, injected her with something that made the pain in her limbs and head go away. Sarah protested for a few moments, then she lost interest in arguing.

All the while, the *ba-boom* noises continued, and inside this steel tube the explosions sounded terrifyingly close and dangerous. Each concussion caused the hull to vibrate and everything not welded into place rattled where it hung. Sarah watched the radio operator as each whispered call came—

Wasserbombe im Wasser.

—and she saw his concern, his sliver of fear, before the crashing came. But then he just smiled and shrugged.

"Nowhere near us," he whispered. The inescapable implication being that a closer, more accurate attack would be louder and more destructive.

The captain's cabin was little more than a wooden closet with a mattress, but it was the best bunk on the boat, so they gave it to her. It also had a curtain, which meant that once she rehydrated, she could pee unseen into her bucket. The toilets were off limits when they were submerged, she was told. Besides, one still stored fresh food.

The smell of vomit and sewage in such close proximity was lost in a thick, nauseating funk of sweat and diesel oil that permeated the air like smoke, and Sarah was just too tired to care. She slept. A real, deep, dream-free and comfortable rest undisturbed by wakeful anxiety or confusion.

On waking, between warm sheets, she discovered a gift of dry clothes, an emptied waste bucket and a bowl of cold vegetable soup. She was famished.

The *Schiffskapitän* came to see her. He was absurdly young to be in charge, but everyone she'd met onboard so far was little more than a boy.

He was unshaven, like all the crew, but he also *looked* unwashed...and exhausted. Those unlined eyes were bloodshot and red-rimmed with dark smudges under them.

Like the radioman who had tended to her, he smelled of stale sweat, yeast and diesel, but contrarily he also smelled of cologne, a crisp, fresh scent of flowers and lemon. It was absurdly feminine.

He crouched next to the bunk. By this time Sarah was sitting up and dressed in her borrowed clothes. Someone on the crew was very small, because these were a much better fit than anything the Royal Navy had managed.

"How are you feeling?" he asked.

"Better...still alive, thanks to you," she said after a moment.

"No thanks necessary, I couldn't leave you there. Although you scared me, appearing in the periscope like that," he said with a chuckle. "You were aboard that *Shoreham*-class sloop?"

"A British ship? The...*Godalming*, yes..."

"But you're German? With a French passport?"

Sarah had forgotten she'd pushed her papers into the pocket of her borrowed trousers before falling asleep on the *Godalming*'s mess deck.

"It's...complicated. How did you know I was German?"

"You talk in your sleep."

Sarah shuddered. This was a dangerous habit of hers. She wondered what she might have revealed.

"How long have I been here?"

"Two days, just under."

"Is that British ship still there?"

"Yes, but we're losing them, so not long now," the *Schiffskapitän* continued.

Losing.

Sarah did not want to lose. She had not truly accepted defeat, not while there seemed hope of living. Even at the end of his nightmare, Ngobila had not surrendered.

"Losing the ship?" A pinprick of panic pierced Sarah's calm. It tore in two at the weakest point. "Let *Virulent* go? No..."

After the gently belly-tickling joy and the weightless relief of rescue, Sarah felt the responsibilities and anxieties crawling back to claim what had once been theirs.

"No," she said, sitting forward and putting a hand on his arm. "You have to...you *have to* sink them too."

How many people on that ship? What are you asking? The passengers alone—

She closed the door on the little girl and her protests, the one who agonized over each loss of life. It was easier this way but it was colder on the outside.

"Why? I mean, no—" he said in surprise.

"Because they're the enemy."

"Yes they are." He nodded. "A very dangerous enemy. Not one I need to sink."

"You sank *Godalming*."

"Yes, and that was a mistake. I wouldn't have attacked if I'd spotted the destroyer, too. Worst still, it had passengers, or prisoners, or whatever you are..." He leaned forward, too. "What are you?"

"As I said, it's complicated," was all Sarah could manage. She knew that word was tainted.

"Complicated, as in trying to give me orders?"

"You need to listen to me—" she cried, voice still hoarse.

"I don't have time for this." He stood.

The impossibility of what Sarah needed, the cooperation

required…it wasn't realistic. Sarah felt defeat. The surrender didn't bring her ease or comfort. Behind Sarah's eyes, those fifty million people waited, staring at her. The women had stopped in the streets, shopping bags in hand. The children stood, the football rolling away into the road. The cars were stationary, their drivers peering out through the windshields.

"We have to surface very soon," he continued. "There's way too much carbon dioxide in the atmosphere. You never know, maybe your British friends will see us… Get some rest, Élodie."

"Ursula, Ursula Haller," she corrected.

"*Oberleutnant* Jansen," he said, nodding to her.

He was about to pull the curtain back across the door, but stopped. "Who is *Sarah*?"

Sarah dropped the half-empty cup of water she had picked up. "I'm sorry, what?" she said, wiping away the water onto the deck.

"You kept saying 'Sarah is a dead girl' in your sleep."

"Uh, she's a friend – was a friend—"

"A *Jewish* friend…"

Lies will tie you up—

"Yes," Sarah said quietly.

"I had Jewish friends," he stated, very softly.

"Had?" Sarah couldn't help herself.

"Not allowed, now…is it?" He almost whispered it, a tone that made it impossible for her to infer anything.

The inside of the U-boat was less a vehicle and more a complex machine between whose components men squeezed themselves.

Even the deck was often little more than a mesh, as if the human parts deserved only the same utilitarian treatment as its other mechanisms.

The silence was eerie. It wasn't silence at all in the traditional sense, as there were creaks and clunks and bubbling as the hull shifted and even the noise of the sea above them could be made out. It was that the fifty odd men sat or lay or stood, without talking or walking or even moving if they could avoid it.

The silence was essential. She was told in no uncertain terms that there could be no noise, no shouting, no banging, no movement of metal on metal, nothing percussive, nothing mechanical. Sound was crucial. It carried through the water and told tales, gave away those who wished to hide, as it gave away those who hunted for them. One loud noise could draw a listening destroyer from many kilometres away.

She learned that there weren't even bunks for everyone, just those who were off duty, but the waiting – and everyone was waiting – meant there was little for the men to do but sleep, and wait to sleep.

Sarah grew restless and wanted to wander round more, but she repeatedly found herself in the way and was, as politely as possible, shepherded back to the captain's nook.

It was growing hot as well, stuffy in a way Africa had not been. Sarah found herself panting if she moved. This must be what the *Oberleutnant* had meant by *too much carbon dixoide* in the atmosphere. Many of the crew wore respirators or gasmasks as they slept or worked, anything to reduce their poisonous exhalations.

A meaty hand appeared through the curtain to the captain's

bunk and waved. Then it made a tilting palm-up gesture of enquiry.

"Come in," Sarah whispered.

A round man with a big smile pushed his head through the curtain. His hair was greying at the temples and unlike the *Schiffskapitän* he had earned a hundred lines on his face from a lifetime of laughter. He was by far the oldest man aboard, but even then he was just hitting middle-age. He also had that mix of sweat and perfume about him.

"The skipper thought you might be bored," he whispered, and shooed her to the back of the captain's bunk. He smoothed out the blanket and laid a thin card gameboard onto it, along with some tokens, which were chess pawns.

"*Sternhalma.*" Sarah smiled. The continued popularity of this game always made her chuckle, as the shape of the playing grid made a Star of David. "You really don't have to do this. I'm sure you're busy, Herr...?"

"Esser. I am off-duty, as we're not quite at *Gefechtsstationen*, when everyone's busy," he said, setting up the board. "A smelly friend has been in my bunk, and I have another so tired that he doesn't care, so everyone's happy."

"Surprised anyone can smell anything, over the...you know."

"*Gestank.*" He laughed, wrinkling his nose. "Yes, if you're not used to it, I can imagine it's very unpleasant. Here," he said, reaching into his top pocket and pulling out a small bottle of clear liquid with a green and gold label. It read, *Echt Kölnisch Wasser, No.4711.*

Sarah pulled the gold-and-red top off and inhaled. She smiled. "Oh, this is why the *Oberleutnant* smells like..."

"A brothel? Yes, we all smell like that. Except for the ones who choose to send it home and stink the place up instead."

Sarah sprinkled it liberally on the collar of her borrowed shirt.

The game began and the sailor immediately started to make mistakes. Sarah assumed that he was letting her win.

"Everyone's talking about you," he began.

"Are they? And what are they saying?"

"That you're lucky to be alive." He sighed. "Thirty-six hours in the water is one thing but being found floating in the sea alone...that's a real miracle. Sailors, particularly *U-Boot-Fahrer* are very superstitious. They think you're good luck." He winked. "And these children are glad they got to rescue someone. Doing your job in wartime is one thing, but leaving people in the water...gives no one any pleasure."

"You're not supposed to rescue anyone?"

"War Order number 154... *Do not rescue any men; do not take them along; and do not take care of any boats of the ship.* It's too dangerous, you see. Most *U-Boot-Fahrer* in the fleet are too young to have fought in the *Weltkrieg*, they have no idea that compassion gets you killed out here."

"But you fished me out?" Sarah asked, completing a series of triumphant hops with one of her pieces.

"We're only human, and the new *Oberleutnant* is *very* human," he said, smiling. Then the smile faded. He placed a finger on Sarah's arm. Not an invasion of her space, not an attack of any kind, but an unmissable signal to listen. "It was a real risk surfacing to get you with that destroyer out there. I hope you understand that."

Sarah nodded and he withdrew the finger.

"Now everyone thinks you've made them untouchable." He chuckled. "They're baying to get that destroyer." He took his turn and, without looking up, he continued. "And so are you apparently."

"Jansen said that?"

"No, but there's no such thing as a private conversation on a U-boat. What's so special about this *Virulent*?"

Sarah felt there was nothing to lose.

"There's a bad person on board. They have to be stopped."

"And what do little girls know of such things?" he murmured.

Mitgefangen, mitgehangen, thought Sarah. *Commit.*

"I'm twenty years old and an agent of the *Abwehr*."

He snorted and went to laugh, then he met Sarah's gaze and stopped dead. "And who is on the destroyer?"

"A defecting scientist. A mass-murderer. Bad news for the Reich."

Esser motioned to the board. "Why are you playing this game with me?"

"Because I *am* bored." She smiled...but realized that with the lie she had irreparably changed the dynamic of this relationship. The man was now uncomfortable, had made himself vulnerable to a woman, not a girl. There was a way of using that distinction, Sarah knew, but how that worked was beyond her.

"You're winning," he said, sitting back.

"No, I'm really not," Sarah said with a sigh.

CHAPTER FORTY-THREE

Sarah was feeling stronger, but she noticed that she was now panting like a dog even when she wasn't moving. She also developed a twitch in her eye. She was not alone in this. The crew was beginning to twitch too, as well as argue, and lose the thread of conversations, and those were the ones who didn't look like part of *Dornröschen*'s court after she had pricked her finger on the spindle.

Sarah entered the control room. She had found plans and manuals in the captain's closets, and now knew her way around, to a point. *A library tells you about the person*, she had always thought, and the *Oberleutnant*'s shelves revealed someone preoccupied, even anxious about the operation of his boat. The cheap novel he had brought was unread, the pages still uncut.

It was a large compartment by the standards of the U-boat, but it was still a claustrophobic tin-box of a room, walls made of tubes, wire and cables, now lit by two rows of red lights.

The space was dominated by two large columns, the oiled steel tube of the observation periscope, and beyond the ladder to the conning tower, the casing for the attack periscope. There were dozens of valves and wheels and a score of dials, switches and levers. There were nine men present, two map tables, six hanging joints of smoked meat, three boxes of fruit, and everywhere she stood she was shooed away. She finally squeezed between two hams and leaned against the damage control station that was unmanned.

Distracted by the moving food, Esser turned and spotted her. His smile was conciliatory and he moved over to where she stood.

The *Oberleutnant* was draped over the periscope.

"Carbon dioxide reading?" he asked.

"Five per cent," one of the sailors replied.

"Now or never," huffed the skipper. "Surface the boat."

"*Jawohl, mein Kaleun,*" called Jansen's First *Wachoffizier* quietly. This red-headed officer then turned to the crew. "*Auftauchen.*" They went to work around him.

Jansen let the periscope slide into the floor, rubbing his forehead.

Esser leaned over to Sarah. "We have to pump out the carbon dioxide and charge up the batteries. We've been waiting for the dark and for the destroyer to move far enough away," he whispered.

"*Oberleutnant?*" Sarah spoke up over the metallic clang, bubbling and hissing of blowing tanks. The skipper did not hear her, or chose not to. Sarah walked towards him. "*Oberleutnant!*"

"Shh, *Fräulein*," warned the *Oberbootsmann*.

Jansen looked up, his anxiety turning to irritation. "*Fräulein* Haller, I'm very busy—"

"You're surfacing, so you can send a radio message now?"

Jansen looked at Esser, looking for someone to blame. The other man shrugged and shook his head – *nothing to do with me.*

"Too risky to use the transmitter and whatever you want to send isn't going to be important enough." He turned to Esser. "*Oberbootsmann,* would you—"

"I need you to send a message to Admiral Canaris of the *Abwehr*—"

"Enough now." Jansen had raised his voice. The crew had stopped, listening to the exchange.

"*Macht weiter!*" shouted the *Wachoffizier* at the men, and everyone got back to work.

"Really, *Fräulein*," Jansen continued in a more measured tone. "I've heard your fairy tale, but I have things to do, the lives of fifty-five men to protect—"

"And what do you think will happen to them when the *Abwehr* discover you obstructed one of their agents?" Sarah interrupted. "Or maybe it'll only be *you* getting sent to the camp at *Sachsenhausen*?"

"Five metres," called the planesman.

The hatch opened in the conning tower above them with a *clank* and a sheet of seawater splashed down and ran across the deck towards the drains. The sound of the ocean filtered down to them.

Jansen threw up two hands in exasperation.

"Esser, take her and—" he exploded, and then stopped and gritted his teeth. "Just get her from under my feet. She can send her RT message, but it gets coded and done quickly." He followed a crewman up the ladder, then stopped halfway. "If I have to dive before she's done, then it's done."

Sarah nodded and Esser saluted.

When the *Oberleutnant* was gone, Esser swung on her with a look of undisguised antipathy.

"You better be the *Abwehr*'s top agent, or I will throw you overboard myself."

The radio operator had spent many hours tending to Sarah, so he was unfazed, even pleased that it seemed his work hadn't been wasted. He declined to accommodate Esser's anger and began taking Sarah's message like it was for the Führer himself.

"So what do you need to say?" he asked without looking up from the pad.

"Erm…" Even though a breeze had begun to blow through the vessel, Sarah still felt her brain was working two steps behind itself. "It's to Admiral Wilhelm Canaris. Most urgent. *Die Drei Hasen* request the use of U-boat…what is this boat called?"

"U-113," the radioman prompted and continued writing.

"*The Three Hares* request the use of U-113 and for its crew and captain to render all possible assistance to them." She paused. There needed to be something personal, that only Canaris would recognize. "For *no war is pleasant though, surely,* especially for our *expanding clientele*...can you emphasize those last bits?"

"Yes, I'll think of something..." the *Funkgast* replied and did some arithmetic. "Two hundred and twenty-eight characters, fifteen minutes to code, three minutes to send. *Oberbootsmann*, do we have time for this?"

"If we don't, we don't," Esser replied. "Says the *Schiffer*," he added for clarity.

"Fine, *mach ich ja*. Go," the radio operator said, waving them away from his tiny room.

"How long will we be surfaced?" Sarah asked Esser.

"Fifteen minutes to get rid of the carbon dioxide, but then we'll be running the diesel engines to charge up the batteries for underwater propulsion. We were down more than twenty hours and they are flat. I suspect we'll do that right up until they see us, or hear us."

On cue, the hull shivered with the gentle throb of the pistons starting up. The rise and fall of its tone was like the rocking noise of train wheels on rails. The sound of the ocean on the hull grew.

Esser looked up.

"He's a brave one...or a stupid one. Too early to tell yet," he sighed. "Let's just hope he's a lucky one."

The clock ticked on. Fifteen minutes became twenty. The carbon dioxide gauges dropped to zero, the oxygen reserve dial crept upwards. The men who had gathered in the control room to breathe the fresh air began to fidget and drift back to their diving stations. Esser warned Sarah not to stand in the gangway when the alarm inevitably sounded, as the hands would run to the front of the boat to make it nose-heavy for the dive.

Sarah looked at the battery gauge and it had hardly moved. If the destroyer spotted them, they would have very little power to evade it underwater…they couldn't hide.

Sarah climbed the ladder to the conning tower, waving away protests from Esser and others, and then pushed past the nonplussed crew at the firing station to mount the ladder to the bridge.

The first blast of cold sea wind reinvigorated Sarah in a way that she wouldn't have imagined possible.

The darkness was total. Only the dim red light filtering up from the control room allowed Sarah to see the five man-shapes at the rail.

"I don't want you up here," the *Oberleutnant* said quietly. "It's nothing personal, but if we have to dive, you *will* get in the way. You'll get hurt, or you'll slow us down enough that we all will."

"I needed air," Sarah said flatly. "Are they still out there?"

"Plenty of air on the boat now…and yes, off to starboard. That's your right—"

"I know what starboard is," Sarah said tersely.

In the vast swallowing blackness, there was a smear of grey, an Impressionist's interpretation of a ship-shaped light on the horizon. Then it became two flashes and rays of piercing white. The sea danced briefly.

Ba-boom. Ba-boom.

"Chasing fish," laughed one of the lookouts behind Sarah.

"I'll give them one thing, they're persistent," the *Schiffskapitän* grunted. He mumbled something into one of the voice pipes and a few moments later the light began to move to the stern.

"You really think we can just steam away, Skipper?" Another voice, that of a nervous man.

"Maybe. Maybe."

The men needed certainty, Sarah thought. *A comforting lie. Even naked optimism.*

"RT message, *Herr Kaleun,*" a voice announced.

There was a pause in which Sarah's heart began to race.

"I'll read it later," Jansen grunted.

Sarah grew angry and frustrated, not even knowing if the message signalled the end of her hopes. She looked at the flashing searchlights on the horizon and imagined Lisbeth there, believing herself safe and on the verge of achieving hers.

The messenger coughed.

"*Herr Kaleun*...the message is marked *immediate.*"

Jansen swore softly and moved to the hatch. "Come, Ursula Haller, let's find out what your friends in high places think."

Sarah watched the *Oberleutnant*'s expression carefully. Surprise. Confusion. And anger. In any game of bluffing, Jansen would lose heavily.

As he looked up, all those emotions had gone. He scrunched up the piece of paper in one fist. "It says nothing. They don't know what you mean."

"Show me," Sarah insisted.

"No," Jansen said, and he put a foot on the ladder to the bridge.

"Show me," she cried and grabbed his arm.

He seemed to consider throwing her off, or even striking her, but instead he threw the paper on the deck and carried on climbing. She let him go and retrieved the message.

TO: U-113
FROM: BdU
IMMEDIATE
U-113 AT USE OF THE THREE HARES
CAPTAIN AND CREW TO RENDER ALL POSSIBLE
ASSISTANCE
INCLUDING LOSS OF BOAT AND HANDS
XX BEWARE THE NEST OF VIPERS XX
WC

Canaris's exact words from the briefing. He had written this personally. Sarah was now in charge.

The *Schiffskapitän*'s shape did not move from the rail as she climbed onto the bridge.

"*Oberleutnant*," she began quietly. "As you have read—"

"I have read something that could mean anything. Who are the Three Hares? Who says that's you?"

"That is me," Sarah said impatiently. "How would I have known the code otherwise?"

"I picked you up from a sunken *British* ship. You could be anyone...Élodie, Ursula, *Sarah*, whoever you are."

Sarah squirmed as he used her real name.

"And if I message them back," Jansen continued, "and say that *Die Drei Hasen* ask that we shut up and go home, what would my instructions from *BdU* be then?"

"Then you'd end up being court-martialled when you got home and probably shot."

Sarah was just making it up now, but confidence, certainty, the comforting lie was the way to go. She couldn't see his face, couldn't read him. She didn't know if he was about to cave in or become more belligerent.

"I could throw you back in the water, tell them anything."

Sarah looked about her, at the rigid shapes of the lookouts and the ginger *Wachoffizier*. Listening.

"Your orders, the orders of your crew are clear," Sarah said loudly. "*Immediate: U-113 at use of the Three Hares. Captain and crew to render all possible assistance.* Do you think they'll take kindly to you ignoring orders from *BdU*?"

No one moved. No one breathed.

"If they knew it also said, *including loss of boat and hands*, then they might," Jansen retorted.

"Isn't that a standing order? Aren't you always risking the boat, the crew? Isn't that *the job*?"

"I'm steaming away, surfaced, from a ship I can't beat in a straight fight. Captain's discretion applies."

"*All possible assistance*," she hissed. "It says so right here. Engage that destroyer."

"No."

"Is that your last word?"

The *Oberleutnant* was silent.

Sarah looked at the unmoving grey smudge on the invisible horizon to the stern.

She lifted the Beretta into the air and began to fire.

CHAPTER FORTY-FOUR

THE GUN WORKED, despite all the seawater and the rough treatment.

She fired four times into the air, four flashes that illuminated the bridge and three percussive, clapping grunts that seemed to die as soon as they happened. With her other hand she struck the flare she was holding. It ignited, a painfully bright red light, burning white at its centre.

The others had turned, but no one had moved.

Sarah levelled the gun at the nearest sailor, who moved away from her, and she lifted the flare to the sky.

"Nobody moves," she hissed.

"What are you doing?" asked the *Wachoffizier*, aghast.

"Ensuring the orders of *BdU* are carried out. We engage the destroyer. Is it moving yet?"

There was a clamour below. Shouts of alarm. Frantic reports.

Sarah tossed the flare over the stern rail so it landed on the deck below them. The conning tower, the shape of the deck, the anti-aircraft gun…*everything* was illuminated.

Sarah's silhouette, gun in hand, waited.

"So we're bait for you, is that it? Is that all we are?" the *Oberleutnant* sneered. "I should have left you in the water."

"You'd have done your country a great disservice if you had," Sarah declared.

"*Herr Kaleun*, the contact is turning," the nervous voice reported, now with an equally nervous face.

"Have they got us?" Sarah asked.

A star shell streaked upwards and exploded silently high above them, a small artificial sun.

Jansen stepped forwards and in the light he saw the slide of Sarah's pistol was open. He put a hand on the empty gun and, tugging it out of her grip, tossed it over the rail into the sea.

He looked to the stern horizon and then bent down to the hatch.

"*Alarm!*" he screamed.

The boat protested as it sank steeply into the ocean; the hull clanked and the water boiled around it, inside its tanks.

"Put her under arrest, right now." Jansen looked at Esser and pointed to Sarah, a vehemence in the finger's motion.

The *Oberbootsmann* stepped in towards his skipper.

"*Herr Kaleun*…I've read the orders—" Esser whispered.

"Screw the orders!"

That declaration was heard throughout the control room and the adjoining compartments.

But no one moved.

"Sonar contact, bearing 176 degrees, warship, closing fast," a voice interrupted.

"You've a job to do, *Oberleutnant*," Sarah stated. "Doesn't matter how we got here. Just sink that ship."

"*Verpiss dich*, little girl," Jansen spat. "Batteries?" he called out.

"Twenty per cent, *Herr Kaleun*."

"You've killed us...we've no margin for error," he whispered to Sarah.

"Then make no errors."

The next few hours were hellish.

The U-boat drifted, sprinted, slowed, changed course and depth, stopped and lingered.

In their red-lit steel coffin Sarah and the rest of the crew stood and crouched and sweated and prayed and closed their eyes.

The *ping*. The falling, high-pitched metallic ring of sound hitting hull.

Meaning that they had been found.

Ping.

Meaning they still had them.

Ping.

Meaning anything they did now until the destroyer was right above them was pointless.

Ping.

Ping.

Meaning they were attacking.

Ping.

Ping.

Ping.

Ping. Ping. Ping. Closer and closer together as the distance contracted and the net started to close.

The brief silence where they lost the boat.

The renewed urgency as it was reacquired.

The *ping, ping, ping, ping*—

In their shark-belly tomb, Sarah and the crew she had condemned waited, listening to the approaching pulsing *pada-pada* hum of the destroyer's propeller, rising in volume until the rushing, roaring vibrated the water overhead.

Then the orders. The frantic changes in depth, direction, the rush of speed, while their movements would be concealed by the exploding sea...and then the silence. Waiting for the noise of depth charges hitting the water and the call—

Wasserbombe im Wasser.

And the pause.

The pause.

The pause.

The fear.

Was this the one to—

The *boom*. The crashing. The crunch of metal.

The shudder, the shake, the beads-in-a-rattle movement, the walls moving so fast the eyes couldn't focus and only darkness numbed the pain. The sway, the drop of the floor, the walls become ground, the ceiling the walls.

The bruising, bleeding and falling, the dropping objects and shattering steel.

The shouts, the screams, the murmurs and the white-knuckle squeezes of the silent.

The second boom.

The third.

Fourth.

And the rolling thunderous impacts that just became one long and ceaseless cacophony.

The seawater jets and leaks, the hissing, the cries, the panicked joists and jacks, propping up cracking bulkheads and failing valves.

The repairs, the make-do, the brief calm—

And the ping.

Over and over again.

Over.

Again.

Sarah grew more and more frightened, with each and every sound, benign or malignant making her flinch and sweat. The bulkheads seemed to close in on her, a mausoleum that she was locked into, another hell in the here and now. Eventually, even breathing felt like an attack.

Then she moved beyond fear to a numb and quiet place, where she watched the jets of water, the bruises and blood, the swinging deck and felt nothing.

No. Irritation.

The only thing that mattered to her was sinking *Virulent*. Stopping Lisbeth.

But they were just hiding and evading. A gamble had to be

made...or rather the stake had already been placed. All that remained was to roll the dice.

She moved next to Esser, who was stretching by hanging onto one of the ceiling pipes in one corner.

"Thank you for the flare," she murmured.

"Didn't do it for you. Did it for him." He nodded to Jansen. "The *Schiffer* is a good man and he doesn't deserve to end up in a concentration camp." He shrugged. "We'll probably end up dead instead, but..."

Sarah had watched the *Oberleutnant*. Throughout it all, he had leaned against the periscope, arms folded and eyes shut, like he was dozing. As each attack began, he had stirred and stretched, before looking at his watch and yawning. Then he'd quietly issue some orders and wait. She felt this calm radiate from him to the crew. He had learned to lie.

"Why are we just hiding?" she whispered to the *Oberbootsmann*.

"No choice, little girl...big girl, whatever you are."

"You need to explain to me how we're going to sink this ship." Esser snorted derisively, but she pushed on. "Just talk me through it. Why don't we shoot back?"

"By the time we get the periscope up, even at the end of one of her sweeps, she'll be zigzagging and pulling turns in the water. They know we're here and until they think we're not, we won't hit them."

"Is that why they're not hitting us properly?" she asked. "Because they're thrashing about?"

"They're not hitting us because they are not good at this... yet," he added. "When they speed up at the end and the pings vanish, they go in a straight line to drop the charges."

"So...they're vulnerable *then*," Sarah exclaimed.

Every problem has an answer. It's just a question of information.

"What? No...we can't attack them then, that's when we need to be diving and evading."

"And what if we didn't?" she asked.

"They'd ram us if we didn't move, or drop a dozen depth charges onto us if we did."

"Except, if we'd already sunk them..." Sarah mused.

"They'd be head on to us. You're talking about a *bow shot*. The smallest possible target. Impossible."

"At point-blank range?" Sarah said, envisioning a paper ball and a wastebasket.

"The torpedoes have to arm in the water, there's a minimum range – they could be armed before firing." Esser was thinking now. "Incredibly dangerous."

"Let's just wait for the next *ping*, then...or until they get *good at it*."

She looked at him, into his eyes, and saw a moment of serious consideration. A mind going through a set of practical steps, thinking something through.

He believes it.

She approached Jansen.

The captain was angry, then resentful of the suggestion, but unable to ignore her, he listened. He tried to look sceptical throughout, but as Sarah continued he couldn't conceal his growing interest.

"This isn't all your plan, is it?" Jansen looked around and

saw Esser nodding slowly to him. He straightened up, his fingers beginning to tap on the periscope.

"It's too dangerous," he said finally.

"We're dead if we don't try." Sarah sighed. "How much battery power is left?"

"But why would we sit there waiting for them?"

"What if they thought we were damaged?"

He had stopped pouting.

"We'll put oil in the water...and we'd need distance," Jansen said, almost to himself. "Could run ahead full speed, because it wouldn't need to be quiet, we'd want them to know where we are...open up a gap...then full reverse..."

There was a light in his eyes now.

Esser came over and leaned on the periscope.

"A V and W class destroyer, twelve hundred tons...be a good story to tell, wouldn't it?" he murmured.

"Flank speed," the *Schiffer* called.

CHAPTER FORTY-FIVE

14TH NOVEMBER 1940

IT TOOK AN HOUR or more to build up any kind of space between them. The crew felt better now that they were doing something other than hiding. Esser said that just showed how inexperienced they were.

They needed to loop away from an attack in the opposite direction to that of the destroyer. This was guesswork, as the enemy could not be seen while they were underwater, but eventually the destroyer passed over them from bow to stern, and they made the correct move. They ran at flank speed in the opposite direction to the ship, under cover of water still boiling from the depth charges. Then they had to guess the course of the ship's next loop back towards the sub and, going the other way, put more distance between them.

Sarah had to close her eyes to imagine how the game was playing out, the two vessels turning in big curves, the submarine using the destroyer's speed and overenthusiasm — its overconfidence — against itself.

At some point the U-boat would have to turn to face its enemy in one of those long, looping curves, with *Virulent* closing on it. There was an aft torpedo tube, but the odds were better face on. Should they wait and hope they could increase the distance or risk losing the hard-won metres between them?

A moment came and the *Schiffer* made the call. *Now.*

Sarah knew she had nothing to offer at this point, but she couldn't sit by idly and blind, while others decided, acted and witnessed.

Jansen was about to climb into the conning tower to use the attack periscope with something approaching a skip in his step.

"*Oberleutnant*, can I watch?" Sarah asked cautiously. She tried being the needy child, rather than the bullish tyrant. "There *are* two periscopes…"

The *Schiffskapitän* was about to refuse but clearly felt magnanimous, or exhausted.

"*Oberbootsmann*," he called to Esser. "She can watch down here, but no higher than twelve so she doesn't get in my way." He jabbed a finger at Sarah. "If all you see is water, so be it."

"You have a way with him," Esser said, calling her over.

Looking into the periscope was harder than it seemed. If you didn't hold your head at just the right angle and distance from the lens you could see nothing. Then the bright image fluttered into being, eerily close in a way that made you want to step back from it. Sarah seized the hand grips on either side to hold her eye in place.

It was early dawn. All Sarah could see was water, the rolling surf and the silver grey of the lightening sky. The waves sloshed over the scope, blurring everything to a dark green shadow, before dropping again to leave a view obscured by running droplets.

"I can't see anything," Sarah moaned.

"Look to port, 250 degrees and rising," Esser suggested, pushing her shoulders to help her move.

The seascape swept by as she sidestepped to the right and moved the viewfinder around, which drifted with oiled effortlessness.

Virulent hove into view, a dark and alien blight on the organic greys, and disappeared again. It made Sarah jump, and it took her a while to find it again.

The destroyer was in three-quarter view by this point, slicing through the water from left to right as Sarah watched, and creating a giant bow wave.

It was turning towards them. The change in orientation appeared slow, but it was inevitably and inescapably steady.

"It seems far enough away," Sarah said.

Esser turned something on the viewfinder. The destroyer filled the image, snapping into something much more menacing. Again Sarah wanted to flinch away but squeezed the hand grips instead. She could see the men aboard, the flapping jack, the rust streaks from the anchor chains. The searchlights blinded her as they swept between the shortening gap.

The men aboard. The men.

Soldiers, *dumme Schlampe*. In a war.

Passengers. Innocents.

Vichy supporters. Enemy.

People—

Sei still! Lisbeth is there. Lisbeth must be stopped.

The real activity in the U-boat was now in the tower compartment. Sarah had read that the torpedoes were programmed and fired from there, the calculations made based on the instructions from Jansen at the attack scope. All the voices – the story – was now filtering down the ladder, and the crew without a job to do then and there were gathering near the control room to listen.

"We're both turning to meet each other. To turn quickly, we need to be at full speed, but then we're closing the gap quicker. It's a gamble," Esser whispered.

"Range 656 metres...650...639..."

"Bearing 275."

"Range 550."

"We need to be facing them, bearing zero degrees, that's also 360 degrees, before they get within 150 metres," Esser went on. "Any closer and the impact will damage us, too."

"Range 520 metres...510...500..."

"Bearing 300..."

Sarah could smell her own sweat, overpowering the flowery cologne, as the room warmed and she dripped inside her shirt.

Virulent crashed into a breaking wave and rocked, listing hard to port, but even this obstacle seemed incapable of stopping her inexorable turn.

"They're nearly face on to us..." Sarah gasped.

"And then they'll cross the distance faster, and stop travelling to meet our bow as we turn."

"Range 450...440...425..."

"Bearing 320 degrees..."

Sarah juggled the figures in her head but couldn't make them tally against one another.

"Will we make it?" she asked.

"Right now, yes. When she starts romping in a straight line, who knows? This was your idea."

Sarah smiled without humour.

"Range 400...375...345..."

"Bearing 330 degrees..."

Sarah willed the destroyer to move from left to right, willed the numbers above the image to count up faster.

But *Virulent* was now all bow, all guns, all superstructure, a slim and deadly profile, coming right at them. It blotted out the sky behind.

"Range 315...285...255..."

"Bearing 340 degrees..."

Sarah could see the lookouts on the destroyer's flying bridge, watched them drop their glasses and grip the rail.

"Range 220...190...160..."

"Bearing 350 degrees..."

"Open tubes one to four!" called Jansen.

"We aren't going to make it," Sarah groaned.

"Festhalten!" came the call.

Esser put a hand on Sarah's shoulder but she shrugged him off. The destroyer's propeller was now audible through the hull.

"Range 130...100...70..."

"Fire all tubes!"

The boat shook and the bubbling whooshes drowned out the coming ship.

The periscope whirred and began sliding into the floor out of Sarah's hands.

"Hey!" she cried.

"Got to protect it," Esser shouted. "Hold onto something."

"*Alarm!*"

The floor sagged downwards. And Sarah fell forwards.

The torpedoes detonated.

The instant the blast smacked against the hull, the lights shattered, showering everyone with glass and turning the compartment into a black hole.

The screams, the rattle of splintering steel, the jets of water filling the room as multiple seals and valves failed, Sarah's short journey to the deck, the waves of heat, the sparks and frantic torch beams in the smoke and orders and shouts – all these things painted their own picture. The smell of burning electrics and oil filled the nostrils.

The U-boat rocked again with a new concussion and began listing to port, shaking as the keel of the destroyer scraped over the top of their hull, with an extended shriek of tearing metal. Fingernails down a blackboard.

Sarah, who seemed to be sitting against a bulkhead of dripping pipes with that same excruciating howling in her ears, couldn't stand and did not know how to pull herself up. She drew her legs up to her and wrapped her arms around them.

She felt the sea rising over her boots and bottom. She promised herself she would stand before the water reached her knees.

You did it, dumme Schlampe. Are you happy now?

Hello, Mutti...I don't know I did anything yet.

That's going to be your excuse for going on? To be sure?

Isn't that what you do? Even when the play is going to be cancelled and you know there's no future, you just get up onstage every night and give it everything...

Did I say that? I was an old fool, a stupid romantic. You can go through the motions, no one cares.

But people do, Mutti. They're beginning to see me now, I can't hide any more. What do I do?

Stop listening to ageing failures, as if they know anything more than you. Stop trusting. Did I not teach you anything? Everything is a lie, everything is artifice, no one is telling the truth, they're just reciting lines they've learned. Sometimes they're the right ones and they can proceed. Sometimes they're not and the audience boos and shouts and throws things. People get their lines wrong and that ruins your cue, so know the story and carry on as if they hadn't messed up. Don't trust them with your part. Don't. Trust. Them.

My part is to stop Lisbeth.

Then get the play back on track...or lie down in this water now and get it over with.

Sarah reached up out of the water and seized a pipe above her. She pulled.

The screaming became shouts and then talking. The water stopped spraying out of the walls and ceased to rise. The lights came on. The boat slowly, noisily began to surface.

Sarah tasted iron and grasped that it had not been seawater running down her face but blood. She thought of *der Werwolf* painting themselves in her gore at her initiation in the chapel at Rothenstadt, of her filthy Jewish blood all over their faces. *Drink it down and choke on it.*

Then she thought about the vow, the *two* vows she took that night, one written by the Ice Queen, and one created by Sarah to counteract the other.

To hide among the weak and overlooked, only to rise when called to devastate, to decimate, to dominate...to rise like vengeance...to commit whatever acts are necessary...to destroy all that is within my power to destroy...

She couldn't remember which vow was which, in whose interests she was really fighting. All she knew was that she was indeed a *Werwolf, the fastest and most feared hunter of the forest.*

She rubbed her eyes, but left the rest of the blood where it was.

She found Jansen in the tower room. He was leaning into the attack periscope.

"*Oberleutnant,*" Sarah said respectfully.

He did not look up.

"Did we get them?" she continued.

"I lost six men in the bow compartment," he said flatly.

"I'm sorry," Sarah said. She felt it, but packaged the grief and guilt for later.

"No, I don't think you are. Not really. This is your job, isn't it? For the Reich?"

"Yes. I'm still sorry though. Do you believe me?" she asked.

"Do you honestly care, one way or the other?"

Sarah paused.

"No, no I don't," she stated and folded her arms against the spiked emotions. "Did we get them?"

"Yes. It ploughed on for a few kilometres or more but couldn't keep the bow out of the water."

The relief...no, there was no relief. No feeling of triumph or achievement.

Slowly, as if meat had rotted in an adjoining room, a sense of unthinkable wrongness permeated Sarah's being. The hundred lives she had ordered snuffed out were going nowhere. They were going to stay and taint everything.

But Jansen continued. "One lifeboat made it off. Maybe forty sur—"

"Let me see, *verdammt nochmal!*" Sarah snapped and pushed the *Schiffer* from the viewfinder.

Virulent was sliding into a sea slick with oil and covered in debris. Only its smoking stern was visible now, its red-painted keel stained with soot and covered in limpets, visible to the world one last time. One lifeboat filled with men was paddling slowly away.

"I need to see...closer," she ordered. Jansen sighed and increased the magnification.

Among the grubby and miserable sailors, slick with oil, soot-stained or bleeding, was a burst of bright gold. In the lifeboat sat Lisbeth Fischer.

CHAPTER FORTY-SIX

THE U-BOAT WAS BARELY MORE than a wreck. As well as the crushed bow, it had lost the deck gun entirely, as if a giant had dragged its claws across the hull and torn it away, along with the planking and great slivers of the superstructure. The bridge rail had been torn in two and one side hung over the conning tower as if the steel was canvas. It had surfaced, slowly and with some difficulty, as well as a noticeable list. It was difficult to believe that it had been the victor of the encounter.

The *Wachoffizier*, who spoke passable English, had hailed the lifeboat, and the survivors had drawn it sluggishly towards the drunken predator.

"Did you manage to get an RT message out in time?" he asked through a megaphone as they closed in.

"Not a chance, you sneaky bastard," called the chief petty officer at the tiller, in a loud cockney accent. There was only one commissioned officer aboard that Sarah could see, a damp youngster who looked aghast and stunned by events.

"We'll put a call out for you after we leave…" the German continued genially. "But first we believe you have a citizen of the Reich with you that we want returned to us. Do you have Dr Lisbeth Fischer aboard?"

There was some looking around and muttering aboard the boat, some elbows and pointing.

"No, we ain't," the man at the tiller stated over the others.

The *Wachoffizier* looked to Sarah, who pointed unambiguously to the woman now sitting hunched under a blanket near the bow.

"We believe that Dr Fischer is four rows from the bow, second in from the port side. Dr Fischer is a Reich citizen whom you were good enough to rescue when her ship was… sunk…and it is time for her to return to Germany. She is not a refugee or a defector, and she certainly cannot remain as your prisoner. Please help her aboard."

There was more muttered discussion on the lifeboat. There wasn't much support for the leader's defiance.

"I don't know the legal position here," the *Wachoffizier* said, leaning in to the *Schiffer*. "We should just start threatening them, I guess?"

"Are you taking her by force then, *Mine Hurr*?" the coxswain in the lifeboat asked the U-boat.

"If you want us to," the German called, smiling.

Lisbeth stood in the boat as if she was surrendering and looked at the bridge. It took her a second but then she saw Sarah and looked right into her eyes.

"*Liebchen*," she called, waving. "You're safe! I'm so happy."

Sarah turned to Jansen. "She gets off that boat, nobody else.

Then they keep their distance. And no one goes near her, or me, until I know what she has or has not done."

"Please," sniffed the *Oberleutnant*.

"*Ach, bitte, bitte, bitte...*" Sarah spoke deliberately. *Pretty please.*

Sarah stood on the torn bow deck, arms behind her back, as the lifeboat struggled to pull alongside the listing submarine. The crew were behind her and out of the way.

One of the British sailors was arguing with the others about letting Lisbeth go. *She works fast*, Sarah thought. Given a few more days, would they all have done what she wanted?

Sarah felt the need to urinate. It came strongly and out of the blue. It brought a breathlessness and a weakness in her legs.

Stage fright. It's stage fright. Control your breathing.

It's what I'm about to do...

THIS IS THE SHOW. Cancelled, runaway success, no crowd or an audience of thousands. PLAY YOUR PART.

Finally, Lisbeth was helped over the side of the lifeboat, clambered onto the hull, and up onto the deck. She was dressed in borrowed sailor's clothes with the necklace lying over a woollen sweater. She held it like it was a lifeline.

With her other hand she rubbed at her face nervously, removing a streak of make-up and revealing the scars on her cheek. Sarah reminded herself that her physical appearance meant nothing. It didn't represent her state of mind or whether she was good or evil. In fact Sarah felt a pang of sympathy... then she understood that this was the desired effect.

Jansen's crew had pushed the lifeboat away with poles and were retreating as ordered, but she could feel the eyes of the *Schiffer* and the bridge crew on them, not to mention the British sailors twenty metres away.

"Come here, *Liebchen*," Lisbeth cried after a pause, holding her arms wide and stepping forward.

"Don't come near me," Sarah growled. She could feel a loss of control humming in her cheeks, making her want to whine and cajole and cry. She squeezed her teeth together until it stopped.

"What's the matter, Ursula?"

"I know who you are, what you've really done. You're the White Devil."

"Who told you that? It was Klodt who—"

"The mask had your make-up inside. You killed all those people, hundreds that I saw and how many more before then? You've been in Africa for ten years? Fifteen?"

Lisbeth closed her eyes and screwed up her face.

Before, Sarah would have accepted this action immediately as something born of pain and suffering, something that she needed to repair, to fix, to drive away. Now it looked twisted and inauthentic, like a small child trying to manipulate an adult.

"Every medicine there has ever been has cost lives at some point," Lisbeth managed.

"Medicine?"

"All medicine is poison. It's a question of dose. *Ursula*," Lisbeth said more urgently, stepping forward. Sarah fought the urge to retreat and stood her ground. The woman's voice dropped, grew cloying, tearful. "We can pay them back, all of them. The English and the Americans. *Then* we can start on the Nazis, and then Stalin and his thugs, then the Japanese and that Ishii. You and me, we can scrub the earth *clean*. Ursula, please."

Lisbeth reached out to her.

Sarah could step forward into her arms, receive her love. She could tell Jansen there had been a terrible error, and they could travel together—

"Imagine, everyone who ever hurt you, everyone who ever hurt someone you love, punished, stopped from hurting anyone again," Lisbeth continued, a tremor in her voice. "We could rescue the Slavs, the blacks, *the Jews* if you want. You can decide. We'll do it together."

Sarah could...control her, maybe, or stop her worst excesses, convince her to give up on infecting England, then...figure out the best way to use the weapon. The appropriate victims—

The spell was broken.

"A kind of *triage*?" Sarah sneered.

"No, not triage...but if a limb is beginning to rot, you saw it off. You cut out the tumour before it grows. To save the patient—"

"As if you care about those people..."

"Of course I care. I'm a doctor, I care about everyone. I just have to make hard decisions, that's all."

"But you didn't ask about your father."

"Why...what happened to my stepfather?"

"Your father didn't make it, but you never even thought of asking."

"He wasn't a good man..."

"No. Weak, craven, nasty and evil...but you could forget all about him because...you have to *remind yourself* that you're supposed to care," Sarah said, the understanding seeping into her voice. "Give me the sample," she demanded, holding out a hand.

Lisbeth changed in an instant, like she had torn off a mask. There was rage in her eyes, and it was cold.

"I don't have it," she answered, eyebrows raised, eyes wide.

"It's around your neck," Sarah said flatly.

"Oh, this." Lisbeth touched her necklace. "This is empty, *Liebchen*. I poured the contents into the water barrel of that lifeboat."

Sarah turned to look at the British sailors. Forty men, among them several of the refugees from Libreville. They were watching, confused but exhausted. No one was drinking. Yet. Or no one was drinking *any more*.

"One of them could be infected. Maybe they all are. What are you going to do, Ursula?" Lisbeth crowed. "Are you going to let them live and see? Or are you going to *cut* the infection out? Are you going to be strong or hard? Which is which?"

The woman was daring her to do something about it. The tactic required Sarah to be overwhelmed, to be unable to take the next step. Lisbeth thought Sarah too compassionate, too human, to do what needed to be done.

Sarah had struggled with the idea that Lisbeth had seen something of herself in *Ursula*... That Lisbeth might have believed that *Ursula* could be corrupted, or had already been corrupted by her experiences, as Lisbeth had been.

She could have had Lisbeth shot immediately, but she hadn't, and not just because she wanted to know the fate of the sample. Sarah had wanted to know if Lisbeth really had infected her with her own tainted soul. Had she fallen for Lisbeth's artifice because she was also contaminated?

But...she thinks I'm too good to kill them all, thought Sarah.

The realization was like an absolution.

She felt unburdened. Weightless.

She had been judged by evil and found wanting, by its own standards. Sarah was never part of Lisbeth's plans, or at least she had shown herself incompatible with them.

The relief was total.

It made the next act an easy one.

"You think I'll let them go, you think I'm too *nice*." Sarah hissed the last word and smiled.

Lisbeth shook off the last vestiges of her disguise. "Let me make this easy for you." She pulled her necklace from her neck. She began to unscrew the top. "I've got a little bit left, enough for me and *you*."

Sarah took her other arm from behind her back. In her hand was Lady Sakura's derringer.

"That's tiny!" Lisbeth laughed.

Sarah took a step forward, aimed and squeezed the trigger as Clementine had taught her.

The low-velocity bullet moved so sluggishly Sarah could see it travel through the air.

Lisbeth watched it, too, right up until it struck her face.

In that moment Sarah saw Lisbeth *horrified* and realized that nothing about Lisbeth up until that point had been real.

It had all been an act, to provoke a desired response.

As Lisbeth slumped to the deck at Sarah's feet, there was a cry from the lifeboat, where several of the British sailors had stood in shock, and a gasp behind her from the bridge. Sarah pushed the necklace clear of Lisbeth's chapped hand with a foot. Seeing it was still sealed, she picked it up and cast the stone as far as she could into the ocean.

Sarah had been cold, but not from the wind or the spray. From her core to her skin, she had felt a chill that didn't hurt or discomfort her. An unemotional resolve. But standing over Lisbeth's corpse, it was fading fast, like the last sand running through an egg timer, leaving behind an empty glass. At the bottom, she filled with doubt, guilt and nausea.

She didn't need a rain of fire, the lake of ice, or the mouth of Satan that Dante described. She had no need of a cursed valley of dead babies, a dark abyss, or the waiting room of shame that her mother talked about.

Hell was in the here and now. A place of lamentation of her own making.

She thought of *der Werwolf*, and the end of her vow, realizing now what it meant.

Kill all those it is within my power to kill.

And, finding myself in hell, deliver you to the devil myself.

EPILOGUE

16TH DECEMBER 1940

THE U-113 CRAWLED INTO THE HARBOUR at Kiel on a bitterly, painfully cold morning. Only the very robust, or the very in love, were waiting to greet the returning crew on the frost-rimed quayside. A few dockworkers and sailors of the *Kriegsmarine* stopped to see the apocalyptic damage suffered by the iron coffin wheezing into port, but it was no weather for spectating. It was shaping up to be a winter for hunkering down and getting on with things.

The four-week voyage had been an exercise in sustained fear and miserable tension, as the U-boat had limped home, the long way around the British Isles, barely capable of submerging if attacked and probably incapable of surfacing again if it had. Yet the journey continued unmolested, unseen and unremarked upon by the Royal Navy or the Royal Air Force.

After a brief heated argument, they towed *Virulent*'s lifeboat and new water barrel behind them for two weeks. The *Oberleutnant* wouldn't countenance killing the survivors on the off-chance that they were infected, and Sarah was gratified to discover that she could not bring herself to order it. It was hugely dangerous, the extra time cutting them loose in the event of an attack would probably have been fatal, but the bizarre convoy was left alone long enough to ensure that no one aboard became ill, just more and more irritated. When they cut the boat loose, there was a profound sense of relief and no little satisfaction that they had not erred on the side of caution.

After Lisbeth's death the crew would not look Sarah in the eyes and avoided her where they could. Now Sarah stood on the torn bow deck under the conning tower, as had become her habit. A murderer returning to the scene of the crime. She was wrapped in multiple clothing layers and a leather smock coat that trailed on the floor behind her. Nobody had volunteered to give her warmer clothing as they sailed north, so in the end she just took some. She was surefooted now and unconcerned by the pitch and roll of the boat in the winter waters. Somewhere in what felt like the incineration and extinguishing of her soul, she hadn't lost her seasickness so much as no longer cared about it. This, she presumed, was what they meant by getting your sea legs.

She had watched the smooth, curved, thirteen-storey tower of the Laboe Naval Memorial grow on the horizon until it towered over the estuary, silhouetted by the rising sun. It was impossible to miss. It marked home and safety for many. But it also demanded attention, a remembrance.

So Sarah had made herself remember.

Her mother. Schäfer. Stern. The other guards of Schäfer's

estate. Foch. The Bateke boy who ran. Lieutenant La Roux and his men. Hasse. Bofinger. Jansen's six men. The crew of *Virulent* and half the passengers from the *Ittenbach*, save the forty survivors.

Lisbeth Fischer.

She made that 170 people. Give or take two or three.

Ngobila. Though she had not caused his death, this man, like the infected villages, and millions of others round the world, had suffered and died in European imperial hands. Sarah felt sullied and implicated by it. She felt remembrance was the least she could do.

How many had she saved? Thousands. At the very least. But was that the way that the mathematics of death worked? How many need she save to strike off the casualties? How many saved lives needed to justify the murders?

She'd saved millions of Slavs, too...but that figure seemed ridiculous. Fantastical. How would they kill *millions*? Who would do that? And why?

But she did know, after a moment's thought. She had seen it happening, heard how it had happened before and knew how it would all happen again. *People* would do that. The Nazis for land and racial purity. The Belgians for money. The British and French for not much more than that, wrapped up as a patronizing racist paternalism – imagined fathers to a whole continent, but with all the secrets and horrors of Professor Schäfer behind closed doors.

She had watched the port grow in front of her, seen the warships, the busy cranes, the new U-boats and their bombproof pens. There was a war happening, here and now.

This country she was returning to was not just the master of Europe. It was hungry for more and would stop at nothing to make that happen. Nothing.

Sarah took this knowledge and hugged it close, warmed it and would feed it, in the hope that it would guide her in the months to come.

It was with these thoughts that Sarah saw the Captain standing on the quayside, in the cold, with the lovers.

What was this man now? Safety? A mentor? Her family? Was he any of these things any more?

As the ship tied off, the crew – *the remains of the crew* – were lining up for dismissal. Sarah decided to take her leave immediately, but as she reached the gangplank, something made her turn to the bridge, where Jansen stood with the ginger *Wachoffizier*. She straightened up and saluted.

"Get off my boat," Jansen growled.

Sarah turned back to the land, unsurprised, but a voice behind her made her stop.

"Thank you for not damning us all," Esser said.

"Thank you for your help. You've saved…lives, many lives," she managed.

"You know," he said, shrugging, "some people believe that hell is just somewhere you have your sins burned away, so you can finally be with God. That there is only shame in this life."

Esser stood a distance from the others, and they couldn't be overheard. She leaned in. "The *Jews* believe that, *Oberbootsmann*." She sighed dismissively.

He offered a hand. "Lev Herschel Esser. Pleased to meet you," he said quietly.

She took his hand and shook it. "I'm an agent of the *Abwehr*. Why are you telling me this?"

"Take care, *Sarah*," he whispered. "And mind you don't talk in your sleep any more."

She had trouble crossing the gangplank and climbing the quayside steps.

The Captain looked healthy. There was colour in his cheeks and a clarity to his eyes – not the knife-edge focus of the Pervitin, but something approaching his previously centred, single-minded self.

He also looked pleased to see her, but that could have been one of his many masks.

"I had a very interesting chat with Admiral Canaris," he said. "He wanted to know why I was on my way back from the Bay of Guinea on a U-boat I'd requisitioned, and yet coming to see him in his offices on the *Tirpitzufer* at the same time."

"Things got complicated, but rest assured the admiral will be happy with the results." Sarah shrugged. "Depending on what he was actually asking us to do, of course."

"Of course. A long story for a long car ride probably."

"Probably. Britain is still in the war?" she asked.

"And will remain so. The Reich is returning my barges unused until further notice. I will still be charging."

"Of course you will."

"And bombs have fallen on Berlin. Another promise broken to the German people." He smiled. "Those are stacking up now."

"So where's your racist friend? Back in Paris, or back in the *Dreckloch* he hates so much?"

The Captain missed a beat. "Claude got sick. He... It was quick. Turns out I had a lot of leftover morphine..." He smiled, evidently without feeling it. "So he didn't suffer."

The hairs on Sarah's neck prickled and she had to catch her breath. If Claude had contracted the disease, she must have been very, very close to death. She remembered Claude pouring the bleach over her head. In all probability that had saved her life, at the expense of his own.

"I'm sorry, I know he was your friend."

"Yes, I need to choose those more carefully... He was a good man, once. But he let the world make him hard."

A chill filled her chest, like a gust of the winter wind had entered her. Had Clementine been infected after all? Had she escaped only to spread the disease inadvertently? She pictured Clementine, dying alone, far from home.

Sarah wobbled, struggling between sympathy and panic, as if on a loose roof ridge tile, high above the pavement below. She quashed the emotions. Clementine had survived everything else life had thrown at her, even if others had paid the price. Sarah would not have bet against her now.

Sarah found herself with eyes closed and screwing up her face. She had to break this new habit, borrowed from a monster.

"Do we get hard, or do we get strong, that's the question..." She looked back at the submarine. "What do we do now, Captain Floyd?"

"I thought you'd like to go back to Berlin."

"No, I mean, how do we fight the Nazis when the cost of doing it is *so high*?" she said softly. "When I've done such terrible, *terrible* things and that's a *success*. That's *the job*."

He looked at her with an expression that might have been sympathy but could easily have been the confusion of not understanding, a lack of empathy.

"I mean, you've done terrible things—" she continued.

"Thank you," he said flatly.

"How do you live with yourself? How do you *forgive* yourself?"

"I think I've demonstrated recently that dealing with those things remains a work in progress. But you fight for what's right, no matter how it's done. Then you commit, you own it. Own your deeds."

Commit to the move.

"And what do *we* do? Are you yourself again?"

"I'm six weeks clean."

"You cannot *ever* do that again. This" – she waved a hand in between them – "it doesn't work without you, the real you... whoever that really is," she added with a chuckle. Then she looked right up at him, the last of the little girl. "I *have* to be able to rely on you. Promise me it's over, for ever."

"I promise."

A promise. From a liar, who sometimes told the truth. Which of these was it? Did she trust him?

Not at all.

Faith. Not trust.

Sarah did not trust anyone, any more. This had really always been the case, she had just forgotten it. It was a spell cast by Clementine's proximity and agitation, by Sarah's unexpected need to be liked. An illusion built of Lisbeth's lies and Sarah's need to be held. No longer.

Yet she had felt the rush of recognition and homesickness in Lady Sakura's arms. She was an old friend, the echo of a better mother...but Atsuko Takeda was now a spy, a double agent and therefore a liar. In reality she could be anybody. Sarah buried those feelings. Concealed her longing.

She was the little girl on the warehouse roof in Friedrichshafen once more. Alone, accompanied by voices that were probably her own.

The Captain was her colleague, her *handler*. Close but apart. She would deal with the rest as and when it came up. She was growing. *Had grown*. Soon she would need no handling.

Sarah stepped towards him and opened up her arms.

He opened his.

They shuffled into each other and closed them. They held on and, after a few seconds, tightened their grip.

"Your new coat makes an unnecessary amount of noise. And you smell of diesel oil."

"And there was me thinking I was wearing too much *Echt Kölnisch Wasser*." She sighed, letting go.

"Anyway...I've brought a *different* friend," the Captain said, motioning to the Mercedes.

"Oh good, we need friends. I'd come to miss Sergeant Norris. Turns out he's a wise man."

Sarah smiled and looked at the car. At the small, fragile, pale little girl who stood next to it.

"Hello, Haller," said the Mouse.

AUTHOR'S NOTE

The creation of *Devil Darling Spy* was driven by my discovery of two horrific moments in history: the Nama and Herero genocides, and the war crimes of Japan's Unit 731. These atrocities resonated with me, not only for what they represented at the time but for how their echoes continue in the world today. The research that followed showed me some of humanity's other dark corners, and they became part of the book.

I became aware of the extermination of the Nama and Herero peoples by German authorities when I read David Olusoga and Casper W. Erichsen's *The Kaiser's Holocaust: Germany's Forgotten Genocide and the Colonial Roots of Nazism.*

At the heart of the Namibian genocides was the belief that some humans are seen as less valuable, *less human* than others. What really chilled me to my core on reading *The Kaiser's Holocaust* was the extent to which that belief was not limited to the atrocity's instigator General von Trotha, the settlers, or even the Kaiser's Germany. That thinking was the defining factor in the notion of colonization, of empire. Swanning into someone else's world and stealing everything out of a sense of superiority and entitlement at gunpoint – all the European powers had done this. It was what empire *meant*.

While von Trotha terrorized what is now Namibia in 1904, Belgians in the Congo were simultaneously unleashing a reign of terror that would cost some ten million lives, as revealed by campaigner E. D. Morel in his book, *Red Rubber: The Story of the Rubber Slave Trade Which Flourished on the Congo for Twenty Years, 1890–1910.* There was an international outcry that led to changes, but in practical terms, these only brought about a more sanitized method of forced labour and more subtle abuses.

Hitler and the National Socialists were likewise obsessed with colonies and territorial expansion – they called it *Lebensraum*, or "living space". They chose to go east, into Poland and the Soviet Union, rather than into Africa or Asia, where colonial territory would have to be taken from other major European powers.

While Samuel's testimony in these pages is a true and accurate description of events, including the Shark Island camp and the collection of human skulls there, there is no evidence that the German settlers were behind the outbreak of rinderpest that so weakened the Herero.

But to a mind already reading about chemical and biological warfare, Shirō Ishii and Unit 731, it sounded like a textbook use of bioweapons. It would not have been the first time that a colonial power had done so, after all.

The real Shirō Ishii believed in biological and chemical weapons as a vehicle for his country's imperial ambitions from the very start, and as a well-connected and persuasive personality, he almost single-handedly drove the entire programme. After the Japanese invasion of Manchuria and the creation of the puppet-state Manchukuo, Ishii saw somewhere he could work in secrecy and a population that he could experiment on with impunity. So Unit 731 was created.

The image of the White Devil was born from the descriptions of his doctors arriving in stricken Chinese villages. Dressed in protective gear, they promised medical help and sophisticated treatment, but they were only there to experiment, study and murder...much like the doctors on Namibia's Shark Island were more skull exporters than healers.

With the exception of the clandestine visit to Berlin described in *Devil Darling Spy*, everything relating to Shirō Ishii and his Unit 731 in this book is based on fact. The human experimentation, infecting the city of Ningbo with the plague, and giving contaminated sweets to children – these are all true, and only a sample of his crimes.

Ishii's eventual fate revealed much about the moral complexity – or moral vacuum – that surrounded the Second World War. He was captured by the US occupation authorities, but escaped prosecution for war crimes by offering up his research – data gained by experimenting on and vivisecting humans – in exchange for immunity. The US government considered his work "absolutely invaluable" as it prepared itself for a war with the USSR that seemed imminent. He almost certainly went to work at Fort Detrick, Maryland, home of the

US biological weapons programme, where testing of biological agents on human subjects continued until 1974.

Conceived and written as the Ebola Virus Disease outbreak in Guinea, Liberia and Sierra Leone was reaching its zenith, *Devil Darling Spy* absorbed that tragedy. The Western lens of the media coverage and the way NGOs ignored local cultural sensibilities to the detriment of their medical efforts seemed clear echoes of colonial thinking. Meanwhile the real Millies waited for news outside the clinics and hospitals, as others withheld their sick in fear. I knew that the very first documented outbreak of EVD in 1976 was spread by missionaries reusing their needles. That overconfident disdain seemed very symbolic.

Dr Chisomo Kalinga, an academic specializing in colonialism and illness narratives, who acted as a reader on *Devil Darling Spy*, has pointed out that the existence of a German medical mission in the AEF is unlikely, Albert Schweitzer's rather paternalist mission in Gabon being the exception rather than the rule. She also noted that medical missions were usually designed to get Africans well enough for work, and that was the extent of the philanthropy.

Dr Kalinga likewise maintains that the average rural Africans of the period would have been more superstitious than I had initially portrayed them and less likely to have trusted Western medical staff. I have acted to redress this balance, and hope that the population of Central Africa depicted in *Devil Darling Spy* does not seem anachronistically compliant.

As for the White Devil, like the stories around the

Ngontang, it would have been more a recent folktale than true mythology, which in Bantu traditions tended towards animal spirits. Dr Kalinga suggests that it would have become a story akin to an "urban legend" of today.

Some elements of the story are unambiguously true, such as the anti-fascists hidden by the Hotel Victoria in Rome, the state-induced famine in the Soviet Union in 1932, or the horrors of Backe's Hunger Plan. Some are still a subject of debate to this day, such as the extent of the real Admiral Canaris's aid to the Allied cause. Certainly, the head of the *Abwehr* disapproved of Hitler and the actions of the *Wehrmacht* and SS in the East, but the idea that he was actively plotting against the Nazi machine from day one pushes the bounds of credibility. He remains an enigmatic figure.

However, there is no evidence that the Japanese Ambassador in Berlin was having an affair with his secretary. Although I am describing the real ambassador, Saburō Kurusu, that detail is a fictional convenience.

There were very few black Germans when the Nazis took power, and despite their appalling treatment and their genocidal mass-sterilization, their small numbers probably saved them from a formal extermination programme. This may have been because the Nazis believed the sterilization had solved their "problem" or because they were preoccupied by what they called "the Jewish question". The lives of those growing up black in Nazi Germany were nonetheless horrendous, as Hans J. Massaquoi recounts in his unique memoir *Destined to Witness: Growing Up Black in Nazi Germany*.

The so-called "Rhineland Bastards" were overwhelmingly

the beloved children of consensual relationships, and the French soldiers, including the black colonial troops, were tolerated, even liked by the Rhinelanders, for their respectful behaviour – not that the converse would have justified the children's later treatment in any case. But in a vivid demonstration of how even the most liberal voices of the era were mired in racist thinking, it was E. D. Morel, the whistle-blower on the atrocities of the Congo Free State, who was one of those responsible for creating the "Black Shame" narrative and the subsequent moral panic. Putting black soldiers in positions of authority over white people appeared to be a world gone mad, and the intellectuals of the era were happy to embroider the truth to make their point.

Devil Darling Spy is littered with horrendous attitudes and the deeply racist words and labels spoken by the characters who hold them. Even sympathetic characters employ problematic terms, because they were widely used at the time. The term *Gypsy*, for example, to describe the Roma, Sinti and Lalleri peoples murdered by the Nazis in the *porajmos*, is now considered pejorative. Notions of the *exotic* and *exoticism* are also problematic, as is the repeated geographical ignorance of the characters and their references to Africa as if it were Devon or New Jersey, rather than a massive, diverse continent of widely differing landscapes, peoples and mindsets. It is, hopefully, clear when characters are speaking, or Sarah's own thought process is being revealed by the narration, and that the book is critical of them.

Rather naïvely, I thought that setting a book in Central Africa during World War Two would be merely a case of research, similar to the work I did for *Orphan Monster Spy* on Germany, Austria and the Holocaust. I was unprepared for the paucity of books, documentaries and articles upon which to base my studies. This scarcity of sources and of accessible, mainstream work is representative of a very real Eurocentric bias that permeates Western culture. Google Maps, for example, has no street view available in the vast majority of the African continent. There are settlements in the Sahara that can be seen in the satellite view but do not even warrant a *name* in Google Maps. It's indicative that the global North still views some parts of the world as inherently less important. Their thought process is still, to paraphrase the Captain in his moment of weakness, that "it's just Africa".

Colonialism has tainted everything that has followed it. It was in part the cause of both world wars. France's failure to decolonize, with the US caving in to pressure from de Gaulle, caused decades of death and misery. The UK's clumsy handling of Indian independence led to misery and bloodshed on an unimaginable scale. The last century of history is the story of broken promises by everyone, everywhere.

And colonialism is over in name only, with rampant corruption enabled by the West and the way that corporations continue to enact colonial-style practices in the global South.

It is a perfectly reasonable viewpoint that I simply should not be writing about colonialism, setting books in Africa, or depicting black or mixed ethnicity characters. Kit de Waal wrote a brilliant piece on the challenges of writing the other and cultural appropriation and included the anonymous quote, "Do not dip your pen in somebody else's blood."

I have benefited from the privilege colonialism has brought, as have millions of others. My country's wealth was almost exclusively built on stolen resources and the suffering of its subjects, including the murder, rape and enslavement of a quarter of the world. Rather than dipping a pen in the blood of Africa, I feel like I'm trailing that blood, the blood of those who have paid colonialism's heavy price, wherever I go. I feel those red footprints across everything I own, both earned and handed to me. I can no longer live with doing so and not trying to do anything about it.

I encourage everyone to seek out explorations of Africa and colonialism by writers of colour, whose history or lived experience I cannot hope to replicate. Spanning the adult, YA and children's sections, and cutting across genres and time periods a start can be made with the work of Nadifa Mohamed, Jennifer Nansubuga Makumbi, Desmond Ohaegbulam, Marguerite Abouet, Elizabeth Orchardson-Mazrui, Chimamanda Ngozi Adichie, Chinua Achebe, Nuruddin Farah, Wayétu Moore, Naivo, Yaa Gyasi, Leila Aboulela, Ben Okri, Aminatta Forna, Ousmane Sembène, Abdulai Silá, Bessie Head, Abdourahman A. Waberi, Zetta Elliott, Ngũgĩ wa Thiong'o, Nnedi Okorafor, Zetta Elliott and Nisi Shawl.

The ubiquity of colonialism's oppression and murder should not, in any way, detract from the crimes wrought by Nazi Germany or the specific horrors of their mechanized death camps. The late David Cesarani, talking to historian Laurence Rees, said of the Holocaust that "never before in history, I think, had a leader decided that within a conceivable time frame an ethnic group would be physically destroyed, and that equipment would be devised and created to achieve that. That was unprecedented." That said, the complicity of one in the birth of the other should be recognized. Especially now.

When I started writing *Orphan Monster Spy*, creeping authoritarianism and the far right were making themselves felt. Free-market economics had just bankrupted the world. But rather than taking the economic model to task in any way, those invested in the model were allowed to turn and blame the poorest and most vulnerable for what happened. By the time I was writing *Devil Darling Spy*, anti-immigrant rhetoric and racist, homophobic and misogynistic dog-whistling from the far right had become the mainstream discourse. The marginalized are beaten and abused on the streets. Politics entirely disconnected from reality holds court in both the UK and the United States. Meanwhile the super-rich get richer, people go hungry and the planet gets hotter.

We need truth – real, verified and evidence-based – as well as real understanding – of colonialism, of the Holocaust, of history. We need to read, as that means knowledge and empathy. Empathy and compassion are the enemy of "looking after our own", because we are all "our own".

If you assume or even hope that you would have been the kind of person to defy the Nazis, now is the time to find out.

FREE EBOOK

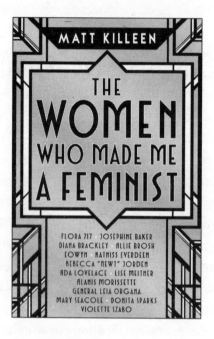

Learn about the incredible historical, contemporary and fictional women who inspired Matt Killeen to become a feminist and create his own feminist hero Sarah in *Orphan Monster Spy* and *Devil Darling Spy*. From WWII secret agent Violette Szabo to *The Hunger Games'* Katniss Everdeen, Crimean War nurse Mary Seacole to physicist Lise Meitner and musician Alanis Morissette, their stories are eye-opening and empowering.

Search online for
THE WOMEN WHO MADE ME A FEMINIST

ACKNOWLEDGEMENTS

For a few moments I thought that this would be nice and easy, having already thanked the people and organizations upon whose shoulders I had climbed to become a published author. Then I realized that I probably have to thank more people this time around than ever before – the people who helped *Orphan Monster Spy* after publication, as well as those who assisted and advised me on *Devil Darling Spy*. The resulting 2,500 word essay was, in practical terms, far too long for publication. So, to the booksellers, bloggers, media outlets, librarians, teachers, award organizers, reviewers and blurbing authors who helped with my debut – thank you. If you've in any way supported my work and I haven't expressed appreciation below, please know that it has meant the world to me.

Many thanks to Professor Timothy Parsons for his knowledge and insights on the Second World War in Africa and forced labour in French colonies, beginning with his published work and ending with his notes on the embryonic *Devil Darling Spy*, via English football and the reasons to prefer Blues to Villa.

Thank you to Kyle Hiller of Angelella Editorial for his invaluable authenticity read and generous after-sales care.

Especial gratitude goes to Dr Chisomo Kalinga, doyenne of African illness narratives, who battled a horrific cyclone that devastated three countries and still managed to deliver her notes on the entirety of *Devil Darling Spy* just a day behind schedule.

Thanks also to academic and author Mary Ononokpono for her wise advice, Dr Afaf Jabiri for helping me approach the Libyan community. Thanks also to Pascale Yammine and Dr Hisham Fakir for their help with the pilots' Arabic.

I'm grateful to Dr Emma-Kate Yates for providing the research on smallpox in Berlin between the wars and for general epidemiology backup; to Dr Lesley Alborough for all things related to ocean swimming, submersion and hypothermia; and of course, to Sarah's namesake, my consultant on all matters Jewish, Deborah Goldstein.

Thank you to translator extraordinaire Kyoko Pallash for generously acting as my reader for all things culturally and linguistically Japanese and for assisting in the hunt for the pre-1960s version of the "Takeda Lullaby"...which only went and got itself cut in the line edits. *Sore ga jinseida.*

Arigato gozaimashita to my old Japanese teacher Yasuko-san and her giant papier-mâché syringe, for being the voice and face of Lady Sakura. One day Mr Giraffe will learn the counters for three-dimensional objects, but I fear the Japanese people should not hold their breath.

As ever, thank you to the Facebook hivemind for the on-tap, sum knowledge of humanity – to the countless Chanel No. 5 describers, child's hand measurers, food-scare rememberers and grammar police. Special gratitude goes to Vanessa Plaister and Alison McKay for vintage hair advice and, of course, Fiona Barker for telling me *precisely* how many times the word "realize" should appear in my book and for showing her working out.

Danke to the volunteers and admins at Subsim for getting me back in the control room of a Type VIIC submarine so I could run the attack on HMS *Virulent* over and over until I could prove it was possible. As with all the sites I've visited that study Axis and Third Reich history, I see you keeping those real Nazis off your forums. Keep at it and don't let up for even a moment.

Thank you to *my* Scooby Gang – Anna Mainwaring, Luci Nettleton, Kim Hutson and Paula Warrington – and the other SCBWI gang, far too numerous to name individually, for their help and support. Thank you to all the other writers who have looked after me and showed me how this author thing is done.

Thank you to my publishers on both sides of the Atlantic:

To Kat, Jacob and Jessica at Usborne's publicity department for their patience and appearing with a bottle of water before I knew I needed one.

To Stevie Hopwood, Anna Howorth, Hannah Reardon Steward, Anne Finnis, Rebecca Hill, Stephanie King, Becky

Walker, Peter himself and everyone else in the multicoloured hot-air balloon.

To designer extraordinaire Will Steele for all the lovely foil.

To all the Usborne Independent Organisers, especially Dionne Lakey and her crew for rescuing me in Milton Keynes.

To everyone at Viking, past and present – Janet Pascal, Jody Corbett, Marisa Russell, Bree Martinez, Kristin Boyle, Vanessa Carson, Mary Raymond and Summer Ogata to name just a few. Thank you for your belief. And for sending my son *Sleep Train*, the sound of bedtime ever since. *Clickety-Clack.*

To the teams in Italy, Spain, Poland, Romania, Czech Republic, Portugal and Brazil for bringing Sarah to the majority non-English speaking world.

As for my editors and the serial killers of my darlings, Kendra Levin at Viking and Sarah Stewart at Usborne, my gratitude and admiration knows no bounds. I hope I continue to make you proud and annoy you with my ellipses...

And down there at the abyssal level of gratitude is my agent Molly Ker Hawn. Thank you. I am relieved, every day, to have passed your asshole test and hope to continue to.

Thank you to the whole team at TBA, especially Amelia Hodgson in London, fellow Mets fan Victoria Cappello in the Big Apple, and their co-agents, especially Diana Spector in Los Angeles.

To the ultimate repositories of appreciation... Thank you to my amazing children and extended family and friends, without whom all this, not to mention my life, would seem hollow and empty. As for my wife-slash-best-friend-slash-business-partner-slash-muse-in-chief Anne-Marie...what can be said that I didn't say last time? Words are inadequate, and that's an admission filled with existential horror, coming from a *writer*. So, I shall keep it simple: Thank you for everything. I love you.

And you, Coco-Mojo, *sit, stay, good girl*.

As a postscript, and climbing onto my soapbox, thank you to the professional librarians of now and my past for nurturing me and a billion other children. Libraries and their custodians widen horizons, democratize knowledge and understanding. They provide quiet spaces for those who may not be privileged enough to have their own, not to mention delivering access to local and national public services. There is no substitute for professionally run libraries, and anything that threatens them is a threat to society.

ABOUT THE AUTHOR

Matt Killeen was born in Birmingham and, like many of his generation, was absorbed by tales of the war and obsessed with football from an early age. Guitars arrived at fourteen, wrecking any hopes of so-called normality.

He has had a great many careers – some creative, some involving laser guns – and has made a living as an advertising copywriter and largely ignored music and sports journalist. He fulfilled a childhood ambition and became a writer for the world's best-loved toy company in 2010.

He lives near London with his soulmate, children, dog and musical instruments, looking wistfully north at a hometown that has been largely demolished and rebuilt in his lengthy absence.

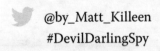 @by_Matt_Killeen
#DevilDarlingSpy

DON'T MISS SARAH'S
FIRST MISSION

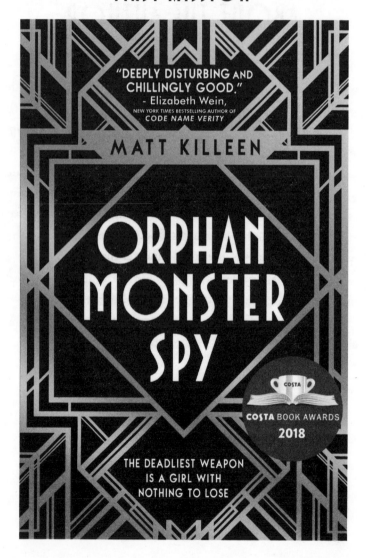

A TEENAGE SPY.
A NAZI BOARDING SCHOOL.
THE PERFORMANCE OF A LIFETIME.

Sarah has played many roles – but now she faces her most challenging of all. Because there's only one way for a Jewish orphan spy to survive at a school for the Nazi elite. And that's to become a monster like them.

The Nazis think she is just a little girl. But she is the weapon they never saw coming. With a mission to destroy them all.

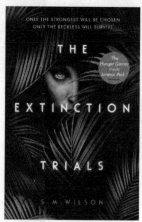

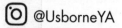